Jessie Fothergill

Kith and kin

A Novel

Jessie Fothergill

Kith and kin
A Novel

ISBN/EAN: 9783337032869

Printed in Europe, USA, Canada, Australia, Japan

Cover: Foto ©Andreas Hilbeck / pixelio.de

More available books at **www.hansebooks.com**

KITH AND KIN

A Novel

BY

JESSIE FOTHERGILL

AUTHOR OF

'THE FIRST VIOLIN,' 'PROBATION,' 'THE WELLFIELDS,' ETC.

'God be thanked, the meanest of His creatures
Boasts two soul-sides ; one to face the world with.
And one to show a woman when he loves her.'
                                        BROWNING

London

MACMILLAN AND CO., LIMITED

NEW YORK: THE MACMILLAN COMPANY

1899

First Edition, 3 vols., *crown 8vo.*, 31s. 6d., 1881. *Second Edition*, 1 vol., *crown 8vo.*, 6s. (⑤), *May*, 1882. *Reprinted* 1886 ; 1891 ; 1897. *Transferred to Macmillan & Co., Ltd.*, 1898. *Reprinted* (2s.), 1899.

CONTENTS.

CONTENTS.

KITH AND KIN.

'HOLLOA, Aglionby! whither away?'

'Me? I'm off to the Palace of Ceres, to testify my allegiance to the Liberal cause.'

'Oh, the Liberal Demonstration! I wish you joy, I am sure!'

'Thank you. I don't say that I shall agree with all I hear, but I want to know what they have to say for themselves.'

'Contradictious, as usual.'

'Aren't you going too?'

'Why on earth should I go? We had our turn last week, my boy. You seem to forget that there has been a Conservative Demonstration already, and that we had a great triumph at the Palace of Ceres last Saturday. Ours is an accomplished fact, while yours has yet to come off.'

'A great triumph, had you?' returned Aglionby, a gleam of humour, of a kind the reverse of angelic, lighting up his dark, lean visage. 'I know there was a great row, because I was there, and helped to make it; if you like to call it a triumph, I've no objection, I'm sure.'

'I'll go bail you never were at so enthusiastic a meeting in your life,' was the vehement retort.

'Never at such a noisy one, I admit. I hope your chief speaker felt soothed and cheered altogether with his Irkford reception. That scene on the platform——'

'A fine scene!' said the other, reddening angrily all over his fair and ingenuous countenance. 'A fine display of English feeling, to hoot down a respectable, honest man, just because his opinions happen to differ from yours!'

'Now, my dear fellow, don't let your feelings carry you away. I was there as well as you, and I'm proud to own that I groaned as loudly as anybody, not just because my opinions differ from his—heaven forbid! That *was* a meeting, Percy! I congratulate you.'

'It was what we wanted—a demonstration,' replied his friend, chafing.

'Very much so,' said Aglionby politely. 'The question is—a demonstration of what?'

'Our party have clearly-defined principles, which they know. They don't want expounding over and over again, like yours. I hope you may get at something this afternoon—something definite, I mean. At any rate, you will have a good chance of hearing. You see, we had ninety thousand of an audience. To-day, there will be you, the speakers, and the reporters.'

'Thanks for that sparkling gem of banter. "Won't you join the dance?" Will you really not come and save the meeting from irretrievable disgrace? If we could proudly embellish our report in Monday's paper with the distinguished name of Percy Golding, Esq., we should feel that our exertions had not been made in vain.'

'I can tell you, you won't get the chance of doing any such thing,' said Mr. Golding, in a huff. Then, rapidly changing the subject, he added in milder tones: 'Where is Miss Vane? Isn't she going with you?'

'Miss Vane is at home. She cares nothing about such things, I am happy to say. Women have no business at political meetings—especially young women.'

'Lots of ladies are going. Half the reserved seats are taken up with them,' said Percy; but his expression showed that he was at one with his friend on the last point, if not as to political principles in general.

'Oh, then there will be one or two others in addition to myself and the reporters, after all. I haven't got a reserved seat; they are too expensive. I'm going with the cads, in the shilling places, and, in case anyone else should happen to do the same thing, I will go on and secure a place. Farewell! Can't I persuade you, really? I would stand between you and suffocation from overcrowding.'

' My opinions on political matters are formed, thank you,' said Mr. Golding stiffly.

'Happy man! Mine are only in the process of development. Once more, farewell !'

Percy Golding returned his nod, and the two young men separated. Bernard Aglionby, warehouseman in an Irkford firm, Radical and freethinker, took his way towards the city; Percy Golding, his friend, banker's clerk, Conservative and Churchman, took his way out of it, humming a tune the while, and hastening his steps more than he had done when he had met Aglionby. They were fast friends, and had been so for many years. They squabbled incessantly, but quarrelled never.

As Aglionby's long legs carried him quickly down the broad and busy thoroughfare, which gradually, as the town grew thicker, became less broad and more busy, there was at first a strongly-perceptible smile visible upon his dark, keen face—and that smile a sarcastic one. He had a remarkable face, with sharp, handsome, clear-cut features, a firm mouth, a fine brow, and dark eyes, which were often seen brilliant, but rarely soft, and which were illumined oftener than not with a glowing spark of malice and mockery. They darted from one object to another with a keenness and quickness which were remarkable. Nothing seemed to escape their scrutiny; yet there was rarely any pensiveness to be seen in their expression. Eyes and mouth, too, were given to smiling frequently, and a hearty laugh was by no means a rare event in this young man's life. Yet his laugh was not contagious, and was oftenest heard when others were perfectly grave, giving his company an uncomfortable sensation that he laughed at, rather than with, them.

'I wonder if we shall muster a hundred and fifty thousand this afternoon?' he speculated within himself, as he strode onwards, and kept passing pieces of hoarding covered with monstrous broadsheets, conspicuous amongst which was a huge poster in red letters on a white ground—'Palace of Ceres, Knottley, near Irkford. This day. Grand Liberal Demonstration. Speeches will be made by Messrs. —— and ——. Lord John Ponsonby in the chair. Proceedings to commence at three o'clock precisely.'

'The Tories had ninety thousand after all deductions were made,' he reflected, 'and that's a big crowd. I should like us to beat it.'

He whistled softly to himself as he strode on in the brisk, pleasant air of the October afternoon; brisk and pleasant even in the smoky streets of the huge, dingy, manufacturing town.

'I hope it will be over in time for me to take Lizzie to the theatre,' he again reflected. 'As she has got her new toggery, she will want to show it, sense or no sense. Girls are so odd.'

He was in the thick now of the great, dirty town, and turned off down a street inscribed 'City Road;' very long, very straight, dingy, and uninviting in appearance. Here the walls were enlivened with a constant succession of the red and white posters, announcing in terms impossible to be

misconstrued, more and more particulars as to the approaching 'Grand Liberal Demonstration at the Palace of Ceres,'
to be held that afternoon. By-and-by this road became
more and more crowded. Cabs, carriages, and foot-passen-
gers were all increasing in numbers, and all steadily throng-
ing in one direction. From the steps of a railway-station
poured a continuous stream of persons—men and women
both—all turning towards one point, where in the dim distance could be seen looming through the smoke a huge,
dome-shaped roof, that of the great hall belonging to the
euphoniously-named 'Palace of Ceres.'

Aglionby recognised an acquaintance here and there,
nodded briefly, and stalked onwards, his great height and
his long strides giving him an advantage over most of the
others. Inside the wall, the very large grounds belonging to
the palace were thronged to overflowing with an enormous,
surging crowd. There was a lane, preserved by the exertions
of sorely-tried policemen, just wide enough to admit of two
lines of carriages, one going to, the other coming away from,
the door of the hall.

Aglionby appeared to know his way well. He wasted no
time in struggling through this densely-planted forest of
humanity; but skirting it, came to a side-door, presented
his shilling to the guardian who stood there, was admitted,
and found himself at once within a vast hall, capable of
holding twenty-five thousand persons. There was a great
platform at the upper end, about which were distributed a
few gentlemen, eagerly conversing; a large space in the
centre of the hall was devoted to the reserved seats, about
half of which were already occupied, and that very largely
by ladies, as Mr. Golding had predicted. The space all
around these seats was already filled almost to overflowing;
but Aglionby, again skirting the crowd, made his way to a
most convenient corner, admirably adapted both for seeing
and hearing, and in close proximity to one of the reserved

benches. In this place a youth was standing whose face lighted up as he saw Aglionby approach.

'Here I am!' observed the latter. 'Did you think I was never coming?'

'I knew you wouldn't miss this,' said the boy, slipping out of his place; 'and I was only just in time to keep the place for you. I've been here just an hour.'

Aglionby had told Golding that he was 'going with the cads in the shilling places,' and he had certainly paid one shilling for his place, or rather, for permission to enter at the door and try to secure standing-room. But at the present moment he drew forth a shabby-looking little leather purse (indeed, his whole costume betokened anything but a super-fluity of means) and took from it a half-crown, saying:

'Thank you, you've earned your money well, Bob,' and tendered it to the youth, who looked like a respectable shop-boy.

He flushed a little, looked rather sheepish, and stammered: 'I don't like to take it, Mr. Aglionby, really. It's but a little thing to do for you, and——'

'Pooh! pocket it, and see that no professional gentleman relieves you of it on your way home. A bargain's a bargain; and clear out, my lad, for your room is more desirable than your company at the present moment.'

The youth murmured something; looked with more than gratitude up into the dark, sharp face of Aglionby, who appeared at that moment to be abstractedly gazing towards the platform, and then, wriggling off, made his way through the crowd, and was soon trudging gaily down City Road, turning the coin over in his pocket, perhaps to institute an intimacy, as rare as it was agreeable, between it and two pennies, a piece of string, and a buck-handled knife.

Aglionby propped himself up against a pillar and surveyed the proceedings. There was a band, which played popular melodies, to the airs of which a portion of the audience sang political songs.   He joined in now and then, in snatches, in a voice which was pleasant, and which had in it more bass than baritone, but he was too intently observing the faces around him to take much interest in the singing.

Two seats at the end of the reserved bench by which Aglionby was standing, and from which nothing but a stout cord separated him, remained empty for some little time. Then came an elderly gentleman, accompanied by a young lady, and took their places there—the elderly gentleman next to Aglionby.   He was the very image of a country gentleman, thought the pale-faced denizen of streets and offices, and suburban lodgings.   His fresh, hale complexion, bright, frosty blue eye, and white hair ; his upright attitude ; his whole appearance, bespoke the countryman.   And Aglionby had noticed, as he made his way to his place, that he was a huge man, tall and broad, and stalwart, with such a physique as is rarely bred in a town.   So tall and so big was he, as to make the lady beside him look almost small, although she too was of a stature that was 'more than common tall,' and of a stately carriage to boot.   Aglionby only noticed her passingly, at first.   He remarked her height and her dignity of mien ; he saw that she was young, and had fine and rather large features, and the expression upon her lips and in her eyes, he saw, was not one of girlish timidity, though far removed from boldness.   Still, she had more self-possession and a steadier gaze than he altogether admired —or thought he admired—in woman.   For, though politics were his pastime, and the Radical cause his darling, he was in many matters a martinet in theory, and a staunch Conservative in practice—which is exactly what might have been expected.

He amused himself with the contrast in the conversations on either side of him, scraps of which came to his ears.

'You see we are in plenty of time, uncle,' said the lady

in a contralto voice, and with a clear and polished accent. ' I hope they will be punctual.'

' Trust them !' replied the old gentleman, a little gruffly. ' It's a sight worth seeing, this ! Does my eyes good to behold it. You never saw the like before, Judith, and you never may again.'

' No. And what order they keep, and how they all turn towards that platform, as if it were a magnet ! And what earnest, intent faces, most of them ! How different from the people at home, uncle !'

The old gentleman indulged in a series of chuckles, which made his face red, and his blue eyes moist, and Aglionby glanced sideways at the young woman, attracted by her voice, and pleased with what she said. Certainly she was not wanting in intelligence, but what a contrast to Lizzie—his lovely Liz !

At his right, amongst those who, like himself, were standing, were two rough-looking fellows in the garb of operatives. A stunted, keen-faced man was talking to them :

' Have you come far ?' he asked.

' We've tramped it from Huddersfield,' replied one. ' Th' young measter giv' us th' tickets, and we coom afoot. We can't afford railway fares i' these bad times.'

' Well, you'll not repent it,' was the consolatory reply. ' How do you think of passing to-night ?'

' On the road. We must be back by Monday morn, you see.'

' Well, come and have some tea with me, when it's over. I live close by, in City Road. I'm a watchmaker, and I'll be glad to give you a meal.'

The invitation was apparently accepted, but the band began again, and drowned further conversation.

The great hall was filled now, until not another soul could press in. The most perfect order prevailed. In a momentary stillness, a booming sound in the distance told those who knew that the clock of the Town Hall, two miles away, in the city, was striking three. Almost as the sound ceased, the door behind the platform opened, and the principal speakers came on. Many members of Parliament and local celebrities who had already appeared, had been warmly welcomed. Here was the chairman, Lord John Ponsonby. They received him with manifest pleasure but there was an electricity, a subtle thrill which told that they were waiting for some one, for something yet to come. More celebrities, or otherwise; more short, sharp, absent-minded cheers. More and more heads, known and unknown, crowd forward. Then comes he whom they are waiting for. Here is the 'brave white head'—the 'grand, calm, proud face' of their best-beloved, and then bursts forth the roar that deafens, and stuns, and is never forgotten of them who have once heard it. A roar, a thunder, a prolonged storm of exultation, that has something fierce and fearful in it, as well as glad, greets that veteran champion of beautiful liberty.

Twenty-five thousand throats cheered at the full pitch of their power, as if to fling all the praise they could upon that one head, as if to bow with weight of glory that well-known brow. All else were forgotten. At Irkford the old love is very faithfully loved.

There are others about and around him who are great and good, but that is the man who fought for them and their fathers years ago, to give them bread; and who has fought for them since, in many a battle. They have not forgotten it: they never will forget it. Aglionby felt the enthusiasm run like lightning, in a subtle red-hot current, through every vein. He too cheered—cheered at the top of his voice—his eyes all the time fixed upon that form and that face, whose appearance had called forth all this storm of fierce and passionate delight. Even while he was cheering, he had observed how some of the women's faces blanched, and their eyes blenched before the tremendous roar of joy—and he looked instinctively at the girl who sat so near to him. There was no blenching in her face. It was a little flushed, out of its pallor, and there was a clear light in her eye, and a repressed smile upon her lip, which told of enjoyment, not fear. The prolonged roar, which lasted more than five minutes, and would not be hushed, had no terror for her nerves.

At last there was a momentary silence, before the first speaker had opened his mouth, and Aglionby heard her say quickly :

'Don't you remember, uncle, those lines about, "How any woman's sides can hold the beating of so strong a throb"? I wonder how any man's glance can meet this approbation, and not quail.'

'Ay, ay! But hush, my dear. There's Lord John speaking.'

The meeting, unparalleled in the annals of public meetings—even of Anti-Corn Law, and O'Connell meetings—lasted two hours. Those on the platform described afterwards, how they were haunted by the sea of faces turned up to them; by the wave-like surgings of the great multitude. This was the smallest section of the crowd which had assembled. In other halls, and in the grounds outside, receiving scraps of oratory from disinterested speakers, were as many as made up the whole gathering to more than one hundred thousand. The speakers were strictly limited as to time, and punctually at five o'clock the meeting dispersed.

Aglionby, slowly making his way out, paused near the great door, watching the carriages of the celebrities and noncelebrities as they drove away; observing the throng and hearing the comments.

The carriages and cabs went by numbers, and as he stood there a hired landau drove up, and the number, ' 137,' was called out; but as no response was made, it was quickly hurried on, to come round again in its turn, which would not be for a long time yet. Just when it had disappeared, there was some pushing from behind, and turning, Aglionby beheld the elderly gentleman and stately young lady beside whom he had stood during the meeting.

'Come along, Judith !' said the old man irascibly. 'We can slip between the horses' heads, and overtake the carriage.'

'Oh, but, my dear uncle——'

But the rash and impetuous old gentleman, who looked as if he could not brook having to wait for anything or any-one, dragging his niece by the hand, was down the steps, and under the heads of a couple of prancing steeds belong-ing to an approaching carriage. With a repressed exclama-tion she wrenched her hand out of his, and while he darted forwards, she darted back again, and up the steps, alone. The disconsolate visage of the ruddy-faced gentleman was visible, peering at her between horses' heads, jostled by the crowd, and looking very helpless, despite his great stature and herculean dimensions.

Aglionby was conscious of a vague interest in these pro-ceedings. He watched her as she came to the top of the steps, and stood there, frowning a little, and biting her lip.

'Provoking !' he heard her murmur. 'But perhaps, if I wait——'

She looked a little anxious, and glanced uncomfortably around her. Aglionby's theories upon the subject—woman —included one which proclaimed her helplessness in a crowd. He thought the better of her for looking uneasy. Lizzie would have been frightened to death, poor little thing !

As this thought crossed his mind, his lips moved, and he suddenly and impulsively stepped forward, raising his hat, and remarking :

'If you will take my arm a moment, I will help you across to your companion.'

She looked a little surprised, glanced for a moment into his face, and said :

'Thank you. If you would not mind !'

She placed her hand lightly within the arm which he extended, and he led her quickly and skilfully between the
carriage then advancing, and the one behind it; and despite
expostulating policemen and disapproving coachman, handed
her in safety to the other side. A few moments' search sufficed to discover the old gentleman, who exclaimed:

'I wish we had never left the steps, Judith! The crowd
here is most rough and unpleasant, and how we are ever to
find the carriage, I don't know.'

'Your carriage is just over there, if you like to come to
it, and sit in it till your turn comes round again,' said Aglionby politely, and secretly much amused at the mixture
of reckless impetuosity and nervous helplessness characteristic of the country cousin in a great crowd.

'Where? How? Thank you, sir!' said the elderly
gentleman, crimsoning in his agitation, and looking excited.

'There,' said Aglionby, his eyes gleaming with subdued
mockery, as he stretched a long arm, and pointed a long
forefinger towards the spot where he saw the carriage clearly
enough. 'Suppose you follow me—I can show you the
way,' he suggested, and the old gentleman, tucking the young
lady's arm through his own, and glaring (no other word will
describe the look) with sudden interest at Aglionby's back,
and up to his close-cropped dark hair, followed him whither
he led him through the masses of the crowd, until, by what
seemed to the bewildered strangers nothing short of a miracle,
they stood beside their own chariot, which, hired though it
was, was still a haven of refuge, with the tall, dark, young man
holding the door open, composedly, and smiling slightly.

'Thank you, thank you, sir!' said the old man, handing
his niece in, and still staring at Aglionby with a fixedness,
and withal a suspicious expression, at which the latter could
with difficulty refrain from laughing aloud.

'The old boy must think me a plausible member of the
swell-mob,' he thought. 'He's thinking that he would not like

to meet me alone on a country road, late at night, and armed with a stick. *She* looks as if she didn't care what happened, so long as she got out of the crowd, and away from the reek of the many-headed—of whom I am one, and she knows it. I saw her look at me during the meeting.'

Aloud he said :

' If you will sit here, your man will drive you on as soon as he can, and you will be all right. Good-afternoon !'

' Sir, pardon me, but will you not—can we——'

' Thank you, I'm walking,' replied Aglionby, slightly lifting his hat, and striding away.

CHAPTER II.

MEETING THE SECOND.

AGLIONBY carried himself homewards as fast as might be, through a tortuous maze of side streets and short cuts. He lived in lodgings in a southern suburb of Irkford, in a quiet, modest, dingy-looking street, called Crane Street, and in apartments suited to his very moderate means. As he bent his steps towards Crane Street, his mind was running eagerly and delightedly on the spectacle, the excitement of that afternoon. He was not given to airing any crotchets or enthusiasms ; his fault was extreme reserve and taciturnity ; but at the same time he silently cherished ardent longings, wishes, ambitions.

' I call that *life*, that sort of thing, for those who take part in it,' he said within himself. ' One afternoon of that would be worth a hundred years of selling grey shirtings and towellings, and being badgered if your sales don't come up to the mark you are expected to reach. It's a life for a galley-slave, by gad ! and nothing better. I wish I saw my way out of it. " Aglionby this !" " Aglionby that !" ' His face darkened. 'And then old Jenkinson, who's rolling in money, can go canting to people about its being a misfortune for any young man to have anything to depend upon but his own exertions! Hum! Ha! I wish he'd just let one of his own sons exchange with me, and see where his own exertions landed him. I should like to cut the whole concern, and go off to Canada or New Zealand; only I like Irkford, and I like the life there is here. I like the politics, and the stir and the throb of a big city like this. And then Liz—poor little Liz!—she would scream at the very notion of such a thing.'

A smile dawned in Aglionby's face and eyes, which for a few moments had been preternaturally grave, and even severe. This smile was unquestionably a tender one; it transfigured his face, and made it look that of another being, gave a softness and graciousness to the hard, sharp outlines, and melted away the cynical little lines about the mouth. He looked up, rousing himself from his abstraction, with a vague consciousness that he must be near home, and found himself within a few paces of the house. He strode up the little walk, and opened the door with a latch-key.

Apparently its rattle in the lock had been heard, for as he was pulling it out, and standing just within the narrow little passage, about to close the door, some one came tripping out of a back parlour and said:

'How late you are!'

'I'm sorry, my child! Couldn't afford so many 'bus fares in one day, so I had to walk,' he replied, putting the latch-key into his pocket with one hand, and with the other possessing himself of her slim fingers; then his arm by some means slipped round her waist, and thus pinioned, he led her into the dark little back parlour whence she had emerged.

'Come, let me go, sir! You and I are going to have our teas all alone, and that's more luck than you deserve. And

then off we go !   Oh, I'm dying to be off, and we shall get
no places if we're not in lots of time.'

'Well, stop—you can spare time for me to have one look
at you.   Let's see how your new finery suits you.'

He held her off at arms-length, and gazed at her, with
his keen eyes softening visibly.   Handsome though his own •
features were, his hard and cynical expression made his face
almost a plain and decidedly a sombre one.   Surely she
compensated for his want of attractiveness ; for she was an
exquisitely pretty creature.   Tall, lithe, and *svelte*, her form
was enchanting, while the long, slender white throat supported a lovely little head.   She was fair, with a delicate
complexion, untouched by the smoke and closeness of the
town.   She had one of those faces, child's and woman's at
once, which appeal irresistibly to all male hearts, and to
most feminine ones.   Soft blue eyes ; a lovely mouth,
pensive, yet pouting, and a dreamy smile ; abundance of
pale hair, which, however, just failed to have the true corn-
coloured tinge which makes the difference between flax and
gold—all these charms she possessed, together with that
other charm usually wielded by woman at nineteen years of
age.

So much for the first view ; the real, undeniable advantages—and they were all that Aglionby had ever seen. From
the hour in which he had been betrothed to her, he had been
firmly convinced that she embodied his ideal of womanhood.
Perhaps a feminine eye would have been required to perceive, a feminine finger to point out, certain other charac-
teristics, which, however, *she* might read who ran.

Miss Lizzie Vane wore a dress which faithfully followed
every worst point of the prevailing fashion ; and exaggerated
all of them a little, by way of originality.   Her gown was the
gown of the present day   It fitted her almost half the
length from her throat to her heels, like a skin ; it was well
tied back just behind the knees, and on the ground behind

an abundance of perfectly meaningless little frills, arranged upon a spoon or wedge-shaped piece of stuff, waggled and whisked about with her every movement. This was the 'train' of Miss Vane's gown; for a young lady moving in her exalted sphere, and living, too, in one of the palatial family mansions of Crane Street, could hardly be expected to dispense with so useful, so necessary an appendage.

Her waist was—let us say, very slim indeed; her bust and hips forced into a prominence displeasing in itself, and out of all proportion with the rest of her figure. Her plentiful hair was gathered behind into as small and shabby a round knob as it could by any means be screwed into; in front a great wisp of it was pulled forward, relentlessly cut short, and then curled, frizzed, piled and towered both on the front of her head and over her pretty white forehead. Certainly a pair of liquid blue eyes look at you with a very bewitching glance from out a forest of such little ringlets; and so Aglionby thought.

So much for Miss Vane's appearance while in repose.

The exigencies of her sub-skirt arrangements, the position of what she called her 'kicking-straps,' necessitated a side-long, crab-like movement, which, if gracefully managed, is amusing for a short time as a novelty, but he who would call it soothing or agreeable as a permanent form of locomotion in one who is to be a companion for life, must be a man who is very much in love indeed.

It was upon this sinuous-looking form that Aglionby gazed with admiring eyes. Then his glance left her form and fell upon her face. That at least was lovely, since it had no waist to be compressed into an attenuation suggestive of the most painful results in case of any unlooked-for accident. No frizzing and no torturing of hair could make it otherwise. Ill-temper now, old age in the future, could alone have the power to make Lizzie Vane's face an ugly one, and—to tell the truth—no power in the heavens above, or in the earth beneath, would ever make the said face a noble one, or put a spark of intellectual fire into the sweet blue eyes.

'*Do* come and get your tea!' she implored him, wriggling impatiently. 'Ma has gone out. I've been waiting for you for such a time. I should have died of dulness, if Mr. Golding hadn't looked in, and cheered my solitude.'

She laughed a little affectedly.

'Percy came, did he? Ah! your society would suit him better than the home-truths we've been hearing this after-noon. There was too much of the sledge-hammer about our proceedings to suit friend Percy,' he said, smiling sardoni-cally, as he seated himself; and Miss Vane, bending in an elegantly serpentine attitude, stood before the tray, and poured out the tea.

'Why don't you sit down, too?' he asked. 'I thought you were going to get tea with me.'

'So I am; but I shall stand. I can't sit down, I'm so impatient, and I must be off to get ready,' replied Lizzie, conscious of a treacherous tension about the knees, which she knew by experience meant a crack, and a sudden un-seemly expansion of garment, in the event of sitting down, or of assuming any other than an upright posture. 'How do you like my dress? You don't even seem to see it,' she said, bending into a graceful curve, and looking affec-tionately over her shoulder at the spoon-shaped train before alluded to.

'It's—well, I don't understand such things. I suppose it's very pretty, but I don't think it suits you quite so well as some you've had. It looks a little too tight, as if there hadn't been quite enough stuff, doesn't it?'

'There's a compliment!' cried she, with more heat than the occasion seemed to demand. 'But you're no judge. Mr. Golding said he had never seen anything in more per-fect taste.'

'Well, Percy's more of a judge than I am, and then he

2

has sisters,' said Bernard with ready acquiescence, 'so I
suppose it must be right.   And,' he added, in the most perfect innocence and good faith, 'I suppose they know what's
what in a big shop like Lund and Robinson's, eh?'

'Yes,' said Lizzie eagerly, and all smiles; 'why? did you
see anything like it in their windows?'

'N—no.   At least I didn't observe anything, but when I
went to buy that ribbon for you last week, the girl who served
me had on a dress exactly like this of yours—only black, you
know.   She reminded me of you, somehow.'

He smiled, thinking he had paid an unexceptionable compliment.   Indeed, a year ago, the idea of his going into a
draper's shop to buy ribbon for a girl would have been
scouted by him as being out of the range of possibility.   But
flimsy creatures have, ere this, wielded considerable power
over other creatures which were anything but flimsy.   Lizzie
Vane's influence had tamed him, not only to the buying of
ribbons, but to a feeling of anxiety to understand her and
sympathise with her, in her own particular province—that of
dress and millinery.

To his surprise and discomfiture, his last well-meant effort
produced only an angry pout :

'Really, your ideas are so odd, Bernard.   To think of
comparing me to a shop-girl!' she expostulated.

It was Bernard's turn to look surprised.

'I didn't compare you with a shop-girl,' he said, 'and if
I had—I don't know much about such things—but that girl
I speak of was infinitely superior to some of her customers.
Why not a shop-girl, Lizzie?' he added reflectively.   'Suppose you had been obliged to go out, as they call it, to
earn your living—I'd rather be a saleswoman in one of those
big shops full of pretty things, than a nursery governess,
with a lot of impudent squalling brats to tyrannise over me.'

'I've never considered the subject, not having felt the
necessity of it,' retorted Miss Vane loftily.

Bernard smiled slightly. If anybody but Lizzie had been talking, scathing would have been the comments upon pampered ignorance and upstart vanity. As it was, he let the observation pass, and spreading a slice of bread-and-butter, attacked another topic—one which he had tried before with scant success. He spoke out of the fulness of his heart, not because he hoped that Lizzie would feel interested in the subject.

'We *had* a meeting this afternoon, Liz. I don't believe there ever was such a meeting.'

'Oh, I know nothing about meetings,' she replied with temper.

'No; I'm glad of it, my child.'

This was his usual reply to such announcements on the part of his betrothed. He made it, not because it was what he really felt, but rather what he thought he ought to feel under the circumstances. Perhaps he cherished a hope that frequent repetition of the words would produce the desired sensation.

'There were lots of ladies there, though,' he added, and the face of the young woman who had sat near him was vaguely present in his mind as he spoke.

'I expect they were frights,' she said, not yet appeased.

'Not a bit of it. There were some very fine ladies indeed there, I can tell you. A very fine-looking young woman sat close to me.'

'How was she dressed?' asked Miss Vane.

'Oh, how do I know? In black, I think.'

'Had she a hat or bonnet on?'

'I don't know. She'd something that shaded her eyes—a low, round thing.'

'A *round hat with a brim!* At a large meeting! Impossible! No one would wear such a thing.'

'Now you give it a name, it was a hat with a brim,' he rejoined. 'White straw it was, with a white feather laid

2—2

round it, somehow, flat-looking. And a little silk shawl quite loose round her shoulders.'

'She could not have been young, and she must have been a dowdy. I said they were all frights,' said Lizzie, interested for once in her life in a public meeting.

'She was young, handsome, and no dowdy,' he replied composedly, but with more tenacity of the point than he was wont to display in matters relating to dress and appearance. 'You know, my dear, ladies who are somebodies often dress much more plainly than people in our position. I dare say a countess's daughter would be more simply dressed than you and Lucy Golding, when you go to town in the omnibus. My aunt, Mrs. Bryce——'

'Well! commend me to public meetings for making a man too polite for anything,' was the exasperated reply. ' *When* you've done, if you do not *very* strongly object, we *might* be thinking of setting off.'

'Any time; I'm ready as soon as you are,' he answered, promptly jumping up.

Miss Vane floated sideways from the room, and presently returned attired in a large white hat, turned up at one side with a large pale blue feather, and a bunch (also large) of blush roses. Over her pale-grey dress she had flung a buff-coloured *dolman* of so gorgeous a show as at the first glance to belie its very moderate cost. This garment was richly braided, and further adorned with large buttons and a narrow bordering of a fur which, with the best intentions, did not quite succeed in matching the colour of the cloak it was supposed to trim.

Gathering up the cataract of little frills which hung behind her, Miss Vane announced herself ready, and after giving a critical glance at Bernard, and rather mournfully remarking that she 'supposed he must do,' they set out together; presently found an omnibus, and in it went down to the town again, and descended at the entrance of one of the Irkford theatres.

As may be supposed, the more select and expensive seats were beyond their means: they occupied places in the upper circle, and being very early, secured them in the front row of the same, forming one of innumerable couples in similar circumstances who that evening chose that means of amusing themselves.

They were, perhaps, a rather noticeable pair, certainly a strong contrast to one another. His sombre face with its gleaming eyes and occasional smile ; his careless dress, and nonchalant unconventional attitudes, might have struck some eyes. Anyone who had cared to observe him so far, would also have remarked that, underlying all the carelessness of dress and mien, there was a pride which could not be concealed—a certain imperious hauteur in the glance which scarcely agreed with his ostensible station, occupation, and surroundings. His heart was not in the place, or the play, or the scene at all ; he went to please her, and for nothing else. She was an almost startling contrast to her lover— fair, delicate-looking, and pretty to admiration, despite her ridiculous dress, and absurdly vulgar and affected airs and graces. She could not, and did not fail to attract attention. Aglionby never noticed that people looked at her. Miss Vane was, however, fully conscious of the fact. This evening, after they had sat waiting for some time, she drew his attention to it, saying plaintively :

'Bernard, that odious man on the other side has never taken his eyes off my face. It is so disagreeable. What am I to do ?'

'A—what ?' he asked abstractedly. 'Oh, that man is staring at you ? don't look at him, and then you can't see him.'

Brutal retort thought Lizzie, in despair. Mr. Golding had more than once wondered at some 'fellow's' impudence in staring at her, and expressed a wish to knock the offender down ; a style of argument which appealed, as it seemed to her, to more elevated, chivalric feelings than that used by Bernard.

'Well, you might try to enliven me a bit!' she exclaimed, rather impatiently. 'What am I to do *but* sit and look at people, if you never open your lips?'

'I beg your pardon, I'm sure. The fact is, this seems rather flat after this afternoon. I wish you could have seen the ovation they gave to ——. It was grand; and he was grand too! He smashed the Government all to atoms.'

'Dear me! The Government is always being smashed to atoms, according to what you say; but it seems to me to keep on governing all the same,' observed Lizzie, unconsciously touching a sore spot.

'Of course it does,' he growled; 'and will do, unless it is kicked out.'

'I wish political meetings didn't make people so awfully grumpy,' observed the young lady, rather ruefully. 'You do seem to think of nothing but politics.'

'There's nothing else much worth thinking of. When a fellow's like me, Liz——'

'I wish you wouldn't call me "Liz."'

'No? What then?'

'Lilian is what I like to be called.'

'But if Lilian is not your name—which it isn't——'

'Never mind, I shall never get you to understand. When a fellow's like you—well, what happens?'

'A slave in a warehouse, and with absolutely no prospects, except to sell grey shirtings till he's superannuated, he's apt, if he has not something to take his mind outside his daily drudgery, to get either despondent or dissipated. Now, politics take me out of myself, and—holloa! Why, there she is!'

'She? who?' asked Miss Vane, forgetting her superfine manners and craning forward as eagerly as he did.

'Why, she—the girl I was telling you about. They must have got home safely then.'

'Which? Where? Do show me! Do you mean the girl that had the hat with a brim? I should like to see *her*.'

'The same. Look at her, going into that box with the old gentleman ; and tell me, if you dare, that she isn't a fine looking girl.'

'I can see nothing fine-looking about her,' said Miss Vane crushingly, and not altogether truthfully, as a dismal suspicion began to form itself in her mind that there was something more admirable about the perfect simplicity of the lady in question than in even her own truly *recherché* toilette.

'Come, come, Liz ! you're jealous !'

'Jealous, Bernard ! Why, she has on one of those plain washing silks that look no better than a brown holland. And nothing in her hair, and no colour, no eyes, no *go !*' said Lizzie, becoming energetic in her contempt.

' My dear child, she has far more than what you call "go"! Look at the way in which she moves. Look at the glance of her eyes—how she measures everything so calmly and deliberately! I tell you that woman would look just the same, only rather cooler, if every soul in this theatre was one of a mob thirsting for her blood.'

'Well, to be sure ! What next ! A quiet, plain-looking girl like that! *I* am better-looking than she is, and I'm no beauty.'

This was one of Miss Vane's favourite remarks, and was always made in the firm conviction that since there was not a word of truth in it, it must be magnanimous.

'And I declare, Bernard, she's looking at you. She is ! And she is pointing you out to her pa. Oh, and you are blushing ! He's blushing, for the first time in his life ! Eh —h—h ! what fun !'

There was certainly a heightened colour in his face, as he turned to her, with a curling lip, and in a voice which was new to her in its coolness and disdain, observed that she was behaving like a child.

Lizzie's mirth was checked for the moment. At that tone she experienced the same constrained sensation, the same quickened breath and beating heart, though in a lesser degree, as when he had one night suddenly upset all her calculations, and claimed her love and her life, in a manner which had subdued her. She became silent, and her lip quivered for a moment. This great clumsy Bernard, at whose awkwardness she many a time laughed, had sometimes a way of looking at her, and speaking to her, which sent her heart into her mouth.

He leaned back in his seat, and studied the playbill until the curtain went up, and then he looked towards the box before he looked at the stage. They were not looking at him now; they were intently watching the first scene of 'Diplomacy' with the absorbed interest of country folk, who do not often get the chance of seeing a play.

The curtain went down on the end of the first act.

'Oh, my! What lovely dresses that Mrs. Kendal has, to be sure! I wish I'd had this made a long plain princess robe, like that grey and gold one she has. Don't you think it would have suited me better, Bernard?'

'It might have suited you; the question is, how would the passages and the size of the rooms at your mother's house have suited it?' he answered, honestly endeavouring to go deeply and conscientiously into the subject.

'Tsh!' she replied impatiently.

During the remainder of the performance she was sulky and silent. Aglionby did not perceive it. He was interested in his late neighbours at the Liberal Demonstration. He could not help seeing that they looked at him more than once, and exchanged remarks about him. It was the old gentleman who looked at him oftenest, and who even once levelled his opera-glass, and looked long and intently through it in his direction. The young lady, as Bernard saw, looked exceedingly grave, when her features were not animated during the play; but her face was one on which a grave expression sits well, though her smile, when she did smile now and then, was a sweet one. There was something in her countenance which indefinably attracted him, and led him to wonder what she would be like to talk to. He admired the old man, too—his huge stature, and the proud carriage of his head; and the conclusion he came to was still that they lived in the country, and were most likely people of consequence, wherever their home might be.

When the play was over, he made his way, with Liz on his arm, down the stairs. In the large entrance-hall was a great crowd of people going away. Close to the door Bernard jogged elbows with some one, and looking round, saw the old gentleman with the young lady on his arm. This time it was she who was next to him—so near that their elbows touched, and he could look into her very eyes. He saw that she had one of those marble-pale countenances, whose pallor by no means betokens ill-health. How calm and composed the deep, steady grey eye! How steadfast the meeting of her lips one upon the other—steadfast yet sweet! And what a store of intellectual strength was betokened by that smooth, expansive white brow, which had the unmistakable arch that denotes power of thought!

He saw that her eyes were fixed upon Lizzie, who happened also to look round at that moment, flushed with excitement, and a little, perhaps, with vexation—brilliantly, dazzlingly pretty, with that beauty which by gaslight looks ethereal and almost transparent. When she saw the steady eyes of the strange girl fixed upon her, she bridled, tossed back her head, hung upon Aglionby's arm, and said in an affected and audible voice :

' Do let us get out, Bernard dear ! I'm almost stifled.'

' Bern——' broke suddenly from the old gentleman's lips. He made a lunge forward; he stretched out his hand towards Aglionby's coat-sleeve; he cried, ' Sir ! sir ! Mr.—a— !'

But in vain. The crowd closed in between them. The elderly gentleman and his companion were left to wait their conveyance; Aglionby and Miss Vane to make their way through the crowd : she to grumble bitterly as they waited for an omnibus, and to wish ardently that cabs were not so ruinously expensive.

The second meeting had brought them no nearer than the first.

CHAPTER III.

AN INTERLUDE.

> ' But for loving, why, you would not, sweet,
>   Though we prayed you,
>   Paid you, brayed you
> In a mortar, for you *could* not, sweet.'

SUNDAY at Irkford is a day which may or may not be dull, according to the habits of those who have to spend it there, by which I would intimate that the place is so large as to allow of Sunday being spent there in divers and various ways without any scandal accruing therefrom. Some kind of provision is made for the spiritual (or otherwise) entertainment of all, from Christians and secularists, through every denomination of the Jews, Turks, infidels, and heretics who form no inconsiderable item of its population.

It was Bernard's only clear holiday throughout the week, as he had only the half of Saturday. He had got into a groove, as we all get into grooves, and his mode of spending the day seldom varied. The morning he usually disposed of in walking if it were fine ; or in reading, writing, and smoking if it were wet—in either case, alone. Miss Vane was not much to be seen during those morning hours. Bernard usually dined at the timely hour of a quarter past one on this day with Lizzie and Mrs. Vane. In the afternoon

he was supposed to be at the service of his bethothed—
generally, in the evenings also, on which occasions he would
accompany her to a church in some outlying fields, which
church was a favourite walk in summer for hundreds of persons
who attended the service and afterwards walked home in the
evening freshness and coolness. It was the nearest approach
to a ' summer Sunday evening ' in the country which was to
be had. Bernard and Lizzie generally strolled back by
some roundabout route, leading at last into the gas-lighted
thoroughfare, and so quietly and peacefully home to supper,
and, when Miss Vane had retired, to a pipe, a book, and bed.

There were occasional Sunday evenings on which his
fiancée was deprived of his society ; occasions on which he
devoted his attention to the furtherance of the Liberal cause
in politics, and the secular one in religious and philosophical
matters, at a meeting composed of himself and a body of
kindred spirits, or rather, of spirits as nearly akin to his
own as he could find—and that was not very near, for his
was a caustic, lonely, and somewhat bitter nature. This
knot of men—chiefly young, as may be supposed from their
proceedings—called themselves by the somewhat ambiguous
and misleading title of ' The Agnostics.' It was very much
of a misnomer, since their confession of agnosticism certainly
went no further than matters religious ; on all other topics
—social, moral, and political—they professed to have the
newest lights, and to be capable of taking the lead at any
moment. These ' Agnostics ' were all ardent, hard-working
fellows ; Bernard Aglionby was the one cynic in their ranks.
They talked as pessimists of the most terrible and gloomy
school. They acted, hoped, and enjoyed themselves as
optimists of the brightest cheerfulness, again always with
the exception of Bernard, and with him a tinge of pessimistic melancholy was constitutional. It needed a correc-
tive, which neither his life, his companions, nor his surroundings had yet supplied.

Mr. Percy Golding, it need hardly be mentioned, did not belong to the aspiring body of ' Agnostics ' just spoken of.

On the day in question the club did not meet, therefore Aglionby was at liberty to dispose of his time as seemed good in his own eyes. He got his breakfast, and just as the piously-disposed were wending their way to their different temples, he put on his hat, ran upstairs, and knocking at the closed door of the beloved of his soul, said :

' I'm going out, Lizzie. Shan't be back again till dinner-time.'

' All right !' cried Miss Vane ; and Aglionby, whistling set off.

He did not miss Lizzie in these Sunday morning walks. In the first place, they extended so far that certainly no town-bred girl could have joined him in them, however good her will. Next, they were always devoted to meditations— sometimes when he got quite out into the country, to reading—in which she had no part nor lot. His Lizzie was a dear girl ; he never thought of her without a smile and a softened look ; but, equally, there were long hours during which he never thought of her at all. He did not want feminine influence in his deeper thoughts, so he often told himself. What a bewildering thing it would be if Lizzie ever were to take it into her head to pretend that she felt an interest in politics, for instance. What a hopeless muddle would result ! Fortunately, she had better sense. She knew what she was equal to, and with wisdom confined herself to doing it. He never said within himself that she knew what she liked, and never troubled her head about any person or thing outside the sphere of her little, little world. He would have liked dearly to marry her out of hand, give her a carriage, a fine house, a cheque-book, and *carte-blanche* to amuse herself as she chose, and give what entertainments it pleased her to have ; while he would have been very proud of her beauty, would have lived in the utmost harmony with her, and she would never have interfered in the really serious concerns which were outside her sphere—in the business, the politics, and the statesmanship of life. In their mutual bark she was metaphorically to recline in the comfortable, cushioned cabin, with a novel and her fancywork, while he was to be the man at the wheel.

It was a fine, crisp October morning, as he set out, turning his face towards the south, and quickly threading the mazes of streets, till he came to a great high road, full of persons dressed in their best, with their Prayer-books in their hands, and with their Sunday gloves, umbrellas, and expressions in full force. On either side of the road were large houses, residences of rich merchants, fashionable doctors, men of law in large practice, bank directors, and other favoured ones of fortune. There were trees, too, in the gardens, waving over the road, and an occasional Sunday omnibus taking a load of passengers out into the country.

He pursued his way until the last houses were left behind, and those which did now and then appear were really mansions in the country, in grounds or parks of their own. The air was pleasant, and blew with an agreeable freshness upon his face. Far away he could see the soft outlines of blue Derbyshire hills, while to the right extended a flat, smooth, highly-cultivated plain. He met very few persons when he had advanced so far on his way. With his hands in his pockets, and his face occasionally turned upwards to look into the deep field of liquid blue above, he marched on and on, thinking busily of many things—chiefly of the meeting yesterday, and, naturally enough, of those two strangers with whom he had been twice in one day brought into collision.

' I suppose she took an interest in it all,' he reflected. ' I wonder what she thought of it, and whether she agreed or disagreed. She must have come because she was interested —or perhaps the old boy made her come. I shouldn't wonder. He looked as if he were one who wouldn't let anyone out of his sight whom he imagined ought to be in attendance upon him.'

A pause in the thoughts, which presently returned to another but a parallel track.

'I wonder what the Tories will make of our meeting yesterday; I'm awfully anxious to see to-morrow's papers. By-the-way, I wonder, will my letter be in to-morrow morning's *Daily Chronicle?* It should be, and it should touch up those denominational schools a bit. I hope it will draw down a storm of abuse. I like being abused—when I know I am in the right of it. I like battle.' His eyes gleamed with that light—not a mild one—which oftenest illumined them. 'Pity there is so little chance of combat, of any sort, in an Irkford saleroom.'

Of late, these reflections upon that state of life in which his lot was cast had been more numerous and more discontented than usual.

'If I could only see my way to something else, not another day would I remain,' he thought. 'It is slavery—neither more nor less. I should think that father of mine, poor fellow, hardly saw the probable results of *his* decisive step in life, or he might have looked again before he took it. *I* am one of those results'—he smiled in grim amusement—'and some of the others I have to put up with, as a salesman of cotton goods.'

He laughed again, not mirthfully, and, looking at his watch, wheeled round on his heel, and returned over the same ground as that which he had already traversed. He arrived again in Crane Street, and found Miss Vane quite ready to receive him, and dinner almost ready to be eaten. Lizzie was got up regardless of trouble, at least ; one trembled to think of the amount of time which must have been devoted to the frizzing and arranging of the fuzz of hair which projected, like an excrescence, over her forehead, and hung almost into her eyes : trembled because, if she had little leisure, her work must have suffered direly from the tyranny of fashion, and if she had much leisure she occupied it in a deplorable manner. It did not seem to strike Bernard in that light; probably he had not the faintest idea but that her hair grew ready frizzed as he saw it. His eyes lighted, his face softened as she met his view.

'Well, my lass, good-morning; you do look bonny!' he exclaimed, kissing her tenderly.

'*Don't* call me "lass," Bernard dear, as if I were a factory girl!' she said plaintively, raising her blue eyes to his face.

'I won't call you anything that you don't like, my beauty —does that suit you better? What am I to do for you this afternoon? I am at your service.'

'Oh, we are going to Mrs. Golding's to tea, and then I want you to go to church with me.'

The light certainly did die out of Aglionby's eyes as this enchanting programme was unfolded for his delight.

'Tea at Mrs. Golding's?' he said, trying hard not to speak ruefully. 'Have you quite promised? Is there no means of getting out of it?'

'I don't want to get out of it,' said Lizzie candidly. 'I like going there; there'll be others there as well as us, and I've promised Mr. Golding to sing his favourite song.'

'Have you? What is that?' asked Bernard, who was never jealous by any chance—a characteristic not perfectly agreeable to Miss Vane's ideas of a model lover.

'It's called "We sat by the river, you and I,"' she answered. 'Come, dinner's ready; ma's calling.'

'All right, we'll leave the river till afterwards; though what river you and Percy can imagine yourselves by, at Mrs. Golding's, except one of tea, which there always is there, I can't conceive.'

'I shouldn't think you would like to imagine us by any river, unless you were there too,' she said, marvelling at his utter incapacity to comprehend that other men admired her.

' He thinks I'm like him, I suppose. He sees no one but me ; and he thinks I can't even see that others see me. I do wonder sometimes that I ever said " Yes " to him so easily as I did, except that he is so much more of a man than any of the others, and so awfully indifferent to everybody else— and then Lucy Golding said I never could bring him to book, however much I tried. I'll show her this afternoon whether I haven't brought him to book.'

They sat down to dinner. Mrs. Vane, Lizzie's mother was of course present as well. Her aspect might have afforded a timely warning to any man not already in love. She had once been exquisitely pretty in the style of a wax-doll, or a Dresden shepherdess. She had had eyes of forget-me-not blue : it is a colour that does not stand the test of tears and sleeplessness, with both of which ills Mrs. Vane's life had been plentifully troubled. She had had a profusion of flaxen hair, which was now thin, and streaked with grey. She had had a pretty figure and a peach-blossom complexion. Figure and complexion had both vanished like a dream. She had been the essence of the much-bepraised ' womanly woman,' in the sense of not taking the most remote or elementary interest in any question outside personal, domestic, or family gossip. Advancing years had not made her more intellectual ; the ardent hater of the ' strong-minded female ' must have hailed Mrs. Vane as his ideal— no one ever had been able to accuse her of strongminded-ness. In addition to this, she was prone to tell Aglionby, now that he was, as she said, 'like a near relation,' that ' Lizzie is *so* like what I used to be at her age, Bernard : I think I see myself again in her—only for the dress. We wore more stuff in our skirts in those days, and I think it looked better—not but what she's very good taste.'

Mrs. Vane might have furnished a warning to Bernard in more ways than one. She was the widow of a man who had held a somewhat higher position than Aglionby's, in a business of the same kind—such a position as Bernard himself looked forward to attaining before he could make Lizzie his wife. His higher position had afforded him the means of marrying, and had enabled him to save sufficient money to leave a tiny income to his widow and one child, which income they eked out by taking two lodgers, Bernard Aglionby and another young man, who did not trouble them much, and who always went home to the country at the end of the week, and stayed there till Monday.

Lizzie had been at a cheap school, where she had acquired some flimsy accomplishments and a little superficial information—generally incorrect—upon such matters as geography, history, and 'common subjects.' The large and first-rate High School for Girls had been disdained, as not being select enough, since tradesmen's daughters went to it. The other large school in the vicinity, at which a really first-rate education was to be obtained, was a ladies' college, avowedly intended for rich and exclusive pupils, and of which the terms were prohibitory to persons of Mrs. Vane's annual income; therefore Lizzie had gone to the cheap day-school already mentioned, and had flirted at a very early age with the students of the college hard by, with the big boys on their way to the grammar-school, and with the clerks going down to business, specimens of each of which classes she was in the habit of meeting on her way to and from her seminary. She had been the belle of that truly select establishment for a long time before she had left it. Languishing youths had written her notes, and sent her valentines and gloves and goodies in abundance; in fact, Miss Vane was a reigning beauty—in her set. If she had been in another set, the 'society' papers would have chronicled her doings, and told of her costumes, would have disputed about the colour of her eyes, and fought fiercely over her reputation, or want of it.

Just a year ago Bernard Aglionby had come to lodge with

them, replacing another young man who had recommended the place to him. Naturally, they had frequently met. Lucy Golding and she had talked him over. Lucy said Percy knew him well, but that he never came to their house ; that he was well known to be impervious to all feminine charms and womanly wiles. This, and other communications of a like nature, had somewhat piqued Miss Vane, and had inspired her with a deep interest in Aglionby. Soon, existence ceased to be worth having until, at any rate, a smile and a compliment had been wrung from Bernard—some token to show that he was not proof against her, however nearly case-hardened. It had been some little time before the experiment had succeeded—before Aglionby had even thoroughly roused to the consciousness that there was a pretty girl in the house who smiled kindly upon him. Then, whatever he might have felt, he had for some time concealed his sentiments behind a mask of impassive calm, until one day he broke forth, and made love in a fashion so imperious, and so vehement, as, metaphorically speaking, to carry Miss Vane off her feet.

She could not withstand the torrent of his fiery nature. His piercing eyes seemed to burn through her. His voice, and his glance, and his ardour, had for the moment thrilled and subdued her, and it was such a triumph over Lucy and Percy, and all the rest of them—over Bernard's friends, too —those odd ' Agnostics' who never went to church, and who talked about republicanism as if they would not be sorry to see it established, and who all—there was the point—seemed to think that Aglionby was quite above woman's influence— these incentives, put together, formed a stronger influence than she could resist. Aglionby became her accepted lover, and, looking at it all from her point of view, she presently began to find that a great conquest brings its cares and pains as well as its pleasures. Still, it was a conquest, and her power had made itself felt now and then. More than once she had cajoled Bernard into giving up some political meeting or some evening of debate ; or she had withdrawn him from his brother Agnostics in order to take her to the theatre, or go out with her to some suburban tea-party.   Suburban tea-parties and theatre-going were things which she liked, and which Bernard, as she very well knew, disliked, so that every time he accompanied her to either one or the other entertainment, was a new and tangible proof of her ascendency over him.

This afternoon she had what she considered a very convincing proof of this ascendency.   Bernard meekly followed her to Mrs. Golding's, and there there were, as he had prophesied, rivers of tea, many muffins and teacakes, a number of young people, and a little music by way of diversion. Bernard sat in silent anguish during this last form assumed by the entertainment.   He had some scientific knowledge of music ; his mother, while she lived, had taken care of that ; and he had a fine natural taste and discrimination in the matter, thrilling in answer to all that was grand or elevated in the art.   His one solitary personal extravagance was to attend the series of fine concerts which were given every autumn and winter season at Irkford.   The performance this afternoon caused him pain and dejection.   He experienced a sense of something akin to shame ; to him it all appeared a sort of *exposé*.   Lizzie, in the sublime blissfulness of ignorance, boldly sat down and sang in a small voice, nasal, flat, and affected :

> ' We sat by the river, *you* and *I*,
> In the sweet summer-time long ago.

It was terrible.   He was thankful when at last Lizzie arose and said it was time to be going to church.   That was her moment of triumph, or rather, it ought to have been—when Miss Golding, it may be innocently, or it may be of malice aforethought, but certainly with every appearance of ingenuous surprise, exclaimed :

3—2

'To church! I thought you never went to church, Mr. Aglionby.'

'I go with Lizzie whenever she likes,' he said carelessly and haughtily. 'It pleases her, and does me no harm.'

'Oh—h! Bernard!' cried his betrothed, her cup of pleasure dashed from her lips; while a young lady, who was almost a stranger, and who appeared struck with this remark of Bernard's, said severely that she could not understand how going to church could harm anyone. To which he, inwardly annoyed by the silly stupidity of the whole affair, replied nonchalantly that it was nevertheless very bad for some constitutions, his amongst them; and amidst the consternation produced by this statement, he and Lizzie departed.

'Really, Bernard, you do upset me when you come out with those awful remarks of yours. Poor Miss Smith couldn't make you out at all.'

'I dare say not. I am sure it is a matter of complete indifference to me whether she made me out or not.'

'Yes, you will set public opinion at defiance; and it will do you no good, say what you like.'

'My child,' said he, drawing her hand through his arm, and laying his own upon it, 'I think you can hardly be called a judge as to what is public opinion. If you mean that Miss Smith represents it, I don't care to please it. And if I go to church with you at your wish, what do fifty Miss Smiths and their silly ideas matter?'

'Ah, but I don't know whether it is not very wicked in you to come to church when you don't believe in a word of what is going on. I am not sure that I do right to bring you, only I keep hoping that it will have *some* good effect upon you.'

'Well, it has,' he said tenderly. 'It has the effect of making me love you and prize you ten times more for your goodness and your faith.'

They were reconciled, as they entered the gates of the

churchyard, and joined the throng going in, while the loud, clanging bells overhead sounded almost deafening, and the steeple rocked to their clamorous summons.

Bernard liked sitting there, through the evening service, with Lizzie by his side; and he liked the walk home through the fields, under the clear, starlit sky, and then through the streets, between the line of lamps. When she hung on his arm, and they talked nothings together, then he felt at home with her; he forgot her bad singing, and her conventional little thoughts and stereotyped ideas. In the province of talking nothings Lizzie was at home, was natural, unaffected, even spirited. So soon as she left them she became insipid and artificial, and this was what Aglionby had dimly felt for some time, though he had not given a definite name to the sensation. They talked nothings to-night, and he parted from her in the warm conviction that she was a dear, lovely little creature, that she was the woman who loved him, and whom he loved, and to whom he was going to be loyal and true to his life's end.

CHAPTER IV.

MEETING THE THIRD.

THE morning of Monday was half over. Aglionby stood in the sale-room of the warehouse, which at the moment was empty. He had disposed satisfactorily of large amounts of goods already, and now for the first time he found a leisure moment, in which to take up a newspaper, and glance over it. It was the advanced Liberal journal of Irkford, the *Daily Chronicle.* In a conspicuous place at the head of a column, in the middle of the paper, was a letter to the editor, entitled 'Education in Denominational Schools.' This letter was signed 'Pride of Science,' as if with a defiant challenge to the rival 'Pride of Ignorance.' Aglionby's eyes

gleamed as he glanced down the columns, and his most disagreeable smile stole over his face. The letter was from his
own pen, and was not the first, by several, with which he had
enriched the columns of that journal, on that and kindred
topics. He was not aware, himself, of the attention which
these letters had attracted. He knew that generally they
called forth angry replies, accusing him of wishing to under-
mine the whole fabric of respectability ; to explode the secure
foundations of society, and cause anarchy to be crowned :
and to these fulminations he delighted to reply with a pitiless,
slashing acerbity ; an intuitive stabbing of the weak points
in his opponents' armour, which must have made those
enemies writhe. He had never yet paused to ask himself
whether his course of action in the matter were noble or not.
He detected abuses, and those abuses flourishing rankly
under a system which he thoroughly disliked; and he hastened
to expose them, and to hold up them and their perpetrators
to ridicule ; dangling them before such a public as chose to
take an interest in his proceedings, and scourging them well,
with whipping words and unsparing hand. His letter this
morning was a pungent one. He had written it, on the
Thursday night before, in a bitter mood, and the bitterness
came out very clearly in the composition. He had made a
point of investigating the proceedings and system at several
denominational schools, and had collected some significant
facts, which he had used with considerable cleverness to
bring a good deal of discredit on the clerical and denominational party.

' I shall be pelted to death for this, in to-morrow morning's
issue,' he reflected, looking cynically pleased. ' Halloa !
Here's a leader on my precious effusion. What has it got to
say ?'

He had just begun to read, but was interrupted by a call of :
' Mr. Aglionby !'

He looked up and saw one of the principals of the firm

entering the room—and behind him another figure. Aglionby felt slightly bewildered, but not very much surprised, when he recognised the choleric-looking old gentleman of the Liberal Demonstration and the play, on Saturday afternoon and evening.

'The third time of meeting!' he reflected. '*Kismet!* The will of Allah be done!'

He stood silent, while his glance wandered beyond both the men, to the doorway, and the beyond which was visible through it. Blank space. Neither a hat with a brim, nor yet one without : nothing but the remembrance of a pair of deep-set grey eyes, a pale face, and a steadfast-looking mouth.

' Mr. Aglionby!' was repeated.

'Yes,' he answered, as he laid down his paper, and advanced a step.

'I think you are at liberty just now.'

'There are no customers here at the moment,' he replied.

'Then be good enough to take this gentleman round the premises. He is interested in our arrangements, so you will explain them to him as clearly as you can, and give him all the information he desires.'

Then, with a bland smile, Mr. Jenkinson, the senior partner of the firm of Jenkinson, Sharp, and Company, excused himself on the plea of a pressing engagement at that very hour, from going farther with them, and they were left alone together.

Aglionby, turning to the old gentleman, saw that he was regarding him with an intent fixity of expression, which had in it something almost fierce, and which called forth at once the young man's readily-aroused sense of the ludicrous.

' Perhaps you would like to begin at the beginning?' he suggested ; and the old man, meeting his eyes, and hearing his voice, most certainly started and changed countenance.

' As you like—I don't care,' he muttered, still continuing to gaze at his guide.

'Then come this way,' said the latter, conscientiously carrying out his directions. The visitor followed him, and Aglionby explained everything to him very clearly, but very soon came to the conclusion that his trouble was wasted, for so absent-minded a man, he thought, he had never seen. Merely glancing at all the things he was shown, he kept his eyes still persistently fixed upon the face of his guide, occasionally giving utterance to a 'Humph !' when it appeared necessary to say something, but evidently feeling but scant interest in the vast stock and complicated business system of Messrs. Jenkinson and Sharp.

At last they found themselves back in the saleroom. Aglionby remarked :

'I think you have seen everything now.' (This was entirely a figure of speech, for he was convinced that the strange old man had perceived little or nothing of it all.) 'Do you wish to see Mr. Jenkinson again, or shall I show you out ?'

'I should like a few words with you,' was the reply, unexpected but hardly surprising after his peculiar behaviour. 'If we can be alone, that is,' he added. 'I should like to ask you a few questions.'

'Perhaps I may not be disposed to answer them,' remarked Aglionby, a little drily.

'Perhaps not, but I rather think you will. At any rate you might as well hear what they are.'

Aglionby glanced around. It was the dinner-hour and there was no one in the saleroom but themselves and a boy, the boy to whom he had given half-a-crown for keeping his place at the meeting on Saturday. This youth was undoing a blue handkerchief containing two slices of bread and butter, and a bottle of cold tea—his dinner.

'Bob, just clear out, will you, and get your dinner somewhere else,' said Aglionby good-naturedly. The lad raised a pale, delicately-sensitive face, smiled, and picking up his little bundle, departed.

' Now we are alone,' observed Aglionby, propping himself up against a mountain of 'goods,' and sticking his hands into his pockets. The old gentleman seated himself on a solitary wooden-bottomed chair, folded his hands on the top of his stout walking-stick, and said :

' I wish to know your name.'

' My name is Bernard Aglionby,' replied the young man, lifting his head a little, with a gesture of unconscious pride.

' I thought so !' burst from the old man's lips, as he struck his stick upon the ground; and Aglionby, gazing at him fixedly, felt a strange sensation stirring at his heart. A rush of vague recollections—memories strange and potent, partaking both of sweetness and bitterness, came surging up in his mind. Whose spirit was it that looked at him through those frosty blue eyes ? The pause that followed the last words was a long one. Aglionby waited almost breathlessly for the next question. When it came it did not surprise him —now.

' Did you ever hear of a place in Yorkshire called Yoresett-in-Danesdale ?'

Aglionby glanced at him keenly, searchingly, and saw that he was agitated. Then he replied, curtly enough, ' Yes.'

' Were you ever there ?'

' No.'

' Ah ! Never there !' He looked with an indescribable mixture of expression at Aglionby, and went on slowly: ' Perhaps you've also heard of a house called Scar Foot, not a hundred miles from Yoresett ?'

' I have.'

' And of one John Aglionby, who lives there ?' he said, and his tones vibrated, while the glance he fixed upon his interlocutor was a strange compound of defiance and anxiety.

' I've heard of him too,' replied the young man, his face darkening.

'You have? Well, here he is—I am he.'

He tapped his broad chest with his strong forefinger, and a rush of colour covered his face, while his eyes were fixed ever more intently and more eagerly upon the other's face. Aglionby looked at him, his own countenance, so strong a contrast to that of his companion, set in a gravity which amounted to sternness. There was no sarcasm in his eyes now, and no malice upon his lips. He bore little likeness to the hale-looking old man, with his white hair, his ruddy, full face, and yet there was, as one looked at them, a something—a flavour of expression perhaps, a similarity in the way in which their lips closed one upon the other.

'I am he,' he said again. '*I* am your grandfather, lad; I!'

'I knew you must be, as soon as you spoke of Yoresett and Scar Foot,' said the other gravely. 'Well?'

'Well! Have you no word to say to me? The nearest relation you have in the world!'

'What should I have to say to you? Nothing agreeable, surely.'

'And why not? What injury have I ever done you?'

'That is an odd question,' said Aglionby, shrugging his shoulders. 'You turned my father out of doors, and disinherited him when he married my mother; and when you might have been reconciled with her, how did you treat her?'

'How did she treat me?' put in Mr. Aglionby, hastily and wrathfully.

'What a question! Was she tamely to submit to insults? As for me, you have ignored me from the hour of my birth to the present one, except once, when you proposed to do me a deadly injury. My mother treated that effort of yours as it deserved to be treated.'

'This to me! From you—from my own grandson——'

'Pardon me, but I can be no grandson of yours, for you disowned my father for marrying my mother; and when you might have atoned for my father's death, you only pursued an innocent woman with your vindictive hatred and revenge, in asking her to separate herself from her child—from the child she had borne in trouble and adversity—her only comfort, if a poor one. A grandson of yours—no !'

Aglionby the elder was quivering with wrath and emotion. He shook his stick menacingly within an inch of Bernard's face. The latter smiled slightly, drew his hands from his pockets, and folded his arms.

'I suppose that is your view of the case,' said the old man. 'I say that your father was my all—and that he broke my heart.'

'You look as if your heart had been broken long ago !' retorted Bernard sceptically.

'He refused even for one instant to look at the woman whom I wished him to marry.'

'Englishmen generally choose their wives for themselves, and my father just did what you had done before him, and what I have done after him,' said Aglionby, quite convinced that he had stated an undeniable fact.

'What ! You are married ?'

'No, I'm only engaged to be.'

'Bah ! I say an only son has no right to choose indiscriminately. There is policy to be considered, and family interests. When your father scoffed at Marion Arkendale, and took up with——'

'Stop, if you please. You are speaking of my mother. One whisper that savours of disrespect to her, and I leave you on the instant. Indeed, I must decline to discuss her at all with you, in any way.'

Mr. Aglionby chafed under this curb, but nothing in Bernard's expression encouraged him to continue the subject. He bit his lips, and drew his brows together, looking the young man over, from the crown of his sombre, shadowy locks, down to the arched instep of his long, slender foot.

'Why are you called Bernard?' he asked. 'It is no name in our family.'

'My mother's name was Bernarda; and her father's before her was Bernard; mine is the same.'

'And have you no other? No John, for instance, nor Roger, nor Ralph?'

'None but Bernard.'

'Why not John Bernard? It would have made a fine name!'

'I don't suppose John sounded well in the ears of those who gave me my name.'

'Then, when your mother—no, I'm not going to discuss her; don't be afraid—when she told you how she had decided your destiny for you—did you feel content with her decision?'

'Perfectly—why not?'

'Tell me what she said about me. Did she teach you to hate me?'

'No. I remember it well. I was about six years old, and I was learning my lessons in my mother's room. She had been downstairs, but presently came up again, looking pale and determined. She came up to me and took me up in her strong arms, and kissed me often, and asked me if I would like to go away from her and live with some one else? I cried out, "No." Not if I had toys and sweets, she said, and a pony, and a beautiful home? "And you, mother," I answered. "No, not me, my boy." I bawled out lustily that I would not go; and she kissed me with a kind of wild passion, and called me her lion-hearted boy. Afterwards, when I grew older, she told me all about your offer. She said you had sent a messenger to say that if she chose to give me up entirely to you for eleven months in the year, and during that time to hold no communication with me or with you, she might have what was left of me for *one*—and she said she had sent you back the answer that you deserved. I say she did right. If I were begging my bread in the streets, I should say she had done right.'

His grandfather had been gazing intently at him as he spoke, drinking in, as it were, every word that he uttered. As Aglionby ceased, he drew a long sigh, and a strangely subdued look came over his face. He passed his hand across his eyes and said, in a low voice, as if communing with himself:

'Ay! ay! such was my message—such was my message. Then,' he added presently, looking up again, 'since you are called after your mother and her people; since you have been delivered over into their hands, what have they done for you? Perhaps you were too proud to accept their assistance, eh?'

A gleam of hope, pleasure, and approval dawned in his eyes, and he looked eagerly at Aglionby.

'My mother had no people, except her one sister, who was as poor and as brave as herself. I never refused their assistance, for it was never offered me. They had no means of assisting me.'

'No means! I thought——' he began, looking strangely at Bernard, while a dark red colour suffused his face. He muttered something to himself and seemed to ponder upon it.

Then suddenly looking up again, he asked:

'And pray, what do you think of me?'

His choler had subsided, and he looked up into the sombre face above him, with an expression akin to wistfulness.

'Of you? I know absolutely nothing of you, except that one action of yours, which you cannot possibly expect me to think right. For the rest, you are my father's father, and entitled to my outward respect, at least.'

'Humph! Then, when your mother refused my offer, what did she do?' he asked suspiciously.

'She went on with her music-teaching and her drudgery. She worked for me.' said Aglionby, with passionate though repressed emotion. 'And six years ago, when I could have begun to repay her, she died.'

No asseverations were necessary to emphasise the feeling that lay beneath this simple and unadorned statement of a fact. It seemed to cause some reflection to the elder man, who, however, presently said :

'How would you like, when next you have a holiday, to come and spend it at Scar Foot?'

Bernard's eyes suddenly lighted. His face changed. Then he laughed a little, and said :

'Not at all, thank you.'

'No? Why not?' asked the other, in a tone of deep mortification.

'Because I have neither part nor lot in Scar Foot, and will not go near it. I will keep to the friends I know.'

'Sirrah! What friends can you have here? What influence have they? How can they help you? What can they do for you?'

'Nothing; that's just it. I have everything to do for myself, and it is best to remain where nothing can happen to disturb my conviction on that point.'

'Then you don't realise that I still could, if I chose, put you out of the necessity of doing anything, could provide for you amply, without your needing to lift a finger.'

Bernard laughed again, more cynically than before.

'If you chose, and if I chose,' he said. 'You seem to forget that I am Bernarda Long's son, but I do not. Nor do I forget your own character, your caprice, your hardness. All the Aglionbys are hard and obdurate as rocks; my mother has told me so, and I feel it in my own breast. You are not one who could put up with being thwarted. If I saw much of you, I should probably do something to thwart you every day. I have hands to work with '—he held them out—'a head to plan with '—he smiled ambiguously—'health to carry me through adversities, and a will which enables me to restrain my wishes and desires within reasonable bounds. So long as those things are left to me, I am my own master, and my own master I will remain.'

'A bright life, truly!' sneered the other. 'Hard work for a bare subsistence: grinding your brains to powder to keep body and soul together; a strong will to be used for nothing but to repress the natural desires and impulses of a young man of spirit—a pretty life, truly, and I wish you joy of it!'

'It's not much to boast of, is it? "A poor thing, sir, but *mine own.*" Fortunately there are always things in this world, and especially in a big town like this, to take a man outside himself, or he would be in a bad way.'

'Plays, for instance, and concerts. It runs in the blood to be fond of such things.'

'Yes. Luckily for me, it does. They have driven the devil from my elbow more than once, and will do so again, I doubt not.'

'Oh, then he does sit at your elbow sometimes, does he?'

'Often enough; and black enough he looks.'

'What shape does he take now? What does he look like?'

'Many a shape. Once he dragged me through some months of low dissipation—I'm an elevated character, you perceive. He got me into the mire and held me there till I was nearly choked. But I managed to scramble out some-how. That was after my mother had gone,' he added slowly, and with hesitation. 'I had nothing then, not a soul to turn to. Bah! It's a filthy recollection. He takes other shapes now.'

'As what, for instance?'

'Oh, now he oftenest looks like a lean knave, clutching an empty purse, and pointing his finger along a cold road full of mile-stones that get more and more tumbledown-looking as you go on. I passed the twenty-sixth of them the other day.'

'Ha!' said the old man, clutching the round knob of his stick, pursing his mouth and staring down at the dusty floor with round, open eyes, as he shook his head a little. 'I know him. I know those mile-stones, too. You've many yet to pass before you get to the one that *I* tottered by a few weeks ago.'

'Which was that?' asked Aglionby, in a softer tone.

'The seventy-second.'

'Ah! That is a long way from twenty-six.'

'Ay, it is. Well; you haven't made yourself out a smooth or delicate character,' he said, with sudden quickness and keenness.

Aglionby shrugged his shoulders.

'Why should I? You would hardly have believed me if I had, seeing that I am one of your own race. Such as I am, I have told you—why, I couldn't say, whatever you were to give me for it.'

'And your existence here, is it an inspiriting one?'

'No—at least, not that part of it which is devoted to business.'

'It is not a business in which you are likely to rise, then?'

'Not unless I bought my rise. The heavier you are weighted—with gold—the faster you get on in the race,' said Bernard, rather drily.

'H'm! Did you choose it for yourself?'

'Necessity and the length of my mother's purse chose it for me. They bound me over to them for five years, and paid me various salaries during that time, beginning with five pounds, and ending with the dizzy eminence of five-and-twenty. Since then, by screwing hard, I've been able to keep myself.'

'And is this situation pretty secure?'

'It is quite secure, so long as I am the cheapest and hardest-working fellow they can find for it.'

'But why should you submit to such scurvy treatment? A grandson of mine! Monstrous! give them a lesson; offer to leave them.'

Again Aglionby laughed the cynic's laugh.

'They would take me at my word at once, and there would be fifty hungry men waiting to step into my shoes, and to thank heaven on their knees for the work that I was too dainty for.'

'But you could find something else—something more suited——'

'When I can—something more remunerative—I shall cut the present concern without scruple, I assure you.'

'What would you be, if you had to choose ?'

'That's a leading question, but I happen to have an answer ready for it. I'd be a politician, with enough money to help my cause forward, and the opposition one backward.'

'Your cause being—I saw you at the Liberal demonstration on Saturday.'

'Yes, my cause is the Liberal cause, or rather the Liberal cause is mine.'

The old man rose.

'I must go,' said he. 'When I came in here, I was thinking of you, and wondering where in all this great city you were to be found. I guessed who you were, when I heard that girl call you Bernard. Is *she* the girl you are engaged to ?'

'Yes.'

'Ah, well! wouldn't you really like to run over to Scar Foot? I can tell you it is a place well worth visiting—the fairest spot, *I* say, in the fairest county in all fair England.'

'I dare say; it would do me no good to see it—under the circumstances,' replied Bernard curtly, while an intense longing to look upon it rushed over him. Had he not heard its every room described by his father, till he felt that were he dropped down before it, he could find his way through it blindfold! He had heard the doggerel old verse which that father had repeated in his last hours, as he lay senseless and 'babbled of green fields.'

4

'To Fair Scar Foot my thoughts I turn,
  Whence late I walked with you,
  Through fields bedewed——'

There the recollection always broke off short; but
Aglionby, from his earliest childhood, always thought of
Scar Foot as surrounded with 'fields bedewed.' His father,
exiled and banished, had never ceased to love his home,
and return to it in fancy, with a dalesman's deep and
ineradicable love. If he, Bernard, were thus disturbed at
the mere idea of seeing the much-loved spot, what might the
extent of his weakness be, should he ever really behold it?
No; he would keep firm while yet he could; and he added
nothing to his last words, though his lips were parted.

His grandsire watched him keenly.

'Can you unstiffen your fingers so as to shake hands with
me?' he asked.

Bernard paused. Then literally carrying out the old
man's words, he did unbend his obstinate joints, and put
them within the old, knotted hand held out to him.

Their eyes met; there was plenty of dogged obstinacy
in both their faces, plenty of self-opinionatedness, pride,
determination; rugged, twisted characters, both of them, but
honest. As their fingers touched, Bernard remembered—
and the recollection seemed to throw a new light over his
mind—that his father had not been strong and sturdy like
this; who was to say what provocation this irascible old man
might not have received at the hands of his beloved? What
passionately cherished hopes might not have been blighted
when Ralph Aglionby left 'Fair Scar Foot,' at strife with his
father, and after sulking in London for six months took to
wife Bernarda Long, from among what must have seemed to
the retired country squire the daughters of Heth—the ranks,
namely, of poor musical professional people!

As if by one impulse their hands closed upon one another,
in a mighty grip; then, without a word, were unclasped again.

Old John Aglionby walked erectly away, nor turned to look back, whatever his secret yearnings might be. His grandson, left to a few moments' solitude, stalked to a dingy window, and looked out upon the throng in the busy street below. The din became vague in his ears; the sights blurred before his eyes. What had passed seemed like a dream. Never to any human being, save to his mother, when he had been a boy, had he laid bare so much of his heart, or spoken so freely of his thoughts and feelings. Why had he done it? He was roused by a touch on his elbow. Looking round he confronted the boy Bob, holding up a coin, no less an one than a golden sovereign.

'He gave me this!' he exclaimed breathlessly.

'Who? Old Jenkinson?'

'Lord, no! catch him! That old gentleman that was with you. He met me as I was coming back, and he said, was I any friend of yours? and——'

'I know what you said, simpleton,' replied Aglionby, in his softest tone, and in his voice there were notes of the gentlest music.

'I said the truth. I said you were the best friend I had, and that I'd die for you; and he said, "That's right, lad; he's worth it!" and gave me this.'

'Mr. Aglionby, wanted!' sang out a voice at the other end of the room, and Aglionby, having missed his dinner in the parley which had taken place, advanced to attend to the requirements of two specimens of that much-prized visitant, the buyer.

CHAPTER V.

OUT OF HARMONY.

WITH a vague yearning for sympathy and the comments of some fellow-creature, Aglionby that night called Lizzie aside, telling her he had something important to relate to her. They retired into the empty back parlour, and sitting side by side in the firelight, he made his first great confidence to her. She was the woman he loved ; she was to be the partner of his life, his companion for better for worse. To whom else could he have turned more appropriately ?

He felt that it was not right to conceal his true history from her any longer. When he sat down beside her, and began, it was out of a full heart that he spoke, and he looked eagerly for her words of sympathy ; half his trouble would be removed when she should say to him, 'Dear Bernard, you have done right, and I approve of your conduct.'

She heard his narrative with many expressions of astonishment, but with very few questions or interruptions. He told her what had happened that morning, and how his grandfather turned out to be the same old man whom they had seen at the theatre on Saturday night.

'Then you quarrelled with your grandfather ?' said Lizzie.

'It was not I ; but he quarrelled with my father at his marriage ; he disowned and disinherited him, and would never see him again.'

'Then your father married some one whom this old gentleman did not like ?'

'Exactly. My mother was poor ; she gave music-lessons ; she was half English, half Spanish. She had nothing but her goodness, her cleverness, and her good looks, which last you must confess she has bequeathed to me in overflowing measure.'

'Oh, nonsense ! But was the old man so hard as all that ? Did he never get over it ?'

'You see he had wished my father to marry his own cousin, a Miss Arkendale, with whom he had been brought up all his life. My father would not. They quarrelled about that first, and my father left home, and very soon afterwards sent word that he was married to my mother. That brought the matter to a climax. He was forbidden ever to go near Scar Foot again. My father was not a particularly powerful character, but he held out for several years, and would neither compromise nor temporise. Then he died, rather suddenly, as I have told you. My mother went on with her teaching, and kept herself and me. She told me once, when I asked about my father's relations, that she had only once received any notice from the old man, and that notice took the shape of a proposition that she should part with me, give me to him, you know, and not see me or have anything to do with me again except for one month in each year, in which case she was to be handsomely provided for for life. She never told me how she received the proposition, but I can well imagine with what rage it would be. She always told me simply, that it was of course quite out of the question. From that day to this, no notice has been taken of her or me. My grandfather turned to his niece, the niece whom he had wished my father to marry. She married too, a clergyman, I believe, and she and her daughters have become all in all to him. They are his heiresses, quite the heiresses of the country-side. One of them will no doubt have the old house—Scar Foot.'

' Is it a family mansion? Have they lived there long ?'

'Hundreds of years, my dear. I have heard about it till I know it as well as if I had lived there ; but I shall never look upon it.'

' Then, of course, that girl we saw with him, whom you admired so much, will be his favourite niece ; perhaps he'll leave her *all* his money, and then won't she be a catch !' observed Miss Vane, unconsciously hitting right and left at Bernard's susceptibilities. With one of those flashes of intuition which are often most surprisingly brilliant in the most stupid persons, she had hit upon a solution of the question (which Aglionby had been almost unconsciously revolving in his mind, ever since he had parted with his grandfather that morning)—a solution so exceedingly probable, on the face of it, recommending itself to the superior masculine understanding, which had not yet arrived at it by the slower but more infallible route of a process of reasoning, that the possessor of the said masculine understanding, jumping from his chair, cried with emphasis :

'By Jove, I expect you are right! I wish I had taken more notice of her !'

'Well, I think you took about as much as you could. I know I felt quite cut out. By the way, was he very disagreeable to you this morning ?'

'Not at all. He has a rough manner, because he has a rough nature. But if I had encouraged him he would soon have become quite amiable. He invited me to go to Scar Foot in my holidays.'

'Bernard !' her eyes sparkled. 'You will come into your rights in the end of all. If you make yourself agreeable to him while you are there, you will soon thrust these nieces aside, and he'll leave all the money to *you*, as he ought. That will be grand !'

Aglionby experienced a kind of shock in thus discovering how entirely he had failed in his effort to win her sympathy. She understood that he had a grandfather who was rich, and who appeared favourably disposed towards him, and she took it for granted that he would at once endeavour to secure possession of some of that wealth. He patiently endeavoured to put her right, quite sure that she had misunderstood ; he had not explained clearly.

'My dear child, do you imagine that I could or would stoop to him after his years of cruelty and injustice? I declined utterly to have anything to do with him or his caprices. He can confine his attentions to those who are willing to subject themselves to him and wait for what they can get. I am not one of them.'

'Well, I never ! If you call that playing your cards well, I don't. I call it idiotic.'

' My dear !'

'Yes, I do. To think of throwing away a chance like that ! It's all very well to be clever, and to know all about politics, and so on ; but if it makes you neglect your own interests, and behave like a simpleton, I've done.'

She spoke with temper, and added :

' You're not so tremendously rich that you can afford to fling rude words at a grandfather with money. And you might have thought of others that you profess to care for——'

' My dearest Lizzie,' said he, gravely taking her hand, and looking earnestly at her, ' hear me ! You have misunderstood. I have told you this story because I wish you to learn all about me and my belongings, not because I wish to take any part in the matter. I *have* no interests to look after, no cards to play in the case, as you appear to think. My intention is to remain perfectly neutral, just as I always have been. My grandfather treated my father tyrannically and shamefully. I don't say he was utterly without provocation—he may have been provoked to a certain extent ; but, after all, it is not a sin for a man to wish to marry a good and clever and amiable woman, whom he loves. There was no crime in the matter. It simply did not please him, and his nature was so despotic that unless everyone gave way to him he behaved atrociously. He would have been the first to challenge any man who had disputed his own right to choose in such a matter. I have nothing to thank him for, save utter neglect. There are such things as manliness and honour, Lizzie. If I had consented to enter his house, or stooped to accept favours flung at me as you'd fling a bone to a dog, I should have suffered sorely in my honour and self-respect. Understand me—I have nothing to do with this inheritance ; it is no more to me than if it did not exist——'

' But if he left it to you, you'd take it ?' she interrupted, eagerly.

He laughed.

'Take it? oh yes, fast enough! And when the first grape harvest comes off on the Yorkshire moors which surround Scar Foot, I'll take you there to partake in the rejoicings and try the vintage. That's a bargain!'

'How can I understand such stuff as that? But I cannot see what harm there would have been in a little civility to an old man like that, for he must be old to have a grandson twenty-six.'

'He's seventy-two—he told me so. I don't know that I behaved uncivilly to him after the first interchange of compliments. But you have never served under a tyrant, or you would know that civility is a small portion of what they require from those who are beneath them. To serve a tyrant for gain, to wait for dead men's shoes, generally means slavery of the most degrading description while your tyrant lives; and when he dies, to be kicked out by his successor penniless and barefoot still.'

'That sounds very grand, but I know that money is a very good thing.'

'So it is; and being fully conscious of that fact, I am going to set about earning some as speedily as may be.'

'Why earn it, when you could have had it given you?' she said, pursuing the topic with an obstinacy and an urgency which he had never known her display before.

'No one has offered to give me any, that I am aware of,' he answered very gravely. 'And I think, my love, as we don't appear to agree upon the subject, 'we had better let it drop. I do not intend to make the slightest advance to Mr. Aglionby of Scar Foot, nor does he intend taking any further notice of me, unless I am much mistaken; or unless I am ready to lie down and let him trample on me—which I am not.'

Lizzie was silent—less convinced than ever. Bernard's revelations of this evening had awakened in her all kinds of desires and ambitions. She would so like to be rich; to leave this poky little house and live in a large one, and go to the best shops, and never have to ask for an estimate of the cost of a new dress. She would like to go to parties and concerts; into the reserved seats where 'the swells' went ('swells' being her term for all who could afford to live luxuriously). She would like to show Lucy Golding a few things; to open her eyes upon some points regarding which she displayed a lamentable deficiency.

Her mind was overflowing with these thoughts, burning thoughts; but when she looked at Bernard she had to confine them to the sphere of thoughts—she dared not speak them out.

As for Aglionby, the interview of this morning had left upon his mind, too, a deeper impression than he was himself fully aware of. He had been rough and abrupt to his grandfather, had cut short his advances, and steadily refused his half-ungracious overtures; but he had looked the old man in the face, and had not misliked his countenance. He had seen something there which he felt to be in harmony with certain chords in his own nature. He had said that if they were much together he would be certain to thwart his elder every day, but on reflection he felt less certain on that point. He fancied he could have been so far in sympathy with his grandfather as to have put up with a good deal at his hands. Then there rushed over his mind the unchanged, monotonous dreariness of his own prospects. He had described with grim humour how the devil was wont to come and place himself at his elbow, but now the humorous part of it had somehow disappeared, and only the blackness and ugliness of the vision remained.

He tried to pooh-pooh it; to consider it a mere episode, and have done with it. He took up the newspaper containing the leading article upon his own letter, and read it through. And he repeated to himself, 'What does it matter? 'Twill all be the same a hundred years hence.'

CHAPTER VI.

YORESETT-IN-DANESDALE.

JOHN AGLIONBY, going down the stairs of the warehouse, and out at the principal door, found himself in the roar of the crowded street and some ten minutes' walk from his hotel. He paused a short time, and looked blankly around him, like one in a dream ; then took his way to the hotel, where he knew that his grandniece would be waiting for him, prepared to start on their homeward journey. On proceeding to the hall of the hotel, he saw their luggage awaiting them, and on going into the coffee-room he found his niece, Judith Conisbrough, sitting on a sofa, reading the morning paper. She looked up as he came in, and rose.

'I thought you were going to be late, uncle,' she remarked, with a slight smile, as she began to draw on her gloves. 'You look heated,' she added considerately, 'and tired. I hope you have not been overdoing yourself.'

'What should I have been overdoing myself with?' he grumbled. 'Here, waiter ! bring me my bill, and call me a cab There's a stand outside there, I perceive.'

The bill was soon settled, the cab soon called. As they drove to the station Judith glanced more than once in an inquiring manner at her great-uncle, whose whole aspect and demeanour had undergone a subtle change since he had left the hotel, armed with an introduction to view the premises of Messrs. Jenkinson and Sharp. It was true that since the meeting on Saturday afternoon she had noticed an absence in his demeanour more than once, but she had put its cause down to the memories called up in his mind of the days of his youth, of those days when he had been heart and soul an enthusiast for the cause in which the great Irkford politicians had won their spurs. This morning his abstraction was more marked than it yet had been. It amounted to a fixed, brooding gaze before him. Perhaps, she thought, he had met with some old friend of his early days, and was conning over past scenes and past events. She did not speak to him nor question him as to his absence of manner, but she saw that all he said and did was done and said in an almost mechanical way, until they were seated in the train, and it rolled slowly forward towards 'Yorkshire and the North.'

Even then he had nothing to say, but sat gazing forth upon the uninviting prospect which surrounded them for a long time after leaving Irkford—endless dirty suburbs, vast manufactories, great sheds where machinery was made; these followed in their turn by still more depressing-looking localities, half town, half a dismal mockery of the country, where the trees in the beginning of October were already leafless, and had been so for the last three weeks. It all looked very dingy and half-hearted, and so the old man seemed to think, for he suddenly heaved a great sigh, and said :

'It's a go-ahead place, this, and I notice that go-ahead places are generally dirty. My throat feels dry for want of a draught of the fresh air at Scar Foot.'

'Yes ; I don't think a town life would suit you, uncle ; and for my part, I think I should suffocate if I had to live in a street.'

He made no answer, but leaned his head back, and closed his eyes. With what was his mind busied, she wondered, that he should have that pinched, pained look, that sudden appearance of age, and loss of heartiness and vigour?

Whatever his secret thoughts might be, he did not confide them to her, but maintained his gravity and taciturnity during the whole journey, which, by the railway, lasted about three hours. Judith Conisbrough presently ceased to study him ; she knew him too well to attempt to talk with him when he was in that mood, and she leaned back in her seat, and watched the landscape as it grew ever wilder and more beautiful, while the fair and fertile lowlands were left behind, and suddenly she saw, grimly appearing above a high green hill, the round blue head of some great mountain whose height surpassed that of all the others near. It was Peny-gent, and from that she knew that their railway journey would not last much longer.

The train had borne them through all that wild and beautiful district of Craven, and Penygent had been left far behind, when they drew up at a little wayside junction, and got out, to pursue the rest of their journey in a dogcart. Their train had been a slow one, but it puffed them deliberately into fairyland.

Judith, seated beside her uncle, and with their small luggage, and the man-servant behind, enjoyed the pleasure, as she always did, of moving through that beautiful vale. Each village and hamlet that they passed gave one the idea, more and more strongly confirmed as they advanced, that they were rapidly approaching the end of the world.

It was a soft, mellow October afternoon—the sky of that tempered, chastened blue, the sun's beams of that pleasant, far from fervid warmth, peculiar to this most delicious season of the year; and the 'feel' of the air in those limestone regions of romance, how like it is to some delicate wine of which one may drink to repletion, without any after sensation but one of pleasure ! As they left the little wayside station, and the good mare stretched her long legs over the white road, the faces, both of old man and young woman, lighted up and took a brighter glow. On every side of them, as they bowled along, with an occasional slower motion as they breasted some hill, were great green and grey fells, some of them with bare brown summits, showing where the peat-bogs lay, and where the peat was deep ; others crowned by some bleak escarpment of bald grey limestone, grimly con-trasting with the verdant green of the lower slopes and the fertile valleys and fat pastures beside the river, the Yore.

If one stood quite still, one could hear the murmur of rushing waters, coming one knew not whence; but one could guess that the pure springs of those streams and cascades were concealed somewhere amongst the bare folds of the hills, or were leaping down their beds deep in the recesses of the plentiful woods which were visible on every side, and of which the foliage was, not like that of Irkford—a vanished thing; but a ruddy and a golden glory, impossible to surpass. At first they saw the river, now many miles away from its dark and elevated source in the bleak side of Great Shunner Fell, gleaming through grassy meads in a bed which it filled to the brim; while the cattle drank from it, and the reeds bent and swayed in its current.

They had driven for some distance before either of them spoke. The longed-for draught of fresh air they had at last, and an uneasy weight was removed from Judith's mind at least.

'I'll put you down at your mother's door,' said Mr. Aglionby, 'and your luggage with you, and I shall get home myself long before it's dark.'

'Oh, thank you, uncle. But won't you come in and take tea with us?'

'No, I'll go on to Scar Foot at once,' he said decidedly.

'Wouldn't you like Delphine or Rhoda to go with you for a day or two?'

'No, I want no one,' he answered, with a sudden distrustful look sideways from under his bushy eyebrows, which look she did not remark, being fully engaged in glancing joyfully around at the beautiful hills, and the beloved woods, and along the up-and-down limestone road, which would lead at last to the cobble-stoned street of Yoresett, where her home was.

Presently they drove up the said street, into the quaint, sloping, open space which formed the market-place at Yoresett. In the middle was the ancient stone market-cross, around which at the half-yearly 'hirings' the countrymen and wenches stood to be hired as farm labourers or servants. Facing the market-cross on the left hand of the square stood a splendid old stone house—a mansion in size, solidly built, large, commodious, and handsome ; and with a date over the door, of 1558, showing that it had been built in the first year of the reign of good Queen Bess. It rose straight out of the street, its gardens lying behind, and it was called Yoresett House. It was the property of Mrs. Conisbrough, and the residence of herself and her daughters. Over the way there were houses and shops, small village shops, full of the marvellously useless articles only to be found in such shops, and higher up, the winding, roughly paved street narrowed, first up a hill, and then down one, and consisted of an inn or two, and a shop or two, and the post-office, and many odd-looking houses, inhabited by what the denizens of the busy world would doubtless have thought odd-looking people. It was altogether as old-world, quiet, quaint a place as could well be imagined.

The dogcart was pulled up before the door of the old stone house, and before Judith could get down, the said door was quickly opened, and in the frame made by this process appeared a young, fresh, handsome face, with dark, dare-devil eyes, while a young voice, high but not shrill, cried :

' I'm glad to see you, Judith ! I thought it must be you. Be quick in, and tell us all the news. The slippers *are* kept in the same place yet, so you needn't ask that. How do you do, uncle? Come, Judith, we want the news, the news, the news, I say, and we shall turn you out of doors if you haven't got any.'

Judith's box was conveyed into the house by a servant-maid ; she shook hands with her uncle, exchanged some parting words with him, and then she was pulled into the house ; the door was shut, and Mr. Aglionby drove off down the street, to take another road to Scar Foot.

Judith, her arm still grasped by her sister, entered the roomy, stone-paved hall of the old house which was her home, and paused there, as if not quite sure which way she meant to take : whether one that should lead into one of the numerous parlours and sitting-rooms on the ground-floor, or whether towards the staircase. Her course was decided for her. The young lady who had appeared at the door—or rather, part of whose person had appeared at the door, while the remainder of it and her attire were carefully concealed behind the said door—now stood, or rather danced, revealed as a tall, healthy-looking damsel of fifteen or sixteen, still in short frocks, and with a large, coarse kitchen apron tied around her. She wound it into a kind of rope, and danced lightly and bewilderingly around her elder.

'No, you are not going upstairs,' she said decidedly. 'You are coming into the parlour to enjoy a cup of tea, and above all, to tell us the news. So don't attempt to shirk it.'

'Suppose I have no news?' suggested Judith, moving with serene dignity towards a door on the left hand of the hall.

'That is an idea too monstrous to be entertained for a moment. You have spent four whole days in a great city, at an hotel—of course you have news ; I would give the world to stay at an hotel, it must be so grand ! What a swell I should feel, if I were you !'

'My dear Rhoda——'

' "How vulgar you are !" I know what's coming, and am kind enough to spare you the trouble of saying it.'

She laughed, still jumping lightly from one foot to the other. Judith looked at her, and smiled too, indulgently.

'Well, at least take off that apron,' said she, pausing just before the parlour door. 'Don't present yourself before mother with such a thing on.'

'Why not, I wonder ? Besides, I can't take it off till my work is done.'

' What work ? *You* working !'

' Well, I'll tell you,' said Rhoda, a ripple of mirth running over her face. ' Ho, ho, ho !' she burst into a peal of laughter that made the rafters ring ; ' I'll tell you—I am plucking a goose !'

' Plucking a goose !'

' Just so. One came—was sent, I mean ; you could hardly expect the poor thing to walk over of its own accord —from Scar Foot ; and that lazy old Geoffrey Metcalfe had never plucked it. He *is* an aged impostor, if ever there was one. Louisa has plenty to do, poor creature ; so there was literally no one to do it but me, and I've been in the kitchen, lost to all outside things, absorbed in my work and my work alone, as you so often say I should be. Come in ! I think mother and Delphine are both——*Oh !*'

She had pushed open the door, and entered the parlour, but suddenly recoiled on the very threshold, almost falling over upon her sister, who, filled with a somewhat impatient astonishment, put her aside, and entered the room.

' Mother and Delphine' were certainly there ; the former a comely-looking matron, resembling her eldest daughter in features, but with a high complexion, and eyes which lacked the steadfastness of Judith's ; the latter a very lovely, slender, fair-haired creature, who sat in a side-window embroidering.

Rhoda's ' oh !' had been called forth by the fact that they were not alone. Standing in the window recess, and languidly propping himself against the side of it, was a tall young man, who, with his hands clasped behind him, had fixed his eyes upon Delphine's work, and who appeared either too exhausted or too indolent to lift them off it again.

Judith, inwardly as much surprised as Rhoda at the appa- rition, advanced, nevertheless, with her usual composure. Delphine rose and went to meet her, undulating forward with a peculiarly graceful, •sylph-like movement. Rhoda, after her first recoil, took courage, and went forward, her colour high, but her eyes defiantly laughing.

A kiss on the part of the two elder girls. Then Judith went to her mother, stooped over her, and kissed her, remarking : 'I'm glad to see you haven't suffered while I have been away, mother. You look very well.'

' I am very well, my dear, and very glad to see you back ! You are earlier than we expected !'

'We came by the Midland instead of the North-Eastern, mamma.'

'Oh yes. My dear, let me introduce our visitor. Mr. Danesdale, my eldest daughter.' Mr. Danesdale bowed low, rousing himself, apparently, from his languor to do so ; Miss Conisbrough smiled, and asked :

'Sir Gabriel's son ?'

'S—Sir Gabriel has the happiness to call me son,' replied the young gentleman with a very slight stammer, a very slow and pronounced drawl, and a south-country accent which struck with peculiar effect upon Judith Conisbrough's northern ears.

You have been long expected,' she said.

'Yet I came quite unexpectedly after all,' he answered, turning to Rhoda and holding out his hand to her. Not a smile dawned upon his handsome face, which was even sad in its tired solemnity of expression. He had mournful, slowly-moving eyes of dark blue, over which the lids fell thoughtfully—or sleepily ? Judith speculated. His general expression and manner was one of weariness and *ennui* carried to excess.

'Good-afternoon,' he drawled. 'That goose : is it nearly done ?'

'Ah, *you* never plucked a goose, never saw one done, in your life, Mr. Danesdale,' she said, blushing, more with suppressed laughter than embarrassment.

'I've n—never done it myself, certainly ; but I've often

5

seen other fellows do it; or if not geese, pigeons, which comes to the same thing, you know.'

'Fie, Mr. Danesdale!' said Mrs. Conisbrough, smiling with a placid amusement expressing anything but 'fie.'

'But why, mamma?' cries Miss Rhoda, thirsting for information. 'What is there wrong in watching people pluck geese, or pigeons either? You are casting a reflection upon your child when you say "fie." And if Mr. Danesdale's friends——'

'Oh, I beg your pardon; I didn't say "my friends," I said "other fellows." There's a difference,' expostulated Mr. Danesdale.

'Well, it's very funny,' replied Rhoda, while the rest of the company smiled, and the young man placed a chair for Judith, opening his eyes fully at last, and saying:

'You have been at Irkford, Mrs. Conisbrough says.'

'Yes, with Mr. Aglionby, my uncle.'

'Indeed. W—what sort of a place is it? I never was there, though I used to know some fellows at Oxford who had been. They lived there when they were at home.'

'I can hardly tell what sort of a place it is. Very large and very dirty——'

'Oh, what a poor, tame description!' said Rhoda. 'You little know what she did while she was there, Mr. Danesdale; nor what she went for. She is a dangerous person. She went on purpose to go to the Liberal Demonstration.'

'Did she go, or was she taken there?' asked Mr. Danesdale.

'Both,' replied Judith, taking off her gloves. The young gentleman had seated himself, and appeared in no haste to take his departure. He was dressed in a brown velvet shooting-jacket and knickerbockers, and now Judith remembered to have vaguely noticed a gun leaning up against the wall in the hall. Rhoda at this juncture was beckoned to by her mother, and going to her, received some whispered instructions which sent her skipping out of the room.

'D—does she always run?' asked young Danesdale earnestly.

The others laughed.

'Almost always. I wish she would practise walking a little, now that she is such a big girl,' said Delphine, speaking for the first time.

'I don't think I should tell her so,' he said in a tone that was almost animated. 'She looks very nice as she is!'

'Yes, I think so,' Judith said, and Mrs. Conisbrough turned to her.

'Mr. Danesdale has been kind enough to bring us some birds, Judith; so he's going to stay and have a cup of tea, and walk home to Danesdale Castle.'

'To walk!' Judith had said in some surprise, and before she had time to restrain herself.

'You seem surprised,' he remarked. 'I often notice that people do look surprised when they hear that I can walk at all, and then I always feel inclined to say, "Would you rather look a better walker than you are, or be a better walker than you look?"'

'The last for me,' said Judith, laughing. 'It is much easier to answer than the one about being a fool and looking one.'

'Perhaps it is,' he admitted. 'At least it is very beautiful to have it decided for you so promptly. I have heard a great deal about you, Miss Conisbrough. I have pictured you in my own mind, marching on with the multitudes to the Liberal Demonstration at Irkford.'

'Our chariot marched along, and that very slowly, for the multitude was very great, literally.'

'I suppose it would be. Irkford is such a t—tremendous place for that sort of thing.'

'Only Irkford?' suggested Delphine, presenting him with a cup of the tea which, accompanied by Rhoda, had now arrived.

'Yoresett too, it seems,' he answered; 'which is what I

should never have expected. Miss Conisbrough, did you really go because you wished, or on compulsion ?'

' I went because I wished.'

' Judith is the politician of this family,' observed Rhoda. 'She has been known to sit up at night reading political books.'

' And where did you get your politics from ?' he asked.

' Chiefly from my uncle.'

' By the way, Judith, how is your uncle ? I wonder he didn't come in,' said Mrs. Conisbrough.

' He—oh, he seemed rather in a hurry to get back to Scar Foot,' answered Judith, with a sudden constraint in her manner, which Delphine noticed with a quick look upwards.

'Have you seen Mr. Aglionby yet, Mr. Danesdale ?' asked Judith. ' He and Sir Gabriel are great friends, though such very opposite characters.'

' I've heard a lot about him, but I have not seen him. That is a lovely place of his by the lake—what is it called ?'

' Shennamere.'

' Shennamere—yes. I rode over with my father the very day after my return. But Mr. Aglionby was out, they said.'

' I see.'

' And there didn't appear to be anybody else. Has Mr. Aglionby no children ?'

There was a momentary, a more than momentary, pause and silence, during which Danesdale thought to himself :

' Now, why did I ask that question ? I've put my foot in it, somehow.'

At last Mrs. Conisbrough remarked, blandly, but not cordially :

' Mr. Aglionby's only son displeased him exceedingly, many years ago. He married a woman his inferior in every way. Mr. Aglionby quarrelled with him and disinherited him, and some years afterwards the son died.'

' I see. It must be rather slow for the poor old fellow, I

should think.   He must often have regretted the loss of the
only fellow with whom he could constantly quarrel.'

' Oh, I don't think it was his desire to be always quarrelling with anyone, poor old man !   Of course he felt the
misunderstanding.'

' Rather a serious misunderstanding, to quarrel irreparably
with one's only son, wasn't it ?' asked Mr. Danesdale, whose
drawl had almost disappeared, and whose eyes, no longer
half closed, were regarding Mrs. Conisbrough inquiringly.

' Y—yes,' replied the lady, trifling with her teaspoon, and
gazing into her cup.   It was a very terrible misunderstanding.   It cut him up very much.   But I hope we—the girls
and I—have done all that lay in our power to make up to
him for the loss of his son.'

' Ah, y—yes,' said Mr. Danesdale, returning to his drawl
and his hesitation.   ' But an only son's a difficult thing to
replace.   Being one myself, I speak from mournful experience.   My father tells me, often, what an unique article I
am.   I'm sure he finds me a great anxiety, just from that very
feeling that he couldn't replace me if anything were to happen
to me.   Will you have some more tea, Miss Conisbrough ?'

Judith started as she gave him her half-empty cup to put
down.

' No, thank you.   I'm not thirsty, nor hungry either.'

' I should think that lake by Scar Foot must be a glorious
place for skating,' observed Mr. Danesdale.   ' Does it ever
get frozen over ?'

' Oh yes !' Rhoda exclaimed fervently.   ' It does, and
when it is frozen I could live on it.   You can't think what
it costs me to come off it at the end of the day.   I do hope
the next winter will be a hard one, Mr. Danesdale, and then
you would see what it is like, all about here.   I always say
there is no such place as Yoresett and the dale in the world,
but Judith and Delphine vow they would rather live in a
musty town ; and why, do you suppose ?'

'Society, perhaps.'

'Oh no! At least, only the society of dead men. They would like to live in a town because there would be *libraries* there.'

Scorn unutterable was expressed in the accent laid on the penultimate word.

'L—libraries. But you can have a library in the country. At least, there's Mudie's. They send all over the country. Mudie's will send you anything you want.'

Another pause till Mrs. Conisbrough began :

'Well, really, in many ways, Mudie's is such a tiresome institution. They sometimes keep you so long——'

'Mudie's is a delightful institution, but a very expensive one,' said Judith composedly. 'A box for the country, to be worth anything, costs five guineas, and then there's the carriage to and from London.'

'My dear Judith, that won't interest Mr. Danesdale.'

'Perhaps not ; I only wish him to understand.'

'Yes,' said he ; 'in such a case you want a free library.'

'Our library consists of fields and trees, and the running brooks,' observed Delphine, laughing.

'Miss Conisbrough's has been something else as well,' he observed, looking at Judith, putting down his cup, and rising all at once.

'Not much else,' answered she. 'So little else that it will take me a long time to digest all that I saw and heard in Irkford while I was there.'

He shook hands with Mrs. Conisbrough, remarking that he would be just in time for dinner, if he took the short cut across the moor ; and then, bidding adieu to the young ladies, and asking if he might come again, he took his departure.

CHAPTER VII.

THE SISTERS.

Now, Del, I'll go upstairs, and remove the stains of travel,' remarked Judith, putting aside Rhoda's renewed demands for news.

'Yes, do, and I'll come with you,' answered Delphine, as they passed out of the parlour together.

Outside, in the hall, they stood still, and looked each at the other, their hands locked together. Then both bent forward, and exchanged a grave kiss.

'Now I feel as if I really were at home again,' said Judith, in a tone of satisfaction. 'I'll come to your room, Del, since my things have not walked upstairs, and, according to Rhoda's account, there is no one to bring them at present.'

'All right,' said Delphine, flying up the shallow oaken stairs with a rapid motion, and then, arrived at the top, standing still and looking down upon her more slowly-moving sister.

'You are more like some "strange, bright bird" than ever, child,' said Judith, her eyes dwelling upon her with deep pleasure.

'Don't add, "with plumage gay," I pray you,' laughed Delphine, 'for my plumage is very old and shabby, and is likely to continue so.'

'It shows off your beauty the better, then,' replied the other, as they went arm-in-arm down a long, light, broad corridor.

There was abundance of room in Yoresett House. If the girls had not many other luxuries, they could each indulge in that of a separate bedroom, and one or two sitting-rooms apiece as well. The only difficulty about it being, as Rhoda had more than once observed, that there was no furniture in any of them.

Delphine flitted about the room, pouring out water for
Judith to wash her hands in, placing a brush and comb for
her, and so forth, all her movements being instinct with a
grace on which the eyes of the elder girl continually dwelt.
Delphine was more like a ray of sunshine than anything else,
but not the sunshine that is broad and busy and glaring ;
rather like those rays of it which come quietly stealing
through trees on a summer afternoon, as the sun goes
westering.   Her hair was of the real golden hue, and she
wore it braided low down behind, and falling in loose and
natural waves about a delicate and sweet oval face.   She
possessed, too, the great beauty which does not always
accompany such hair and such a complexion, a pair of
limpid, golden-brown eyes, which might be light in their
actual colour, but which, as Judith had often said, 'always
behaved as if they were dark.'

Seen alone, it could not be denied that Judith Conisbrough possessed grace, as well as dignity of carriage.
Seen beside Delphine, the dignity remained, but one
wondered where the grace had gone.   The girls were aged
respectively twenty and twenty-two, and their friendship was
as closely knit a bond as could well exist.

'How did Mr. Danesdale get here, Delphine, and where
does he come from ?' asked Judith.   'How long is it since
he established himself here in this fashion ?   And have I
been away four days, or am I labouring under a delusion,
and been absent four months ?'

'Your questions are numerous, my dear, for you.   I will
answer the last one first.   You left here last Thursday, so
that as to-day is Monday, you have been away just four
days.   Mr. Danesdale got here by the prosaic method of
pulling the bell, and asking Louisa if Mrs. Conisbrough
was at home.   He performed this prodigious deed last
Thursday afternoon—not many hours after you and Uncle
Aglionby had started on your travels.'

'But what brought him here? The Danesdales and we have not had much to do with each other for a long time, now. Surely, he did not deliberately come to call upon us?'

'He came very deliberately, as he does everything,' replied Delphine, with a sudden infectious laugh, which began in her eyes, and ended with her voice. 'He came, as I tell you, and was admitted. He introduced himself, and said he had been shooting, and that in returning, coming through Yoresett, he had been prowling round our back premises, of course not knowing whose they were, and that his dog, in a moment of temporary mental aberration, having perceived our cat, had rushed into the garden after her, and was then planted beneath the big apple-tree, awaiting her descent from it, while she sat aloft and growled. He—Mr. Danesdale I mean, not the dog—thought his personal intervention would be necessary to reconcile the conflicting powers. He had asked a man whose garden it was, and as he knew Mrs. Conisbrough's name perfectly well, he had ventured—and so on. A very elegant speech, but it took him *such* a long time to get through it.'

'Well, did you let him into the garden then?'

'We let him into the garden, and watching him carefully, and in some alarm, as being such a very unusual kind of visitor for us to have, we perceived him go up the walk, call his dog to him, and administer a cuff to it.'

'Beat it? oh, horrid!' said Miss Conisbrough, with a red face of indignation.

'So Rhoda thought, for she ran out to him, and caught hold of his arm, and in a voice trembling with emotion, cried, "For shame!"'

Judith laughed.

'He turned round, took off his hat, and said, "Did you ever t—train a dog?"'

Judith laughed again at the ludicrously exact imitation of Mr. Danesdale's tones.

'Rhoda said "No." "Then," he answered, with the most melancholy drawl, "don't hinder me in the performance of a painful duty." Upon which Rhoda blushed violently, though she indignantly denies it to this day.'

'To this day ! it might have happened a month ago, to hear you talk.'

'It does seem quite a long time ago. He gave his dog a slight chastisement, and sent it in a state of abject repentance out into the road. Then mother asked him to sit down in the parlour and rest, which he did; he stayed quite a long time, and told us where he had been travelling, and what he had been doing, and what he meant to do, now that he had got home.'

'Evidently under the impression that his family and ours were on intimate terms,' interrupted Judith significantly.

'Quite so; and he described the party they had staying at the Castle, and, I'm sorry to say, made great fun of some of his sister's friends.'

'Implying that you were not so dull,' murmured Judith.

'Perhaps so,' said Delphine, who had seated herself on the edge of the bed, and who looked pensively across towards her sister. 'But then you must reflect, Judith, that as soon as he mentioned us at home, which he would be almost sure to do, his darkness would be enlightened, for Philippa Danesdale is not our devoted friend; he would hear all about us, and about our poverty, and our general insignificance.'

'Yes, of course; and what conclusion do you draw from that ?'

'Oh, nothing in particular; only you seemed to think that if he had known at first all about us and our circumstances, he might not have been so polite as he has been.'

'So I did think, and so I do.'

'Cynic ! But in that case, why does he continue to

come? for he has been several times—nearly every day, since, on some pretext or other.'

'True,' said Judith reflectively, standing still with a hair-brush in one hand, and a handglass in the other, and looking with abstracted earnestness at Delphine, who for her part met the glance openly with her luminous eyes, which seemed to reveal everything, while in reality they concealed nearly all that was passing in her mind.

'He must come, then,' said Judith slowly, 'because he likes to come.'

'Or,' suggested Delphine, with a shadowy smile, 'to amuse himself—young men like to amuse themselves, so I've heard; and speaking from my own point of view as a young woman, I should suppose it was true—and if they have inquiring minds, and are in a strange country, they like to amuse themselves by studying the manners and customs of the natives. Now, Mr. Danesdale is in a strange country— I'm sure Danesdale must be very strange to him after the years he's been away—and we, as natives, must be strange too.'

'Ergo?'

'He finds amusement in studying us.'

'It is an ingenious hypothesis, and one which does you credit,' said Judith. 'I have only one objection to make to it.'

'And what is that?'

'That I don't believe, and it would take a great deal to convince me, that Mr. Danesdale was ever amused at anything in his whole life.'

'Oh, Judith! Why, he was intensely amused at Rhoda and her goose this very afternoon.'

'Was he? Well, I beg his pardon, and yours. In the meantime, don't you think mamma will be feeling herself injured at our long absence?' said Judith, giving a final shake to her garments.

The two girls, arm-in-arm again, went down the broad, light passage, which, however, was beginning to be dusk now, and back again into the parlour. Neither of them had said, ' He comes to see some one,' yet the thought had been present in both minds.

' Now,' said Rhoda, as they came into the parlour, ' draw round the fire, and in the twilight tell us the tale of your adventures at Irkford. Give a sensational account of the meeting at once.'

Judith essayed to do so, but succeeded ill, so ill that Rhoda at last said :

' Was it enthusiastic ? I can't picture it. Was the room as large as the whole inside of Yoresett Church ?' (Yoresett Church would seat eight hundred persons at the most.)

Judith laughed.

' I must have told my tale badly indeed, Rhoda. The room held twenty-five thousand people.'

' Oh dear !' said Rhoda, subdued by the picture conjured up. ' I can't imagine it,' she said at last. ' One ought to see such things, and I never shall. And you went to the play ? Oh, *how* I should like to go to the play ! What was it called ? " Diplomacy " ? That sounds political too. Mr. Danesdale says he has been over and over again to every theatre in Europe worth speaking of, and he's going to give me an account of his experience.'

' Indeed ! Then I may as well keep my one little visit quiet. It is sure to fall flat, with such prospects as you speak of looming in the distance.'

' Mean thing !'

' Did uncle seem to enjoy it ?' asked Mrs. Conisbrough.

' He was delighted with the meeting. He saw lots of faces that he knew on the platform, and if he had not been so shy, I am sure some of those gentlemen would have given him a hearty welcome. But, of course, he wouldn't make any advances to them.'

' Just like him !'

' It gave me an odd sensation,' Judith went on, ' to see all those multitudes. We *are* ambitious, you know, Del, you and I.'

' Of libraries ?' suggested Rhoda.

' But surely it would satisfy any ambition to walk on to a platform, and on the instant of one's appearance to be cheered madly by twenty-five thousand voices, as if they never meant to leave off.'

' Yes, indeed. And did they groan? I have often wondered what groaning on a large scale could be like.'

' Oh yes ! They groaned. It has a most extraordinary effect. There's something fearful in it. When anyone whom they didn't like was mentioned, you know, then they hooted and groaned. There was a young man near to us whom I watched a little. He was standing close to the end of our bench; I never saw any face look so earnest, or express such an intensity of interest. I think his eyes had a great deal to do with it. I never saw eyes that gleamed like his, nor any face which took such an expression of scorn and contempt. I am sure that young man has a terrible tongue and a hot temper.'

' Dear me ! This is thrilling !' said Rhoda, holding up a very dilapidated linen table napkin, which she was supposed to be repairing, and then laying it down. ' I see now what you were interested in. It was the young man, not the meeting. Proceed, I implore you !'

' No ; I was interested in him as expressing the opinion of the meeting in a condensed form, as it were. The spirit that I saw in his face was the general spirit felt, I am sure. And, oddly enough, when the meeting was over, he came to my assistance when I had got separated from uncle, for there were about one hundred and fifty thousand in all.'

' Tremendous !' remarked Delphine.

'E—normous!' cried Rhoda. 'And this interesting young man; how many more times did you see him?'

'Once,' replied Judith, repressing a smile.

'You did! This is portentous! I suppose you cried, "Ha! Do I behold my doom? Speak, stranger, whence and *what* art thou?" But where did you see him again? I am interested. Everything's interesting here.'

'At the theatre.'

'No! And did he see you?'

'He saw us; yes, distinctly. I saw him in the upper circle pointing us out to——'

'To his friend—the friend of the hero? What was his friend like? Anyone in whom I could take an interest?'

'I really don't know. She was one of the prettiest creatures I ever saw in my life, despite her vulgarity and affectation.'

'*She!* It was a *she!*'

'Yes. *She* was *his* sweetheart, my dear. No one could possibly have mistaken that fact.'

'Oh—h!' Rhoda groaned. 'How you do dash my hopes to the ground! Upon the whole, I think our hero is more interesting than yours.'

'Yours?' laughed Judith provokingly. 'Which? Who? Where? Do tell me about him.'

'You saw our hero this afternoon. Unreasoning jealousy alone makes you try to deny it. And he is a gentleman by birth and breeding, who lives at home at ease, and is not engaged to a vulgar girl whom he takes to the upper circle; not that I know where that is, but you mention it so sneeringly that I am sure it must be an inferior part of the house. No; I think, taken all in all, Delphine, we prefer our hero to this groaning, hooting, gleaming, bad-tempered one of Judith's.'

Joining in the chorus of laughter which greeted her observations, Rhoda departed, saying she had a little cooking to do.

Judith and Delphine had much to talk about, but Mr. Danesdale's name was not mentioned again until late at night, when they were both in their respective beds, and Judith called from her room to Delphine's, which opened into it :

'By the way, Del, what is Mr. Danesdale's name? His Christian name by which he is known to those who love him best, you know.'

'Randulf,' came sleepily from the other room.

'*Randulf*—what a queer name !'

'It might have been better. Good-night, dear !'

'Good-night. Yes, I remember now, I have heard Philippa speak of " Randulf."'

CHAPTER VIII.

SPECTRES.

THE morning broke fine, but with a delicate white mist over everything, swathing Addlebrough hill and the other great green fells which shut in the dale, and enwrapping the woods which filled the hollows and gorges in the said hills. The Misses Conisbrough, surveying the prospect from the windows of the breakfast-room, decided that it was going to be a glorious day, and that they would go out and spend the morning at High Gill, where it would be sheltered and sunny.

There was absolutely nothing to prevent them from going out when, and for as long as they chose. No numerous engagements; no probable callers, or other claims upon their time and attention existed, to detain them.

Judith and Delphine and Rhoda Conisbrough were girls whose life had its trials. Fatherless, brotherless, and very poor, they had never known any other existence than the one they led now. Mrs. Conisbrough's income was of the

very slenderest proportions. She possessed the house she
lived in ; it had been given by old John Aglionby's father to
his daughter, Mrs. Conisbrough's mother; and she, as an
only child, had inherited it. The years of her married life
had been passed there, with the clergyman her husband.

Her income was sufficient, by strict economy, to maintain
herself and her daughters in respectability ; that sad kind of
respectability which has to be ever on the alert to conceal
the scantiness of the clothing that is beneath the decent
outside garment. They had enough of food, enough of
firing, and a servant to wait upon them and keep up appear-
ances before outside eyes.

There, their comforts might almost be said to end. The
girls had never known what real comfort or plenty meant.
What few and meagre pretences of luxury they had ever
known, had come through the hands of their great-uncle,
whose heiresses they were supposed to be, but who loved to
keep the reins of power in his own hand, and make his
favours appreciated through their very rarity. His help had
procured them an occasional visit to the seaside, an occasional dress for some rare and seldom-occurring festivity,
an unfrequent sudden little expedition like this of Judith's
to some neighbouring town with him.

It was a pinched, cramped, sordid life, and they were one
and all girls of mind and spirit ; girls who could not vegetate
in inactivity without suffering from it, mentally and morally.
They did suffer. Active brains and quick imaginations they
all possessed—possessed also intellect of no mean order,
and apparently these things had been given them for no
other purpose than that they might suppress all their
promptings. Everywhere, turn where they would, even in
this quiet dale at the world's end, there met them beauty
and pleasures, and opportunities for enjoyment, and everywhere and always they were confronted by the one grinding
answer to all wishes of that kind—' There is no money.'

Women like these it is who suffer tortures undreamed of by the busy and active, by those whose hands are full, and whose lives are running over with occupation ; who may use their brains, and turn their talents into money, or exercise them in benevolent works. Such cannot know the degrading, the souring influence of a life of monotonous poverty, of grey care, of the pinching and scraping which results in no gain, no profit, which has for sole object to hide from inquisitive or indifferent neighbours the real extent of the barrenness of the land.

They were young yet; they had rubbed on somehow. Rhoda was still too much a child, lived too intensely in the present, and rejoiced too much in the mere fact of a life of perfect health and perfect ignorance to have suffered much so far. But her sisters suffered, and suffered the more in knowing that the social law was no longer so stringent, which used to decree for women in their position, ' Thus far and no farther. Thou shalt work, not for honourable profit, but to conceal thy inherited poverty. Thou shalt wither and die where thou art—only thou shalt not come forward, nor have thy name spoken, for that is a shame.' And, if circumstances did not change, Rhoda too would suffer in years to come. Mrs. Conisbrough said it was their wretched poverty that was at the bottom of it all. It was poverty which prevented her from dressing her daughters suitably, and taking them out into the society they were fitted for.

' Had I been able to do that,' she often said, ' both Judith and Delphine would marry easily. Anyone can see that Judith goes about like a queen ; and Delphine's face, if she had her proper chances, would set a score of men raving. Instead of which they are wait—waiting here ; seeing no one, doing nothing : and their uncle will do nothing to help me, though you would think that out of sheer self-

6

respect he would wish them to make a different appearance
in the world.'

Judith, tired of these outbursts, and ashamed of hearing
them, occasionally remonstrated. A more than usually
open discussion had taken place on the subject only a day
or two before her departure with her great-uncle for Irkford.

'Political meetings,' Mrs. Conisbrough had complained,
'were not the places where girls found husbands. Their
uncle could take them to such places just to gratify himself,
but he obstinately closed his eyes against doing anything
which was for their real good.'

Judith's indignation had been roused, and she had spoken
out, more plainly than was her wont, to her mother.

'I would not take a penny from my uncle, mother, to do
as you seem to think we ought to do. You mean, I suppose,
to buy dresses, and go to balls and other places for men to
look at us, and fall in love with us. It is disgusting, and,
for my part, if he offered me the invaluable chance to-
morrow, with the alternative of never leaving Yoresett again,
I know which I would choose. But if he would give me a
hundred pounds now, to do as I like with, I would not be
here another week.'

'Why, what in the world would you do with it ?'

'I should do the only thing that I know of as being open
to me. As I have never been properly educated, and all
my accomplishments consist of a few songs which I sing
very badly, no one would take me to teach their children.
Besides, I can't teach, though I can learn as fast as anybody. I should go to some large town, such as Irkford or
Leeds, and go to the principal doctor in it, and tell him
how much money I had got, and ask him whether I could
be made into a nurse.'

'Preposterous !' said Mrs. Conisbrough crossly.

'It would be hateful, and I should loathe it at first. But
I am able to do nothing else, and it is not an expensive

trade to learn. It would earn my bread. I should be of some use to some one; for there must be people to do the drudgery of this world, and it would be, oh, the whole universe higher than selling myself to a man in exchange for a home and clothing. Any girl out of the street can do that.'

'Judith, I forbid you ever to utter such—such coarse, horrible expressions again in my hearing. To speak in that way of marriage—the happiest and holiest institution there is.'

'If that is what you call marriage, give me unholy institutions.'

'I am too much shocked and grieved to say any more,' replied Mrs. Conisbrough, really hurt.

'I am very sorry if you are hurt, mother. Unfortunately, Del and I have so very much time on our hands, and so little to do with it, that we get bitter sometimes, and wish we were housemaids.'

'You little know what you are talking about. This murmuring spirit of yours is shocking, Judith. I can't really imagine what you have to complain of,' said her mother, with the sublime inconsistency of a weak-willed woman, who is tenacious of no proposition except the one which asserts that surely never was mortal vexed as she is vexed. 'You have a house to live in, clothes to cover you, and food to eat.'

'So has a well-to-do-farmer's cow in winter. If I felt like a cow, I should consider myself well off, I dare say.'

'Who said anything about cows? You always wander so far from the point. Not only that, but you have your uncle's money to look to. When he dies, you will, every one, be well off, and I shall perhaps have a little rest, if I'm not killed with trouble before ever he goes—poor, dear old man!'

The last words came hastily, as an after-thought. 'It is

6—2

best to bow at the name of the devil—he can do so much harm.' Mrs. Conisbrough had become suddenly desirous of counteracting the impression which her first remarks might have produced, that she cherished hopes of Mr. Aglionby's speedy demise, or that she considered him a stingy curmudgeon. If any such speeches ever penetrated to his ears, the service of all these years would assuredly go for nought.

'I would far rather that uncle would help me to make myself well off,' said Judith. 'I mean as soon as I get the chance to write to some of the women's rights ladies, and ask them to help me ; only they will very naturally inquire, "What can you do?" and I must perforce answer, "Nothing, madam."'

'If ever you do so disgrace yourself, you—you will break my heart,' said Mrs. Conisbrough, who at the words 'women's rights' beheld in her mind's eye a woman on a platform, dressed in men's clothes, and shouting at the top of her voice.

She herself was one of those women who never look at a newspaper, and viewed them in the light of useful protectors to white-painted pantry-shelves, when not ruined for that exalted purpose by the stupid persons who would cut them, instead of leaving them in the original broadsheet.

But Judith had left the room, far more deeply moved and agitated than her mother, though the latter bore every outward appearance of chagrin. Mrs. Conisbrough was left to fume over her troubles. She accused her girls of being obstinate, self-opinionated, and unconventional ; she did not know where they got that restless spirit from ; in her days young people were much more strictly brought up, and scarcely ventured to open their mouths before their elders— the fact being that her own daughters had never been brought up at all. She always allowed things to drift as far and as long as she could. The girls had grown up, struggled up,

scrambled up—anything that the reader likes. They had
never been brought up by a hand firm and tender at once;
and this fact accounted for some of their defects as well as
for some of their virtues. Then again, though their lives
were even more secluded, their opportunities fewer, their
means narrower than hers had been at their age; though
they lived at the end of the world, in a dale without a railway, their souls had received a sprinkling from the spray of
that huge breaker of the nineteenth-century spirit which we
call progress. How it had reached them it would have been
hard to say, but perhaps the very silence and monotony of
their existence had enabled them to hear its thunder as it
rolled onwards,

> 'In lapses huge, and solemn roar,
> Ever on, without a shore.'

Certain it was that they had heard it, had been baptized
with some drops of its potent brine, and that thoughts and
speculations disturbed their minds, which would never have
entered hers; that things which to her formed the *summum
bonum* of existence, caused them no pang by their absence.
While she was always lamenting their want of money, their
absence of 'chances,' they cried out that they had no work;
nothing to do. She wanted them to be married; they
wished to have employment. The difference of aim and
opinion was a deep and radical one; it marked a profound
dissimilarity in the mental constitutions of mother and
daughters; it was a constant jar, and a breach which
threatened to grow wider.

She knew that this morning Judith and Delphine would
have a weighty confabulation upon certain points which
would not be submitted to her; that aspects of the Irkford
visit would be described and dwelt upon, of which she
would never hear anything. She accused her girls in her
own mind of reserve and secretiveness, oblivious of the fact

that she never gave an opinion upon their aspirations in the matter of work, save to condemn them.

Mrs. Conisbrough watched them as they left the house, and went up the street towards the hill in whose recesses High Gill was hidden—three as lovely, lissom figures as a mother's heart could wish to see.

She heaved a deep sigh. Her comely countenance looked clouded and downcast ; and she shook her head.

'God forgive me !' she thought within herself; 'sometimes I really wish he was dead, and all safe ! Once in possession we should be right, I know. It is all absolutely his, and he can leave it as absolutely to us. No one could set aside any will that he chose to make. Besides, anything else, after all this time, and after all that he has promised, would be so hideously unnatural.'

She went to her seat by the fire, and to a great basket of household linen, every article of which required repair, for all the things at Yoresett House had been in use for many years, and nobody in the establishment had much money wherewith to buy new ones.

The morning droned on, and she sat undisturbed in the breakfast-parlour, whose windows looked, not upon the market-place, but to the back, over a delightful garden in which stood the big apple-tree beneath which Mr. Danesdale's dog had sat and watched Mrs. Conisbrough's cat ; and beyond that, to delicious-looking, rounded, green hills, like those which form the background of some of Mr. Burne Jones's pictures. There were autumn woods, too, to be seen—a blaze of scarlet and gold, from which the mist had now completely cleared away. Deep in one of these woods was High Gill, the favourite resort of the girls. They loved to pass a summer afternoon or an autumn morning there, listening to the lulling roar of the water, and watching the rainbows made by the spray.

Profound silence throughout the old house, till at last

there came the sound of horses' hoofs along the street outside—hoofs which paused before her door.

'It must be Uncle John, I suppose,' she thought, and
very soon afterwards he walked into the room, saluting her
with the words :

'Well, Marion, good-day !'

'Good-morning, uncle ! How good of you to come and
see me so soon ! Sit down, and have a glass of wine.'

'No, thank you. I won't trouble your ever-generous
hospitality,' said the old man, and his smile, as he spoke,
was a sinister one, bearing a great resemblance to Bernard's
most malevolent grimace. His rugged eyebrows came down
in a kind of penthouse over his eyes, effectually concealing
their expression, save when they caught the light, and then
there was that in them which was not the lambent glow of
benevolence.

The old Squire, as Aglionby was called in those parts, was
not famed for the sweetness of his temper, nor for its
certainty. Mrs. Conisbrough had experienced, ere now,
specimens of the defectiveness of this temper ; but though
the men of the Aglionby race were not famed for the in-
gratiating amiability of their manners, she thought she had
never seen her uncle look so uncompromisingly vindictive
as he did now. She misliked, too, the suave and mellifluous
accents in which he spoke, and which belied the expression
in his eyes.

'Well, at least sit down and rest,' she urged him. 'The
girls have all gone out for a walk.'

'Oh, have they? I hope Judith's safe return satisfied
your maternal anxiety.'

'I was not anxious about her, so long as I knew she was
with you. She looked wonderfully brightened up by the
little change. It was so kind of you to take her !'

'Humph ! If it doesn't make her discontented with the
home-coming.'

'Oh, well-regulated minds——'

'Like yours, Marion. I know how admirably you were brought up. And I am sure you have brought up your girls as well as ever you were brought up yourself. They *are* truthful, I think. They ought to be, with a parson for their father, and such a good woman as you for their mother. I am sure you have taught them the sinfulness of telling lies, haven't you, now?'

'Lies——'

'Yes, lies. I always call them what they are. "False-hoods," "untruths"—such rubbish; *lies* is the word for them, and lies I call them.'

'Really, uncle,' she said, with a nervous laugh, 'one would think you were accusing me of telling untruths.'

Mrs. Conisbrough's tongue seemed to refuse to form the rougher word.

'The last thing in the world, my dear, that I should think of. I was just saying that you were so well taught the wickedness of telling lies, that you would be sure to bring up your daughters with a great respect for the truth. And then, having yourself been a parson's wife—you look surprised, my dear,' he added, blandly. 'It was your remark about well-regulated minds, and a humdrum life, which sent my thoughts upon this tack. I'm sure you have taught your daughters the necessity and beauty of truth-fulness.'

'I hope I have indeed, Uncle John. The world would be in a bad way without truthfulness, the most indispensable of moral virtues, I should call it.'

'Ha, ha!' he burst out, and there was something so absolutely malignant in the tone of his laugh, that Mrs. Conisbrough looked at him, vaguely alarmed. 'You never spoke a truer word, my dear. A bad way, indeed—a very bad way. All sorts of relations would be getting wrong with one another, and all sorts of injustice would reign rampant. Did you read the Tichborne case, when everyone was interested in it ?'

'No—I never read newspapers.'

'That's a pity. There are so many interesting little scraps in them, such as ladies like. In the first place, of course, there are the births, marriages, and deaths, and then, for us men, the political news, and the leading articles—you women don't care about such things, of course. But there are all kinds of bits of gossip that women *do* care for—such as long-lost sons turning up again, and all that kind of thing. That Tichborne case was the case of a man who called himself the rightful heir, you know.'

'Yes, I think—of course I heard a great deal about it, though I didn't read it. But, you see, we only have a newspaper once a week,' she faltered, turning pale, and pressing her hand against her heart.

He was remorseless.

'It is just in the weekly papers that they cull together the choicest morsels of that kind,' he said, smiling unpleasantly. 'You consult your paper next Saturday, and I'll warrant that you'll find little bits that will interest you.'

He rose, and grasped his hat as if to go ; held out his hand, and when she nervously placed her own within it, clutched it in a grip of iron, so that her rings cut into her flesh, and staring into her face, with intent eyes, which seemed to flame with anger, said, in a rough, harsh voice :

'Last Saturday afternoon, I saw my grandson. Last Saturday evening, I saw my grandson again. Yesterday morning I found him, and had a long conversation with him, and told him who I was.'

'Oh—oh !' she cried faintly, and nerveless, pale, trembling, she would have sunk backwards into her chair, but that the grip with which he held her hand sustained her.

'He is not at all what I should have expected. He is very poor, and working hard at a warehouse, where he has to slave for a lot of d——d upstart tradesmen, who would kick him out of doors if he uttered a murmur. That's what he's been doing for years, ever since his mother died, and before that too. He may have wanted a sovereign, many a time, while I have been living in plenty. Ah! it's enough to turn one's brain.'

'Oh! Loose my hand! Let me go!' she almost panted, as with labouring breath, and disturbed visage, she tried to get her hand free. 'Uncle, you hurt me!' she at last cried petulantly, as if petulance would relieve the agony of her overstrained nerves.

He laughed roughly, as he flung away, rather than loosed, her hand, and continued in the same grimly jocular strain to banter her concerning her skeleton in the cupboard.

She felt in her heart sickening qualms of fear, as he burst open the door as it were, took the spectre out, and dangled it relentlessly before her eyes, aghast as they were at the unexpected revelation.

'Fancy what lies those relations of his must have told—that mother, you know,' he went on. 'I always said she was a graceless baggage, and she has deceived the lad himself to such an extent that he won't even hear a word in her dispraise. Some people are fools, Marion, and some are liars. That's just the difference in this world. What a *fool* you must have been, once upon a time, to be duped as you were, for a *liar* you couldn't have been.'

He turned towards the door, when she, suddenly springing up, ran after him, seized his hand, and exclaimed, agony and apprehension, pleading and urgency in her voice:

'Uncle John, be pitiful, I pray. Remember my poor girls! What *are* they to do? What will become of us all? Oh, miserable woman that I am, why was I ever born?'

'Ah, why?' he retorted, almost brutally. 'Being a parson's wife, you ought to know more about that than I do. As for me, I'm an old pagan, like a lot of those I knew in

this dale when we were all young together, and if we had no
Christian meekness, we were free from some Christian vices
too—lying amongst them.   Good-day, my dear.'

He did not turn again, but went away, leaving her alone
with her fears, her misery, and humiliation.

'What does he mean?' she kept repeating, beating her
hands together, as she paced about the room.   'What does
he mean, and what does he intend to do?   Why does he
not speak out?   It is enough to kill one to be kept in this
agony of suspense.   After all these years—after all his
promises, and all my servitude—no, it cannot, *cannot* be!
no, it cannot,' she reiterated, catching her breath.   'What
could I tell him?   Why did he not wait, instead of speaking
to me in that manner, as if he wanted to tear the very
heart out of my breast?   How can anyone speak, or explain
—how can a nervous woman collect herself, with a man
glaring at her more like a devil than a human being with
unreasoning rage!   And then they talk about women having
no self-command!   Oh, if I dared, what a tale I could tell
about *men*, and their boasted generosity to those who are
weaker than themselves!   I believe if I said what I thought,
that I could make even a man blush—if that is possible.
But I must not lose my self-command in this way,' she
added, suddenly collecting and composing herself; and
seating herself in her rocking-chair she swayed slightly to
and fro, with clasped hands, and eyes fixed on the ground,
lost in a painful, terrified calculation of chances.

'I must think, think, think about it,' she thought within
herself.   'It is that thinking and calculating which wears
me out more than anything else.   Oh!' (as her mind,
despite the necessity for dwelling on the matter in hand,
persistently reverted to its grief and woes).   'This life is a
hard, dreary business; and what *brutes* men are.   Hard,
gasping wretches!   They keep us in slavery.   They hate to
see us free, lest they should lose our blind submission to

them; I know they do. If we try to make ourselves free, they grind us to powder. Judith and Delphine are right, yes, they are perfectly right in their principles, but they do not know, as I do, what will become of them if they carry those principles out. They talk about selling themselves, and the degradation of trying to please men that they may fall in love with them : but when they are as old as I am, and have lived through what I have, they will know that it is the only way for a woman to find a little ease and comfort in this world. It is the only thing to do, unless they want to be crushed to death for defying the universal law.'

This was the form of reflection into which Mrs. Conisbrough's emotions usually crystallised after they had been deeply stirred, as this morning. She spoke as she felt. She loved ease, and hated discomfort, and nothing moved her so profoundly as the loss of the first, and as having to endure the second. Presently she somewhat calmed down, and when the girls came in from their stroll, she looked not very different from usual, though she was pale and silent. She gathered that they had been at the waterfall all the morning, and (implied, though not expressed) occupied, Judith and Delphine, in what Rhoda called 'talking secrets.' Immediately after dinner, Mrs. Conisbrough retired to her own room, saying she felt tired, and wanted a rest. She did not mention their uncle's visit to the girls, who were thus left for the afternoon as well as for the morning to follow their own devices.

CHAPTER IX.

SCAR FOOT.

RHODA had put on an ancient straw hat and a pair of leather gloves, and gone to 'do a little gardening.' Judith and Delphine were alone in the parlour.

'Then you'll go ?' said the latter.

' I shall go, this very afternoon. We have quite decided that it is the best, and there is no use in delaying it. He was in a very good temper, and, for him, quite gentle all the time we were at Irkford. Yes, I shall go.'

'The sky has turned grey, and it looks as if there might be a storm.'

' I'll put on my old things. I cannot wait.'

' Well, God speed you, I say. I shall be trembling all the time until you return.'

Judith ran upstairs, and soon returned, equipped evidently for a long walk over a rough road, in strong boots, her skirt kilted conveniently high, and her soft rough hat on her head. Delphine came with her to the door, looking wistfully at her.

'Let me go, Judith !' she said suddenly. 'It is always you who have the disagreeable things to do.'

'You, child ! don't talk nonsense, and never fear. I am all right. Good-bye !'

Delphine kissed her hand after her, and watched her down the sloping market-place, till she turned a bend in the road, and was lost to view. Judith stepped forward at a pace which carried her quickly over the ground. There was nothing of what is popularly known as 'masculine' in her movements, but they were free, graceful and untrammelled : she did not hobble on high heels, nor were her garments tied back in such a manner as to impede her every motion. Her gown followed the old Danesdale rule for what a gown should be—it was not long enough to catch the dirt, and it was 'walking width and striding sidth,'* as a gown should be. The walk she had before her was one which required such a gown and such a *chaussure* as she wore. Along a good country road, which kept pretty much on the level until she arrived at a brown, bleak-looking village, which

* That is, for walking, wide enough, and to spare, with space enough to stride in, if necessary, without being pulled up short at each pace.

had a weatherbeaten appearance, a green in the centre, with five old horses grazing upon it. Then the road became a rough one. Beautiful, no doubt, in its varying charm of uphill and downhill, in the grand views of the high hills, and the long, bare-backed fells which spread around on every side ; with the white sinuous roads traced over them— roads which led over wild passes and lonely 'commons' to other valleys and dales, remoter even than this one. Lovely in spring, in summer; lovely, in a way, at every season, but on this grey October afternoon invested with a certain savage melancholy, a bleak desolation unnoticed, probably, by most of those who lived amidst it, but which had its undoubted influence upon their habits and their characters, and which must have stirred an artist's heart, and set a poet's brain working in lines which he might have made as rough and abrupt as he chose, but which, to fully express the poetry of the scene, must have had in them something both of grandeur and of grace.

It was a strange, forsaken country, full of antique grey villages which made no progress, and most of which appeared gradually falling into decay, inhabited by persons many of whom had never been even into the neighbouring Swaledale. All this district, in the early days of English religious dissent, was a stronghold of the people called Quakers. Here and there, in unexpected places, in archaic-looking little towns, in tiny, half-forsaken hamlets, will be found some little square stone meeting-house, often incapable of holding more than from a dozen to twenty persons. There was such a meeting-house, though one rather more considerable in size, in the brown village through which Judith had passed, and in its dreary little yard were mouldering the bones of some of these stern old 'Friends,' unindicated even by a name, with nothing to show them save the grass-covered mound beneath which they lay. Sturdy spirits, Spartan souls they had been—spirits of the kind

known in their day as 'God-fearing,' a kind one seldom
meets with and seldom hears of now. Looking round on
the present race, one feels indeed that they would be hard
set to comprehend those 'God-fearing' men, or any of their
works or ways, or to understand the spirit that breathed into
and animated them. Emasculate orthodoxy faints away on
the one hand in incense and altar bouquets of hothouse
flowers ; on the other, dilutes its intellect in the steam of
'tea-meetings,' in the reek of muffins, and the blasphemous
familiarity with the Deity of revival hymns ; while, opposed
to it, rampant secularism jeers at the notion of a Deity, and
ignorantly points the finger at the word 'fear,' being apparently unable to comprehend that there is a holy awe
which is as far removed from abject terror as the exalted
paganism cf Marcus Aurelius is removed from its own blatant
annihilation of what it is pleased to call the superstition of
a God. Vociferously its adherents denounce the God-
fearing man as a puerile creature, a prey to timid superstition.
Neither that orthodoxy nor this heterodoxy would know
what to make of the stern, cold religiousness, the unyielding
righteousness of those ancient 'God-fearing' men, any more
than they could own anything to be good which lies outside
the pale of their own dogmatism and their own crotchets.
'There were giants on the earth in those days,' as Judith
Conisbrough often thought, for she had a high opinion of
these departed Quaker dalesmen. Where is the hero in the
ranks either of secularism or orthodoxy who will bring the
same concentrated fervour to bear upon his cause ; who will
suffer all things and endure all things, and such things as
were suffered and endured by those early Methodists and
Quakers—those 'God-fearing,' uncultivated rustics ?

Judith left the village behind her, crossed the bridge, and
took the road up the hill to the left, and now, as ever,
though her heart was not light to begin with, the glorious
sweep of country which met her eyes, made that heart bound.

Ay, it was bonny, she often thought; it was solemn, too, this rare, unspoiled dale, this undesecrated temple of nature.

She loved every foot of the road as well as she knew it, and that was by heart; she loved the quaint, bleak shape of barebacked Addlebrough, with his 'scar' of grey rock on the summit. She loved the three or four great hills which brooded over the other side, treeless and cold; and dear to her was the little group of very old houses shaded by a wood of broad-boughed trees, which hamlet went by the name of Counterside. She had heard her great-uncle tell how he and his sister, her mother's mother, used to go to school at a queer little brown house in the said hamlet, trudging with hornbook and slate in hand from Scar Foot to Counterside, and back again from Counterside to Scar Foot.

Then the road grew lonelier and wilder; the birds chirped in the tangled autumn hedgerows: a tiny little crested wren hopped forth and impudently nodded into Judith's face ere it flew away. The spikes of the wild arum, the 'lords and ladies' of our childhood, gleamed scarlet through the lush grass. The brilliant berries and sinister beauty of the black briony cast their charm over the hedges of thorn which in spring had been a waste of hawthorn blossom. The few autumn flowers flourished—the yellow hawkweed, the lilac scabious, the blue veronica in the ditches. But the chiefest and most glorious were the red berries; what is the tale of the number of those bushes, plants, and herbs, which die down in the autumn in the shape of a scarlet berry? There were the aforesaid 'lords and ladies,' the aforesaid black briony, and in addition to them the spikes of the honeysuckle, the broad, flat tufts left by the wild guelder rose: the hips and the haws in their thousands, all helping to make the hedgerows a vivid mass of colour.

Judith lingered because she could not do otherwise. She was one of those people who cannot rush along such a road without pausing or pondering. She felt it a desecration, a

thankless course too, as if a beggar spurned the hand held
out to him, filled with gold.

Turning a corner, she suddenly had in view on the left,
and far below her, a small and lovely lake, perhaps a mile
in length, of an irregular oval in shape, bordered on all sides
by the great fells before spoken of, and, on its margin in
many parts, by trees.   From the moment in which she came
in sight of it, her eyes dwelt upon it with an earnestness
that was wistful in its intensity.   She knew it well, and loved
it, every silver foot of it, with a deep, inborn love given by
the inherited tastes of generations of forefathers, who had
lived and moved and had their being by the side of that
fair sheet of water, in the midst of those pure and elevating
natural surroundings.   For it—this fairy lake, this Shennamere, as it was called, an old corruption of 'Shining Mere'
—and the old house at its head, of which she had not yet
come in sight, were inextricably woven in her mind and
fancy with all of glad and happy, of bright and pleasant,
which her life had contained.

There was no remembrance so far back as not to include
that of Scar Foot by Shennamere.   Infancy, childhood,
little girlhood, young womanhood, large portions of each of
these periods had been passed here, and passed happily.
Influences like these must have sunk somewhat into even a
light nature, and hers was no light one, but deep and
earnest ; calm on the outside, and undemonstrative, but
capable of intensely concentrated feelings—of love and
resentment keen and enduring, of suffering and patience
practically unlimited for that which she felt to be worthy,
noble, or right : tenacious of early impressions which
coloured and modified all her thoughts and feelings.   Should
she live to be a hundred, should she pass through the most
varied, distracting experiences, to the end of her days Judith
Conisbrough's heart would leap up at the sight of this mere,

7

and the name of the beloved old house would be as music in her ears.

For about a mile the road went above the lakeside, then down a long, steep hill, with a rough stone wall at one side, and with shady trees stretching over it, till, still turning a little to the left, the back of a large house came in view; behind it ran a roaring beck; a small wood of large old trees gave it shelter—trees in which the rooks were cawing hoarsely.

There was the farmyard to pass through, and the farmer's wife to greet ere she came to an old stone gateway, and, passing through it, found herself in front of the house. It was a long, low, solidly built old house. Over the stone archway she had passed through, a slab was let in with the initials, J. A., and the date, 1667. John Aglionby of that period had built himself this house, but upon the remains of an older and a smaller one, where his fathers had lived before him. Over the doorway was a larger slab, with the same date carved on it, and ' IOHN AND IVDITH AGLIONBIE, THEIRE HOVSE,' above and below it.

Judith passed several windows, and paused before the door in the porch, before she went in, surveying the prospect. The clouds had lifted a little, and one pale, white gleam of light stole through them, and slipped adown the side of the hill opposite, showing up the bare grey houses and stone roofs of the tiny village called Stalling Busk, and then slid gently on to the lake, and touched it with a silver finger, so that even on this dark afternoon it was veritably ' Shenna-mere.'

Raydaleside and the Stake Fell looked black and threatening, and the clouds that were piled above them seemed big with the coming storm. From where Judith stood, a most delightful old-fashioned flower-garden, with no pretensions at all to elegance, and therefore full of the greater charm of sincerity, sloped down almost to the lakeside. There was just a paling, a little strip of green field with a path through it, and then, the margin of the mere, with a small wooden jetty running into it, to which a boat was moored, with the name *Delphine* painted in white letters on its grass-green side. Many an hour had the two girls passed in it, floating about the lake, with or without their great-uncle. Just now it rocked uneasily ; not constantly, but occasionally. The whole surface of the lake seemed to sway restlessly. It all portended a coming storm, and as Judith looked across the water, there came a sound from Raydaleside like some prolonged, weird whisper. Storm-portents, all. She knew it ; and as the breath of that whisper struck cold upon her face, she turned to the door, and with a strange, unwonted chill at her heart, lifted the latch and walked in.

CHAPTER X.

'IN THE PLOT.'

THOUGH large and solidly built, and with some pretensions to elegance outside at least, the house at Scar Foot was in reality planned more like a large farmhouse than anything else. The door by which Judith entered let her straight into a splendid old square kitchen or houseplace, with flagged floor, warmly carpeted over, with massive beams of oak, and corner cupboards and flat cupboards, wainscoting and chair rail of the same material. There were solid-looking old oak chairs too, black, and polished brilliantly by the friction on their seats and arms, of generations of small-clothes, hands and elbows. This room was furnished comfortably and even handsomely, but it was always used by Mr. Aglionby as a sort of hall or entrance chamber. Over the way on the right, was another spacious, comfortable room, serving as a sort of library, for all the books were

kept there.   Upstairs was the large drawing-room, or recep-
tion-room—'the great parlour' had been its name from time
immemorial.   The master's own favourite den and sanctum,
into which no person dared to penetrate without first knocking and being invited to enter, was a much smaller room
than any of those already described, arrived at by passing
through the houseplace on the left of the entrance.   This
little room was panelled throughout with oak.

Not finding her great-uncle in the houseplace, where a
roaring fire was burning cheerily, Judith knocked at the
door of the sanctum, and a rough voice from within bade
her enter.   She found the old man there, puffing at his
'churchwarden,' with his newspaper beside him, and his
colley dog, Friend, couched at his feet.   He looked up as
she entered, and she saw with surprise that a black look
darkened visibly over his face.   He did not speak.

'Good-afternoon, uncle.   I have walked over to see you.'

'Vastly obliged, I'm sure, my dear,' he replied, with the
urbanity of tone which with him portended anything but
urbanity of temper.

'We have heard nothing of you since our return,' she
pursued.

'I was at your house this morning, anyhow,' he said
snarlingly.

'Were you?' she said, in great astonishment.   'Then
didn't you see mother?'

'Of course I saw her.'

'She did not mention your having been.   How very
extraordinary!'

'Humph!' was the only reply.

Judith seated herself, as she usually did, opposite to him,
in an oaken elbow-chair, and stooping to take Friend's head
between her two hands, and brushing the hair from his eyes,
she said :

'Perhaps she will tell us about it to-night.   She was tired, and went to lie down after dinner, so she doesn't even know that I am here. I came early to save the daylight. Do you know, uncle, I think there's going to be a storm.'

'It is more than probable that your surmise is correct,' he rejoined sententiously.

'Shennamere is restless, and the wind comes moaning from off Raydaleside,' she went on, keeping to commonplace topics before she approached the important one which lay near her heart, and which, after long and earnest discussion with Delphine, they had decided should be broached to-day. She was sorry to see that her uncle was not in the most auspicious mood for granting favours, but she felt it impossible now to turn back with the one she desired, unasked, after all her heart-beatings, her doubts and difficulties, and hesitations, and—she took heart of grace—he never had refused any of her rare and few petitions. He might, perhaps, have grimaced over them a little, in his uncanny way, but in the end they had been granted, always.

'Ay,' her uncle responded to her last remark; 'whoever thinks that Shennamere is always ashine, knows nought of the weather in these parts; and whoever lives at Scar Foot should fear neither solitude nor wild weather.'

'Well, you have never feared them, have you, uncle?'

'What do you know about it?' he returned surlily.

Judith, looking out through the window, saw the storm-clouds gathering more thickly. She must broach her errand. With her heart in her throat, at first, not from fear, to which sensation she was a stranger, but from the tremendous effort of not only overcoming her own innate reserve, but of laying siege to his also, she said:

'Uncle, I came to see you this afternoon, with a purpose.

He looked sharply up, on the alert instantly—his eyes gleaming, his face expressive of attention. She went on:

'You have been very good to us girls, especially to Delphine and me, and most especially to me, all our lives.'

'Humph !'

'And I am sure we have returned your goodness with the only thing we had to give—affection, that is.'

A peculiar sound, between a sneer and a snort, was the answer.

'I am more than twenty-one years old now—nearly twenty-two, indeed.'

'Thrilling news, I must say !'

'I am not a very clever person, and I am a very ignorant one.'

'Some grains of truth appear to have penetrated to your mind, though they have taken a long time to get there, if you have only found that out now.'

'But I don't think I am more stupid than most people, and when one is young, one can always learn.'

'Do you desire a master for Italian and the guitar ?'

'Not at present,' she replied composedly, but her heart grew heavier as she saw no sign of responsiveness or of sympathy on his face ; only a hard, stolid fixity of expression, worse almost than laughter.

'I don't think I should ever care to perform on the guitar,' she proceeded, 'though I should like to know Italian well enough.   But I did not come to you with any such absurd request.   It was a much more serious business that brought me here.   Uncle, mamma has often told us that you are rich.'

'The devil she has !' broke discordantly from him.

'And if she had never said so, we have heard it from numbers of other people.   And mamma has often said that when you died——' she hesitated, faltered.

He removed his pipe from his mouth, and, with gleaming eyes, and lips that had grown ominously thin, relieved her from the necessity of finishing the sentence.

'You lasses would have my money to cut capers with, eh?'

'Oh no, no !   But that, as you have no one else to leave it to—we—you—uncle, you know what I mean ; and do listen to me! You quite misunderstand me. I hope you will live for years and years—for twenty years to come. Why not? And I do not want your money. I hate to think that people point us out as being your heiresses; and when mamma talks about it, it makes me feel fit to sink into the earth with shame. But, uncle, you know—for you cannot help knowing—that mamma has not enough money for us to live upon. We can starve and pinch, and economise upon her income, but we can't have any comfort upon it, and it is terrible. We cannot speak about it to strangers —we don't wish to; but it is none the less misery that we live in. And—I am so tired of being idle, and so is Delphine: we should like to work sixteen hours a day, if we could keep ourselves by doing so. And if you would give me a hundred pounds now, uncle, you should never need to think of spending another penny upon me as long as we both live, nor of leaving me any money when you die; nor to Delphine either. We have a proper plan. We want to work, not to waste the money. Oh, uncle dear, you know what it has cost me to ask this. Surely you won't refuse!'

The pleading in her voice amounted to passion. She laid her hand upon his arm in the urgency of her appeal, and looked with an intensity of eagerness into his face.

Mr. Aglionby put down his pipe and rose from his chair, his face white with anger, his lips and hands trembling.

'What! you are in the plot too, shameless girl!' he said, in a fury which, if not loud, was none the less dreadful.

Judith recoiled, her face pale, her eyes dilated, and gazed at him as if fascinated.

'Your precious mother has bequeathed her impudence and her slipperiness to you too, eh? A bad lot, those Arkendales, every one of them. The men were freebooters, and the women no better, and you are like the rest of them. You thought to come and wheedle something solid out of me before it was too late. I know you. I know what it is to be an old man with a lot of female vultures sitting round him, waiting for him to die that they may pick him clean. It seems some of them can't even let the breath leave his body before beginning their work. But,' his voice changed suddenly from raving in a broad Yorkshire dialect to the treacherously smooth tones of polite conventionality, 'though I am past seventy-two years of age, my dear, I am not a drivelling idiot yet, and so you may tell your respected mother on your return. And——'

'My mother knows nothing about this,' Judith said, or rather, she tried to say it. She was stunned, bewildered by the torrent of anger she had drawn upon herself, and utterly at a loss to comprehend his repeated references to some 'plot,' some 'scheme,' of which he seemed to accuse her of being cognisant.

'Bah!' he vociferated, returning to his raging anger, which appeared to have overmastered him completely. And as he spoke he hissed out his words in a way which irresistibly reminded her in the midst of her dismay of the streaming out of boiling water. And they fell, too, upon her head with the same scalding effect.

She stood still, while he raged on with wild words and wilder accusations; nothing being clear in them, save that she and all belonging to her had played a part to cheat and fleece him, and to 'oust the poor lad from his rights,' all of which accusations were as mysterious to her mind as they were outrageous to her dignity. She had forgotten by now the errand on which she had come, while her mind, in painful bewilderment, sought to assign some reason for this fit of frantic anger.

The accusations and the epithets he used at last roused her indignation beyond control. Raising her head, she fixed her clear eyes unblenchingly upon his face, and standing proudly upright, began in a louder, clearer voice:

'Uncle, listen to——'

'*Begone !*' he almost shouted, with a stamp of his foot, and turning upon her with eyes that scintillated with fury ; ' and may you never darken my doors again.'

She paused a moment, for her mind refused altogether to comprehend his words. Then, as some understanding of what he had said began to dawn upon her, she turned to the door, saying, in an almost toneless voice :

' Good-bye, uncle. You are not yourself. You are making a dreadful mistake. Some day you will repent it.'

CHAPTER XI.

A THORNY PATH.

SHE closed the door after her, and passed through the large houseplace, full of a ruddy, dancing light and a cheering warmth, out at the open door, into the drear October twilight. The lake was rougher now, and its livid surface was covered with flashing specks of foam. The weird whisper from Raydaleside had grown into a long shrill shriek—a prolonged storm-cry. All else was deathly still. Mechanically, as she passed the windows of the old house, she glanced towards them, and saw that ruddy light, that cheering warmth within. Her heart was nigh to bursting. She felt bewildered, battered down by what had taken place. It was all so incredible, so inexplicable—that she had been thrust out, desired never to darken those doors again, called by opprobrious names, there—within those beloved walls, beneath that happy roof! It was like a mortal blow. Still stunned by this stroke, she passed almost automatically out of the garden, under the old archway, through the farmyard, without returning, or even hearing the greeting of the herd, who said :

' Good-naat, Miss Judath. There's a storm on the rooad.'

She was tongue-tied, dumb, powerless to speak. Out in

the shady road again, with the dusk fast falling, with that
long, 'dree,' desolate way before her, and with such a result
to report to Delphine! She walked mechanically onwards,
perhaps half a mile, while confusion reigned in her mind.
Then the whole affair seemed suddenly to start before her
eyes in an almost lurid light. She had descended so low
as to ask for money, and she had been spurned and cast
out—and that by one whom she had truly loved and
honoured all her life, despite his rugged nature, which
ruggedness she had weakly fancied to be but the outward
mask of a great tenderness common to rugged natures. She
had always thought there was sympathy between his nature
and hers, for her innate reserve was as great as his own;
the effort to overcome it had always been like a physical
pang, and in the bitterer and more desponding moments
through which she had often passed, she too had felt repeatedly as if she could be rough, could use harsh words,
and could gird savagely at those who worried her with their
stupidity. She had made a great mistake. The ruggedness concealed no deep wells of tenderness, but a harsh,
hard, yes, a brutal nature.

It was nothing short of brutality to which he had treated
her this afternoon. What trembling hopes she and Delphine had built upon this poor little chance; the possible
result of so tremendous an effort! How they had planned
a course of work, of economy and saving, and patient waiting! They had come to the solemn conclusion that their
present life was wrong and degrading, or at least, that it was
wrong and degrading to make an effort to escape from it.
They did not believe it was what they had been born for.
Delphine had been much moved by Judith's account of
how, while she was at Irkford, a girl had been pointed out
to her, at a picture exhibition, as a young artist of promise,
who painted portraits and got forty guineas apiece for them.

'That would be the height of happiness to me,' Delphine

had said, tears in her eyes. ' I could paint portraits to earn
money to do greater things. Ah, what a happy girl! I
wonder if she knows how happy she is.'

Their plan had been for Judith to secure their uncle's
assistance, and go to Irkford, and, failing other things, adopt
the nursing of which she had spoken to her mother; to
look out all the time with a view to finding some employment for Delphine, which, they were both convinced, was
to be had, however humble. This was their scheme, and
had it succeeded, they would have rejoiced more than if
they had suddenly inherited fortunes twice as large as their
uncle could leave them, and which their mother was always
craving for them.

If it had succeeded ! How quickly would that road have
been traversed, and how high would Judith's heart have
beaten ! But it had not succeeded.

Her thoughts suddenly flew off to what was left—to the
prospect before them of a whole lifetime of this pinching
and scraping and starving, and saving sixpences, till they
grew old, and friends had disappeared, and joys were past,
and death longed for. The effort to change these grinding
circumstances had failed ; that which remained was almost
too fearful to think of. It takes a great deal to chill the
blood and dismay the heart of two-and-twenty, healthy,
resolute, and untroubled by morbid fancies ; but Judith
Conisbrough felt her blood cold, and her heart as wax at
the prospect before her. Nothing gained, and all the few
privileges they had ever had, irretrievably lost.

An indescribable weariness palsied her limbs, a despondency which amounted to despair laid its cold hand
upon her heart. The storm-wind came whistling over the
desolate fells, the lake beneath her looked like a sheet of
lead. Where was now its shining? Where the glory and
the dream which had sustained her on her way to Scar
Foot an hour ago?

Straight before her the bleak, cold mass of Addlebrough rose, and looked like a monstrous barrier which she could not pass—looked like the embodiment of her poverty, her circumstances, her doom. In the dusk her foot struck against a large loose stone. She stumbled, but recovered herself, sat down on a rough log by the roadside, and covered her eyes with her hands, as if trying to shut out all which confronted her—all which had once been so dear and warm, and was now so cold and cruel.

No tears would come.

Her eyes burnt ; her brain was filled with the remembrance of that irate old man, towering over her, pouring upon her angry rebukes for some crime of whose nature she had not the least idea, uttering words of abuse and condemnation. Thrills, hot thrills of passionate indignation, and cold ones of chill dismay, shook her one after the other. Now she felt as if she must go back and beard the old man in his anger, and tell him how wicked he was : that he maligned her, and that she defied him ; and again, she felt as if she must remain there where she was for the rest of the night, too out of heart to rise, or move another step.

The last consideration had grown uppermost, and had at last forced from her a deep, tearless sob, which gave her no relief, and only seemed to set her heart in wilder agitation. No outside sound roused her, or would have roused her, less than that which she now heard—her own name.

' Miss—Miss C—Conisbrough !' came in accents of surprise.

Judith started violently, crimsoning with shame ; the instincts of pride, reticence, reserve, impelling her instantly to subdue and conceal every sign of emotion. But they came too late. Randulf Danesdale had seen her. It was he who reined up his horse close beside her ; his face, wondering and shocked, which looked from his elevation down upon her, as she gave a startled glance upwards.

He was alone, apparently, save for his dog. Air and exercise had a little flushed his usually pale face; surprise gave it animation, and lent expression to his eyes. He looked, as she could not help seeing, very handsome, very manly, very well. Horse and rider were on the best of terms, and they formed a goodly pair.

He had spoken her name half inquiringly, as if he doubted the evidence of his own eyes. But when she suddenly uncovered her face, and looked up at him, and he saw that it was indeed she, he backed his horse a step, and bowed.

She had risen in an instant, but she could not entirely recover her presence of mind in the same space of time.

'I—Mr. Danesdale!'

'Good-evening—I fear I startled you,' he replied, and his presence of mind had not for a moment deserted him.

He had waited for her to speak, that he might know what line to take, and he followed it up at once.

'I must have been sitting there without calculating the time, for I don't possess a watch,' she said, with a faltering attempt at a laugh.

He smiled in answer, and dismounted.

'That is quite evident,' he said, holding out his hand. 'Are you thinking of walking back to Yoresett?'

'Certainly I am; having no other mode of conveyance, I must either do so or remain where I am.'

Judith had recovered her outward self-possession, but her answers were curt, and there was bitterness in her voice, and the mental agony which she was obliged to suppress forced from her certain tones and expressions which were unlike her usual ones.

'Then,' said he, 'since I have been fortunate enough to overtake you' (with as much gravity as if he had overtaken her walking at the rate of three miles an hour), 'allow me to have the honour of escorting you home. I of course have to pass through Yoresett on my way to Danesdale Castle.'

'I cannot think of detaining you. Pray ride on,' said Judith, who, however, had begun to move onwards, while he, slipping the bridle over his arm, paced beside her, and his horse, his friend, followed him.

'I shall enjoy the walk. I rode as far as Hawes, indeed beyond it, this morning, to have lunch with the Sparthwaites. Do you know the Sparthwaites?'

'By name, of course. Not personally—at least, I only just know them to speak to.'

'But your uncle, Mr. Aglionby——'

'Oh, Mr. Aglionby is on terms of friendship with many people whom we don't know at all. When my father was living, he was incumbent of Yoresett, and he and my mother of course visited with all these people. Since his death, my mother has been unable to visit anywhere. She cannot afford it.'

'I beg your pardon——' began Randulf.

'Not at all,' she answered, in the same quick spasmodic way, as if she spoke in the intervals of some physical anguish. 'I only think it foolish to pretend that there are reasons for not visiting people which are not the real reasons, and concealing the real one which covers all the others, and is simply—poverty,' said Judith distinctly.

It was not her wont to speak in this way, to flaunt her poverty, as it were, in the face of one better off than herself. But she was not her usual self at this moment. What she had just gone through seemed to have branded the consciousness of her misfortunes so deeply into her heart, with so burning and indelible a stamp that it would be long before she would be able to give her undivided attention to anything else.

A week ago she would have recoiled with horror from the idea of thus hardly and nakedly stating the truth of their

position to young Danesdale ; she would have felt it an act
of disloyalty to the hardships of her mother, an unwomanly
self-assertion on her own part. Now she scarcely gave a
thought to what she said on the subject ; or if she did, it
took the shape of a kind of contempt for her own condition,
a sort of 'what does it matter ? He knows perfectly well
that we are half-starved wretches—why should he not hear
it, and learn that he had better go away and leave us to our
natural obscurity ?'

But for one slight circumstance, Judith would almost
have supposed that Randulf had really forgotten, or not
noticed, the strange position in which he had found her,
'crying in a hedge,' as she scornfully said to herself. That
circumstance was, that he neither drawled nor stammered
in his speech, but spoke with a quick alertness unlike anything ·she had imagined him capable of assuming. This
convinced her that he was turning the case over in his mind,
and wondering very much what to think of it.

She knew nothing of his character. Of course he was a
gentleman by birth and breeding. Was he a gentleman,
nay, more, a man in mind and conduct ? Would he be likely
to receive a confidence from her as a sacred thing, or would
he be capable of treating it lightly and perhaps laughing
over it with his friends ? She knew nothing about him which
could enable her to give even a conjecture on the subject.
But the confidence must be made, the favour asked.

'Mr. Danesdale,' she said abruptly, after they had walked
on for some little time, and saw the village of Bainbeck'
below them, and the lights of Yoresett gleaming in the
distance, and when she felt that the time for speaking was
not long.

'Yes, Miss Conisbrough.'

'You must have felt surprised when you saw me this
afternoon ?'

' Must I ?'

'Were you not? Pray do not deny it. I am sure you were.'

'Since you speak in that way of it, I was more than sur prised. I was shocked and pained.'

'Poor relations are very troublesome sometimes. I had been troublesome to my uncle this afternoon, and had got well snubbed—more than snubbed—insulted, for my pains.'

'The old r—rascal!' observed Randulf, and Judith almost smiled at the naïve way in which he revealed how readily he had associated the cause of her trouble with Mr. Aglionby.

'I left his house in indignation. I cannot of course tell you what had happened, nor can you have any concern to know it. I was thinking about it. I shall never be able to tell it to anyone but my sister Delphine, for it concerns us alone; so, as you have accidentally seen that something was wrong, would you mind, please—not mentioning—you can understand that I do not wish anyone to hear of it.'

'It is natural on your part to ask it,' said he, 'but I assure you it was unnecessary, so far as I am concerned. But I give you my word, as a gentleman, that whoever may hear of the circumstance will not hear of it from me. Pray regard it, so far as I am concerned, as if it had not happened.'

He spoke with a grave earnestness which pleased Judith extremely, and sent a glow of comfort to her chill heart. The earnestness sat well on the handsome young face. Looking up, as she thanked him for his promise, she thought how young he did look, and happy. She herself felt so old—so incalculably old this afternoon.

'I thank you sincerely,' was all she said.

'The s—storm's close at hand,' observed he the next moment, displaying once more the full beauty of his drawl and his hesitation; 'I shall be in for a drenching, in more ways than one.'

'How?' she asked, in at one almost like her usual one.

'From the rain before I get to Danesdale Castle, and from

my sister's looks when I walk in late for dinner, and take my place beside the lady whom I ought to have been in time to hand in.'

' Oh, and it will be my fault !'

' It will. That is a fact beyond dispute. But they never wait for me, and I shall have the pleasure of mystifying them and seeing their curiosity run riot. That is what I enjoy. D—don't distress yourself.'

They were passing the market-cross in Yoresett. Judith was opposite her mother's door. She shook hands with Randulf ; thanked him for his escort, and wished him well home before the storm broke.

' Thank you, and if J may presume to offer you a little advice, Miss Conisbrough, don't bother yourself about your wicked uncle.'

She smiled faintly, bowed her head ; he waved his hand, sprang upon his horse, and they parted.

*　　*　　*　　*　　*

With her heart low again, she knocked at the door. Insensibly to her perceptions—for she had been so absorbed, first in her own emotion, and afterwards in her conversation with Mr. Danesdale, that she had noticed nothing else—the storm had increased. The wind was alternately wailing a dirge, and booming threats across the fells to the town. There would be floods of rain to-night, and to-morrow Swale and Yore would be thundering in flood through their valleys, fed by a hundred swollen becks from the hillsides. As the door was opened to her, the first cold splash of rain fell upon her face. The storm was from the north-west. It was well that all who had homes to go to should seek them while the tempest lasted.

It was Rhoda who had opened the door.

' Judith !' she exclaimed. ' Mamma and I both said you would be kept all night at Scar Foot. It was only that bird

8

of ill-omen—that croaker, Delphine, who said you would not. Are you wet ?'

' A little, I believe,' replied Judith, anxious for an excuse not to go into the parlour immediately. ' Oh, there's my candle, I see ; I'll go straight upstairs. I wish you'd tell Del to come and help me a minute.'

Mrs. Conisbrough always resented the tendency to ' talk secrets.' Rhoda had rather a respect for it—besides, when her elders were engaged in that pastime, their eyes were not so open to her defects. She alertly answered, ' Yes, to be sure,' and ran back into the parlour, while Judith toiled slowly up the stairs, and along the bare, hollow-sounding passage. She entered her own bedroom, placed the candle upon the dressing-table, and paused. She pulled off her gloves, threw them down, and then stood still, looking lonely and desolate, till a light, flying foot sounded along the passage ; even at that gentle rush her face did not lighten. Then Delphine's lovely face and willowy form came floating in, graceful, even in her haste.

' Judith ?' There was inquiry, suspense in her tone.

' Oh, Delphine !' Bursting into a fit of passionate weeping, she fell upon her sister's neck and cried as if her heart would break.

' Was it of no use ?' asked the younger girl at last, softly caressing her as she spoke.

' Worse than no use ! He not only refused, he insulted me ; he spoke abusively, talked about " plots " and "schemes," and things I could not understand. And at last he got into a fury, and he—oh, Delphine, Delphine !— he bade me begone. He turned me out—from Scar Foot —from my dear old place that I loved so ! Oh, I think my heart will break !'

' He must be *mad*—the horrid old monster !' cried Delphine distinctly, her figure springing erect, even under the burden of her sister's form, and her tones ringing through the room. 'He has not the right to treat you, or any of us, in that way. *Let* him do without us! Let him try how he likes living alone in his den, and getting more and more ill-tempered every day, till he frightens the whole country-side away from him. I will never go near him again, of my own free will; but if ever I meet him, I will tell him what I think of him—oh, I will! Cheer up, Judith! Keep a good heart. We will not be beaten by a tyrant like him! Depend upon it, it was the idea of our wanting to be free, and wanting him to set us free, of all people, that made him so wild. Don't cry more, now. We must go down to tea. Mother seems a little out of sorts just now, too. We will talk it over to-night. Come, my poor dear! Let us take off your things. How tired she must be!' she added caressingly. 'After walking alone, all along that dreadful road, and in such weather. It wasn't fit to turn out a dog. Why, it must have been dark before you got to Counterside, Ju! You would wish for old Abel and his fog-horn. How did you grope your way along the road?'

'That reminds me,' said Judith suddenly, while a deep blush spread over her face and neck. 'I wasn't alone, except for about half a mile from Scar Foot.'

'Not alone! Did Toby from the farm bring you with his lantern?'

'I never saw Toby. It was Mr. Danesdale——'

'*Mr. Danesdale!*'

'Yes. And the worst is, he found me sitting in a hedge, like a tramp who can walk no farther, groaning, with my face in my hands.'

'Oh, Judith! How terrible!'

'He got off his horse and walked with me to Yoresett. He is probably now riding for dear life, to be as nearly in time for dinner as he can.'

'Well, we must go down now,' said Delphine, very quietly.

'You must tell me about that afterwards. There's Rhoda
calling out that tea is ready.'

Arm-in-arm they went downstairs into the warm, lighted
parlour, which, despite its shabby furniture, looked very
comfortable and homelike, with the tea-table spread, and the
urn singing, and the old-fashioned crystal glass full of gracefully arranged yellow-berried holly and glossy ivy leaves.

Mrs. Conisbrough did not inquire anything respecting the
reception her eldest daughter had met with from her uncle.
She cast a wavering suspicious glance towards Judith, as the
girls came in, which glance presently grew more reassured,
but neither cheerful nor inquiring. In her own mind she
was thinking, 'What has he said to her? How far has he
gone?' Judith met her mother's look in her usual manner,
and spoke to her with her usual cordiality. Mrs. Conisbrough
heaved a sigh of relief, but dared not proceed to questions or
any kind. When the meal was over they all sat still in the same
room, some of them working, some of them reading. Their
store of books was small, but they were occasionally able to
borrow a few from a certain Mrs. Malleson, their one and
only intimate friend, whose husband was rector of the great
parish of Stanniforth, which comprised Yoresett and many
other places. The doctor of the district, who also lived some
distance away, and who was a kindly-natured man, would
occasionally remember 'those poor Miss Conisbroughs,' and
would put a volume or two in his greatcoat-pocket for their
benefit. Judith was making a pretence of reading one of
these volumes now. Delphine sat at the old piano, and
touched a chord now and then, and sang a phrase once and
again. Rhoda was embroidering. Mrs. Conisbrough held
a book in her hands, which she was not reading any more
than Judith was reading hers.

Meanwhile, without, the storm had increased. Judith
had heard the first threatenings of the wind which was now
one continuous roar. The rain, in spasms, lashed the panes

furiously. Yoresett House could stand a good deal of that kind of thing. No tempest ever shook it, though it might, as it did to-night, make wild work with the nerves of some of those who dwelt there.

Suddenly Rhoda raised her dusky head; her glowing brunette face was all listening; she held up a warning finger to Delphine to pause in her playing.

' Don't you hear wheels?' she said in a low voice; such as befitted the solemnity of the occasion.

They all listened; yes, wheels were distinctly audible, quickly moving, and a horse's hoofs, as it came down the street. Quick as thought Rhoda had bounded to the window, lifted the white linen blind, and pulled it over her head, in a frenzy of aroused curiosity.

Just opposite the house stood the only public illumination possessed by Yoresett—a lantern, which threw out melancholy rays, and cast a flickering light upon the objects around. It burned in a wavering, uncanny manner, in the furious gusts to-night, but Rhoda's eyes were keen; emerging presently from her retirement, she found three pairs of eyes gazing inquiringly at her.

'Would you ever believe it!' she cried. 'It's old Mr. Whaley's dogcart, with the white mare, *and he is in it.*'

' Old Mr. Whaley' was the family lawyer of the Aglionby clan, and had been so for forty years.

' Nonsense, my dear child!' protested her sisters. ' It is some belated traveller, and the flickering light has deceived you.'

' I tell you, it was old Mr. Whaley. Don't I know his mare Lucy as well as I know my own name? He was sitting muffled up, and crouching together, and his man was driving. Will you tell me I don't know Peter Metcalfe and his red beard?—and they were driving towards the road to Bainbeck.'

' It is strange,' said Delphine.

Rhoda, going back towards her place, looked at her mother. ' Mamma's ill !' she cried, springing to her side.

'No, no ! It's nothing. I have not felt very well all day. Leave me alone, children ; it will pass off. Old Mr. Whaley, on the road to Bainbeck, did you say, Rhoda ? Then he must be going to see your uncle.'

CHAPTER XII.

DANESDALE CASTLE.

RANDULF DANESDALE, after taking leave of Miss Conisbrough, sprang upon his horse again, pulled his collar up about his ears, rammed his cap well on to his head, called to his dog, and rode on in the teeth of the wind, towards his home. Soon the storm burst over him in full fury, and he was properly drenched before arriving at Danesdale Castle. During his ride thither he constantly gave vent to the exclamation, ' Inc-credible !' which might have reference to the weather, he being as yet somewhat inexperienced in the matter of storms as they rage in Yorkshire dales. More probably it was caused by some train of thought. Be that as it may, the exclamation was oft reiterated. At last, after a long, rough ride along country roads uncheered by lamps, he ascended the hill going to Danesdale Castle, and rode into the courtyard where the stables and kennels were, delivered his horse over to his groom, and sauntered towards the house.

'Are they dining, Thompson ?' he inquired of a solemn-looking butler whom he met as he passed through the hall.

'They are dining, sir,' was the respectful reply, and Randulf's visage wore an expression of woe and gravity impossible to describe ; yet an impartial observer must have come to the conclusion that Thompson and his young master were enjoying an excellent joke together.

' If Sir Gabriel should ask, say I am in, and will join them in five minutes,' said Randulf, going upstairs. During his dressing he again gave vent to the exclamation, ' Inc-credible,' and this time it may reasonably be supposed to have referred to the extreme celerity with which he made his toilette.

When he had ridden into the courtyard ten minutes ago, he had looked animated, interested, and interesting, as he perfectly sat his perfect horse. There had been vigour and alertness in his movements, and a look of purpose and life in his eyes. That look had been upon his face from the moment in which he had reined up his horse by the roadside, and seen Judith Conisbrough's eyes looking up at him. When he came into the dining-room, and the assembled company turned their eyes upon him with a full stare of surprise or inspection, or both, and his father pretended to look displeased, and his sister looked so in stern reality, he looked tired, languid, indifferent—more than indifferent, bored to death.

Sir Gabriel looked as if he would have spoken to him, but Randulf's place was at the other end of the table, nearer his sister, Miss Philippa Danesdale. He dropped into the vacant chair left for him by the side of a lady who looked out of temper; a lady with considerable claims to good looks, in the confident, unabashed style of beauty ; a lady, finally, whose toilette bore evidence of having cost a great deal of money. She was Miss Anna Dunlop, Miss Danesdale's dearest friend, and Randulf had had to take her in to dinner every day since his return home.

Glancing around, he uttered a kind of general apology, including Miss Dunlop in it with a slight bow, and then he looked wistfully round the table.

' You appear to be looking for something, Mr. Danesdale,' observed Miss Dunlop, her corrugated brow becoming more placid.

'Only for the s—soup. I am absolutely starving,' was the reply, in a tone of weariness which hardly rose above a whisper.

'If you will be so late, Randulf,' said his sister in the low voice she always used, 'you must expect to have to wait, a minute or two at any rate, for your dinner. The servants are not omnipotent.'

'I hope not, indeed !' he said. 'If they were, where would you be ? Where should I be ? Where should we all be ?'

'You snap up people's remarks in the most unkind manner,' expostulated Miss Dunlop on Philippa's behalf. 'Your sister only meant to calm your impatience, and you misconstrue her remark, and call up a number of the most dreadful images to one's mind.'

'Dreadful images. Isn't there a song ? Oh no, engines ; that's it—not images. " See the dreadful engines of eternal war." Do you know it ?'

'I never heard it. I believe you are making it up,' said Miss Dunlop reproachfully.

'Ah, it's old. It used to be sung long before your time —when I was a boy, in fact,' he returned, with a gravity so profound as to be almost oppressive.

Miss Dunlop paused a moment, and then decided to laugh, which she did in a somewhat falsetto tone, eliciting no responsive smile from him. A dismal idea that Randulf was a sarcastic young man began to distil its baneful poison through her mind. What did he mean by so pointedly saying, 'It used to be sung when I was a boy'?

'Did the Sparthwaites keep you so late, Randulf ?' asked his sister ; but he did not hear her, or appeared not to do so.

Miss Danesdale was a plump, red-haired woman, no longer young. It was said by some of those friends of her youth whom she, like others, found somewhat inconvenient when that youth had fled, that she was forty. This, how-ever, was supposed by those who knew her to be a slight exaggeration. She sat very upright, always held her shoulders back, and her head elevated, nor did she stoop it, even in the act of eating and drinking. She always spoke in an exceedingly low voice, which only a great emergency or extreme irritation ever caused her to raise ; indeed it is useless to deny the fact, Miss Danesdale, from what cause soever, muttered, with what results, on the tempers of herself and of those who had to interpret her mutters or be constantly asking for a repetition of them, may be more easily imagined than described. Her brother, who had seen little of her until this last final home-coming, considered the habit to be one of the most trying and exasperating weapons in the armoury of a trying and exasperating woman.

Miss Danesdale had every intention of behaving very well to her brother, and of making him welcome, and being very kind to him ; but the manner in which she displayed her goodwill took a didactic, even a dictatorial form, which failed to recommend itself to the young man. If it were not sure to be taken for feminine ill-will towards the nobler and larger-minded sex, the present writer would feel obliged to hint that Randulf Danesdale felt spiteful towards his esteemed sister, and that occasionally he acted as he felt. In any case, he appeared on the present occasion not to hear her, and in exactly the same voice and words, she repeated her question, looking at him as he gazed wearily at the pattern of his now empty soup-plate.

' Did the Sparthwaites keep you so late, Randulf ?'

He looked up with a vague, dreamy expression.

' A—! Did some one speak to me ?'

Extreme irritation now came into play. Miss Danesdale raised her voice, and in a far from pleasant tone, cried :

' *Did* the Sparthwaites keep you so late ?'

' I have come straight here from the Sparthwaites,' he replied, mournfully accepting the fish which was offered to him.

' Whom did you meet there ?' she asked.

Anyone who could have performed the feat of looking under Randulf's wearily-drooped eyelids into his eyes, would have been rewarded with the vision of a most uncanny-looking sprite, which suddenly came floating and whirling up from some dark well of wickedness deep down in a per-verted masculine nature. When he raised his eyelids, the sprite had discreetly drawn a veil between itself and the audience. None the less did it prompt the reply :

'Oh, a l—lot of people. I sat next an awfully good-looking woman, whom I admired. One of those big, black women, like a rocking-horse. Ch—champed the bit just like a rocking-horse too, and pranced like one. She said——'

There were accents in Randulf's voice which called a smile to the faces of some of the company, who had begun to listen to his tale. Miss Danesdale exclaimed almost vivaciously :

'Why, you must mean Mrs. Pr——'

'Don't tell me before I've finished. I don't know her name. Her husband had been ill, it seemed, and she had been nursing him, and they pitied her because of it ; and she said, "Oh, I have nursed him before now. I held him in my arms when he was a b—baby."'

'Randulf !'

'I was h—horror-struck ; and I suppose I showed it, for she suddenly gave a wild prance, and champed the bit more than ever, and then she said : "Of course I don't remember it, but they tell me I did. My dear husband is a year or two younger than I am, but *so* good."'

Mr. Danesdale sank again into a reflective silence. Sir Gabriel and the elder portion of the company went off into a storm of laughter, which did not in the least mitigate the deep gloom of the heir. Miss Dunlop's high colour had increased to an alarmingly feverish hue. Miss Danesdale looked unutterable things. Sir Gabriel, who loved a joke, presently wiped the tears from his eyes, and said, trying to look rebuking : 'My dear boy, if you let that sarcastic tongue of yours run on in that way, you'll be getting into mischief.'

'*I* sarcastic !' he ejaculated, with a look of the deepest injury. ' My dear sir !'

'Will you have roast mutton, Randulf ?' asked Miss Danesdale, behind her mittened hand, as if she were putting some very disgraceful question, and dreaded lest the servants should hear it. ' Because if——'

' Roast mutton ? oh, joy!' he exclaimed, with a look of sudden hungry animation, which greatly puzzled some of the company, who saw him that night for the first time, and who said afterwards that really that young Danesdale was very odd. He came in so late to dinner, and sat looking as if he were going to faint, and told a very ill-natured story about Mrs. Prancington (though Mrs. Prancington is a ridiculous woman, you know), and then he suddenly fell upon the roast mutton with an ogreish fury, and could hardly be got to speak another word throughout the meal. They were sure he had astonished poor Anna Dunlop beyond bounds, for she did not speak to him again.

Perhaps Mr. Danesdale had desired this consummation, perhaps not. At least, he did not murmur at it, but attacked the viands before him in such a manner as soon to make up lost time.

Presently the ladies went to the drawing-room, and the men were left to their wine. All the rooms at Danesdale Castle were agreeable, because they could not help being so. They were quaint and beautiful in themselves, and formed parts of a quaint and beautiful old house ; and of course Miss Danesdale did not wish to have vulgar rooms, and had not, unless a certain frigid stiffness be vulgarity, which, in a ' withdrawing-room,' meant to be a centre of sociability and ease, I am inclined to think it is.

Miss Dunlop was staying in the house. The other ladies

were neighbours from houses not too far away.   All belonged
to 'the dale.'   They were not of a very lively type, being
nearly all advanced in middle life, stout, and inclined to
discuss the vexed topics of domestics, children, the state of
their greenhouses, their schools, and their clergy, all of which
subjects they seemed to sweep together in one category, or, as
Randulf had been known irreverently to say, ' These women
lump together infant schools, bedding-out plants, parsons
and housemaids in a way that makes it impossible for any
ignorant fellow like me to follow the conversation.'

These Dowagers, with Miss Dunlop looking bored and
cross (as indeed she felt) and Miss Danesdale looking prim,
as she stepped from one to the other of her guests, to mutter
a remark and receive an answer—these ladies disposed themselves variously about the well-warmed, comfortable drawing-
room, while the one who was the youngest of them, the
most simply dressed, the handsomest, and by far the most
intelligent-looking, the wife of the vicar of Stanniforth, sat
a little apart, and felt amused at the proceedings.

As soon as politeness would allow her, Philippa seated
herself beside Miss Dunlop, and, with a frosty little smile of
friendship, said, in a mutter intended to be good-natured :

' When the men come in, Anna, and if Randulf comes to
you, just ask him something, will you ?'

' Ask him what ?   If he enjoyed the wine and walnuts as
much as the roast mutton, or if he thinks me like Mrs.
Prancington ?'

' Oh no, dear.   And if he did, Mrs. Prancington is a very
handsome woman.   But ask him if he has seen anything of
the Miss Conisbroughs to-day.'

' The Miss Conisbroughs ?   Are they friends of yours ?'

' No, but they are of his—dear friends.   Just ask him how
long he stopped at their house on his way home.   I must
go, dear.   There's old Mrs. Marton looking fit to éat me,
for not having been civil to her.'

She rose, and walked with neat, prim little steps across the room.

Miss Dunlop sat still for a few minutes, her big black eyes fixed upon her big, black-mittened hands, upon her yellow satin and black-lace lap, and upon the black and yellow fan which her fingers held. After frowning at her hands for some time, she arose, and went to the piano, near which sat Mrs. Malleson, the vicar's wife. Miss Dunlop placed herself upon the music-stool, and began to play a drawing-room melody of questionable value as a composition, in a prononcé, bravura style.

By-and-by the men did come in—Sir Gabriel and the vicar first. A fine old gentleman was Sir Gabriel Danesdale. Abundant curly hair, which had long been snow-white; large, yet delicately chiselled features of great strength and power, and somewhat of the old Roman type, and a complexion of a clear, healthy brown, not turned crimson, either with his outdoor sports or his modest potations. He looked as if he could be stern upon occasion. His face and bearing showed that mingling of patrician pride and kindly bonhommie which made him what he was, and which had secured him the love and goodwill of friends and dependents years ago.

Behind him followed Randulf, as tall as his father, and with shoulders as broad, looking at the moment as if he could hardly summon up energy to move one foot before the other. He was listening with the air of a martyr to a stout country squire with a red face; and other country squires— the husbands of those squiresses who sat in an amply spreading ring about the room— followed after him, talking —what do country gentlemen talk about, whose souls are in the county hunt and the agricultural interest?

Randulf, 'promenading' his eyes around the room, beheld Miss Dunlop at the piano, and the vicar's wife sitting close beside her. To the left, he saw the ring of dowagers, 'looking like a peacock's tail magnified,' he said to himself, and fled towards the priestess for refuge.

'I suppose you got here before the storm came on, Mrs. Malleson?'

'Yes, we did. We shall have to drive home in it, though.'

'I'm afraid you will. What roads they are here, too! I know I thought so this afternoon, riding from Hawes . . . Don't let us interrupt your music on any account, Miss Dunlop,' he continued blandly, as she stopped.

'Oh, I've finished,' answered she, somewhat unceremoniously cutting into the conversation. 'Did you ride from Hawes this afternoon?'

'Yes,' said he, instantly becoming exhausted again.

'And that is a rough road?'

'Very.'

'It comes through Yoresett, doesn't it?'

'It does.'

'Philippa has been telling me about your friends, the Miss Conisbroughs.'

'Has she?'

'The Miss Conisbroughs,' said Mrs. Malleson. 'Do you know them, Miss Dunlop?'

'Not at all, but I hear Mr. Danesdale does.'

'Do you, Mrs. Malleson?' he asked.

'Very well indeed. They are great friends of mine . . . . and of yours too, it seems.'

'Of mine? Well, I've known them just as long as I've known you. May I say that Mrs. Malleson and the Misses Conisbrough are great friends of mine?'

'Yes, if you like. If they allow you to become their friend, I congratulate you.'

'They are nieces to that aged r—reprobate, Aglionby of Scar Foot, aren't they?'

'They are.'

'Won't you tell Miss Dunlop about them? she wants to know, dreadfully.'

'I do, immensely.'

'Are they pretty, Mrs. Malleson?' he asked.

'A great deal more than pretty, I should say,' said Mrs. Malleson, in her hearty, outspoken tones—tones which had not yet quite lost their girlish ring. 'I call the eldest one splendid, so handsome, and so calmly dignified.'

'Yes,' said Randulf, whose eyes were almost closed, and his face expressionless, as he recalled the pale, woe-stricken countenance which that 'calmly-dignified' Miss Conisbrough had raised to him that afternoon. He felt a tightening at his heart-strings.

Mrs. Malleson went on :

'As for Delphine, I think she is exquisite. I never saw any lovelier girl, I don't care where. You know, if that girl were rich, and came out in London—I used to visit a great deal in London before I was married—and I am sure, if she were introduced there, she would make a furore—dressed in a style that suited her, you know. Don't you think she would?'

'I should not be surprised,' he returned, apparently on the verge of utter extinction ; 'one never can tell what there will be a furore about in London—Chinamen, actresses, living skeletons, bilious greens — yes, I dare say she would.'

Miss Dunlop laughed a little ill-naturedly, while Randulf, displaying suddenly more animation, added :

'But the youngest, Mrs. Malleson. That little black-browed one. She is just as handsome as she can be. What a life she would lead any man who was in love with her !'

'She will be a strikingly beautiful woman some day, without doubt ; but she is a child, as yet.'

'Now, Miss Dunlop, you have heard an indisputable verdict on the good looks of the Miss Conisbroughs. All I can say is, that to me Mrs. Malleson's remarks appear full of wisdom and penetration. As for anything else —— Father !'

Sir Gabriel was passing. Despite his overpowering languor, Randulf rose, as he called him, and stood beside him, saying :

'Miss Dunlop is inspired with a devouring curiosity about the Miss Conisbroughs. What can you tell us about them and their antecedents ?'

'Miss Conisbroughs,' said Sir Gabriel, knitting his brows. 'Oh, of course. Marion Arkendale's daughters. Parson Conisbrough's girls. Ah ! she was a bonny woman, and a nice woman, was Marion Arkendale, when we were all young. I know them a little—yes.'

'They are Squire Aglionby's grand-nieces, aren't they ?'

'Yes, what of that ?'

'Will they be his heiresses ? You see, I don't know the local gossip yet.'

'His heiresses—I expect so. Old John never confided the secrets of his last will and testament to me, but it is the universal expectation that they will, when anyone ever thinks anything about it. He disinherited his son, you know, in a fit of passion, one day.'

'Lucky for me that you can't,' said Randulf mournfully.

'I'm more likely to disinherit you for inordinate yawning than anything else,' said Sir Gabriel.

'His son married ; did he leave any children ?'

'One boy.'

'Surely he won't ignore him utterly ?'

'But he will. I remember him telling me that the mother and her relations had the boy, and were going to look after it, and that he was sure they hoped by that means to get a pull over him and his money. He added, with a great oath, that the brat might make the best of them, and they of it, for never a stiver of his should it handle. He is the man to keep his word, especially in such a case as that.'

'Will these girls be much of heiresses?' asked Randulf, apparently stifling a yawn.

'Very pretty heiresses, if he divides equally. Some fifteen hundred a year apiece, I should say. But why do you want to know?' added Sir Gabriel 'Has something happened?'

'Nothing, to my knowledge,' replied his son; 'it was only the extreme interest felt in the young ladies by Miss Dunlop that made me ask.'

'Well, that's all I can tell you about it, except a few anecdotes of old John's prowess in the hunting-field, and of his queer temper and off-hand ways.'

Sir Gabriel left them. Randulf implored Miss Dunlop to sing, which she did, thereby reducing him to the last stage of woe and dejection.

*   *   *   *   *   *

That night the tempest howled out its roughest paroxysms. The following day was wet, and hopelessly so, with gusts of wind, melancholy, if not violent. The inmates of Danesdale Castle were weather-bound, or the ladies, at any rate, considered themselves so. Sir Gabriel was out all morning, Randulf was invisible during the greater part of the day, and was reported by his man as having a headache and not wishing for any lunch.

'*Headache!*' cried Sir Gabriel to the ladies, with a mighty laugh, ' at his age I had never even dreamed of a headache. I'd bet something he's on his back on a couch, with a pipe and a French novel.'

The ladies said nothing. In the afternoon Sir Gabriel was out again, and Miss Danesdale and Miss Dunlop yawned in company until dinner-time, when they and their mankind all met together for the first time that day. They were scarcely seated when Sir Gabriel said :

'It's odd, Randulf, that you should have been asking so many questions last night about old John Aglionby and

9

those girls. There does seem to be a fatality about these things sometimes.'

'As how?' inquired his son.

'Old John is dead. He had an apoplectic fit last night, and died at noon to-day. I met the doctor while I was out this afternoon, and he told me. It gave me a great shock, I must confess. Aglionby of Scar Foot was a name so inseparably connected with this dale, and with every remembrance of my life that has anything to do with the dale, that it is difficult to realise that now he must be a remembrance himself, and nothing more.'

'Yes, indeed, it is very strange. And he leaves no one to take his name.'

'He is sure to have made a proviso that those girls shall take the name of Aglionby. I cannot grasp it, somehow, that there will be Conisbroughs at Scar Foot—and women!'

'Do you visit them, Philippa?' asked Randulf, turning to his sister.

'We exchange calls occasionally, and we always ask them to our parties in winter, but they have never been to one of them. Of course I must go and call upon Mrs. Conisbrough at the proper time.'

'I'm not sorry the poor girls will have better times at last,' observed Sir Gabriel, on whom the occurrence seemed to have fallen almost as a blow. 'And, after all, he was seventy-two and over. When I get to that age, boy, you will be thinking it about time for me to clear out.'

Randulf smiled, and drawled out, 'Perhaps I may, sir,' but his eyes met those of his father. The old man and the young man understood each other well already. Sir Gabriel Danesdale slept that night with the secure consciousness that if he lived to be a hundred, his son would never wish him away.

'Ah, there's a deal in family affection,' he reflected. 'If Aglionby had only been a little more lenient to that poor lad of his, the winter of his life might have had more sun in it and less frost . . . . How he used to ride ! Like the devil sometimes. What runs we have had together; and what fish we have killed ! Poor old John !'

CHAPTER XIII.

'THE FIRST CONCERT OF THE SEASON.'

'THE first concert of the season, Bernard, and you mustn't miss it. Really, for the life of me, I can't tell what you hear in those awfully classical concerts. Isn't it classical that they call them ? I've been to some of them. I like watching the swells come in, and I dare say it's very amusing for them, who go regularly to the same places, to meet all their friends, and that sort of thing; but there I'm done. Those concerts send me to sleep, or else they make my headache. It's nothing but a bang-banging, and a squeak-squeaking, without any tune to go by in it. I *can't* tell what you hear in them.'

It was Miss Vane who thus addressed her swain on the Wednesday evening after he had told her about his meeting with his grandfather. He held his hat in his hand, and listened to her smilingly, but without any signs of relinquishing his purpose.

'Perhaps you don't, my love. I hear a great deal in them. To-night I shall hear Madame Trebelli sing "Che farò senza Eurydice?" which is enough to last any fellow for a week, and make him thrill whenever he thinks of it. Likewise, I shall hear Beethoven's symphony, No. 5, which——'

'Oh, those horrid long symphonies. I know them. I can no more make head or tail of them than I can of your books about ethics or agnostics, or something-sticks. But go, go ; and I hope you may enjoy it. I like a play of

a comic opera, for my part. Promise you'll take me to
" Madame Angot " the next time it comes, and I'll be good.'

'To " Madame Angot " you shall go if I am here, and
able to take you,' he rejoined, his eyes smiling darkly beneath
the brim of his hat. 'You won't be gone to bed when I
get back,' he said. 'It won't be late ; and we can have half
an hour's chat ; just half an hour.'

' Well, if you're not too late,' said Miss Vane graciously.

Bernard promised and vowed to return very early ; and
then went off to enjoy his one piece of genuine, un-
adulterated luxury and extravagance—his shilling's-worth of
uncomfortable standing-room in the ' body of the hall ;' which
shilling's-worth, while the great singers sang, and the great
orchestral masterpieces were performed in a style almost
peculiar to Irkford, of all English towns, represented to him
a whole realm of riches and glory, royal in its splendour.

He secured a good place, just behind the last of the
reserved seats, which were filled with a brilliant-looking
audience. From the moment in which the well-known leader
came on and received his rounds of welcome and applause,
to the last strain of the last composition, he was all ear and
all delight.

It was certainly a feast that night for those who care for
such feasts. There was a delicious ' Anacreon ' overture,
full of Cherubini's quaintest thoughts ; and there was the
great cantatrice singing in her most superb style. ' Che
farò,' though, came in the second part of the performance.
Before it was the Fifth Symphony. Bernard, drinking in
the sounds, remembered the old tale of how some one asked
the composer what he meant by those four portentous and
thrilling chords which open the symphony, and how he
replied, ' Thus fate knocks at the door.'

' Si non é vero é ben trovato,' thought our hero, smiling
to himself. ' A fate that knocked in that way would be a
fate worth opening to, whether good or bad. But one

usually hears a more commonplace kind of tap at the door
than that.'

He listened with heart and soul to the grand scena from
' Orpheus.' The cadences rang in his ears:

> ' Eurydice ! Eurydice !
> Che farò senza Eurydice ?'

When it was over, he slipped out, not caring to spoil the
effect of it by listening to anything more. As he marched
home, his pulses were beating fast. The strains of ' Eurydice ' rang in his ears. But the opening chords of the
symphony struggled with them and overcame them. ' Thus
fate knocks at the door,' he repeated to himself many times,
and in a low voice hummed the notes. ' Thus fate knocks
at the door,' he muttered, laughing a little to himself, as
he inserted his latch-key, and opened the door of No. 13,
Crane Street.

He found Lizzie in the parlour, seated on a stool in the
very middle of the hearth-rug, and gazing upwards at a
brown envelope which she had stuck on the mantelpiece, in
front of the clock.

' Bernard,' she said, ' there's a telegram for you.' She
scarcely turned her delicate fair face towards him as she
spoke. ' It came almost the minute you'd gone, and I'm
fairly dying to know what it can be about.'

He was very much surprised to see it himself, but did not
say so, taking it as if nothing could have been more natural
than for it to come.

' Why, it's addressed to the warehouse,' he remarked.
' How did it get here ?'

' That boy, Robert Stansfield from the warehouse, brought
it. He said it came just as he was leaving, and he thought
you might like to have it. I believe that boy would die, or
do anything for you, Bernard,' she added, watching him as
he opened and read the message without a muscle of his
face changing.

' James Whaley, solicitor, Yoresett, to Bernard Aglionby, 15, Fence Street, Irkford. Your grandfather died suddenly this morning, and your presence here is indispensable. Come to-morrow by the train leaving Irkford at 2.15, and I will meet you at Hawes, and explain.'

' What a long one, Bernard! What is it all about?'

' A stupid thing which will oblige me to set off on a business journey to-morrow,' he said, frowning a little, speaking quite calmly, but feeling his heart leaping wildly. Was it fate that knocked at the door? or was it 'but a bootless bene'?

Why did he not tell her, or read her the telegram? It was chiefly because of their conversation on Monday night last. It was because he knew what she would say if she heard the news, and because, rough and abrupt though he was, he simply could not endure to hear her comment upon that news, nor to listen to the wild and extravagant hopes which she would build upon it, and which she would not hesitate to express. He would have laughed loud and long if anyone had told him that his sense of delicacy and of the fitness of things was finer and more discriminating than that of Miss Vane, but it was a fact that it was so.

Meantime, wild and rapid speculations and wonders crowded into his own mind. He tried hard, to see things in what he called a 'sensible light.' He told himself that it was utterly impossible that his grandfather could have done anything to his will which in any way affected him. There had not been time for it. He would have to go to Hawes, and hear what they wanted him for—possibly to attend the funeral—a ceremony with which he would rather have dispensed. Then, when he knew how much he, with his slender salary, was to be out of pocket by the whole affair, he would come back, and reveal the news to Lizzie, thus for ever putting out of her head all hopes or aspirations connected with old Mr. Aglionby and his money. She was quite

satisfied with his explanation : though she girded at him and
teased him and disagreed with him, he had the power of
making her do exactly as he chose *when* he chose, and of
making her see things as he desired her to see them.   But
he could only do it by means of fear—intimidation, and he
knew it, and rarely indeed chose to exert that power.

He thrust the telegram into his pocket, and consulting a
little railway guide, found that the train mentioned by Mr.
Whaley was the only one during the day by which his journey
could be accomplished in reasonable time.   The earlier ones
were slow, and necessitated so many waitings and changings
that he would arrive no sooner.   In the morning he took his
leave of Lizzie, saying he could not give her his address now,
as he did not know where he should be that night, but he
would write as soon as possible.   Lizzie was very sweet and
amiable ; she hung about him affectionately, and held up her
face to be kissed, and he thought what an angel she was,
what a guileless, trusting angel, to confide herself to the
keeping of a rough-hewn, cross-grained carle like him.   Again
his heart fluttered as he gave a flying glance towards the
possibility that Mr. Whaley of Yoresett might have some
solid reason for summoning him thus suddenly to his grandfather's house.   If there were any such reason—he kissed
Lizzie's sweet face with a strange passion of regretful love and
tenderness.

'Good-bye, my own sweetheart !' he said again.

'Good-bye, Bernard dear ; and be sure you let me know
when you're coming home.'

On his way to town he stopped at a post-office, to send off
a telegram to Mr. Whaley, promising to be at Hawes at the
time mentioned.   And then he went on to the warehouse,
and asked for leave of absence with a cool hardihood which
sorely tried the temper and dignity of Mr. Jenkinson ; and
at 2.15 set off on his journey with an unknown object—his
journey which might be the beginning of a new life—or

merely the seal affixed to the relentless obduracy of one train
of circumstances for which he was in no way responsible. It
was in the bitter, sarcastic nature of the man to contemplate
the latter possibility as being the most probable one.

CHAPTER XIV.

DISPUTED.

Mr. Aglionby, of Scar Foot, had died on Wednesday at
noon. He was buried on the Saturday morning following,
in the churchyard of Yoresett Church, beside those of his
fathers who had been buried there before him. He was
laid low with all pomp and respect, and not a town, village,
or hamlet in the dale but sent its quota to the following.
He had been one of the institutions of the dale, one of the
inseparable accompaniments of every gathering, and every
event almost, that took place in it; and if he had not been
tenderly loved, he had been deeply honoured and respected.
Therefore gentle and simple came from far and near, and
saw him laid to his rest.

Bernard had arrived late on Thursday afternoon at Hawes.
There he was met by Mr. Whaley, and driven by him to his
bachelor house at Yoresett. Mr. Whaley was the very model
of an extremely, if not needlessly, discreet country lawyer.
Bernard Aglionby was little less reticent. He asked few
questions, and seemed satisfied with the short and cautious
answers which were given to them. He learned the details
of his grandfather's seizure and death. Then he asked:

'And do you think the funeral will be over in time for me
to return to Irkford on the same day? because, I assure you,
my chiefs don't approve of an understrapper like myself
absenting himself in this style.'

'I have little doubt,' returned Mr. Whaley softly, 'that

should you wish to return to Irkford on the same afternoon, it can be managed.'

On the Friday morning, Mr. Whaley proposed to drive him over to Scar Foot.

'You should not allow your grandfather to be buried without paying him the last respect; you should at least go and see him before he is taken away for ever.'

Bernard agreed, with taciturn gravity. Mr. Whaley's dog-cart was called, and they drove to Scar Foot.

Aglionby's face was like some mask of bronze, as they drove along that road over which Judith Conisbrough had lately toiled so wearily. Not a word did he say; not a comment did he utter. 'Yea, yea,' and 'Nay, nay,' were all that could be wrung from him. One sign, and one only, did he give of being moved or interested. As they came suddenly to the top of the hill, from which they first had a view of Shennamere, from end to end, a light leaped into his eyes, which darted quickly from hill to hill, and then adown the lake. A flash of subtle feeling passed across his face, and he said abruptly:

'That great boulder at the foot of the lake, is it not called the Dipping Stone?'

'Yes, to be sure. How do you know?'

'I've heard of it,' was the laconic reply. He made no further comment until they had gone down the hill, and then pointing to the buildings on the left, embosomed in their trees, he said, more quietly than ever:

'And that is Scar Foot.'

'That is Scar Foot, Mr. Aglionby, and you are the last representative of the name of those who have lived there for so many generations.'

'Yes, I suppose I am,' he answered, as they drove into the farmyard, and got out of the dogcart.

While it was being taken to the other end of the yard, to water the horse, a woman came out of the back door, and looked at them, then greeted Mr. Whaley as an old acquaintance.

'Good-day, Mrs. Aveson,' said he; and added, 'No one here, I suppose?'

'No one, sir, but ourselves. The young ladies hasn't been nigh; not even Miss Judith, nor Mistress Conisbrough.'

'No, I dare say. It's a good way, you see. And——' he laid his hand upon Bernard's shoulder—'Mrs. Aveson, you do not know who this is.'

She gazed intently into Bernard's dark, saturnine visage.

'N—no, sir,' she hesitatingly said; 'but he is—he has surely a look of the old Squire about the een and the mouth.'

'Very likely. He is the old Squire's grandson, Bernard—Ralph Aglionby's son.'

'Lord-a-mercy!' exclaimed the woman, looking startled. 'You don't mean it! His son that he had by that foreign wife that he married. He doesn't favour his father,' she added in a lower voice; 'he's dark and foreign-looking,' as Aglionby turned away, tired of being stared at, and perhaps moved, more than he cared to confess, at hearing that he was like his forefathers: though he was 'dark and foreign-looking,' they could not deny the resemblance. He strolled away towards the front door.

During that short visit, his intensely keen eyes noted every item of every room he went into. He carried the place away with him, as it were indelibly engraved on his memory—carried away, too, a vivid impression of the dead face of the old Squire in his coffin, which he looked upon long and intently, trying hard the while to forgive him his trespasses that he had trespassed against him, Bernard Aglionby, and those who had been dear to him. He did not feel clear in his mind as to whether he had succeeded in this forgiveness; even at the last, when he turned away, he was not sure. His mother's face seemed to rise before him, stern and sad, worn with lines of toil and grief, soften-

ing into an angel's beauty when it turned to him, or when
he had caressed her. No—forgiveness was not easy, and
according to his creed no such thing as forgiveness existed.

As they drove back through Yoresett, Mr. Whaley pointed
out to him Yoresett House, with the blinds down.

'That's where Mrs. Conisbrough and her daughters live,'
he said. 'She was a niece of old John's; it was about her
that he quarrelled with your father.'

'Is one of the daughters a tall, pale girl, with rather
stately manners?'

'That's Judith—Miss Conisbrough. What of her?'

'Nothing. I saw her at Irkford with my grandfather the
other day.'

Later in the evening, Mr. Whaley remarked, 'We shall
have to go back to Scar Foot after the funeral, for the
reading of the will, and'—his brow wrinkled—'I'm sorry
to say, Mrs. Conisbrough intends to be present at that
ceremony too. She sent me word that she should.'

'Why sorry?'

'It is so needless. As if I could not have come straight
back here and called upon her, and told her all about it.
What do women want at such affairs?'

To this Bernard made absolutely no reply, and this was
the last hint, if hints they were, which Mr. Whaley gave to
his guest, as to the disposition of his grandfather's affairs.

      *   *   *   *   *

The funeral was over, and they had returned to Scar Foot.
Mr. Whaley again inquired of Mrs. Aveson, 'Anyone here?'

'Mistress Conisbrough, sir, and Miss Judith—that's all;
and they're in the parlour.'

Bernard, as he followed Mr. Whaley through the house
place, passed his hand over his eyes. It was all so very
strange and dream-like. He followed Mr. Whaley onwards
into the little parlour, where Judith had been received by
her uncle a few days ago. Bernard was not thinking of her

at all, at the moment ; but was considering what was the
secret he was at last going to hear, what this will, so soon to
be read, was to disclose for him. He was not thinking of
her when he followed Mr. Whaley into the parlour, but on
entering it he saw her before he saw anything else. He
might almost be said to see nothing but her at first. He
was not surprised of course ; he was prepared, and he bowed
to her as he entered. But she was more than surprised ;
he saw the look of puzzled bewilderment that passed over
her face, as she gazed at him, blankly at first, and then returned his salute slightly. Next, Bernard saw Mrs. Conisbrough ; these two with himself and Mr. Whaley comprised
the whole of the company. Mrs. Conisbrough was dressed
in the deepest mourning, with crape, and every outward
trapping of woe. Her handsome, rather highly coloured
face was flushed more than usual ; her hands were restless,
and her dark eyes roamed nervously and incessantly around.
She formed in every way a most startling contrast to her
daughter, who looked what she felt, as if she were only there
on compulsion. Mrs. Conisbrough had insisted upon coming,
and her daughters, after due consultation, had decided that
Judith was the proper person to accompany her. Pale,
sedate, and melancholy, she sat beside her mother on the
couch, and Bernard noticed that but for the fact of its
being black, her dress was no mourning dress at all, but a
somewhat worn one without any trimming ; her hat was a
little black straw hat ; she wore a white linen collar, a black
cloth jacket, and black kid gloves. She had refused every
entreaty of her mother to don what the latter considered a
more appropriate garb, for what reason Mrs. Conisbrough of
course could not imagine.

'Mrs. Conisbrough,' observed Mr. Whaley, shaking hands
with her, 'I think you will agree with me that we had better
get this business over at once before any of us take any
refreshment, or do anything else.'

' I quite agree with you, Mr. Whaley,' she said, in a trembling voice. She could not in the least conceal her great agitation. Mr. Whaley turned to Bernard, who was standing, dark, erect, and observant, by the table. He was grave, now, of course, but he was perfectly cheerful. To have curved his features to any pretence of emotion or of lamentation—to subdue his voice to the tones of a sorrow which he did not feel, were things which it was not in his nature to do. The sarcastic smile which frequently twisted his lips was absent, but his spirit of cool and rather bitter cynicism shone in double strength from his eyes. He looked cold, hard, and indifferent—exactly what he felt—as he confronted Mrs. Conisbrough, for he had always understood in a vague way that she had created mischief at the time of his father's marriage. Judith Conisbrough, measuring him with her calm and considerate eyes, clearly read his expression and admitted it in her inmost heart—'He looks a hard, contemptuous, pitiless man,' she decided.

' Before I begin to read,' said Mr. Whaley, ' let me present to you the only near relation of yourselves and the late Mr. Aglionby—his grandson, Bernard Aglionby.'

Mrs. Conisbrough gave a quick look at him, with nervously distended eyes and twitching lips. She inclined her head a little, and her lips moved, but no sound came from them ; they seemed dry and parched. Bernard merely bowed, in profound silence, and Judith did not repeat her original acknowledgment. Then Aglionby sat down, and while Mr. Whaley broke the seal of the will, there was perfect stillness, broken only by the rustle of Mrs. Conisbrough's dress, as she nervously moved now and then.

Bernard, sitting in the window, could see the head of the lake , he looked at it, his elbow resting on the back of his chair, his eyes shaded a little by his hand. And Mr. Whaley proceeded to read the will.

When Mrs. Conisbrough heard the date, October 7th,

18—, she started violently. It was the date of Tuesday last, the day on which he had been to see her, and on which he had so cruelly and remorselessly tormented her. A cold perspiration broke out upon her face, and her lips trembled.

It was a very concise, unelaborate will : it provided for some legacies to servants and old friends, and one or two very distant relatives or connections. Then the testator left the whole of his real and personal estate, without fetter or condition of any kind, to his grandson, Bernard Aglionby, to dispose of during his lifetime, to give, bequeath, or devise in whatsoever manner seemed good to him.

There was no more ; not another word, beyond the necessary little formula, and the signature of the testator and the witnesses. Mrs. Conisbrough's name and the names of her daughters were not even mentioned.

Mr. Whaley's voice ceased. There was a momentary pause. Bernard leaned forward, and looked around the room, with a strange, bewildered sensation ; a very strange sensation, as utterly devoid of triumph, or jubilation, or delight, as any sensation he had ever experienced. Rejoicing might come later ; he supposed it would, for this was great news—it must be. At present the rejoicing was conspicuous by its absence.

Mrs. Conisbrough had now risen. She advanced from the sofa on which she had been sitting beside her daughter, to the table, and supported herself against it with a trembling hand. Indeed, she trembled all over.

'Is that all, Mr. Whaley ?' she inquired, in a fluttering voice.

'I am sorry to say, madam, that that is all, every word.'

'And you consider that a just will ?'

'Pardon me, Mrs. Conisbrough, I do not, and I even went so far as to expostulate with Mr. Aglionby when he desired me to draw it up. I speak plainly, Mr. Bernard Aglionby.'

' Yes, you are right to do so.'

' Pooh ! Expostulating ? What is that ?' she exclaimed, speaking vehemently, and with strong, passionate excitement. 'I tell you, it is monstrous; it is wicked, it is mad. He knew what he had promised, he knew what he had led me to expect—how I had yielded to his wishes many a time, on the tacit understanding that my self-sacrifice was to be made good to me and my daughters at his death. This is a freak, a folly, a frenzy—I shall dispute the will.'

' My dear madam, do nothing of the kind, I implore you. You would cut your own throat. No court would find for you, and you would simply ruin yourself.'

' I shall dispute the will. And you, sir' (turning with passionate fierceness to Bernard, who had risen, and stood gravely listening to and looking at her)—'you, I warn. I warn you not to take possession of this house and property, or to spend the incomes belonging to them, for you shall make restitution of every penny you disburse. No jury of Englishmen will dispute the base injustice of this will. I should wish to be fair, it is what I have always intended ; I would not grasp everything and give you nothing, but before the sight of heaven it is no upstart stranger who——'

' Beware, Mrs. Conisbrough !' said Mr. Whaley, warningly. ' The upstart stranger you speak of is an Aglionby, and, so far as descent goes, the direct heir male to every penny his grandfather left behind him, and to every stick and stone on the estate.'

' No doubt, sir, it will be to your interest to support the strongest.'

' Mother ! mother !' exclaimed Judith, rising, and putting her hand on her mother's arm. But Mrs. Conisbrough was no longer mistress of herself.

' But might is not always right,' she went on, ' and occasionally the innocent win their cause against the guilty.'

" Shall we not discuss the matter some other time, when

you are more composed?' said Bernard, with profound courtesy of tone and manner, as he too bent over the table towards her, leaning the tips of his fingers on the table and looking with grave inquiry directly into her eyes.

Their faces were very near together. As she met this direct, serious gaze, Mrs. Conisbrough's high colour suddenly faded ; she gave a kind of gasp or sob, and shrank away, averting her gaze.

'Dear mother, let us go away now,' said Judith soothingly.

'Not until I have told these men who are in league against us, once again, that I defy them, and that they had better beware what——'

She stopped suddenly, put her hand to her side, for her heart was weak, and strong excitement usually brought on an attack of illness. She sank down upon the sofa now, livid and unconscious.

Judith sprang to her, unfastened her bonnet-strings, loosened her mantle, and bent over her anxiously. Aglionby walked up to her, and asked in a low voice, and one which he evidently constrained, to repress some kind of emotion :

'Can I assist you in any way ?'

'No, I thank you,' replied the young lady, lifting her eyes to his face, with a look of such deep and mournful sadness, that Aglionby, feeling as if he had rashly intruded upon some sacred precinct, said humbly, 'I beg your pardon,' and retired again to Mr. Whaley's side.

For a short time there was an uncomfortable, brooding kind of silence. Then at last, Judith turned round, her face disturbed, despite its set expression, her voice faltering a little.

'I am very sorry,' she said, 'but my mother has had these attacks before, and she—I am afraid—I know she must remain here just at present.'

'On the sofa, for an hour or two,' said Mr. Whaley, almost briskly. 'I am sure Mr. Aglionby——'

'For a day or two, at least, I grieve to say. I must send

for the doctor—at least,' she added hastily, and looking at Bernard with a deep flush of embarrassment, 'it is as much as her life is worth to remove her at present.'

'Mr. Aglionby,' said Mr. Whaley, looking at him, 'you are master here now. What are these ladies to do?'

'I beg them to make use of the house and everything there is in it, as long as it suits their convenience to do so,' he replied, still in the same courteous, almost gentle tone, and looking earnestly at Judith.

'I thank you,' said the latter. 'Then may I ring for Mrs. Aveson, and order a boy to be sent for Dr. Lowther?'

'You know the ways of the place, I imagine, better than I do; will you please take all authority in the matter into your own hands? Pray oblige me by ordering exactly what is convenient to you,' said Bernard. 'Shall I ring the bell for you?' He put his hand upon the rope, and turning to Mr. Whaley, added in a lower voice, 'Shall we not leave these ladies at present, and I will inquire later if they have all they want?'

With that he pulled the bell, and then saying to Judith, 'I trust Mrs. Conisbrough will soon recover,' he followed Mr. Whaley from the room.

As they closed the door after them, and found themselves in the house-place, they met Mrs. Aveson, going to answer the summons. Aglionby paused.

'Do not leave it to Miss Conisbrough to tell her,' he said. And Mr. Whaley, stopping the woman, said:

'Mrs. Aveson, let me present to you your new master, and the old Squire's successor.'

'Sir! I thought the young ladies—Mrs. Conisbrough——' She was paralysed with astonishment and dismay.

'Not at all. Mr. Aglionby's property goes to his grandson. And I think the ladies want you. Mrs. Conisbrough is ill.'

She made a hasty step towards the parlour. Bernard interposed.

10

'Listen!' he said. 'Will you please attend to Miss Conis-brough's orders as if they were my own? Find out every-thing she can possibly want, and see that it is got for her, and——'

'Sir!' exclaimed Mrs. Aveson. 'You may be master here, or not, but I need no *orders* to attend to those ladies that are in there;' and without condescending to give him another look, she swept onwards.

'Good!' remarked Aglionby, with a saturnine smile. 'I like that woman. She's honest. I hope she will stay here.'

CHAPTER XV.

JUDITH.

Mrs. Aveson, closing the parlour-door, bent over Mrs. Conisbrough. 'Eh, but she's very bad, Miss Judith, this bout. Something's upset her, I guess.'

'Yes, indeed!' said Judith abstractedly. She was forced to withdraw her attention from her mother for the moment, while she wrote with a flying pen to Delphine:

Very bad news. *All* is left to uncle's grandson, Bernard Aglionby, of whose existence we hardly knew till to-day. I have seen him before. Not one of our names is mentioned. Mamma has taken it to heart, made an awful scene, and had one of her attacks in consequence. She is unconscious now, and cannot be moved. Prepare some things for us, and I will instruct Toby to call for them as he returns from the doctor's. Mr. A. is very courteous and gentle, despite the terrible things mother has said to him. He has placed the house at our disposal. If the doctor thinks you ought to come, I will get him to call and tell you so on his way back.

                 'Yours, sorrowfully,

                       'JUDITH.'

'Now, Mrs. Aveson, will you give this to Toby, and tell him to make all speed with it to Yoresett House first, then on to the doctor's; then he must return to Yoresett House, and wait for a parcel? Let him go as fast as he can.'

Mrs. Aveson took the note, and very soon Toby rode out of the yard, on a stout brown cob, which he astonished by his liberal use of a tough switch. Mrs. Aveson returned to the parlour, where Mrs. Conisbrough still lay unconscious. Sometimes these attacks lasted two hours, or rather, once she had had one that lasted so long, and this seemed likely to be as tedious. In vain they applied all the restoratives they could think of, or knew of; she lay rigid, and with a livid, deathly hue upon her face.

Judith was not at first alarmed, nor Mrs. Aveson, who was in every sense of the word 'a friend of the family.' In the intervals of their exertions the woman asked:

'Miss Judith, tell me, is this true, what old Mr. Whaley says? Was the old Squire's will so very unjust?'

'Very unjust, from a moral point of view, Mrs. Aveson. Legally, there was no fault to be found with it.'

'It's a bad hearing. Do you really mean that he has left *all* to that black-looking young man?'

'Yes, all. He is his grandson. I know nothing of where he found him; yes, I do, though. He must have seen him when we were at Irkford, a week ago to-day! But I know nothing of what passed between them. All I know is that this will was made the night he died——'

'Ay! We were witnesses, me and John Heseltine, who happened to be in the kitchen at the time. Had I known how it was going, never would I have signed. It's a crying shame! People have no right to act in that way, I say; though he was my master, and I liked him well enough for all his queer ways. And this stranger, he's no Aglionby in looks, except that he has a glint of the een something like old master, and a twist in the mouth that's a bit akin to him that's gone. But that long thin body, and that lean black face! No Aglionby was ever like that before. I don't know how we shall tak' to him, I'm sure. M'appen we'll have to flit.'

'Oh, I hope not, Mrs. Aveson, or we shall have lost all our friends indeed. But see! is she not coming round a little?'

The hope was deceptive. For two long hours Mrs. Conisbrough lay without consciousness, until her daughter, without losing her presence of mind, began to grow almost faint with fear, and Mrs. Aveson openly expressed her opinion that Mrs. Conisbrough was either dead, or in a trance which would end in death.

She went out of the room at last, in search of some restorative which occurred to her mind, and to look up the road at the back in the hope of catching sight of the doctor on his roadster at the top of the hill; and it was during this absence that at last a flicker of life appeared in the lips and eyes of the unconscious woman.

Her eyes at last opened, slowly and fully; she moved them deliberately and blankly round, fixed them upon Judith without appearing to recognise her, and said, in a toneless voice:

'Bernarda told me so, uncle. She said they would take him, and that sooner than touch a crust of your bread she would starve.'

'Mother dear, it is I. You are at Scar Foot. Try to remember.'

'And if you had only waited that morning, instead of going off in a passion without leaving me time to explain, I

could have told you all about it. But you were selfish and
tyrannical to the last, to the last! Oh dear! It is a weary,
weary world, and weariest of all for women that are poor!'

She turned her face to the wall, and closed her eyes, but
Judith saw two large tears force their way from under the
lids and course slowly down her cheeks. All her soul went
out in love and pity. Her mother's wandering remarks were
for the moment forgotten, though they at first struck her as
strange and inexplicable. 'Bernarda!' Surely that was the
name of the woman her uncle Ralph had married. This grandson was called Bernard, too. And her uncle in a passion with
her mother? What did that mean? But she could think
of none of these things now; she could only stoop over her
mother, and wipe her eyes, and kiss her hand, and conjure
her to look up. To her great relief, too, she heard the
sound of a horse's hoofs, and directly afterwards the doctor
was in the room.

The doctor's orders were what Judith had expected. Her
mother must be carried upstairs and put to bed, where she
must have the most absolute quiet and repose. A state of
the most alarming weakness and prostration had succeeded
to the intense agitation and excitement which had brought
on the attack. It was long before all was arranged, and
before Dr. Lowther could leave his patient, white and weak
and hardly conscious where she was, or what was going on
around her. He promised to call the next day, Sunday,
enforced again and again the necessity for the most absolute
rest, strictly forbade almost all conversation, and departed.

Never had Judith experienced such a feeling as overwhelmed her when she was at last left alone with her mother
in the bedroom—the well-known blue bedroom which she
had occupied many a score of times—with the lamp lighted
on the table, and the dusk outside rapidly gathering into
darkness. When the last echo of the horse's hoofs had died
away over the hill, there fell upon the place a silence utter

and profound, such as can only be known in the very heart
of the country—far away from men that strive, from clanging
bells remorselessly summoning the multitudes to their toil,
from railways that deafen, and traffic that makes weary the
heart of man.   She went to the window—the broad deep-set
window—and leaning one knee on the window-seat, she
curved her hands upon the pane into a kind of arch, and
pressed her aching forehead upon them.   Indistinctly, by
the light of a young moon, she could see what Sir Bedivere
called 'the waves wap, and the waters wan,' of silent
Shennamere, and the shadowy forms of the great fells on the
other side, and one solitary, steadily burning light from the
village of Busk on the hill across the lake.

It was beautiful, and she loved it—loved it dearly: but
was it always to be thus?   Was her prospect never to be
larger than this? and even this she now no more felt to be
her own.   In the house of her forefathers she had suddenly
become a stranger, a casual guest, and every hour that she
now passed there was like a fresh load upon her heart.
Surely there must be some way of getting out of it all.
Even now her mind was busy with thoughts of escape, as
the minds of prisoners and caged birds are wont to be,
and will be, to the world's end.   Shennamere, and Scar
Foot, and Yoresett, and her own home, and this existence,
which was neither life nor death, without either the fulness
of the one or the repose of the other—they had long been
bitter realities to her ; would the time ever come when they
would seem but as a dream that has vanished ?   Would she
ever be able to look back upon them from some height
attained of usefulness, or hopefulness, or successful endeavour,
and to say with a smile, 'Once upon a time I had no more
than those in my life ; no prospect wider than Shennamere
Water and Raydaleside Fell'?   The wonder, the longing,
the strenuous effort to force the future to lift its veil were at
that moment more passionate, more intense than she had

ever known them. Hard hours she had passed, when her heart had fretted as if it must burst with impatience to snap its bonds—bitter hours of self-interrogation : 'Why am I here? What was I born for? Who wants me? What is there for me to do?' Such hours as thousands of young women fight through or sink under every day that dawns, in this glorious kingdom of England, under the model laws, protected by the immaculate social institutions of which we are so proud, in this grandest and greatest of great empires.

Some, whom Fortune favours, come out of the storm into a clear haven, but generally battered more or less. Others are rescued by a man's hand : they marry, have children, and rear them, and we are wont exultantly to point out these cases, and to say, 'See, would you alter the laws under which flourish so beautifully all these talented women who make money, and earn honourable fame ; these happy wives and mothers, loved and looked up to by husbands and children and friends?' We are chary of inquiring whether the talented and successful authoresses and artists, the happy wives and mothers, may not have attained their proud position rather in spite of than in consequence of some of our supremely wise and benevolent legal and social institutions, and we most distinctly do not turn to the other side and look over the edge into that grey twilight country where the failures dwell—the withered-up old maids ; the disappointed strugglers after fame or even independence ; the heaps and heaps of spoiled lives, of vitality crushed, of promptings of intellect, or talent, or genius repressed—the dreadful limbo of the spirits which have failed to make good their claim to a place in the world.

Judith Conisbrough, though she did not put the situation tangibly before herself, even in her own mind, vaguely felt herself trembling on the brink which divides these two worlds ; for it is a narrow ledge, though we trip so carelessly along it; trembling on the verge of that path which separates the 'successful women,' 'the happy wives and mothers,' from this holocaust composed of the failures; of those who had not found favour in the eyes of the world or of men, and who had withered, or were withering away without having any joys, whether of love or maternity, or of published books, pictures that sold, or establishments that succeeded. Sometimes she viewed the matter in a half-bantering, half-cynical way, and was inclined to smile—as we are all inclined to smile—at the failures; but to-night deeper emotions were astir—she felt in deadly earnest; she could see no smiling side to the matter; she told herself that she had been suffered to grow to womanhood in the hope that an old man would leave her some of his money when he died; that he had died and left her none, and that she was worse than useless—she was as a withered tree that cumbered the ground; that she must make a struggle soon, or it would be too late; and she asked herself by what right had those who had doomed her to this fate done so?

Thus she stood, leaning against the window, her eyes straining out into the night, her heart beating fast with a vague excitement, her spirit stretching invisible hands towards heaven, uttering an inaudible but passionate, terrible cry, 'Lord, help me!'

A footstep behind her roused her; she turned, bewildered, as one who wakens from a dream, and saw Mrs. Aveson.

'Miss Judith,' said she softly, ' you're doing wrong to be standing here, tiring yourself, and you're in want of food. You've tasted neither bite nor sup since breakfast-time. Go yer ways down into t' parlour, and there you'll find some coffee, and something to eat, as I've got ready for you. Now go, honey, and I'll bide with Mistress Conisbrough the while. And don't be in any hurry back again. I've nought to do. Go and rest a bit. You'll want your strength.'

'Thank you, very much, Mrs. Aveson,' she said, in a voice

weak from fasting and exhaustion following upon excitement and suspense.

Mrs. Aveson took her seat by the bedside, and Judith slowly went downstairs and into the parlour—the fatal parlour in which she had endured so many hard blows. How pleasant it looked! How cosy, and homely, and dear it was, with the glowing, generous Yorkshire fire, and the bright lamp, and the oaken rafters and panels; the white cloth on the table, and the inviting little meal which Mrs. Aveson had spread for her—coffee in the old square silver coffee-pot, and cream in the ancient ewer of the same shape; the white and the brown bread-and-butter, the egg and the marmalade, and the cold fowl—creature-comforts, no doubt, and infinitely beneath the dignified notice of a romance-writer of the highest order, but to Judith the sight of them was overpowering. They were so exactly what she had always been used to see at Scar Foot; they were what had been at her service all the years of her life whenever she came there, and now they every one belonged to a stranger, one with whom, she foresaw, they were to be at strife—at daggers-drawn—unless her mother's bitter resentment subsided; this stranger's bread she was forced to eat, to sustain bodily weakness, with a feeling that it would almost choke her. Truly, it seemed as if she were destined to eat her bread with tears, and she foresaw no end to the grief in store for them all.

She leaned her elbows on the table, breaking down utterly, and cried piteously; not loudly, but with silent intensity. Her head ached, her heart throbbed—she was wretched!

The handle of the door turned; a footstep paused, a voice, curt and surprised, said:

'Oh, Miss Conisbrough, I beg your pardon. I will not intrude upon you.'

Judith started up, and saw Bernard Aglionby, this 'new master'; this strong man, who seemed to her to have stepped to the front, and put his hand with remorseless grip upon the one chance of peace and happiness there had been for them all, and crushed it as if it had been a fly. Her tears dried as if by magic.

'Pray come in !' she said; 'Mrs. Aveson asked me to come down and have something to eat, and I had forgotten——'

She had almost added, 'your very existence,' but paused in time.

He accepted her invitation, came forward, and closed the door; acting upon her hint, and taking no open notice of her tears, though she dried them without disguise before his very eyes.

He looked at her, and his face wore a keen, sharp, hard expression, as it always did when he was studying those whom he did not know; an expression which by no means betokened dislike of the said persons, but was simply a mask which his own face took in his reserve. To show himself as he was, to those of whose nature he knew nothing, was a thing which it was not in his nature to do. To fulfil the duties of host could however commit him to nothing, and he had decided quietly to ignore poor Mrs. Conisbrough's warnings, and distinctly to assume the position of master in the house which now belonged to him.

'I am glad Mrs. Aveson has persuaded you to come down,' he said. 'You must have fasted long, and, after all your anxiety, must stand in need of something. Would you not prefer wine to this coffee ?'

'No, thank you; I seldom touch it,' said she, seating herself, and pouring out the coffee.

'Pray send me away, if my presence annoys you,' he added, standing against the mantelpiece, his back to the fire, and his face in the shade.

'Not in the least,' replied Judith coldly, as she leaned back, languid and exhausted, too exhausted to eat. He saw this, and stepping forward, urged her to try to eat something.

'You must eat,' he said. 'Dr. Lowther—that is his name, isn't it——?'

'Yes.'

'I saw him, and he told me that Mrs. Conisbrough would require many days of absolute repose before she could possibly leave.'

'I—yes—I am afraid so. I—we—you cannot imagine how I regret having thus to inflict my mother and myself upon you, at such an inopportune time, and—and after such a scene.'

She spoke with a deep blush of mingled pride and embarrassment, and her last words came with difficulty.

'Pray do not think of that. Mrs. Conisbrough's recovery must be your first consideration,' said Bernard, who was, unaccountably to himself, fascinated by the voice and manners of his guest.

There was something in the situation which appealed to his fancy. He had imagination enough to understand that he saw Miss Conisbrough under exceptional circumstances—trying ones, also—and he felt a keen interest in watching her behaviour under those circumstances. So far he had found it admirable.

He took cynical views of life and human nature, which views his new prosperity and easy circumstances would be sure to mellow and modify. As yet there had not been time for this effect to take place. He was still the old Bernard Aglionby, sardonic and mocking; and he thought he had found confirmation of his views on human nature in Mrs. Conisbrough's fury at being left penniless—even in Mr. Aglionby's brutal caprice (as such he regarded it, though it so greatly benefited him) in thus leaving her penniless—in her threat to dispute a will which no English court would for a moment think of setting aside.

So far, he felt his theories as to the predominance of self-interest over all other interests strongly supported by facts.

As for Miss Conisbrough, he did not know yet. He very much wished to know. He had not been able to forget the sadness, the deep sorrow of her eyes, as she had turned to look at him while her mother lay fainting. All these various considerations prompted his words, ' Pray do not think of that,' to which she answered :

'You are very kind, but I do and must think of that. It is the sort of thing one cannot help thinking of.'

' Is it ?' said he.

He had been watching her as she leaned back in her chair, trifling with her knife and fork, and now with his usual impetuousness he exclaimed :

'You really must excuse me, but you are my guest, and I must look after you. Do have some more cold fowl. I beg you will. You will need your strength ; and you must not starve yourself.'

He seized the dish, and placed another piece on her plate.

Judith looked surprised, but overcoming her languor, tried to eat the fowl, and succeeded better.

' Nothing like trying,' observed the new ruler of Scar Foot, rubbing his nervous-looking hands together, and with a gleam of encouragement in his dark eyes.

Judith, looking at him ever more and more attentively, came to the conclusion that his was a face of which it was impossible to say whether the agreeable or disagreeable in feature and expression predominated in it. Now and again the lips relaxed in their cynical curve, and the dark eyes softened, and the corrugated brow grew smooth and pensive. Then, seizing this fleeting moment of softness, one was tempted to say, ' Good !' Again the cynical curve returned to those lips and marred their carving. The eyes were filled with a spark of anything but kindly feeling, and the brow was wrinkled up in lines which seemed to imply that its owner had ceased to expect the sun to shine, or the moon to be bright again, and that he experienced a faint wonder at finding others who still cherished any delusions on those points; and then Judith and others must infallibly have said of that face, 'Not good.' Of one thing alone she felt sure, and that was that his face was neither a common nor an uninteresting one.

She smiled faintly in answer to his last remark. It had not occurred to her to wonder how she should treat him. For her own part, she was not sorry for the result of her Uncle Aglionby's will—all that she regretted in it was that Scar Foot had passed to a stranger, and that her mother had said things to that stranger, of such a nature as to offend the meekest of men; and, however doubtful she might be as to some points of his character, she was very sure that meekness was not one of them. What had overwhelmed her, had been the utter upsetting of all that had appeared to her most trustworthy and most stable—her uncle's regard, his good intentions, his plighted word. And she was terribly ashamed of the display of anger made by her mother that morning.

'It is strange that we should have met before,' she observed, not wishing to maintain a churlish silence.

'Yes, very. I little thought, as I stood beside you at the Liberal Demonstration, that you were the nearest relation I had.'

'*I*—a near relation?'

'Surely you are my third cousin. That's near, when one has no others nearer.'

'Third cousins—I suppose we are,' said Judith musingly. 'I had not thought of it in that light.'

'And you are resolved that you never will think of it in that light,' he said, a flash of sarcasm in his smile. 'Well, I cannot wonder at that. To you, my conduct in turning up at such a time must have appeared more scurvy than cousinly, to say the least of it.'

'I never said so,' said Judith gravely. 'I do not wish to

say so ; for I do not understand the circumstances. How
did you meet my uncle ?   The next time we saw you you
were at the theatre with——'

She stopped suddenly short, and looked at him.

' With Lizzie—Miss Vane, I mean—the girl I am engaged
to,' replied Bernard composedly. ' Did you notice her ?'

' Yes, but I scarcely saw her, really.   I caught a glimpse
of her face, which seemed to me exceedingly pretty.   But
you did not speak to my uncle then.'

' He came to see over the warehouse in which I was one
of the salesmen ; I was deputed to show him round.   We
got into conversation.   But I think he saw some likeness, or
something, that made him suspect who I was.   He asked
my name.   Then he told me by degrees who he was, and invited me to come and visit him here, which proposal I declined with scant courtesy, I fear.   He pressed a few home-
truths upon my consideration ; I returned his presents in
the same coin ; we shook hands, as a concession on either
side, and parted.   You must know the rest better than
I do.'

' Yes, we all know the rest pretty well, I imagine.   We
know the end of it.'

' I hope not, Miss Conisbrough,' he said earnestly.   Judit
seemed to him so calm, so staid and eminently reasonable a
person, that he felt he could speak to her on terms of almost
business-like equality ; it struck him that here was an admirable opportunity for declaring his views upon the vexed subject of his grandfather's will, to one who would hear them
without heat or prejudice.   As for Mrs. Conisbrough, he
considered, with an inward feeling of some contempt, that
a woman who could conduct herself as she had done that
morning, was quite hopeless : he was resolved not to have
any further consultation with her.   If he could enlist Judith
on his side, no doubt she could bring about an arrangement.
She must have some influence over her weaker mother, and

he would infinitely prefer to conduct the negotiation he contemplated through her.

'I hope not,' he repeated. 'If you suppose that I consider my grandfather's will a just one, or that I am capable of taking advantage of it to the full extent, you do me injustice indeed. I am a very rough fellow, I know. I have had to fight the world inch by inch, and have been battered about from my childhood up, and I know it has soured me, and made me an uncivil, pessimistic creature. The only time Fortune ever smiled upon me was when she threw me in the way of my sweetheart, and made her take pity on me and promise to marry me.' ('His face is more good than bad, I am quite certain now,' Judith decided.) 'But in all my knockings about, I don't think I ever took a mean advantage of anyone weaker or worse off than myself—at least, I hope not. Mrs. Conisbrough is unfit to speak of business at present; indeed, to me it seems that with her evident tendency to become violently agitated, she ought not to speak of it at all. Perhaps she will name you her delegate. I am sure you have a cool head. At any rate, we must have a discussion as soon as may be. I cannot consider anything settled until that has been settled. Mr. Whaley will help us, I am sure, for so monstrously unjust a will cannot possibly be literally carried out.'

'I see you wish to be fair,' said Judith calmly, 'but such things are difficult to arrange. I cannot answer for my mother; I think she has been iniquitously treated. But for myself and one of my sisters I can answer. I know that nothing short of starvation would induce us to touch a penny of Mr. Aglionby's property.'

She said this without heat, but with a calm determination which he saw was earnest.

'Because that property has been left to me?' he said hastily, 'because you would not——'

'Not at all; but because of certain events which have

lately occurred—certain things which passed between my uncle and me. This will is a decisive thing at last. I hope that now my sister and I will be able to carry out the desire we have always had, and work, as we should have been taught to do, and made to do from our childhood.'

'I am sorry you do not altogether agree with me. But,' he added quickly, 'you will not oppose my wish that your mother, at any rate, should receive the treatment which is her due?'

'No, I shall not oppose that,' replied Judith. And so impressed was he by her manner, and by every word she said, that he felt as if the cause were gained whose side she took.

'Thank you very much for that promise,' he answered. 'It will make it much easier for me. You will of course be the best judge as to when it is fitting to speak to Mrs. Conisbrough of the matter.'

'It must not be now, nor for some days to come,' replied Judith, rising. 'I will wish you good-night, Mr. Aglionby, and go to my mother, who I am sure must want me.'

'Must you go? Then good-night.' He rose too. 'Miss Conisbrough, are you my enemy?'

'No.'

'Then will you prove it, and acknowledge our cousinship by shaking hands with me?'

Judith looked at the hand he held out—at him—at the hand again; put her own into it, and repeated, 'Good-night.'

'I hope you will rest well,' he replied, holding open the door as she passed out.

'I have shaken hands with him—what will Delphine say?' was Judith's reflection as she went upstairs. She found her mother asleep. She let Mrs. Aveson go, and seated herself beside the bed, folded her hands together, and thought.

'No, he does not know,' she reflected. 'I should be paralysed by the possession of that money—of any of it. But it shows a generous mind to wish to give us some of it, after what mamma said this morning. He has had his troubles too—anyone can see that. I dare say he could tell a tale of how he has been neglected, and disappointed. His eyes are good—they are not afraid to meet yours. When they are not mocking you they are pleasant. Oh, I hope mamma will come to terms with him! A long strife would be so fearful—and then if he did get angry with her, he could crush her to atoms.'

CHAPTER XVI.

A LANDOWNER.

WHEN Judith had gone, Bernard felt he had a duty to fulfil. His conversation with Miss Conisbrough had brought it again to his mind. It was the duty of writing to Lizzie Vane, to acquaint her with his new fortunes—and hers, for of course she was to be the partaker for the future of all his joys and sorrows. He distinctly felt it to be a duty : was it not also a pleasure? As that thought occurred to him, he started up, muttering :

'By Jove! of course it is !'

And he seized pen and paper, and scrawled off these lines, in the fulness of his heart:

' MY DEAREST LIZZIE,

'You will see from the date of this that I am in the house of my fathers. You will wonder, too, what I am doing here, after all I have said to you about my determination never to enter it. What I have to tell you, my darling, is a very serious matter for both of us. You remember my telling you last Monday about my accidental meeting with Mr. Aglionby of Scar Foot, my grandfather. On Wednesday last he died They telegraphed for me to attend the funeral. He was buried this morning, and on his will being read, it turns out that he has left the whole of his property to me. I was astonished, I own, and in a measure gratified; one naturally is gratified at finding one's self suddenly rich when one had least reason to expect to be anything of the kind.

'But there are shades to the picture, and drawbacks to the advantages, and you, my dear Lizzie, with your tender heart, will easily understand when I explain that my joy is not unmixed. It seems that the Mrs. Conisbrough whom I told you about, and who lives with her daughters at Yoresett, the market-town, had always been given to understand that she would inherit the property.

'My grandfather's will was made only the night before he died, in a fit of pique, for some reason which no one seems able to understand. They are entirely ignored—not even mentioned in it. Mrs. Conisbrough and her eldest daughter were present at the reading of the will. The poor lady has taken it very much to heart: her means are exceedingly small, and she thinks the will a most unjust one. (So do I, for that matter—an egregiously unjust will.) And she threatens to dispute it. She will have no chance, of course; but I feel my hands in a measure tied until I know the worst she can do, and until some compromise is come to for her benefit. Meantime, she is ill upstairs in this very house—her agitation having brought on an attack of the heart. She is attended by her daughter, for whom I feel very sorry. I feel sorry for them all. They are gentlewomen, and evidently have had a hard struggle all their lives.

'There is such a sad, patient, yet dignified expression upon Miss Conisbrough's face. She cannot but command respect and admiration. I wish you knew her. One dreams fast sometimes, and since this morning I have been dreaming of you settled here, and myself having effected a compromise with Mrs. Conisbrough, and proved to her that I am not the rapacious upstart she takes me for—and of you and the Misses Conisbrough getting on very well together, and being great friends. I think this is not so foolish as most dreams. I see no reason why it should not come true. Miss Conisbrough is as far as possible from being forbidding, though she looks so grave, and I am sure your winning ways would soon make her love you.

'This is a most beautiful old place—very different from the din and dust of the town. To-morrow I must try to make a little sketch of the lake and the house, and send you them. As soon as I can snatch the time, I shall run over to Irkford and see you, and discuss future plans. I can hardly realise yet that our wedding, which we thought must wait for so many years, need not now be long deferred—no longer than a certain wilful young woman chooses to put it off.

'Remember me to your mother ; and Heaven bless you, my own darling, is the wish of your faithful sweetheart,

'BERNARD AGLIONBY.'

His heart warmed as he wrote the words, and thought of his beautiful Lizzie, and cherished his little plan of making her and the Misses Conisbrough into great friends. Poor Bernard! He wrote out of the innocence and the fulness of his heart, not out of his knowledge of either men or women.

He had chosen to remain at Scar Foot rather than accept Mr. Whaley's invitation that he would return with him to Yoresett and be his guest. Mr. Whaley may easily be pardoned for not having surmised for a moment, what Aglionby's demeanour certainly did not suggest, the unspoken impulse which urged him to remain—the longing which lay deep at his heart, to become better acquainted, in silence and undisturbed, with this old place where his fathers had lived, and where now he was to live after them ; to imbibe, as it were, some ideas of the life, of the home, that was to be his.

Unspoken though it was, the sentiment, the desire, was there. Deep down in his rough heart, and crusted over with the bitterness which with him came too readily to the surface, there were wells of something very like romance and sentiment. Since this morning a thousand schemes had come crowding into his mind, a thousand not wholly selfish plans and purposes, which now he could carry out to his heart's content. All his poetic instincts had been cramped, if not warped, by the life he had led, but under his unpromising exterior they were there—they did exist; and it was they and they alone which had prompted him to refuse Mr. Whaley's invitation.

His sleep, on that first night that he rested under this roof, was sweet and undisturbed. When Sunday morning dawned, and he awoke, he at first could not imagine where he was, so profound was the silence, except for the chirping birds and the smothered rush of the brook at the back of the house. Gradually his senses returned to him. He remembered it all, sprang out of bed, went to the window, and lifted the blind.

The air of the October morning was sharp; the sun was brilliant, the atmosphere clear; the view before him struck with a strange thrill upon him—a thrill half-pleasure, half-pain. The clear moors just opposite; the dimmer forms of the great fells behind them; the glittering silver surface of the little lake; the garden just under his eyes, filled with homely flowers, and with the green field beyond, sloping down to the water's edge—it was indeed very fair for anyone who had eyes to see ! But to him it was more—it was a revelation ; there was the peculiar stillness of a country Sunday morning over it all ; it was the end of the world. Most of us are acquainted with one sensation—that of arriving when it is dark at some seaside place—of sleeping soundly all night ; of awakening the next morning, and on looking out, finding one's self confronted by the open sea.

That is a sensation which never grows old or stale. Something of the thrill and joy which attends its first time of being experienced, hangs also about each recurrence of it.

It was with just such a sensation that Bernard Aglionby's eyes rested now on the prospect before him. Vague, unconscious contrasts were formed in his mind—this place and that—Scar Foot on a Sunday morning, and 13, Crane Street, on a Sunday morning! He opened the window, and inhaled the pure, frosty, fragrant air—Arcadian air. It was very early, he found, not yet six o'clock ; but going to bed again was a thing not to be thought of; and he dressed, went downstairs, and out of doors, and walked to the lakeside with the feeling that he was in a dream. It was as wonderful to him, and certainly quite as agreeable, as her first ball to a girl of seventeen who has been brought up in strict seclusion. He wondered at the intensity of his own enjoyment, and its *naïveté.*

'It is hereditary, I suppose,' he thought, 'and I can't help it. It's the stock I come of. When a man's forefathers have lived and moved and had their being for hundreds of years in a spot like this, and have appreciated it, a love of such things must be implanted in that man's nature at his birth. So it is with me, I suppose. I fear Lizzie won't delight in it as I do.'

Bernard spent almost the whole of that day out-of-doors, literally ' exploring ' with the avidity and the interest of a schoolboy who has found a promising place for birds'-nests. He walked completely round the lake, and thus, from under the village of Busk at the opposite side, he got a fine view of Scar Foot, and gazed at it till he could gaze no longer.

He met a farmer's boy, and asked him the names of some of the great grey fells in the distance, and the boy told him, and added that there must have been rain in Lancashire, for ' look at t' Stake,' which, as Bernard saw, was flecked with irregular white lines. ' All the becks is oot,' added the boy, and Aglionby smiled. At Irkford—for miles around Irkford —the 'becks' were black as ink, and foul as only the streams of a town can be with all manner of pollution.

He went in again, to his dinner, in the middle of the day, and sent a message by Mrs. Aveson to inquire after 'those ladies.' The answer brought by the housekeeper was, 'Miss Conisbrough's compliments, and she was quite well; but Mrs. Conisbrough was rather poorly this morning.' On her own account, Mrs. Aveson added that Mrs. Conisbrough was terribly weak, and had to lie on her back as still as a mouse, or palpitations would come on again. Dr. Lowther had called, and said that complete rest was still necessary. Miss Conis brough had been reading the Morning Service to her mamma, ' and she was going to have her dinner with her upstairs.

With this he had to be satisfied. Then, after dinner, he sat at the open window of the parlour for an hour or two smoking, and making believe to read a county newspaper, with which Mrs. Aveson had supplied him ; but it was as if a spell drew him out-of-doors, and he again set out for what he intended to be a short walk, but on what developed into a long, aimless ramble over hill and dale : he got by mistake on to the road which leads to the great waterfall at Hardraw Scar, which was thundering in indescribable splendour, hurling itself over the rocky ledge into its deep and dark and fearful basin below.

Then he climbed a long road, over some great hiils ; dis- covered some vast and awful-looking 'pots,' crevasses of lime- stone, sinking for unknown depths into the ground—fearsome places indeed, bearing the unromantic title of ' Butter-tubs ;' and a little farther on, found himself just beneath bleak Shunner Fell, gazing down into dark Swaledale, and in full view of such a 'tumultuous waste of huge hill-tops' as he had never seen before. Then he thought it was time to return, and retraced his steps downwards, and by the light of the moon, homewards.

CHAPTER XVII.

'*GODEN ABEND, GODE NACHT !*'

HE crossed the farmyard and went into the garden, under the old archway, and then, just as he was about to enter, he heard a voice singing, and was arrested. The window of the large room on the right was open, and a glow of firelight warmed the background. From it came the sound of a piano being played, and of a woman's voice accompanying it. Aglionby trod softly up to the window and looked in. The fire burnt merrily. Judith Conisbrough sat at the piano, with her back to him, softly playing ; her voice had ceased, and presently the music ceased also. Then she began again, and sang in a contralto voice, sweet, natural, and strong, if uncultivated, a song which Aglionby was surprised to hear. He would not have expected her to sing foreign songs—if this could be called foreign. He folded his arms upon the window-ledge and gazed in and listened, and the music, after all the other strange and dreamful incidents of that day, sank into his inmost soul.

'Oever de stillen Straten,
  Geit klar de Glockenslag.
God' Nacht ! Din Hart will slapen ;
  Un' Morgen is oock een Dag.

'Din Kind liggt in de Wegen,
  Un' ik bin oock bi' Di' ;
Din Sorgen un' Din Leven
  Sind allens um uns bi'.

'Noch eenmal lat uns spräken,
  Goden Abend, gode Nacht.
Di Maand schient up' de Däken,
  Uns Herrgott hält de Wacht.'*

---

* 'Clear sounds adown the silent street,
  The bell that tells the hours.
Good-night ! Thy very heart sleep deep !
  To-morrow is also ours.

Aglionby was not a sentimental man, but he was a man intensely sensitive to simple pathos of any kind. None could jeer more cruelly at every pretence of feeling, but none had a keener appreciation of the real thing when it came in his way. And this little German dialect song is brimming over in every line with the truest pathos. Sung in these surroundings by Judith Conisbrough's rich and pathetic voice, her own sadness heavy upon her and in her heart, it was simply perfect, and Bernard knew it. Like a flash of lightning, while the tears rushed to his eyes at this song, he remembered last Sunday evening, and Miss Vane warbling of how they had 'sat *by* the river, *you* and *I*,' and he shuddered.

There was a long pause, as she laid her hands on her lap, a long pause, and a deep sigh. Then she slowly rose. Aglionby's impulse was to steal away unobserved, even as he had stolen there, but he feared to lose sight of her; he longed to speak to her, to have her speak to him; to tell her, if she would listen to him, something of the pure delight he had this day experienced. So he said, still leaning into the room :

' May I thank you, Miss Conisbrough ?'

He saw that she started, though scarce perceptibly ; then she closed the piano, and turned towards him.

' Have you been listening to my singing? I hope it did not annoy you. It was for mamma. It soothes her.'

' Thy child within its cradle sleeps,
    And I am by thy side.
Thy life—its cares, and hopes, and loves
    Around thee all abide.

' Again the words of peace we'll speak,
    " Good-even, love, good-night."
Each quiet roof the moonbeams streak,
    Our Lord God holds the watch.'

'Annoy me!' he echoed in a tone of deep mortification. You must take me for a barbarian. It did even more than you intended. It soothed *me*. Perhaps you grudge me that?'

'Oh no!' said Judith calmly. 'I am glad if it gave you any pleasure.'

She stood not far from the window, but did not approach it. Inside, the firelight glowed, and threw out the lines of her noble figure and shabby dress, and flickered upon her calm, sad, yet beautiful face.

'Are you going upstairs just because I have appeared upon the scene?' he asked, with a slight vibration in his voice. 'You have ignored me all day, now you are about to fly my presence. You certainly snub me sufficiently, Miss Conisbrough.'

Judith at last came nearer to the window, and held out her hand, which he took with a feeling of gratitude.

'I think you are very ready to invent motives for people's conduct,' she said, 'and those motives most extraordinary ones. I was not even thinking of going upstairs. I was going into the other room to have my supper, at Mrs. Aveson's orders.'

'Were you?' exclaimed he, with animation. 'Then, if you will allow me, I will come and have mine at the same time, for I feel very hungry.'

'As you like,' replied Judith, and if there was no great cordiality in her tone, equally there was no displeasure—she spoke neutrally.

Bernard hastened to the front-door, and met her crossing the passage.

'I think we had better fasten it,' he remarked. 'It is growing dark.'

'We have no thieves in these parts,' said Judith, a little sarcastically.

'But there is the cold,' he replied, with a townsman's

horror of open doors after dusk ; and he shut it, and followed her into the house-place where this evening the supper-table was laid.

Judith walked to the fireplace, and stood with her hand resting against the mantelpiece.   She looked pale and tired.

' Have you been out to-day ?' he asked.

' No.   I have been with mamma.   She was nervous, and afraid to be left.'

' I have been out of doors almost the whole day,' he said.

' Have you ?   Exploring, I suppose ?'

' Yes, I have been exploring.   It is a beautiful place, to me especially, who have been all my life cooped up in streets and warehouses.   I dare say you can scarcely believe it, but I have hardly seen any country.   My mother was always too poor to take me away—allow me !'

Judith looked up quickly as he uttered these words, and placed a chair for her at the table.   She laid her hand on the chair-back, as she said :

' But you had friends who were wealthy, had you not— other relations ?'

' My grandfather, Mr. Aglionby, was my only rich rela- tion.'

' But your mother—Mrs. Ralph Aglionby—had rich rela- tions, I think.'

' If she had, I never heard of them.   Indeed, I know she had none.   Her relations were very few ; and such as they were, were all as poor as herself.   Her sister, Mrs. Bryce, is the only one who is left.   She is a good woman, but she is not rich—far from it.'

' Then I was mistaken,' said Judith, in so exceedingly quiet a tone that he said abruptly, as he did most things :

' I really beg your pardon for boring you with such histories.   Here is the supper.   May I give you some of this cold beef ?'

He helped her, and noticed again how pale her face was, how sad her expression. He poured her out some wine, and insisted upon her drinking it. Every moment that he spent with her deepened the feeling with which she had from the first inspired him—one of admiration. In her presence he felt more genial, more human and hopeful. He scarce recognised himself.

As for Judith, the simple question she had put respecting his rich relations, and the answer he had given her, had filled her mind with forebodings. A dim, dread suspicion was beginning to take shape and form in her brain, to grow into something more than a suspicion. As yet, though it was there, she dreaded to admit it, even to herself. She had a high courage, but not high enough yet to give definite shape to that which still she knew, and which oppressed and tormented her. She must never speak of it. If she could prove herself to be wrong, what terrible repentance and humiliation she would have to go through ; if right—but no ! It could not be that she would be right.

At the present moment, she strove to put down these feelings, and exert herself to be at least civil to this young man who had so strangely stepped into her life, whom she had already begun to study with interest, and who, if her as yet unformulated suspicions should prove to be true, was one whom she could never know on terms of cordiality or friendship, even though all he said and did went to prove that he was no bragging heir, no odious hectorer over that which had suddenly become his.

'Were you at church this morning ?' she asked.

'I ?' He looked up quickly. 'No. Ought I to have been ?'

'I really don't know. Perhaps you are not a churchman ?'

'I am not. And I suppose that almost everyone here is.'

'Yes ; I think that all the gentry go to church, and most of the working people too.'

'Miserable black sheep that I am! I realise from your simple question, that I ought to have presented myself, in the deepest mourning——'

'Mr. Aglionby,' she interrupted, almost hastily, 'pardon me, but you speak of your grandfather as if you felt some kind of contempt for him.'

'Not contempt, but I should lie most horribly if I pretended to admire, or even to respect him. I do consider that he showed himself hard and pitiless in his deeds towards me during his lifetime, and that finally he behaved towards Mrs. Conisbrough with a cruelty that was malignant. And I can't respect a man who behaves so.'

'But it was not so,' said Judith, pushing her plate away from her, clasping her hands on the edge of the table, and looking intently at him.

'Not so?' He paused in the act of raising his glass to his lips, and looked at her intently in his turn, in some surprise. 'I don't understand you.'

'I cannot explain. It sounds odd to you, no doubt. But I have reason to think that when you accuse my grand-uncle of vindictiveness and injustice, and then of malignant cruelty, you are wrong—you are indeed. He was passionate. He did all kinds of things on impulse, and if he believed himself wronged, he grew wild under the wrong, and then he could do things that were harsh, and even brutal. But he was not one of those who cherish a grudge. He was generous. His anger was short-lived——'

'My dear Miss Conisbrough,' said Bernard, with his most chilling smile upon his lips, his coldest gleam in his eyes, 'it is most delightful to find what generosity of mind *you* are possessed of—and also, what simplicity. But don't you think you appeal more to my credulity than to my common sense, when you affirm what you do—and expect me to believe it? Have I not the experience of my whole lifetime? have I not my poor mother's ruined life and premature death from grief and anxiety, to judge from ? And did I not only yesterday hear the will read, which has brought on your mother's illness ?'

He tried not to speak mockingly, but the conviction of Judith's intense simplicity was too strong for him. The mockery sounded in his voice, and gleamed in his eyes.

'If I were in my usual crabbed temper,' he added more genially, 'I should say that you were quixotic and foolish.'

'No, I am neither generous, quixotic, nor foolish. I told you I could not explain. All I can say is, that when I hear you speak in that half-sneering, half-angry tone of him, I feel —I cannot tell you what I feel.'

'Then I am sure you shall never feel it again. I promise you that, and I beg your pardon if I have wounded you,' he said earnestly; and, hoping to turn away her attention from that topic, he added :

'But you said something about going to church. Do you think the neighbours expected me to be at church this morning, instead of rambling round the lake, and talking about the fells with the farmers' boys ?'

'I dare say people would be a little surprised, especially as it was the day after Mr. Aglionby's funeral. These small places, you see——'

'Have their unwritten law, which is very stringent. Yes, I know. I ought to have gone. I would have done, if I had thought of it.'

'Are you a dissenter ?' asked Judith, 'because there is a chapel—Methodist, I think—at Yoresett, and a Quaker's meeting-house at Bainbeck.'

'I am not what you would call a dissenter, I suppose, but a freethinker : what it is now fashionable to call an Agnostic —a modish name for a very old thing.'

'Agnostic—that means a person who does not know, doesn't it ?'

'Yes. At least, with me it does. It means that I acknowledge and confess my utter and profound ignorance of all things outside experience, beyond the grave ; beyond what science can tell me.'

' But that is—surely that is atheism—rank materialism, isn't it ?'

' Scarcely, I think, is it ? Because I don't presume, or pretend to say that those things which believers preach do not exist—all those things in the beyond, of which they so confidently affirm the existence—I do not deny it ; I merely say that for me such things are veiled in a mystery which I cannot penetrate, and which I do not believe that any other man has the power to penetrate. My concern is with this life, and this life alone. I have a moral law quite outside those questions.'

' Have you ? Then you do affirm some things ?'

' One thing, very strongly,' he answered, with a slight smile ; ' a thing which partly agrees, and partly disagrees, with what you affirm—I am supposing you to be a Christian.'

' And what is that ?' asked Judith, neither affirming nor denying her Christianity.

' This : that, to use the words of the Old Testament, " The sins of the fathers shall be visited upon the children unto the third and fourth generation," ay, and a good deal beyond that ; and that, in our system of belief or disbelief—whichever you like to call it—there exists *no* forgiveness of sins. That is all. It is not an elaborate creed, but I think anyone who really comprehends it and accepts it, will find that he must lead a life, to come up to its spirit, as stern and as pure as that which any system of theism can offer to him.'

' *No* forgiveness of sins,' faltered Judith, more struck, apparently, by his words than seemed reasonable. ' That is surely a hard lesson. Not even by repentance ?'

He shook his head. ' I don't see how even repentance can bring forgiveness,' he said. ' " The soul that sinneth, it shall die," and " The wages of sin is death." There is no getting out of it, is there? The man who leads a sinful life does not do it with impunity, I think. If he seems to escape pretty well himself, look at his children—his children's children. Look at the punishments that are transmitted from generation unto generation " of them that hate me and despise my commandments."'

' That is God,' said Judith.

' I know you call it so. To me it means the laws of science and nature : reason, morality, righteousness, clean hands and a pure heart.'

' And you think that would be sufficient to deter people from doing wrong and wicked things ?' she asked, still with an absorption of interest in the theme which surprised him, for after all it was a very old and hackneyed one—a subject which has been disputed thousands of times, and he had certainly not thrown any new light upon it by his words.

' I do not know,' said he; ' I am an Agnostic there, too. It is to be hoped that if it were not efficacious now—which it hardly would be, I dare say—it may become so in the course of time, as the world grows what I call wiser, what you denominate more sceptical, I suppose. At any rate the fact remains, which no theologian can deny, that the sins of the fathers *are* visited upon the children daily, hourly, inevitably; and that if a man wish his descendants to escape punishment —if he wish to escape it himself—he must walk circumspectly : he can't be a drunkard or a profligate all his life, and by re-penting on his death-bed wipe out all the consequences to himself and others ; despite all that is preached about its being never too late to mend, and never too late to be for-given, he cannot do it. He has sinned, and the effects are there. Surely you will own that ?'

' It cannot be denied.'

' Well, and a man or a woman cannot live a dishonest life —cannot go on with a lie in their right hands—without con-sequences ensuing. They may repent, sooner or later, in

dust and ashes, and may swear, like Falstaff, to eschew sack
and live cleanly, but it takes two, at any rate, to tell a lie or
to act one : the effects spread out in rings—none can know
where or how they will end. It cannot be escaped. Some
one must be punished.'

'Then those who come after—is it of no use for them to
try to expiate the sins of their fathers?' she asked, with the
same anxious, eager intentness ; ' or, would it not be natural
and right for them to say, " Since my parents left me with
this blight in my life, I'll even live recklessly. No repentance
will cure it. There is no justice. I will get what pleasure
I can out of my maimed existence, and the future may look
after itself"?'

'I told you the creed was a hard one,' he said. 'We
have no God of mercy to go on our knees to for forgiveness. What we have sowed, we must reap, God or no God.
It is open to us to do as you say—" Eat, drink, and be merry,
for to-morrow thou shalt die." Or, it is open to you to take
your stand as firmly as may be, to *do without* the cakes and
ale ; to say, " Whatever I may suffer for my parents' sin,
none shall have to suffer for mine," and to live righteously.'

'And the reward?' asked Judith, looking at him eagerly
and intently, even anxiously.

'There is no reward, that I know of, except the one which
Christianity says is not sufficient to keep a man straight—the
conviction that you have done right and been honest, cost
what it might, and that whatever you have suffered from
others, no others shall suffer by you. That is all that I
know of.'

'Then do you recommend this creed to others?'

'I recommend it simply as I would recommend truth, or
what appeared to me truth, before a lie—as I would recommend a man setting out on a journey to fill his wallet with
dry bread, or even dry crusts, rather than with macaroons
and cream-cakes.'

She leaned her head on her hand, in silence, and at last said :

'It is a hard doctrine.'

'Yes, I know. It is the only one that I ever found of any service to me in my life.'

'It seems to me that it might be good for strong spirits, but that it would altogether crush weak ones.'

'Then, Miss Conisbrough, it should be good for yours ; it should be the very meat to sustain it,' said Bernard, involuntarily and eagerly.

Judith smiled, rather wanly.

'You imagine mine to be a strong spirit?' she asked.

'I am convinced of it.'

'You never were more mistaken in your life. I am a faint-hearted coward.' She rose slowly, and paused near the fire. 'I think, Mr. Aglionby, that there is a great deal of reason in your agnosticism. I wish people—some people, I mean—had known of it and realised it a long time ago.'

There was a dreary hopelessness in her tone, a blank sorrow in her expression, which went home to him. Like many a strong soul which had been scarred in battle, he shrank from seeing others exposed to the ordeal he had gone through. He thought she was going, all desolate as she was and looked. He could not endure the idea of sending her comfortless away, and he strove to detain her yet another moment.

'Do you mean,' he hastily asked, and in a low voice—'do you mean about my grandfather ? Because, you know, I try to live up to my convictions. He did wrong, I know—and those who come after him must suffer from it more or less ; but I have elected to take the side of not letting others suffer by me, and——'

'I was not thinking of my great-uncle at all,' was the unexpected reply. 'You are harping on the way in which he has left his money. And you would like to make it right.

12

You cannot. I never realised until now, how utterly impossible it is. Yes, the sins of the fathers *shall* be visited upon the children. But you have committed no sin. Do not trouble yourself. If it were merely money—though I am nearly a pauper, I never felt to care so little for money as I do now. It seems to me to make so little difference. I think I shall try your creed, Mr. Aglionby ; it seems to me to be a manly one.' She held out her hand.

'But you want a womanly one,' he urged eagerly, yet not too boldly.

'No ; I want as strong, as manly, as virile a creed as I can find. I want a stick to lean upon that will not fail me, and I believe you have extended it to me this night, though I will not deny that it has a rough and horny feeling to the hand. Good-night.'

'I am greatly concerned——' he began, and his face, his voice, and his eyes all showed that concern to be profound.

'Do not be concerned. I thank you for it,' said Judith, smiling for the first time upon him. Aglionby hardly knew what the feeling was which seemed to strike like a blow upon his heart, as he met that smile, exquisitely sweet and attractive, like most smiles of grave faces. He could not speak a word, for the emotion was altogether new to him. Passively he allowed her to withdraw her hand and to walk out of the room.

He sat with his elbow on his knee, his chin in his hand, gazing into the fire, and would have sat there till the fire had expired, had not Mrs. Aveson at last wonderingly looked in to ask if he had finished supper.

'Yes,' he answered abruptly, and the words of the song came tenderly into his mind :

> 'Noch eenmal lat uns spräken,
> Goden Abend, gode Nacht.
> Di Maand schient up' de Däken
> Uns Herrgott hält de Wacht.'

CHAPTER XVIII.

DANESDALE GOES TO SCAR FOOT.

ABOUT noon the next day, Sir Gabriel Danesdale and his son, riding down the hill behind Scar Foot, left off a lively discussion on politics, which had hitherto engrossed them, and turned their thoughts and their conversation towards the house which had just come in sight.

'I wonder how we shall like him,' observed Sir Gabriel. 'At the funeral I took good notice of him—you were not there.'

'No, I don't go to them, on principle.'

'That is a mistake,' said his father; 'there is never any harm in occasionally confronting in another, what must sometime be one's own latter end. When I fairly realised that it was old John who was being laid under the ground there, my own contemporary, and the friend of my youth, I assure you that the things of this present, the roast and the boiled, the lands and the houses, seemed to shrink away into remarkably small compass. It puts things before one in another light.'

Sir Gabriel spoke with a tempered cheerfulness, and Randulf replied :

'I never thought of it in that way; I have no doubt you are right.'

'You are young, it is no wonder you have never thought of it in that way. But, as I was saying, I took remarkably good notice of this young fellow, and it was strongly borne in upon my mind that if he and old John had been much together, the roof of Scar Foot must have flown off under the violence of their disputes. He is not one of us, Randulf; not one of my kind, though he may suit your new-fangled notions.'

'Did he look like a gentleman ?'

12—2

'Upon my word, I can hardly tell. Not a finished
gentleman, though he had some of his grandfather's pride
of bearing. But everything about him tells of the town;
anyone would have picked him out as belonging to a different world from ours.'

'Are you obliged to call upon him?' asked the young man.

'No, I suppose not, but I choose to do so, though I am
sorry for Mrs. Conisbrough and her daughters. If I find
the fellow is amenable to influence, I shall let him see that
the whole place would approve of his sharing his inheritance with them.'

'I hope you won't burn your fingers,' said his son
sceptically. 'For my part I am very glad not to have made
the acquaintance of this redoutable "old John," for, from
all I can hear, he seems to have been a most odious character, and to have behaved disgracefully to these ladies.'

'Well, I'm afraid there is not much to be said for him, in
that respect; but after all, a son is a son, Randulf, and I
can pardon a man almost anything when it is done for a
son, or a son's son.'

Randulf made no answer. He had been glancing aside,
occupied in looking for the spot where he had found Judith
Conisbrough weeping. He had seen and recognised it, and
with the sight of it came the remembrance of her face.
Unknown 'sons and son's sons' appeared to him insigni-
ficant in comparison with a woman whose sorrow he had
beheld, and whose individuality had profoundly impressed
him. They rode into the courtyard, at the back of the
house.

'I hope he won't be away,' said Sir Gabriel, with an
earnestness which amused his son. 'It has been an effort
to me to come, and I don't want to have made it for nothing.'

He pulled a bell, and while they waited for a man to
come, Judith Conisbrough walked into the courtyard, having

come from the front part of the house. Neither Sir Gabriel
nor his son knew of the presence at Scar Foot of Mrs.
Conisbrough and her daughter, and were therefore proportionately surprised to see her there. She was going past
them, with a bow; but Sir Gabriel, quickly dismounting,
shook hands with her, and wished her good-day. She
gravely returned his greeting.

'Are you—are you staying here?' he asked, at a loss to
account for her presence.

'I am, at present, with my mother, who was unfortunately
taken ill here, on Saturday.'

'Dear, dear! I'm sorry to hear that. Then I fear we
shall not find Mr. Aglionby at home?'

'He is at Scar Foot—Mr. Bernard Aglionby. Whether
he is now in the house, or not, I have not the least idea,'
replied Judith composedly.

'Ah! I hope Mrs. Conisbrough is not seriously ill,'
pursued Sir Gabriel, uncomfortably conscious that the young
lady looked careworn and sad, and with a sudden sense that
there might be more circumstances in the whole case than
they knew of, complications which they had not heard of.

'No, thank you. I hope she will be well enough to be
moved in a day or two. She is subject to such attacks. As
you are going to see Mr. Aglionby, I will not detain you any
longer.'

She bowed to both father and son, and was moving on.
Randulf's horse had been taken. He returned Miss Conisbrough's bow, and made a step after his father, in the direction
of the house. Then, suddenly turning on his heel, he over-
took Judith, raised his hat, and held out his hand.

'You looked so stern, Miss Conisbrough, that at first I
thought I had better go after my papa, and not say anything
to you, but—see, allow me to open this gate for you, if you
are going this way—are you?'

'Yes,' replied Judith, repressing a smile; 'but if you are

going to call upon Mr. Aglionby, do you not think you had better follow Sir Gabriel ?'

'Directly—no hurry ; I never expected I should have the good fortune to meet you, or I should have ridden here more cheerfully. My father was wondering how we should get on with this man here. You know, he has the kindest heart in the world, has my father ; he thinks Mrs. Conisbrough has been treated badly. There !' as Judith's face flushed painfully. ' I have said the thing I ought not to have said, and offended you.'

'No, you have not ; but I think we had better not talk about it.'

'Well, we won't,' said Randulf, deliberately pursuing the subject. 'But everybody knows that the aged r—rascal who lived here——'

'Hush, hush, Mr. Danesdale !'

'I beg your pardon—he behaved scandalously to Mrs. Conisbrough. Have you had speech with this new man ? What is he like ? Is he horrible ?'

'Oh no ! He—I like him.'

Randulf was scrutinising her from under his sleepy eyelids. After this answer, he did not pursue the subject further. Judith asked him to open the gate, and let her go for her walk. He did so, and added, with a slower drawl than usual, ' And, Miss Conisbrough, how is your s—sister ?'

'Which sister ?' asked Judith, surveying him straitly from her large and candid eyes.

'Your sister Delphine,' answered Randulf, leaning on the gate in a leisurely manner, as if he never meant to lift himself off it again.

'I have not seen her since Saturday. I had a note from her this morning, though—I want her to meet me. I won't have her come here ; and that reminds me,' she added, ' that I want to find Toby, the farm boy, to take a message——'

'I am going home that way. Couldn't you intrust the message to me ?'

'I'm afraid it would be a bore,' said Judith, who perhaps saw as clearly out of her open eyes as did Randulf from his half-closed ones.

'I never offer to do things that are a bore,' he assured her.

'Well, if you really don't object, I should be very glad if you would call and tell her that if it is fine this afternoon, she must set off at half-past two, and I will do the same, and we shall meet at Counterside, just half-way. I want very much to speak to her, but you can understand that I don't care to ask anyone into this house, unless I am obliged, nor to send Mr. Aglionby's servants on my errands.'

'So you employ your own most devoted retainer instead,' said Randulf composedly, but unable to repress a smile of gratification. 'I will deliver the message faithfully. Now the gate stands open. Good-morning.'

Judith passed out of the gate, and Randulf hastened after Sir Gabriel, the smile still hovering about his lips, and inwardly saying, 'I'm glad I turned back. It was a good stroke of business, after I'd racked my brains for an excuse to call there, without being able to find one.'

Mrs. Aveson received him with a smile and words of welcome, and ushered him into the state parlour where already his father and Aglionby were together.

Certainly more strongly contrasted characters could hardly have been found, than the three then assembled in the parlour at Scar Foot. Each, too, was fully conscious of his unlikeness to the other. There was a necessary constraint over the interview. Sir Gabriel spoke in high terms of the late Squire. The late Squire's successor listened in courteous, cool silence, bowing his head now and then, and smiling slightly in a manner which the candid Sir Gabriel could not be expected to understand. Aglionby did not protest, when this incense was burnt at the shrine of his grandfather, neither did he for one moment join in the ceremony. When, however, Sir Gabriel remarked that

Mr. Aglionby had been hasty and inconsiderate sometimes, the new-comer rejoined, 'I am quite sure of it,' in a voice which carried conviction. Then Sir Gabriel remarked that he supposed Mr. Aglionby had not lived much in the country.

'My fame seems to have preceded me, in that respect,' replied Aglionby, laughing rather sarcastically. After which Sir Gabriel felt rather at a loss what to say to this dark-looking person who knew nothing of the country, and cared nothing for country-gentlemen's pursuits, who could not even converse sympathetically about the man from whom he had inherited his fortune. Mrs. Conisbrough was a tabooed subject to Sir Gabriel. And he had just begun to feel embarrassed, when Randulf came in, and afforded an opportunity for introducing a new topic, and a powerful auxiliary in the matter of keeping up the conversation, for which his father could not feel sufficiently thankful. He introduced the young men to each other, and Randulf apologised for his tardy appearance.

'I wanted to speak to Miss Conisbrough,' he said, 'and stopped with her longer than I meant to. She had an errand for me, too, so I stayed to hear what it was.'

'It seems to me that you and Miss Conisbrough get on very well together,' observed his father good-naturedly.

Bernard sat silent during this colloquy. What could Judith Conisbrough or her friends possibly be to him? Had he not Lizzie at Irkford? His for ever! Yet his face grew a little sombre as he listened.

'Do we, sir? Well, it is but a week to-day since I made her acquaintance, but I think that any man who didn't get on with her and her sisters—well, he wouldn't deserve to. Don't you?' he added, turning to Aglionby, and calmly ignoring the possibility of any awkwardness in the topic.

'I know only Miss Conisbrough, and that slightly,' said Bernard, very gravely. 'She seems to me a most—charming——'

'You are thinking that "charming" isn't the word, and it is not,' said Randulf. 'If one used such expressions about one's acquaintances in these days, I should say she was a noble woman. That's my idea of her : exalted, you know, in character, and all that sort of thing.'

'I should imagine it; but I know very little of her,' said Aglionby, who, however, felt his heart respond to each one of these remarks.

Sir Gabriel found this style of conversation dull. He turned to Aglionby, and said politely :

'I believe you have always lived at Irkford, have you not?'

'Yes,' responded Bernard, with a look of humour in his eyes. 'I was in a warehouse there. I sold grey cloth.'

'Grey cloth,' murmured Sir Gabriel, polite, but puzzled.

'Grey cloth—yes. It is not an exciting, nor yet a very profitable employment. It seems, however, that if my rich relation had not suddenly remembered me, I might have continued in it to the end of my days.'

'Rich relation?' began Sir Gabriel ; 'I thought——'

'That I had others, perhaps?' suggested Bernard ; while Randulf listened with half-closed eyes, and apparently without hearing what was said.

'Well, I certainly have a vague impression – I may be quite wrong—I suppose I must be.'

'It is an odd thing that Miss Conisbrough also accused me of having rich relations the other day,' said Bernard, and then carelessly changed the subject.

The guests sat a little longer. The conversation was almost entirely between Aglionby and Sir Gabriel ; but secretly the young men also measured one another with considerable eagerness, and the conclusion left in the mind of each concerning the other was, 'I don't dislike him—there is good stuff in him.'

At last they rose to go, and with wishes on the Danesdales'

side to see more of Mr. Aglionby, and promises on his part
to return their visit, they departed.

Bernard looked at his watch, paused, considered, muttered
to himself, 'Of course it is all right;' and ringing the bell,
asked Mrs. Aveson if Miss Conisbrough were out, and if she
had said whether she was coming in to dinner.

'She went out for a walk towards Dale Head, sir, and she
didn't say when she would be back,' responded Mrs. Aveson.

'Thank you,' said Aglionby; and with that he went out,
and by a strange coincidence, his steps, too, turned in the
direction of Dale Head.

But he was not successful in meeting Miss Conisbrough
(if that were the intention with which he set out). He saw
no trace of her; though, as he passed along the beautiful
road, catching occasional glimpses, here and there, of the
lake, his lips parted involuntarily now and then, in the desire
to utter to some companion shadow what he thought of it all.

But it is thin work, talking to shadows, as he felt. He
returned home, found that Miss Conisbrough had come in,
and was going to dine with him, and that a messenger who
had been to Yoresett had brought him a letter from the post-
office of that metropolis, addressed, in a sprawling hand, to
Bernard Aglionby, Esq. Rapture! It was from Lizzie!

CHAPTER XIX.

LOOKING FORWARD.

AFTER she had said good-morning to Randulf, Judith
walked along the rough, stony lane with its gaps in the
hedge, showing the rugged fells in the distance, and her
gaze had lost some of its despondency. Indeed, she felt
cheered by the little interview.

She distinctly liked young Danesdale (though to her, old
in care and sorrow, he seemed more like a very charming

boy than a man grown, with a man's feelings), and she was conscious, with a keen thrill of sympathetic conviction, that he liked her—liked her sisters, liked everything about her. It was a delightful sensation, like the coming of a sudden, unexpected joy in a sad life. She dwelt upon his words, his manner, his gestures, from the moment in which, with the languor gone from his eyes, he had overtaken her, to his last delighted expression about her sending her own devoted retainer on her messages, instead of Bernard Aglionby's servants. It was perhaps rather a cool thing to say—at least it might have savoured of impertinence if some people had said it. From Randulf Danesdale it came agreeably and naturally enough.

She would see Delphine that afternoon—an interview for which she longed greatly; she had gratified Randulf by allowing him to give her message about the meeting, and Delphine would be pleased to learn her sister's wishes from such a courier. Altogether, things looked brighter.

She presently turned off to the right, into a little dell or gorge, and wandered along some paths she knew, half-woodland, half-rocky. She had come out for her health's sake, but remembering the walk in prospect in the afternoon, did not stay very long, and was utterly unconscious that at one moment, just as she was standing beneath a faded beech-tree, whose foliage was yellow and sere, and holding in her hand some variously-tinted autumn leaves which she had picked, the footsteps which she heard in the road below, and not far distant, were those of Bernard Aglionby.

Returned to the house, she went to her mother's room, who still lay white and weak-looking, though free from pain and breathlessness, upon her bed.

'See, mamma, here are some lovely leaves, which I found in the clough this morning.'

She put them in a little glass, and placed them near her mother.

'Thank you, Judith . . . . What were all those voices
I heard below? I am sure I feel as if I ought to know
them.'

'Sir Gabriel and Mr. Danesdale come to call upon Mr.
Aglionby.'

'You do not mean it?' exclaimed Mrs. Conisbrough,
with animation; and then, after a pause, 'Really to call
upon him? To welcome him?'

'I suppose so, mamma. I don't know why else they
should have come.'

'No doubt! "The king is dead: long live the king!"
It would have been the same if we had been in possession,'
said Mrs. Conisbrough, in an accent of indescribable bitterness.

Yet she had ceased to speak of Bernard with the passionate indignation and resentment which she had at first expressed. Perhaps reflection had convinced her that opposition would be folly. Perhaps—with women like Mrs.
Conisbrough, many perhapses may have an influence.

'As you seem so much better, mother, I have asked
Delphine to come to Counterside, and I shall go and meet
her, so that we can have a chat this afternoon. Then I can
tell her how you really are.'

'As you like,' responded Mrs. Conisbrough, rather peev-
ishly. 'I am aware that you and Delphine cannot exist
apart, or think you cannot, for more than a day, without
repining. In my young days, girls used to think less of
themselves.'

'If you do not wish me to leave you, I will send word to
Delphine not to come.'

'On no account stay in for me,' was the logical and con-
sistent reply. 'The walk will do you good. Did you say
you had seen Mr. Danesdale?'

'Yes. It is he who has promised to call at our house, and
ask Delphine to meet me.'

'Ah, I see!' said Mrs. Conisbrough, in a tone so distinctly pleased and approving, that Judith could not but
notice it.

• She turned to her mother with parted lips, then, as if suddenly recollecting herself, closed them again, and took up her
sewing, at which she worked until Mrs. Aveson came to say
that dinner was ready.

'Thank you. Is Mr. Aglionby going to dine now, do you
know?'

'Yes, he is, Miss Judith. If you'd prefer me to bring
yours up here——'

'Oh no, thank you. I'm not afraid of him,' said Judith,
with a slight smile.

'I should think not, Miss Judith. If there's any cause
for fear, I should think it would be more likely on the other
side.'

'Why, I wonder?' speculated Judith within herself; and
her mother's voice came from the bed, as Mrs. Aveson
withdrew.

'Just straighten your hair, Judith, and fasten your collar
with my little gold brooch. It will make you look tidier.'

'I'll straighten my hair, mamma; but as for the brooch,
I really don't think it is necessary. If you could see the
careless, and I might say shabby, style in which Mr.
Aglionby dresses, you would know that he did not think
much about what people wear.'

She had made her beautiful brown hair quite smooth,
and without further elaboration of her toilette, she went
downstairs.

Bernard was standing in the dining-room waiting for her.

'Mrs. Aveson told me I was to have the pleasure of your
company at dinner,' he said, with the graciousness and
politeness which, when he was with her, seemed to spring
more readily than other feelings within his breast.

'I am going out at half-past two,' answered Judith.

'Are you? and I at a quarter to three. I am going to Yoresett to see Mr. Whaley.'

'Indeed. I have a sort of message for you from mamma. She did not send it to you in so many words, but when I. suggested it, she agreed with me ; and that is, that after to-day I think we need not tax your kindness any further. My mother is so much better, that I think she will be fit to go home.'

'Oh, do you think so? She must not on any account move before she is quite able to do so without risk.   I would not be in any hurry to remove her.'

'You are very good to say so. But if you will kindly allow us to have the brougham to-morrow afternoon——'

'I am sure you had better say the day after to-morrow. From what Dr. Lowther said, I am convinced of it. I—I don't think I can spare the brougham to-morrow afternoon, though I really wasn't aware that there was such a carriage on the premises, or anything about it.   But I shall be sure to want it to-morrow afternoon.'

His dark eyes looked at her very pleasantly across the table, and there was a smile upon his lips, all playfulness, and no malice.

Judith met the glance, and thought :

'How *could* I have thought him hard and stony-looking? And if only all these miserable complications had not come in the way, what a very nice relation he would have been !'

But she said, aloud :

'You are very kind ; and since you really wish it, I accept your offer gratefully.   The day after to-morrow, then.'

'That is a much more sensible arrangement, though I call even that too soon.   But I like to have my own way, and I have really got so little of it hitherto, that I dare say there is some danger of my using the privilege recklessly. However, since I have prevailed so far, I will see that all is ready at the time you wish.   And—Miss Conisbrough?'

' Yes ?'

' Do you think Mrs. Conisbrough will strongly object to my seeing her ?'

' You must not speak to her on any matters of money, or business,' said Judith hastily.

' I had not the slightest intention of doing so, though I still hope that in time she will fall in with my views on the matter ; and I hope, too, you have not forgotten your promise to help me in it.'

Judith said nothing. Her eyes were cast down. Aglionby paused only for a moment, and then went on :

' What I meant was, that perhaps you would prefer—she might be very angry if I put in any appearance when she goes away. In plain words, do you think she still so strongly resents my presence here, that it would be unwise for me to pay my respects to her, and tell her how glad I am that she is better ?'

' No,' said Judith, her face burning, her eyes fixed upon her plate. ' She has considered the matter while she has been ill. I think—I am sure you might speak to her, only please do not be offended if——'

' If she snubs me very severely,' said he, with a gleam of amusement. ' No, indeed I will not. Whatever Mrs. Conisbrough may say to me, I will receive submissively and meekly.'

' Because you feel that the power is on your side,' said Judith rapidly, involuntarily, almost in a whisper, her face burning with a still deeper blush. ' It must be easy to smile at a woman's petulance when you are a man, and feel that you have the game all in your own hands.'

She had not meant to say so much. The words had broken from her almost uncontrollably. Almost every hour since the moment in which she had seen her mother cower down before Bernard's direct gaze, her sense of his power and strength had been growing and intensifying. Hours of

brooding and solitude, apart from her accustomed companions; long and painful meditations upon the past and
present, and thrills of dread when she contemplated the
future—these things, broken only by her two or three inter-
views with Bernard, and with him alone, had strengthened
her feeling, until now, though she was neither dependent,
clinging, nor servile by nature, the very sight of Aglionby's
dark face, with its marked and powerful features, made her
heart beat faster, and brought a crushing consciousness of
his strength and her own weakness.   Had he been overbearing or imperious in manner, all her soul would have rebelled.
She was one of those natures with whom justice and for-
bearance are almost a passion; the moments would have
seemed hours until she could break free from his roof and
his presence.   But he was the very reverse of overbearing
or imperious.   The strength was kept in reserve; the
manner was gentle and deferential—only she knew that the
power was there, and she would not have been a woman if she
had not had a latent idolatry of power.   The combination of
strength and gentleness was new to her ; the proximity to a
man who wielded these attributes was equally foreign to her,
and all these things combined had begun to exercise over
her spirit a fascination to which she was already beginning,
half-unconsciously, to yield.

Aglionby's only answer at first to her remark was a look,
slow and steady; but he had looks which sank into the
souls of those at whom they were levelled, and haunted
them, and it was such a glance that he bestowed upon
Judith Conisbrough now.   Then he said :

'That remark shows me very plainly that "petulance," as
you are pleased to call it, forms no part of *your* character ;
but I guessed that some time ago.   I am glad to have you
on my side.'

Judith wondered whether he was saying these things on
purpose to try her to the utmost.   She was glad that at that

moment she perceived, on looking at the clock, that she had only a few minutes in which to get ready, if she were to set off at the time she had appointed with Delphine. Making this an excuse, she rose.

'Are you walking?' he asked.   'I am sure you ought not to walk so far.'

'Oh, thank you, I have been accustomed to it all my life,' said she, going out of the room, and slowly ascending the stairs.

'Child, you look quite flushed,' cried her mother.   'What have you been doing?   Quarrelling with Mr. Aglionby?'

'No, mother.   It would be hard to quarrel with Mr. Aglionby.   No one could be more considerate . . . . but I wish we were at home again.   By the way, he will not hear of your going until the day after to-morrow.'

'I shall be very glad of another day's rest.   I feel dreadfully weak.'

Judith made no reply, but put on her things and went out just as the big clock on the stairs notified that it was half-past two—that is, it said half-past three, as is the habit of clocks in country places—a habit which had perfectly bewildered Bernard, who had tried to get Mrs. Aveson to put it back, but had been met by the solemn assurance that any such course would result in the complete *bouleversement* of all the existing domestic arrangements.   Indeed, he saw that the proposition excited unbounded alarm and displeasure in Mrs. Aveson's mind, and he had to admit that in a Yorkshire dale one must do as the natives do.

It was a fine afternoon.   Judith walked quickly along the well-known road, and in her mind she kept seeing Bernard's eyes directed to her face, after her own hurried remark about woman's petulance.   She could not satisfy herself as to what that look meant, and sighed impatiently as she tried to banish it from her mind.

At last she came to the dip in the road, which, with its

13

shade of overhanging trees, its quaint, nestling old houses and cottages, and tiny whitewashed Friends' Meeting House, was known as Countersett or Counterside. Halfway down the hill she saw something which banished egoistic reflections, and caused a smile to break out upon her face : a slim girl's figure, with the shabby old gown, which yet always looked graceful, and the thick twists of golden hair rolling from beneath the ancient brown straw-hat. That was no unusual sight, and her heart leaped with joy as she beheld it ; but the figure with that figure—not Rhoda's slender height, not her audacious, Irish-grey eyes, and defiantly smiling young face—not a girl at all, but Randulf Danesdale. Surely there was nothing to laugh at, the meeting was a simple one enough ; yet on the faces of all three as they met there was a broad irrepressible smile, which soon became a hearty laugh. Instead of saying anything, the three stood still in the wooded road, and laughed loud and clear—light-hearted laughs. The young people of the present day are generally too learned and careworn, too scientific or æsthetic, to laugh very heartily; but in some country districts there are still left a few rustics who can and do laugh loudly at nothing in particular.

It was Judith who first ceased to laugh, and said :

'Why are we behaving so absurdly ? Surely there is nothing to laugh at !'

'Yes, there is,' said Delphine, her golden-brown eyes dancing. There is Mr. Danesdale to laugh at.'

'Who is too happy to make himself useful in any way,' he murmured.

' He hates walking. Coming up this hill he has been so exhausted, that I am glad Sir Gabriel could not see his degenerate son. He came, Judith—Mr. Danesdale presented himself at Yoresett House, and said you had desired him to give your love, and to say that he was to stay lunch, and see that I set off at half-past two, as you had no trust at all

in my punctuality. I thought it rather odd, but allowed him
to remain. And then he said that part of his commission
had been to come with me until we met you, as you know
my habit of loitering on the wayside. Rhoda said she
didn't believe him, and it was an insult. What I want to
know is, did he tell the truth ?'

Here the sound of wheels just behind them caused them
to turn. Coming down the hill was a dogcart, which Bernard Aglionby was driving, his man sitting behind him.
His piercing eyes glanced from one to the other of the
group, till they rested upon Judith. Randulf and Judith
returned his salutation. Then the dogcart flashed past,
and disappeared round a bend in the road.

'Who is that ?' asked Delphine, in surprise.

'Our new cousin, Bernard Aglionby,' responded Judith,
in a sharp, dry tone. At this juncture Randulf remarked
that he would not detain them any longer He wished
them good-afternoon, and took his way back to Yoresett.
The girls were left alone.

Arm-in-arm they paced about the tiny square courtyard of
the equally tiny Friends' Meeting House before alluded to.

'Well !' said Delphine, pressing her sister's arm, with a
quick excited movement, which the other at once remarked,
'what is it ? I suppose you would not ask me into that
man's house, and quite right, too. He looks a stern, hard
creature, with his dark face and frowning eyes. How has
he treated you ?'

'Most kindly. His appearance is a little against him, I
think. But had he known that I wished to see you, he
would have offered to send a carriage for you, I know. I
think he has behaved admirably !'

'Really, Ju ! You astonish me ! How would you have
had him behave ? He has got all Uncle Aglionby's money
and property. The least he could do was to behave with
courtesy towards those whom he had supplanted.'

'Well, you know, when the will was read, mamma's behaviour really was enough to try a saint, let alone a young
man with a sharp temper, as he has.'

'You seem to know all about his temper very quickly.'

'I've had opportunities, you see.'

Judith then told her sister all about that most unpleasant
scene, and her mother's behaviour throughout, and how well,
as she thought, Mr. Aglionby had behaved.

'You know I did feel inclined to hate him.   One does
long sometimes to be able to feel one's self an unqualified
victim and martyr.   And I did then.   If I could have sat
down, and on surveying my past life and future prospects,
could have found that I had been wronged and ill-used all
along, the victim of oppression and injustice, I should have
been positively glad, because then I could have railed at
everyone and everything, and refused to be comforted.   But
you know, Del, it is a fatal fact that there are *almost always*
two sides to a question.'

'I don't see how there can be another view of this question.   Surely, Judith, you will not try to make it out to be a
just will.   If he had never led us to expect—never cheated
my mother into the belief——'

'True, my dear.   All that is true on the outside.   But
there is another side to it, and a most miserable one, for us.
If what I think is true, it is not we who have to complain.
I can't tell you what I think, until I am more certain on
one or two points.   Delphine, I have something to tell you
that is not pleasant.   I believe I am on the brink of a discovery: if I find myself right, I shall tell you of it, and no
one else.   Our life will then be still less smooth for us than it
has been hitherto; but mamma will make no further opposition to our working, if we wish to do so.'

'You are very mysterious, Judith.'

'I know it must sound both odd and unreasonable.   Well,
if, as I expect, I find myself right (I don't know how I can

speak so calmly of it all, I am sure), I shall then explain to you, and I am absolutely certain of your agreeing with me, that it will be best, not only for you and me to go away and try to find some work, but for all of us to leave Yoresett— sell our house, go to a town and work, even if the work were plain sewing or lodging-house keeping.'

'Judith !' exclaimed Delphine, and there was a tone of horror in her voice.

'You will own that I am not in the habit of saying things without good reason ?'

'Oh yes !'

'Then think about this, dear. It would be painful for many reasons to leave Yoresett.'

'It would be awful—ghastly,' said Delphine, with a shudder.

'Why, Del, that is a new view of the case from you,' said her sister suddenly, looking keenly at her. 'You always used to be more ardent than even I was about it.'

'Of course I should be as willing as ever to go, if it were proved to be the best thing. But we should miss so many things—the freedom, the country air, and——'

'Freedom and country air may be bought too dear,' said Judith, with so sad and earnest a ring in her voice, that Delphine was fain to acquiesce, with a prolonged sigh of reluctance.

'I will not tell you now what I think,' said Judith ; 'I will give myself time to find out whether my conjecture is wrong; and if so, I will indeed repent towards the person whom I have wronged; though Mr. Aglionby holds strange views about repentance. But if I am right, you and I, Del, will be glad to hide our heads anywhere, so long as it is far enough away from Yoresett.'

Delphine made no answer to this. There was a silence as they paced about under the trees, now thinned of their foliage, while the shrivelled, scattered leaves rustled beneath their feet. Scarce a bird chirped. The sun had disap-

peared ; the sky was grey and sad. The inhabitants of the
hamlet of Counterside appeared all to be either asleep or
not at home.

Up and down the little paved courtyard they paced, feeling vaguely that this quiet and peace in which they now
stood was not to last for ever ; that the tiny square Friends'
Meeting House, where the silence was disturbed, it might
be once a week, perhaps not so often, by a discourse, or a
text, or an impromptu prayer from some Friend whom the
spirit moved to utterance of his thoughts, that this was not
the kind of arena in which their life's battle was to be fought.
This was a lull, a momentary pause. Delphine at last broke
it by saying :

'You say Mr. Aglionby has strange notions about repentance—how do you mean ?'

'Oh, it would take too long to explain. We were talking
together on Sunday night—we had supper together——'

'You had ! Then you are not at daggers-drawn ?'

'Dear Delphine, no ! If you had been placed as I have
been, you would understand how it was impossible for me
to remain at daggers-drawn with him, besides the disagree-
ableness of such a state of things. We dined together to-
day. He thinks his grandfather's will was very unjust,
and——'

'Mr. Danesdale said he was not half bad,' said Delphine
reflectively. 'Then, am I to like him, Ju ?'

'How absurd !' cried Judith, in a tone of irritation most
unusual with her. 'As if you could like or dislike a man
whom you did not know ! He wishes to repair the injustice
if he can ; to get mamma's consent to some arrangement by
which she should receive an allowance, or an income from a
charge on the property—or whatever they call it ; I don't
know whether it will do, I am sure.'

'I don't see how it can be prevented, if mamma chooses
to enter into such an arrangement, Judith.'

'Oh, I do, though. I should prevent it if I thought it wrong.'

'You, Judith?'

'Yes, I, Delphine. I think I shall have to prevent it.'

'You speak somehow quite differently,' said Delphine. 'I do not understand you, Judith. I feel as if something had happened, and you look as if you had the world on your shoulders.'

Judith looked at her, strangely moved; Delphine was the dearest thing she had in the world—her most precious possession. To-day's interview marked a change in their relations to one another, an epoch. For until now they had always met on terms of equality; but this afternoon Judith knew that she was holding something back from her sister— knew that she stayed her hand from inflicting a blow upon her, which blow she yet felt would have to be dealt.

'I feel as if I had a great deal on my shoulders,' she answered, trying to speak carelessly. 'And now I must go, Delphine, or mamma will grow uneasy, and darkness will overtake me. And you must run home too.'

'Then, the day after to-morrow, in the afternoon, Judith?'

'Yes. Mr. Aglionby has promised that we shall have the brougham. Give my love to Rhoda, and good-night.'

The two figures exchanged a parting kiss in the twilight, and went their several ways.

CHAPTER XX.

'MY COUSIN JUDITH!'

BERNARD did not return to Scar Foot that night. He had left word with Mrs. Aveson that he might not do so. He remained all night at Mr. Whaley's, at Yoresett, discussing business matters with him. Judith, after her return, sat

upstairs with her mother, and wondered what made her feel
so wretched—what caused the sensation of fierce desolation
in her heart. Mrs. Conisbrough was quickly recovering,
and had begun to chat, though scarcely cheerfully. Her
conversation was hardly of a bracing or inspiriting nature,
and the blow dealt by the old man's will was still felt almost
in its full force. Likewise, she was a woman much given to
wondering what was to become of them all.

But she no longer raged against Aglionby, and Judith did
not know whether to be relieved or uneasy at the change.

On Tuesday morning Dr. Lowther called, and pronounced
Mrs. Conisbrough quite fit to go home on the following day,
as arranged; he added, that she might go downstairs that
day if she chose. Judith trembled lest she should decide to
do so, but she did not. She either could not, or would not
face Bernard Aglionby, and, in him, her fate. So Judith
said to herself, trying to find reasons for her mother's
conduct, and striving, too, to still the fears which had sprung
up in her own breast, to take no heed of the sickening
qualms of terror which had attacked her at intervals ever
since she had seen her mother on the morning of the reading of the will—her expression, and the sudden failing of
her voice; her cowering down; the shudder with which she
had shrunk away from Bernard's direct gaze. That incident
had marked the first stage of her terrors; the second had
been reached when her mother had opened her eyes, and
spoken her incoherent words about 'Bernarda,' and what
Bernarda had said. The third and worst phase of her secret
fear had been entered upon when Aglionby had solemnly
assured her that, save his grandfather, he had never possessed a rich relation, on either father's or mother's side.
She had pondered upon it all till her heart was sick. She
saw the deep flush which overspread Mrs. Conisbrough's
face, every time that Bernard's name was mentioned, and
her own desire to 'depart hence and be no more seen,' grew

stronger every hour. Late in the afternoon of Tuesday, Mrs. Conisbrough, tired of even pretending to listen to the book which Judith had been reading to her, advised the latter to take a walk, adding that she wished to be alone, and thought she could go to sleep if she were left. Judith complied. She put on her hat and went out into the garden. Once there, the recollection came to her mind, that to-morrow she was leaving Scar Foot—that after to-morrow it would not be possible for her to return here ; she took counsel with herself, and advised herself to take her farewell now, and once for all, of the dear familiar things which must henceforth be strange to her. Fate was kind, in so far as it allowed her to part on friendly terms from Bernard Aglionby, but that was all she could expect. If, for the future, she were enabled to stay somewhere in shelter and obscurity, and to keep silence, what more could be wanted ? 'By me, and such as me, nothing,' she said inwardly, and with some bitterness.

In addition to this feeling, she was wearied of the house, of the solitude, and the confinement. Despite her grief and her foreboding, she being if not a 'perfect woman,' at least a 'nobly planned' one, felt strength and vigour in every limb, and a desire for exercise and expansion, which would not let her rest. She wandered all round the old garden, gathered a spray from the now flowerless 'rose without thorns,' which flourished in one corner of it, sat for a minute or two in the alcove, and gazed at the prospect on the other side with a mournful satisfaction, and then, finding that it was still early, wandered down to the lake-side, to the little landing-place, where the boat with the grass-green sides, and with the name 'Delphine' painted on it, was moored.

'I should like a last row on the lake, dearly,' thought Judith ; and quickly enough followed the other thought, 'and why not ?' So thought, so decided. She went to the little shed where the oars were kept, seized a pair, and sprang into the boat, unchained it from its moorings, and with a strong, practised stroke or two, was soon in deep water. It gave her a sensation of joy to be once more here, on the bosom of this sweet and glistening Shennamere. She pulled slowly, and with many pauses; stopping every now and then to let her boat float, and to enjoy the exquisite panorama of hills surrounding the lake, and of the long, low front of Scar Foot in its gardens. A mist rushed across her eyes and a sob rose to her throat, as she beheld it.

'Ah,' thought Judith, 'and this is what will keep rising up in my memory at all times, and in all seasons, good or bad. Well, it *must* be, I suppose. Shennamere, good-bye!'

She had rowed all across the lake, a mile, perhaps, and was almost at the opposite shore, beneath the village of Busk. There was a gorgeous October sunset, flaming all across the heavens, and casting over everything a weird, beautiful light and glamour, and at the same time the dusk was creeping on, as it does in October, following quickly on the skirts of the sunset.

She skirted along by the shore, thinking, 'I must turn back,' and feeling strangely unwilling to do so. She looked at the grassy fringe at the edge of the lake, which in summer was always a waste of the fair yellow iris: one of the sweetest flowers that blows, to her thinking and to mine. She heard the twittering of some ousels, and other water birds. She heard the shrill voice of a young woman on the road, singing a song. She raised her eyes to look for the young woman, wondering whether it were any acquaintance of hers, and before her glance had time to wander far enough, it rested, astonished, upon the figure of Bernard Aglionby, whose presence on that road, and on foot, was a mystery to her, since his way to Scar Foot lay on the other side of the lake.

But he was standing there, had stopped in his walk evidently, so that she knew not from which direction he came, and was now lifting his hat to her.

'Good-afternoon!' cried Judith quickly, and surprised to feel her cheeks grow hot.

'Good-afternoon,' he responded, coming down to the water's edge, and looking, as usual, very earnest. 'You are not rowing about here all alone?' he added, in some astonishment.

This question called up a smile to Judith's face, and she asked, leaning on her oars :

'And why not, pray?'

'It is dangerous. And you are alone, and a lady.'

Judith laughed outright.

'Shennamere dangerous! That shows how little you know about it. I have rowed up and down it since I was a child; indeed, any child could do it.'

'Could it? I wish you would let me try, then.'

'Would you like it, really?' asked Judith, in some surprise.

'There is nothing I should like better, if you will let me.'

'Then see! I will row up to the shore, and you can get in and pull me back if you will, for I begin to feel my arms tired. It is some time since I have rowed, now.'

This was easily managed. He took her place, and she took the tiller-cords, sitting opposite to him. It was not until after this arrangement had been made, and they were rowing back in a leisurely manner towards Scar Foot, that Judith began to feel a little wonder as to how it had all happened—how Bernard came to be in the boat with her, rowing her home. He was very quiet, she noticed, almost subdued, and he looked somewhat tired. His eyes rested upon her every now and then with a speculative, half-absent expression, and he was silent, till at last she said :

'How came you on the Lancashire road, Mr. Aglionby, and on foot? I thought you would be driving back from Yoresett.'

'I did drive as far as the top of the hill above the bridge, and then I got out to walk round this way. You must know that I find a pleasure which I cannot express, in simply wandering about here, and looking at the views. It is perfectly delighful. But I might say, how came you to be at this side of the lake, alone and at sunset ?'

'That is nothing surprising for me. We are leaving to-morrow, after which we shall have done with Scar Foot for ever. I have been bidding good-bye to it all. The house, the garden, the lake, everything.'

That 'everything' came out with an energy which smacked of anything but resignation pure and simple.

'Bidding good-bye? Ah, I must have seemed a bold, insolent intruder, at such a moment. I wonder you condescended to speak to me. I wonder you did not instantly turn away, and row back again, with all speed. Instead of which—I am here with you.'

Judith did not reply, though their eyes met, and her lips parted. It was a jest, but a jest which she found it impossible to answer. Aglionby also perhaps judged it best to say nothing more. Yet both hearts swelled. Though they maintained silence, both felt that there was more to be said. Both knew, as they glided on in the sharp evening air, in the weird light of the sunset, that this was not the end ; other things had yet to happen. Some of the sunset glow had already faded ; perhaps it had sunk with its warmth and fire into their hearts, which were hot ; the sky had taken a more pallid hue. At the foot of the lake, Addlebrough rose, bleak and forbidding : Judith leaned back, and looked at it, and saw how cold it was; but while she knew the chillness of it, she was all the time intensely, feverishly conscious of Aglionby's proximity to herself. Now and again, for a second at a time, her eyes were drawn irresistibly to his figure. How rapidly had her feelings towards him been modified! On the first day she had seen him, he had struck her as an enthusiastic provincial politician : he had been no

more a real person to her than if she had never seen him.
Next she had beheld him walking behind Mr. Whaley into
the parlour at Scar Foot ; had seen the cool uncompromising curve of his lips, the proud, cold glance in his eyes.
Then he had suddenly become the master, the possessor,
wielding power undisputed and indisputable over what she
had always considered her own, not graspingly, but from
habit and association. She had for some time feared and
distrusted his hardness, but gradually yet quickly those
feelings had changed, till now, without understanding how,
she had got to feel a deep admiration for, and delight in his
dark, keen face ; full of strength, full of resolution and pride;
it was all softened at the present moment, and to her there
seemed a beauty not to be described in its sombre tints,
and in the outline, expressive of such decision and firmness,
a firmness which had just now lost the old sneering vivacity
of eye and lip.

It all seemed too unstable to be believed in. Would it
ever end ? Gliding onwards, to the accompaniment of a
rhythmic splash of the oars and ripple of the water, with
the mountains apparently floatingly receding from before
them, while the boat darted onwards. A month ago this
young man had been an obscure salesman in an Irkford
warehouse, and she, Judith Conisbrough, had been the supposed coheiress, with her sisters, of all John Aglionby's
lands and money : now the obscure salesman was in full
possession of both the lands and the money, while from
her, being poor, had been taken even that she had, and
more had yet to go. She felt no resentment towards
Aglionby, absolutely none ; for herself, she experienced a
dull sensation of pain—a shrinking from the years to come
of loneliness, neglect and struggle. She pictured the future,
as she glided on in the present. He, as soon as he had
settled things to his pleasure, would get married to that tall,
fair girl with whom she had seen him. They would live at

Scar Foot, or wherever else it list them to live; they would be happy with one another; would rejoice in their possessions, and enjoy life side by side :—while she—bah! she impatiently told herself—of what use to repine about it? That only made one look foolish. It was so, and that was all about it. The sins of the fathers should be relentlessly and unsparingly visited upon the children. He—her present companion, had said so, and she attached an altogether unreasonable importance to his words. He had held that creed in the days of his adversity and poverty, that creed of 'no forgiveness.' If it had supported him, why not her also? True, he was a man, and she was a woman, and all men, save the most unhappy and unfortunate of all, were taught and expected to work. She had only been forced to wait. Perhaps, if he had not had to work, and been compelled to forget himself and his wrongs in toil, he might have proved a harder adversary now than he was.

The boat glided alongside the landing-place. He sprang up, jumped upon the boards, and handed her out.

'It is nearly dark,' he observed, and his voice, though low, was deep and full, as a voice is wont to be when deep thoughts or real emotion has lately stirred the mind. 'We will send out to have the things put away.' He walked beside her up the grassy path, as silent as she was, and her heart was full. Was it not for the last time? As he held the wicket open for her, and then followed her up the garden, he said:

'Miss Conisbrough, I have a favour to ask of you.'

'A favour, what is it?'

'Only a trifle,' said Aglionby. 'It is, that you will sing me a song to-night—one particular song.'

'Sing you a song!' ejaculated Judith, amazed. And the request, considering the terms on which they stood, was certainly a calm one.

'Yes, the song I overheard you singing on Sunday night. "Goden Abend, Gode Nacht!" I want to hear it again.'

They now stood in the porch, and as Judith hesitated, and looked at him, she found his eyes bent upon her face, as if he waited, less for a reply, than for compliance with his request—or demand—she knew not which it was. She conquered her surprise; tried to think she felt it to be a matter of indifference, and said, 'I will sing it if you like.'

'I do like, very much. And when will you sing it?' he asked, pausing at the foot of the stairs. Judith had ascended a step or two.

'Oh, when Mrs. Aveson calls me down to supper,' she answered slowly, her surprise not yet overcome.

'Thank you. You are very indulgent, and I assure you I feel proportionately grateful,' said Aglionby, with a smile which Judith knew not how to interpret. She said not a word, but left him at the foot of the stairs with an odd little thrill shooting through her, as she thought :

'I was not wrong. He does delight to be the master—and perhaps I ought to have resisted—though I don't know why. One might easily obey that kind of master—but what does it all matter? After to-morrow afternoon, all this will be at an end.'

Aglionby turned into the parlour as she went upstairs, the smile still lingering on his lips. All the day, off and on, the scene had haunted him in imagination—Judith seated at the piano, singing, he standing somewhere near her, listening to that one particular song. All day, too, he had kept telling himself that, all things considered, it would hardly do to ask her to sing it; that it would look very like impertinence if he did; would be presuming on his position—would want some more accomplished tactician than he was, to make the request come easily and naturally.

Yet (he thought, as he stood by the window), whether he had done it easily or not, it had been done. He had asked

her, and she had consented. What else would she do for
him, he wondered, if he asked her? Then came a poignant,
regretful wish that he had asked her for something else. In
reflecting upon the little scene which was just over, he felt a
keen, pungent pleasure, as he remembered her look of surprise, and seemed to see how she gradually yielded to him,
with a certain unbending of her dignity, which he found
indescribably and perilously fascinating.

' I wish I had asked her for something else !' he muttered.
'Why had I not my wits about me? A trumpery song !
Such a little thing ! I am glad I made her understand that
it was a trifle. I should like to see her look if I asked her
a real favour. I should like to see how she took it. Something that it would cost her something to grant—something
the granting of which argued that she looked with favour
upon one. Would she do it ? By Jove, if her pride were
tamed to it, and she did it at last, it would be worth a man's
while to go on his knees for it, whatever it was.'

He stood by the window, frowning over what seemed to
him his own obtuseness, till at last a gleam of pleasure
flitted across his face.

' I have it !' he said within himself, with a triumphant
smile. ' I will make her promise. She will not like it, she
will chafe under it, but she shall promise. The greatest
favour she could confer upon me, would be to receive a
favour from me—and she shall. Then she can never look
upon me as " nobody " again.'

He rang for lights, and pulled out a bundle of papers
which Mr. Whaley had given him to look over, but on trying
to study them, he found that he could not conjure up the
slightest interest in them ; that they were, on the contrary,
most distasteful to him. He opened the window at last,
and leaned out, saying to himself, as he flung the papers
upon the table :

' If she knew what was before her, she would not come

down. But she has promised, and heaven forbid that I should forewarn and forearm her.'

The night was fine ; moonless, but starlight. He went outside, lit his pipe, and paced about. He had been learning from Mr. Whaley what a goodly heritage he had entered upon. He was beginning to understand how he stood, and what advantages and privileges were to be his. All the time that he conned them over, the face of Judith Conisbrough seemed to accompany them, and a sense of how unjustly she had been treated, above all others, burnt in his mind. Before he went to Irkford, before he did anything else, this question must be settled. It should be settled to-night, between him and her.

He meant first to make her astonished, to see her put on her air of queenly surprise at his unembarrassed requests ; and then he meant her to submit, for her mother's and sisters' sake, and incidentally, for his pleasure.

It was an agreeable picture ; one, too, of a kind that was new to him. He did not realise its significance for himself. He only knew that the pleasure of conquest was great, when the obstacle to be conquered was strong and beautiful.

He was roused from these schemes and plans by the sound of some chords struck on the piano, and he quickly went into the house. Judith had seated herself at the piano : she had resumed her usual calmness of mien, and turned to him as he entered.

'I thought this would summon you, Mr. Aglionby. You seem fond of music.'

'Music has been fond of me, and a kind friend to me, always,' said he. 'I see you have no lights. Shall I ring for candles ?'

'No, thank you. I have no music with me. All that I sing must be sung from memory, and the firelight will be enough for that.'

She did not at once sing the song he had asked for, but

14

played one or two fragments first ; then struck the preluding chords and sang it.

'I like that song better than anything I ever heard,' said he emphatically, after she had finished it.

'I like it too,' said Judith. 'Mrs. Malleson gave it me, or I should never have become possessed of such a song. Do you know Mrs. Malleson ?' she added.

'No.   Who is she ?'

'The wife of the vicar of Stanniforth.   I hope he will call upon you ; but of course he is sure to do so.   And you will meet them out.   I advise you to make a friend of Mrs. Malleson, if you can.'

'I suppose,' observed Bernard, 'that most, or all, of the people who knew my grandfather will call upon me, and ask me to their houses ?'

'Of course.'

'How odd that seems, doesn't it ?   If I had not, by an accident, become master here—if I had remained in my delightful warehouse at Irkford, none of these people would have known of my existence ; or if they had, they would have taken no notice of me.   Not that I consider it any injustice,' he added quickly, 'because I hold that unless you prove yourself in some way noticeable, either by being very rich, or very clever, or very handsome, or very something, you have no right whatever to complain of neglect—none at all.   Why *should* people notice you ?'

'Just so ; only, you know, there is this to be said on the other side.   If all these people had known as well as possible who you were, and where you lived, and all about you, they would still have taken no notice of you while you were in that position.   I don't want to disparage them.   I am sure some of them are very good, kind-hearted people. I am only speaking from experience.'

'And you are right enough.   You are not going ?' he added, seeing that she rose.   'Supper is not ready yet.'

'Thank you. I do not want any supper. And it is not very early.'

' Then, if you will go, I must say now what I wanted to say. You need not leave me this instant, need you? I really have something to say to you, if you will listen to me.'

Judith paused, looked at him, and sat down again.

' I am in no hurry,' said she ; ' what do you wish to say to me ?'

' You said this afternoon that you had gone to say good-bye to Scar Foot, to the lake—to everything ; that after you left here to-day you would have " done with " Scar Foot. It would no longer be anything to you. You meant, I suppose, that you would never visit it again. Why should that be so?'

They were seated : Judith on the music-stool, on which she had turned round when they began to talk, and he lean-ing forward on a chair just opposite her. Close to them was the broad hearth, with its bright fire and sparkling blazes, lighting up the two faces very distinctly. He was looking very earnestly at her, and he asked the question in a manner which showed that he intended to have an answer. It was not wanting. She replied almost without a pause :

' Well, you see, we cannot possibly come here now, as we were accustomed to do in my uncle's time, just when we chose ; to ramble about for an hour or two, take a meal with him, and then go home again, or, if he asked us, to spend a few days here ; it would not do.'

' But you need not be debarred from ever coming to the place, just because you cannot do exactly as you used to do.'

She was silent, with a look of some pain and perplexity— not the dignified surprise he had expected to see. But the subject was, or rather it had grown, very near to Bernard's heart. He was determined to argue the question out.

' Is it because Scar Foot has become mine, because I could turn you out if I liked, and because you are too

proud to have anything to do with me?' he asked, coolly
and deliberately.

Judith looked up, shocked.

'What a horrible idea! What could have put such a
thought into your head?'

'Your elaborate ceremonial of everlasting farewell, this
afternoon, I think,' he answered, and went on boldly,
though he saw her raise her head somewhat indignantly:
'Do listen to me, Miss Conisbrough; I know that in your
opinion I must be a most unwelcome interloper. But I
think you will believe me when I say that I have nothing
but kindly feelings towards you—that I would give a good
deal—even sacrifice a good deal to be on kindly terms with
Mrs. Conisbrough and you, and your family. I wish to be
just, to repair my grandfather's injustice. You know, as we
discovered the other night, we are relations. What I want
to ask is, will you not meet me half-way? You will not
hold aloof—I beg you will not! You will help me to con-
ciliate Mrs. Conisbrough, to repair in some degree the injustice which has been done her. I am sure you will. I
count securely upon you,' he added, looking full into her
face, 'for you are so utterly outside all petty motives of spite
or resentment. You could not act upon a feeling of pique
or offence, I am sure.'

She was breathing quickly; her fingers locked in one
another; her face a little averted, and flushed, as he could
see, by something more than the firelight.

'You have far too good an opinion of me,' she said, in a
low tone; 'you are mistaken about me. I *try* to forget
such considerations, but I assure you I am not what you
take me for. I am soured, I believe, and embittered by
many things which have conspired to make my life rather a
lonely one.'

'How little you know yourself!' said Bernard. 'If I had
time I should laugh at you. But I want you to listen to

me, and seriously to consider my proposal. Will you not
help me in this plan? You said at first, you know, that you
would not oppose it. Now I want you to promise your co-
operation.'

'In other words,' said Judith quietly, 'you want me to
persuade mamma to accept, as a gift from you, some of the
money which she had expected to have, but which, as is very
evident, my uncle was at the last determined she should not
have.'

Aglionby smiled. He liked the opposition, and had every
intention of conquering it.

'That is the way in which you prefer to put it, I suppose,'
he said. 'I do not see why you should, I am sure. You
did not use such expressions about it the other night, and,
at any rate, I have your promise. But I fear you think the
suggestion an impertinent one. How am I to convince you
that nothing could be further from my thoughts than impertinence?'

'I never thought it was impertinent,' answered Judith,
and if her voice was calm, her heart was not. Not only
had she not thought him impertinent, but she was strangely
distressed and disturbed at his imagining she had thought
him so.

'I thought,' she went on, 'that it was very kind, very
generous.'

'I would rather you took it as being simply just. But, at
any rate, you will give me your assistance, for I know that
without it I shall never succeed in getting Mrs. Conisbrough's consent to my wishes.'

He spoke urgently. Judith was moved—distressed—he
saw.

'I know I gave you a kind of promise,' she began slowly.

'A kind of promise! Your words were, "I shall not
oppose it." Can you deny it?'

'No—those were my words. But I had no time to think

about it then. I have done so since. I have looked at it in every possible light, with the sincere desire to comply with your wish, and all I can say is, that I must ask you to release me from my promise.'

'Not unless you tell me why,' said he, in a deep tone of something like anger.

'I cannot tell you why,' said Judith, her own full tones vibrating and growing somewhat faint. 'I can only ask you to believe me when I say that it would indeed be best in every way if, after we leave your house, you cease to take any notice of us. If we meet casually, either in society or in any other way, there is no reason why we should not be friendly. But it must end there. It is best that it should do so. And do not try to help my mother in the way you proposed. I—I cannot give any assistance in the matter, if you do.'

This was not the kind of opposition which Aglionby had bargained for. For a few moments he was silent, a black frown settling on his brow, but far indeed from having given up the game. Nothing had ever before aroused in him such an ardent desire to prevail. He was thinking about his answer ; wondering what it would be best for him to say, when Judith, who perhaps had misunderstood his silence, resumed in a low, regretful voice :

'To spend money which had come from you—to partake of comforts which your generosity had procured, would be impossible—to me, at any rate. It would scorch me, I feel.'

Again a momentary silence. Then the storm broke :

'You have such a loathing for me, you hate me so bitterly and so implacably that you can sit there, and say this to me, with the utmost indifference,' with passionate grief in his voice ; grief and anger blended in a way that cut her to the quick. And so changed was he all in a moment, that she was startled, and almost terrified.

'What!' she faltered, 'have I said something wrong? I hate you? Heaven forbid! It would be myself that I should hate, because——'

'Because you had touched something that was defiled by coming from me. Because it had been mine!'

'Thank God that it is yours!' said Judith suddenly, and in a stronger tone. 'It is the one consolation that I have in the matter. When I think how very near it was to being ours, and that we might have had it and used it, I feel as if I had escaped by little short of a miracle from ——'

She stopped suddenly.

'I do not understand you.'

'Do not try. Put me down as an ill-disposed virago. I feel like one sometimes. And yet, I would have you believe that I appreciate your motives—it is out of no ill-feeling——'

'It is useless to tell me that,' he broke in, in uncontrollable agitation. 'I see that you have contained your wrath until this evening; you have nourished a bitter grudge against me, and you feel that the time has come for you to discharge your debt. You have succeeded. You wished to humiliate me, and you have done so most thoroughly, and as I never was humiliated before. Understand—if you find any gratification in it, that I am wounded and mortified to the quick. I had hoped that by stooping—by using every means in my power—to please you, I should succeed in conciliating you and yours. I wished to put an end to this horrible discord and division, to do that which was right, and without doing which, I can never enjoy the heritage that has fallen to me. No, never! and you—have led me on—have given me your promise, and now you withdraw it. You know your power, and that it is useless for me to appeal to Mrs. Conisbrough, if you do not allow her to hear me, and——'

'You accuse me strangely,' she began, in a trembling

voice, forgetting that she had desired him to look upon her
as a virago, and appalled by the storm she had aroused, and
yet feeling a strange, thrilling delight in it, and a kind
of reckless desire to abandon herself to its fury. Even
while she raised her voice in opposition to it, she hoped it
would not instantly be lulled. There was something more
attractive in it than in the commonplace civilities of an
unbroken and meaningless politeness. She had her half-
conscious wish gratified to the utmost, for he went on :

'Strangely, how strangely? I thought women were by
nature fitted to promote peace. I thought that you, of all
others, would encourage harmony and kindness. I appealed
to you, because I knew your will was stronger than that of
your mother. It only needs your counsel and influence to
make her see things as I wish her to see them. And you
thrust me capriciously aside—your manner, your actions,
all tell me to retire with the plunder I have got, and
to gloat over it alone. You stand aside in scorn. You
prefer poverty, and I believe you would prefer starvation, to
extending a hand to one whom you consider a robber and
an upstart——'

'You are wrong, you are wrong!' she exclaimed vehemently and almost wildly, clasping her hands tightly
together, and looking at him with a pale face and dilated
eyes.

'Then show me that I am wrong!' he said, standing
before her, and extending his hands towards her. 'Repent
what you have said about benefits derived from me *scorching*
you!' (He did not know that the flash from his own eyes
was almost enough to produce the same effect.) 'Recall it,
and I will forget all this scene—as soon as I can, that is.
Judith——' She started, changed colour, and he went on
in his softest and most persuasive accent. 'My cousin
Judith, despite all you have just been flinging at me of hard
and cruel things, I still cling to the conviction that you are

a noble woman, and I ask you once more for your friendship, and your good offices towards your mother. Do not
repulse me again.'

She looked speechlessly into his face. Where were now
the scintillating eyes, the harsh discord of tone, the suppressed rage of manner? Gone; and in their stead there
were the most dulcet sounds of a most musical voice; eyes
that pleaded humbly and almost tenderly, and a hand held
out beseechingly, craving her friendship, her good offices.

A faint shudder ran through Judith's whole frame. His
words and the tone of them rang in her ears, and would
ring there for many a day, and cause her heart to beat
whenever she remembered them. 'Judith—my cousin
Judith!' His hot earnestness, and the unconscious fascination which he could throw into both looks and tones, had
not found her callous and immovable. While she did not
understand what the feeling was which overmastered her,
she yet felt the pain of having to repulse him amount to
actual agony. She felt like one lost and bewildered. All
she knew or realised was, that it would have been delicious
to yield unconditionally in this matter of persuading her
mother to his will; to hear his wishes and obey them, and
that of all things this was the one point on which she must
hold out, and resist. Shaken by a wilder emotion than she
had ever felt before, she suddenly caught the hands he
stretched towards her, and exclaimed brokenly :

'Ah, forgive me, if you can, but do not be so hard upon
me. You do not know what you are saying. I cannot obey
you. I wish I could.'

She covered her face with her hands, with a short sob.

Aglionby could not at first reply. Across the storm of
mortification and anger, of good-will repulsed, and reverence
momentarily chilled, another feeling was creeping—the
feeling that behind all this agitation and refusal on her part,
something lay hidden which was not aversion to him ; that

the victory he had craved for was substantially his : she did
not refuse his demand because she had no wish to comply
with it.   She denied him against her will, not with it.   She
was not churlish.   He might still believe her noble.   She
was harassed evidently, worn with trouble, and with some
secret grief.   He forgot for the moment that a confiding
heart at Irkford looked to him for support and comfort;
indeed, he had a vague idea, which had not yet been
distinctly formulated, that there were few troubles which
Miss Vane could not drive away, by dint of dress, and
jewellery, and amusement.   He felt that so long as he had
a full purse, he could comfort Lizzie and cherish her.   This
was a different case ; this was a suffering which silk attire
and diamonds could not alleviate, a wound not to be
stanched for a moment by social distinction and the envy of
other women.   His heart ached sympathetically.   He could
comprehend that feeling.

He knew that he could feel likewise.   Nay, had he not
experienced a foretaste of some such feeling this very night,
when she had vowed that she could not aid him in his
scheme, and he had felt his newly-acquired riches turn poor
and sterile in consequence, and his capacity for enjoying
them shrivel up ?   But there was a ray of joy even amidst
this pain, in thinking that this hidden obstacle did not
imply anything derogatory to her.   He might yet believe her
noble, and treat her as noble.   His was one of the natures
which can not only discern nobility in shabby guise, but
which are perhaps almost too prone to seek it there, rather
than under purple mantles; being inclined to grudge the
wearers of the latter any distinction save that of inherited
outside splendour.   The fact that Miss Conisbrough was a
very obscure character ; that she was almost sordidly poor ;
that the gown she wore was both shabby and old-fashioned,
and that whatever secret troubles she had, she must neces-
sarily often be roused from them, in order to consider how

most advantageously to dispose of the metaphorical six-
pence—all this lent to his eyes, and to his way of thinking,
a reality to her grief, a concreteness to her distress. He
had no love for moonshine and unreality, and though Judith
Conisbrough had this night overwhelmed him with contra-
dictions, and vague, intangible replies to his questions, yet
he was more firmly convinced than ever that all about her
was real.

If she had to suffer—and he was sure now that she had—
he would be magnanimous, though he did not consciously
apply so grand a name to his own conduct. After a pause,
he said slowly :

'I must ask your forgiveness. I had no business to get
into a passion. It was unmanly, and, I believe, brutal. I
can only atone for it in one way, and that is by trying to do
what you wish ; though I cannot conceal that your decision
is a bitter blow to me. I had hoped that everything would
be so different. But tell me once again that you do not *wish*
to be at enmity with me ; that it is no personal ill-will
which——'

'Oh, Mr. Aglionby !'

'Could you not stretch a point for once,' said Bernard,
looking at her with a strangely mingled expression, 'as we
are so soon to be on mere terms of distant civility, and
address me like a cousin—just once ? It would not be
much to do, after what you have refused.'

There was a momentary pause. Aglionby felt his own
heart beat faster, as he waited for her answer. At last she
began, with flaming cheeks, and eyes steadily fixed upon the
ground :

'You mean—Bernard—there is nothing I desire less than
to be at enmity with you. Since we have been under your
roof here, I have learnt that you at least are noble, whatever
I may be ; and——'

At this point Judith looked up, having overcome, partially at least, her tremulousness; but she found his eyes fixed upon hers, and her own fell again directly. Something seemed to rise in her throat and choke her; at last she faltered out:

'Do not imagine that I suffer nothing in refusing your wish.'

'I believe you now, entirely,' he said, in a tone almost of satisfaction. 'We were talking about creeds the other night, and you said you wanted a strong one. I assure you it will take all the staying power of mine to enable me to bear this with anything like equanimity. And meantime, grant me this favour, let me accompany you home to-morrow, and do me the honour to introduce me to your sisters; I should like to know my cousins by sight, at any rate—if Mrs. Conisbrough will allow it, that is.'

'Mamma will allow it—yes.'

'And I promise that after that I will not trouble nor molest you any more.'

'Don't put it in that way.'

'I must, I am afraid. But you have not promised yet.'

'Certainly, I promise. And, oh! Mr. Aglionby, I am glad, I am *glad* you have got all my uncle had to leave,' she exclaimed, with passionate emphasis. 'The knowledge that you have it will be some comfort to me in my dreary existence, for it is and will be dreary.'

She rose now, quite decidedly, and went towards the door. He opened it for her, and they clasped hands silently, till he said, with a half smile which had in it something wistful:

'*Goden abend!*'

'*Gode Nacht!*' responded Judith, but no answering smile came to her lips—only a rush of bitter tears to her eyes. She passed out of the room; he gently closed the door after her, and she was left alone with her burden.

CHAPTER XXI.

AN AFTERNOON EPISODE.

'WE must not go out this afternoon, because they are coming, you know,' observed Rhoda to Delphine.

'I suppose not; and yet, I think it is rather a farce, our staying in to receive them. I cannot think it will give them any joy.'

'You are such a tiresome, analytical person, Delphine! Always questioning my statements——'

'Sometimes you make such queer ones.'

'I wish something would happen. I wish a change would come,' observed Rhoda, yawning. 'Nothing ever does happen here.'

'Well, I should have said that a good deal had happened lately. Enough to make us very uncomfortable, at any rate.'

'Oh, you mean about Uncle Aglionby and his grandson. Do you know, Del, I have a burning, a consuming curiosity to see that young man. I think it must have been most delightfully romantic for Judith to be staying at Scar Foot all this time. I don't suppose she has made much of her opportunities. I expect she has been fearfully solemn, and has almost crushed him, if he is crushable, that is, with the majesty of her demeanour. Now, *I* should have been amiability itself. I think the course I should have taken would have been to make him fall in love with me——'

'You little stupid! When he is engaged to be married already!'

'So he is! How disgusting it is to find all one's schemes upset in that way. Well, I don't care whether he is engaged or not. I want to see him awfully, and I think it was intensely stupid of mamma to quarrel with him.'

'No doubt you would have acted much more circumspectly, being a person of years, experience, and great natural sagacity.'

'I have the sagacity at any rate, if not the experience. And after all, that is the great thing, because if you have experience without sagacity, you might just as well be without it.'

'I know you are marvellously clever,' said Delphine; 'but you are an awful chatterbox. Do be quiet, and let me think.'

'What can you possibly have to think about here?'

'All kinds of things—about which I want to come to some sort of an understanding with myself. So hold your peace, I pray you.'

They had finished their early dinner, and had retired to that pleasant sunny parlour where Judith had found them, little more than a week ago, on her return from Irkford. Delphine, being a young woman of high principle, had pulled out some work, but Rhoda was doing absolutely nothing, save swaying backwards and forwards in a rocking-chair, while she glanced round with quick, restless grey eyes at every object in the room, oftenest at her sister. Not for long did she leave the latter in the silence she had begged for.

'Won't you come upstairs to the den, Delphine? It is quite dry and warm this afternoon, and I want you so to finish that thing you were doing.'

'Not now, but presently, perhaps. I feel lazy just now.'

Pause, while Rhoda still looked about her, and at last said abruptly: 'Delphine, should you say we were a good-looking family?'

Delphine looked up.

'Good-looking? It depends on what people call good-looking.'

'One man's meat is another man's poison, I suppose you mean. I have been considering the subject seriously of late,

and on comparing us with our neighbours, I have come to
the conclusion that, taken all in all, we *are* good-looking.'

'Our good looks are all the good things we have to boast
of, then,' said Delphine unenthusiastically, as she turned her
lovely head to one side, and contemplated her work—her
sister keenly scrutinising her in the meantime.

'Well, good looks are no mean fortune. What was it I
was reading the other day about—"As much as beauty
better is than gold," or words to that effect.'

'Pooh !' said Delphine, with a little derisive laugh.

'Well, but it is true.'

'In a kind of way, perhaps—not practically.'

'In a kind of way—well, in such a way as this. Suppose
—we may suppose anything, you know, and for my part,
while I am about it, I like to suppose something splendid at
once—suppose that *you* were, for one occasion only, dressed
up in a most beautiful ball-dress ; *eau de Nil* and wild roses,
or the palest blue and white lace, or pale grey and pale pink,
you know—ah, I see you are beginning to smile at the very
idea. I believe white would suit you best, after all—a billow
of white, with little humming-birds all over it, or something
like that. Well—imagine yourself in this dress, with everything complete, you know, Del,'—she leaned impressively
forward—'fan and shoes, and gloves and wreath, and a
beautiful pocket-handkerchief like a bit of scented mist—
and jewellery that no one could find any fault with ; and
then suppose Philippa Danesdale popped down in the same
room, as splendid as you please—black velvet and diamonds,
or satin, or silk, and ropes of pearls, or anything grand, with
her stupid little prim face and red hair——'

'Oh, for shame, Rhoda ! You are quite spiteful.'

'I, spiteful !' cried Rhoda, with a prolonged note of in-
dignant surprise. 'That *is* rich ! Who has drawn Miss
Danesdale, I wonder, in all manner of attitudes :—" Miss
Danesdale engaged in Prayer," holding her Prayer-book

with the tips of her lavender-kid fingers, and looking as if she were paying her Maker such a compliment in coming and kneeling down to Him, with an ivory-backed Prayer-book and a gold-topped scent-bottle to sustain her through the operation? " Miss Danesdale, on hearing of the Més-alliance of a Friend "—now, who drew *that*, Delphine? and many another as bad? My sagacity, which you were jeering at just now, suggests a reason for your altered tone. But I will spare you, and proceed with my narrative. Sup-pose what I have described to be an accomplished fact, and then suppose a perfect stranger—we'll imagine Mr. Danesdale to be one, because I like to make my ideas very plain to people, and there's nothing like being personal for effecting that result—suppose him there, not knowing any-thing about either of you, whether you were rich or poor, or high or low—now, which of the two do you think he would be likely to dance with oftenest?'

' How should I know?'

' Delphine, you used to be truthful once—candid and honest. The falling off is deplorable. " Evil communi-cations "—I won't finish it. You are shirking my question. Of course he would dance with you, and you know he would. There's no doubt of it, because you would look a vision of beauty——'

'Stuff and nonsense!'

' And Miss Danesdale would look just what she is, a stiff, prudish *plain* creature. And so beauty *is* better than gold.'

' Yes, under certain conditions, if one could arbitrarily fix them. But we have to look at conditions as they are, not as we could fix them if we tried. Suppose, we'll say, that he had been dancing with me all the evening——'

' Which he would like to do very much, I haven't a doubt.'

' And suddenly, some one took him aside, and said : " Friend, look higher. She with whom thou dancest has not a penny, while she who stands in yonder corner neglected, lo! she hath a fortune of fifty thousand pounds, which neither moth nor rust can corrupt." After that, I might dance as long as I liked, but it would be alone.'

'I call that a very poor illustration, and I don't know that it would be the case at all. All I know is, that it pleases you to pretend to be cynical, though you don't feel so in the very least. I do so like to dream sometimes, and to think what I would do if we were rich! Delphine, *don't* you wish we were rich?'

'Not particularly; I would rather be busy. I wish I was a great painter, that's what I should like to be, with every hour of the day filled up with work and engagements. Oh, I am so tired of doing nothing! I feel sometimes as if I could kill myself.'

Before Rhoda had time to reply, Louisa, the maid, opened the door, remarking:

'Please, miss, there's Mr. Danesdale.'

The girls started a little consciously as he came in, saying, as Louisa closed the door after him:

'Send me away if I intrude. Your servant said you were in, and when I asked if you were engaged, she replied, "No, sir, they are a-doing of nothing." Encouraged by this report, I entered.'

'We are glad to see you,' said Delphine, motioning him to take a seat, and still with a slight flush on her face.

'I called for two reasons,' said Randulf, who, once admitted, appeared to feel his end gained: 'to ask if you arrived at home in safety after that confabulation with Miss Conisbrough, and to ask if you have any news from Mrs. Conisbrough. How is she?'

'Much better, thank you. So much better, indeed, that we expect her and Judith home this afternoon——'

'Yes,' interposed Rhoda, 'so far from doing nothing, as Louisa reported, we were waiting for mamma's return.'

15

'Ah, I can tell Philippa then. She has been talking of calling to see Mrs. Conisbrough.'

It was Rhoda's turn to cast down her eyes a little, overcome by the reflections called up by this announcement. There was a pause ; then Rhoda said :

' How thankful Judith and mother will be to come away from Scar Foot, and how very glad Mr. Aglionby will be to get rid of them !'

' Had you just arrived at that conclusion when I came ?'

' Oh no ! We were at what they call "a loose end," if you ever heard the expression. We were exercising our imaginations.'

Rhoda pursued this topic with imperturbable calm, undismayed by the somewhat alarmed glances given her by Delphine, who feared that her sister might, as she often did, indiscreetly reveal the very subject of a conversation.

' Were you ? How ?'

' We were imagining ourselves *rich*,' said Rhoda, with emphasis. ' You can never do that, you know, because you are rich already. We have the advantage of you there, and I flatter myself that this is a new way of looking at it.'

' I beg your pardon, Rhoda—I was not imagining myself rich. I was imagining myself——' she stopped suddenly.

' Imagining yourself what ?' he asked, with deep interest.

' Oh, nothing—nonsense !' said Delphine hastily, disinclined to enter into particulars.

He turned to Rhoda. Delphine looked at her with a look which said, ' Speak if you dare !' Rhoda tossed her head and said :

' There's no crime in what you were wishing, child. She was imagining herself a great painter. That's Delphine's ambition. Like Miss Thompson, you know——'

' Oh no !' interposed Delphine hastily—' not battle-pieces.'

' What then ?'

'Landscape, I think, and animals,' said Delphine, still in some embarrassment.

'Del draws beautiful animals,' said Rhoda, turning to him, and speaking very seriously and earnestly. Randulf was charmed to perceive that the youngest Miss Conisbrough had quite taken him into her confidence, and he trusted that a little judiciously employed tact would bring Delphine to the same point.

'Oh, not beautiful, Rhoda! Only—' she turned to Randulf, losing some of the shyness which with her was a graceful hesitation, and not the ugly awkward thing it generally is. 'Not beautiful at all, Mr. Danesdale ; but it is simply that I cannot help, when I see animals and beautiful landscapes— I absolutely can't *help* trying to copy them.'

'That shows you have a talent for it,' said Mr. Danesdale promptly. 'You should have lessons.'

He could have bitten his tongue off with vexation the next moment, as it flashed into his mind that most likely she could not afford to have lessons.

'That would be most delightful,' said Delphine composedly, 'but we can't afford to have lessons, you know, so I try not to think about it.'

Randulf was silent, his mind in a turmoil, feeling an heroic anger at those 'ceremonial institutions' not altogether unallied to those with which Mr. Herbert Spencer has made us familiar—which made it downright improper and impertinent for a young man to say to a young woman (or *vice versâ*), 'I am rich and you are poor. You have talent ; allow me to defray the expenses of its cultivation, and so to put you in the way of being busy and happy.'

'And do you paint from nature ?' he asked at last.

'Of course,' replied Delphine, still not quite reconciled to being thus made a prominent subject of conversation. 'Why should I paint from anything else ? Only, you know, one can't do things by instinct. Uncle Aglionby let me

have some lessons once—a few years ago—oh, I did enjoy
it ! But he had a conversation with my painting-master one
day, and the latter contradicted some of his theories, so he
said he was an impudent scoundrel, and he would not have
me go near him again. But I managed to learn something
from him. Still, I don't understand the laws of my art—
at least,' she added hastily, crimsoning with confusion, 'I
don't mean to call my attempts art at all. Mamma thinks
it great waste of time, and they are but daubs, I fear.'

' I wish you would show me some of them. Where do
you keep them ? Mayn't I look at them ?'

' Oh, I could not think of exposing them to your criticism !
you, who have seen every celebrated picture that exists, and
who know all about all "the schools," and who make such
fun of things that I used to think so clever—you must not
ask it indeed ! Please don't.'

Delphine was quite agitated, and appealed to him, as if
he could compel her to show them, even against her will.

' You cannot suppose that I would be severe upon anything of yours !' he exclaimed, with warmth. ' How can you
do me such injustice !'

' If you did not say it, you would think it,' replied
Delphine, ' and that would be worse. I can imagine
nothing more unpleasant than for a person to praise one's
things out of politeness, while thinking them very bad the
whole time.'

' I never heard such unutterable nonsense,' cried Rhoda,
who had been watching her opportunity of cutting in. ' To
hear you talk one would imagine your pictures were not fit
to be looked at. Mr. Danesdale, I should like you to see
them, because I know they are good. Delphine does so
like to run herself down. You should see her dogs and
horses ; I am sure they are splendid, far better than some of
the things you see in grand magazines. And I think her
little landscapes——'

'Rhoda, I shall have to go away, and lock myself up alone, if you will talk in this wild, exaggerated way,' said Delphine, in quiet despair.

'But you can't refuse, after this, to let me judge between you,' said Randulf persuasively. 'An old friend like me—and after rousing my curiosity in this manner—Miss Conisbrough, you cannot refuse !'

'I—I really——'

'Let us take Mr. Danesdale to your den !' cried Rhoda, bounding off her chair, in a sudden fit of inspiration. 'Come, Mr. Danesdale, it is up a thousand stairs, at the very top of the house, but you are young and fond of exercise, as we know, so you won't mind that.'

She had flung open the door, and led the way, running lightly up the stairs, and he had followed her, unheeding Delphine's imploring remonstrances, and thinking :

'By Jove, they are nice girls ! No jealousy of one another. I'll swear to the pictures, whatever they may turn out to be.'

Delphine slowly followed, wringing her hands in a way she had when she was distressed or hurried, and with her white forehead puckered up in embarrassed lines. Rhoda flew ahead, and Randulf followed her, up countless stairs, along great broad, light passages, and even in his haste the young man had time to notice—or rather, the fact was forced upon his notice—how bare the place looked, and how empty. He felt suddenly, more than he had done before, how narrow and restricted a life these ladies must be forced to lead.

Rhoda threw open the door of a large, light room, with a cold, clear northern aspect. It was bare indeed ; no luxurious *atelier* of a pampered student. Even the easel was a clumsy-looking thing, made very badly by a native joiner of Yoresett, who had never seen such a thing in his life, and who had not carried out the young lady's instructions very intelligently.

Randulf, looking round, thought of the expensive para-
phernalia which his sister had some years ago purchased,
when the whim seized her to paint in oils; a whim which
lasted six months, and which had for sole result, bitter
complaints against her master, as having no faculty for
teaching, and no power of pushing his pupils on; while
paints, easel, canvases and maulstick were relegated to a
cockloft in disgust. Delphine's apparatus was of the most
meagre and simple kind—in fact, it was absolutely deficient.
Two cane-bottomed chairs, sadly in need of repairs, and a
rickety deal table, covered with rags and oil-tubes, brushes,
and other impedimenta, constituted the only furniture of the
place.

'It's very bare,' cried Rhoda's clear, shrill young voice,
as she marched onwards, not in the least ashamed of the
said bareness. 'And in winter it's so cold that she can
never paint more than an hour a day, because fires are out
of the question. With one servant, you can't expect coals
to be carried, and grates cleaned, four stories up the house.
Now see, Mr. Danesdale. I'll be show-woman. I know
everything she has done. You sit there, in that chair.
We'll have the animals first. Most of them are in water-
colours or crayons. Here's a good one, in water-colours, of
Uncle Aglionby on his old " Cossack," with Friend looking
at him, to know which way he shall go. Isn't it capital?'

Despite his heartfelt admiration for all the Misses Conisbrough, and for Delphine in particular, Randulf fully
expected to find, as he had often found before with the
artistic productions of young lady amateurs, that their
'capital' sketches were so only in the fond eyes of partial
sisters, parents and friends. Accordingly he surveyed the
sketch held up by Rhoda's little brown hand with a judicial
aspect, and some distrust. But in a moment his expression
changed; a smile of pleasure broke out; he could with
a light heart cry, ' Excellent !'

It was excellent, without any flattery. It had naturally the faults of a drawing executed by one who had enjoyed very little instruction ; there was crudeness in it—roughness, a little ignorant handling ; but it was replete with other things which the most admirable instruction cannot give : there was in it a spirit, a character, an individuality which charmed him, and which, in its hardy roughness, was the more remarkable and piquant, coming from such a delicate-looking creature as Delphine Conisbrough. The old Squire's hard, yet characteristic features ; the grand contours of old Cossack, the rarest hunter in all the country-side ; and above all, the aspect of the dog : its inquiring ears and inquisitive nose, its tail on the very point, one could almost have said in the very action, of wagging an active consent ; one paw upraised, and bent, ready for a start the instant the word should be given—all these details were as spirited as they were true and correct.

'It is admirable !' said Randulf emphatically. 'If she has many more like that, she ought to make a fortune with them some time. I congratulate you, Miss Conisbrough '—to Delphine, who had just come in, with the same embarrassed and perplexed expression. 'I can somehow hardly grasp the idea that that slender little hand has made this strong, spirited picture. It shows the makings of a first-rate artist—but it is the very last thing I should have imagined you doing.'

'Ah, you haven't seen her sentimental drawings yet,' said Rhoda, vigorously hunting about for more. 'Oh, here's one of her last. I've not seen this. Why—why—oh, what fun ! Do you know it ?'

'Rhoda, you little—oh *do* put it down !' cried the harassed artist, in a tone of sudden dismay, as she made a dart forward.

But Rhoda, with eyes in which mischief incarnate was dancing a tarantella, receded from before her, holding up a spirited sketch of a young man, a pointer, a retriever, a whip, an apple-tree, and in the tree a cat, apparently in the last stage of fury and indignation.

'Do you know it, Mr. Danesdale? Do you know it?' cried the delighted girl, dancing up and down, her face alight with mirth.

'Know it—I should think I do!' he cried, pursuing her laughingly. 'Give it to me, and let me look at it. 'Tis I and my dogs, of course. Capital! Miss Conisbrough, you must really cement our friendship by presenting it to me— will you?'

He had succeeded in capturing it, and was studying it laughingly, while Delphine wrung her hands and exclaimed, 'Oh dear!'

'Splendid!' he cried again. 'It ought to be called "Randulf Danesdale and Eyeglass." And how very much wiser the dogs look than their master. Oh, this is a malicious sketch, Miss Conisbrough! But, malicious or not, I shall annex it, and you must not grudge it me.'

'If you are not offended——' began Delphine confusedly.

'I offended?' Rhoda was rummaging amongst a pile of drawings with her back to them. Mr. Danesdale accompanied his exclamation with a long look of reproach, and surely of something else. Delphine pushed her golden hair back from her forehead, and stammered out:

'Then pray keep it, but don't show it to anyone!'

'"Keep it, but keep it dark," you mean. You shall be obeyed. At least no one shall know who did it. That shall be a delightful secret which I shall keep for myself alone.'

Here Delphine, perhaps fearful of further revelations, advanced, and, depriving Rhoda of the portfolio, said she hoped she might be mistress in her own den, and she would decide herself which drawings were fit to show to Mr. Danesdale. Then she took them into her own possession, and

doled them out with what both the spectators declared to be
a very niggard hand.

Randulf, apart from his admiration of the Miss Conisbroughs,
really cared for art, and knew something about pictures. He
gave his best attention to the drawings which were now shown
to him, and the more he studied them the more convinced
he became that this was a real talent, which ought not to
be left uncultivated, and which, if carefully attended to,
would certainly produce something worthy. She showed
him chiefly landscapes, and each and all had in them a spirit,
an originality, and a wild grace peculiar to the vicinity, as
well as to the artist. There were sketches of Shennamere
from all points of view, at all hours and at all seasons: by
bright sunlight, under storm-clouds, by sentimental moonlight. There was a bold drawing of Addlebrough admirable
as a composition. The colouring was crude and often incorrect, but displayed evident power and capacity for fine
ultimate development. Now and then came some little
touch, some delicate suggestion, some bit of keen, apprecia-
tive observation, which again and again called forth his admiration. Some of the smaller bits were, as Rhoda had
said, sentimental—full of a delicate, subtle poetry impossible
to define. These were chiefly autumn pictures—a lonely
dank pool, in a circle of fading foliage ; a view of his own
father's house seen on a gusty September afternoon struck
him much. He gradually became graver and quieter, as he
looked at the pictures. At last, after contemplating for
some time a larger and more ambitious attempt, in oils—a
view of the splendid rolling hills, the town of Middleham,
and a portion of the glorious plain of York, and in the fore-
ground the windings of the sweet river Yore, as seen from
the hill called the 'Shawl' at Leyburn—he laid it down and
said earnestly, all his drawl and all his half-jesting manner
clean gone:

'Miss Conisbrough, you must not take my judgment as

infallible, of course, but I have seen a good deal of this kind of thing, and have lived a good deal amongst artists, and it is my firm conviction that you have at any rate a very great talent—I should say genius. I think these first sketches, the animals, you know, are admirable, but I like the landscapes even better. I am sure that with study under a good master you might rise to eminence as a landscape-painter; for one sees in every stroke that you love the things you paint—love nature.'

'I do !' said Delphine, stirred from her reserve and shyness. 'I love every tree in this old dale; I love every stick and stone in it, I think ; and I love the hills and the trees as if they were living things, and my friends. Oh, Mr. Danesdale, I am so glad you have not laughed at them ! I should never have had courage, you know, to show them to you. But it would have been misery to have them laughed at, however bad they had been. They have made me so happy—and sometimes so miserable. I could not tell you all they have been to me.'

'I can believe that,' said Randulf, looking with the clear, grave glance of friendship from one face to the other of the two girls, who were hanging on his words with eager intentness—for Rhoda, he saw, identified herself with these efforts of Delphine, and with the sorrow and the joy they had caused her, as intensely as if her own hand had made every stroke on the canvases. 'But you must learn ; you must study and work systematically, so as to cultivate your strong points and strengthen your weak ones.'

The light faded from Delphine's eyes. Her lips quivered.

'It is impossible,' said she quietly. 'When one has no money one must learn to do without these things.'

'But that will never do. It must be compassed somehow,' he said, again taking up the view of Danesdale Castle, with the cloudy sky, which had so pleased him. 'Let me——'

'Oh, *here* you are! I have been searching for you all over the house,' exclaimed a voice—the voice of Judith—breaking in upon their eager absorption in their subject.

She looked in upon them, and beheld the group: Delphine sitting on the floor, holding up a huge, battered-looking portfolio, from which she had been taking her drawings; Rhoda standing behind her, alternately looking into the portfolio and listening earnestly to Randulf's words; the latter, seated on one of the rickety chairs before alluded to, and holding in his hand the view of Danesdale Castle.

'I could not imagine where you were,' continued Judith, a look of gravity, and even of care and anxiety, on her face.

'Well, come in and speak to us, unless you think we are very bad,' retorted Rhoda. 'Come and join the dance, so to speak. We are looking over Delphine's drawings, and Mr. Danesdale says they are very good.'

'Of course they are,' said Judith, coming in with still the same subdued expression. 'I am quite well, I thank you' (to Randulf, who had risen and greeted her); 'I hope you, too, are well. But, my dear children, you must come downstairs at once.'

'To see mother?' said Rhoda. 'Oh, I'll go; and I'll entertain her till you are ready to come down. Stay where you are. Del has not shown Mr. Danesdale all.'

'To see mother—yes,' said Judith, striving to speak cheerfully. Delphine saw that the cheerfulness was forced, and became all attention at once.

'Of course you must come down and see mother at once,' proceeded Judith. 'But you have to see Mr. Aglionby too. He asked mother to present him to you, and she consented, so he has come with us. Therefore don't delay: let us get it over. And I am sure Mr. Danesdale will excuse——'

'Mr. Danesdale understands perfectly, and will carry himself off at once,' said Randulf, smiling good-naturedly.

'Wants to be introduced to us!' repeated Rhoda wonderingly. 'Of all the odd parts of this very odd affair, *that* to my mind is the oddest. Why should he want to be introduced to us? What can he possibly want with our acquaintance?'

'Oh, don't be silly!' said Judith, a little impatiently.

'But I am very cross. I wanted Mr. Danesdale to see Delphine's "morbid views." She has some lovely morbid views, you know. Delphine, just find that one of a girl drowned in a pond, and three hares sitting looking at her.'

'I shall hope to see that another time,' observed Randulf; 'it sounds delightfully morbid.'

Delphine had begun to put her pictures away, and her face had not yet lost the grieved expression it had taken when she had said she could not afford to have any lessons. Rhoda, mumbling rebelliously, had gone out of the room, and Judith had followed her, advising or rebuking in a lower tone. Thus Randulf and Delphine were left alone, with her portfolio between them, he still holding the drawing of the Castle. Delphine stretched out her hand for it.

'Don't think me too rapacious,' said he, looking at her, 'but—give me this one!'

'Why?'

'Because I want it for a purpose, and it would be a great favour. At least I should look upon it as such.'

'Should you? Pray, is that any reason why I should accord it to you?'

'Make it a reason,' said he persuasively. 'I should prize it—you don't know how much.'

'As I say,' said Delphine, still rebelliously, 'that constitutes no reason for my giving it to you.'

'If I take it——'

'That would be stealing the goods and chattels of one who is already very poor,' said Delphine, half-gaily, half-sadly.

'And who is so noble in her poverty that she makes it

noble too,' he suddenly and fervently said, looking at her with all his heart in his eyes.

She shook her head, unable to speak, but at last said hesitatingly :

'I do not know whether I ought—whether it is quite—quite——'

'In other words, you rather mistrust me,' said he gently. 'I beg you will not do so. I want to help you, if you will not disdain my help. Since you will have the bald truth, and the reason why I want your sketches, I have two reasons. The first is, that I should prize them exceedingly for their own sakes and for that of the giver ; next, if you would trust me and my discretion, I will engage that they should bring you profit.'

'Do you mean,' said Delphine, with a quick glance at him, and a flushing face, 'that I could earn some money, and—and—help them ?'

'That is what I mean.'

'You mean,' she persisted rather proudly, 'that to oblige you, some friend would buy them, and——'

'Good heavens ! do you know me no better than to suppose that I would sell what you had given me ! What a cruel thing to say !'

'I beg your pardon !' she murmured hastily, and overcome with confusion ; 'but—but—I do not see how——'

'You can paint others as good as these,' he said, unable to resist smiling at her simplicity. 'When these have been seen and admired——'

'But you must not tell who did them—oh, you must not do that !'

'Again I implore you to' trust my discretion and my honour.'

'I feel afraid—I dare say it is very silly,' she said.

'It is very natural, but it is needless,' he answered, thinking at the same time that it was very sweet, very bewitching, and that he was supremely fortunate to be the confidant of this secret.

'And you would not be ashamed—you do not think that a woman—a lady—is any the worse if she has to work hard?' she began tremulously.

'All honest work is good; and when it is undertaken from certain motives, it is more than good, it is sacred. Yours would be sacred. And besides,' he added, in a lower, deeper tone, 'nothing that your hands touched could be anything but beautiful, and pure, and worthy of honour.'

Her face was downcast; her eyes filled with a rush of tears; her fingers fluttered nervously about the petals of the flower that was stuck in her belt. She was unused to praise of this kind, utterly a stranger to compliments of any kind, from men; overwhelmed with the discovery that some one had found something in her to admire, to reverence.

'When you are a well-known artist,' he added, in a rather lighter tone, 'with more commissions and more money and fame than you know what to do with, do not quite forget me.'

'If ever—if ever I do anything—as you seem to think I may—it will all be owing to you.'

This assurance, with the wavering look, the hesitating voice with which it was made, was unutterably sweet to Randulf.

'Then I may keep the sketch?' he said

'Yes, please,' said Delphine.

He rolled them both up, and they went downstairs to the hall, where they found the two other girls waiting for them.

Randulf made his adieux, saying he hoped he might call again, and ask how Mrs. Conisbrough was. Then he went away, and Judith led the way into the parlour.

*　　*　　*　　*　　*　　*

Aglionby, left alone with Mrs. Conisbrough, while Judith went to call her sisters, sat in the recess of the window which looked into the street, and waited for what appeared to him a very long time, until at last he heard steps coming down-stairs and voices in the hall. He had a quick and sensitive ear, and besides that, Randulf's tones, with their southern accent and their indolent drawl, were sufficiently remarkable in that land of rough burr and Yorkshire broadness. So then, argued Bernard within himself, this young fellow was admitted as an intimate guest into the house which he was not allowed to enter, despite his cousinship, despite his earnest pleadings, despite his almost passionate desire to do what was right and just towards these his kinswomen. He had told Judith that he would comply with her behest. He was going to keep at the distance she required him to maintain—after this one interview, that is. But he felt that the price he paid was a hard and a long one. His joy in his in-heritance was robbed of all its brightness. He sat and waited, while Mrs. Conisbrough leaned back and fanned her-self, and observed :

'Why, that is Randulf Danesdale's voice. He is always here. Where can they have been ?'

Mrs. Conisbrough, as may already have been made ap-parent, was not a wise woman, nor a circumspect one. Perhaps she wished to show Aglionby that they had people of position amongst their friends. Perhaps she wished to flourish the fact before him, that Sir Gabriel Danesdale's only son and heir was a great ally of her daughters. Be that as it may, her words had the effect of putting Bernard into a state of almost feverish vexation and mortification. It did appear most hard, most galling, and most inexplicable that against his name alone, of all others, *tabu* should be writ so large. He saw Randulf go down the steps, with a smile on his handsome face, and a little white roll in his hand, and saw him take his way up the market-place, towards the inn where he had left his horse, and then the door of the parlour was opened, and his ' cousins' came in.

There were greetings and introductions. He found two lovely girls, either of them more actually beautiful than her who was his oldest acquaintance. Beside their pronounced and almost startling beauty, her grave and pensive dignity and statuesque handsomeness looked cold, no doubt ; but he had seen the fiery heart that burnt beneath that outward calm.

He was much enchanted with the beauty of these two younger girls ; he understood the charm of Delphine's shadowy, sylph-like loveliness ; of Rhoda's upright figure, handsome features, and dauntless grey eyes. He talked to them. They kept strictly to commonplaces ; no dangerous topics were even mentioned. Aglionby, when they were all seated, and talking thus smoothly and conventionally, still felt in every fibre the potent spell exercised over his spirit by *one* present. Judith sat almost silent, and he did not speak to her—for some reason he felt unable to do so.

All the time he was talking to the others, he felt intensely conscious that soon he must leave the house—for ever, ran the fiat—and in it he must leave behind him—what? Without his knowing it, the obstacle which prevented his answering that question, even to himself, was that viewless but real fact—Miss Vane.

By-and-by, he rose ; for to stay would have been needless, and, indeed, intrusive under the circumstances. He shook hands with Mrs. Conisbrough, expressing his hope that she would soon be, as he bluntly put it, 'all right again.' He might not say, like Randulf Danesdale, that he would call again in a few days, and inquire after her. Then, with each of the girls, a handshake—with Judith last. When it came to that point, and her fingers were within his hand, it was as if a spell were lifted, and the touch thrilled him through from head to foot, through brain and heart and soul, and every inch of flesh ; electrically, potently, and as it never had done—as no touch ever had done before. He looked at her; whether his look compelled an answering one from her—whether she would have looked in any case, who shall say? Only, she did look, and then Bernard knew, despite her composed countenance and steady hand and eye—he knew that it was not he only who was thrilled.

'Good-afternoon, Miss Conisbrough,' and 'Good-afternoon, Mr. Aglionby,' sounded delightfully original, and pregnant with meaning. Not another word was uttered by either. He dropped her hand, and turned away, and could have laughed aloud in the bitterness of his heart.

'I'll open the door for you, Mr. Aglionby,' came Rhoda's ringing voice; and, defying ceremony, she skipped before him into the hall.

'We've only one retainer,' she pursued, 'and she is generally doing those things which she ought not to be doing, when she is wanted. Is that Bluebell you have in the brougham? Yes! Hey, old girl! Bluebell, Bluebell!'

She patted the mare's neck, who tossed her head, and in her own way laughed with joy at the greeting. With a decidedly friendly nod to Aglionby, she ran into the house again, and the carriage drove away.

'Well?' cried Miss Rhoda, rushing into the parlour, panting.

Judith was not there. Doubtless she had gone to prepare that cup of tea for which Mrs. Conisbrough pined.

'Well?' retorted Delphine.

'I like him,' chanted Rhoda, whirling round the room. 'He's grave and dark, and fearfully majestic, like a Spaniard; but he smiles like an Englishman; and looks at you like a person with a clear conscience. That's a good combination, I say; but, all the same, I wish Uncle Aglionby had not been so fascinated with him as to leave him *all* his money.'

To which aspiration no one made any reply.

16

CHAPTER XXII.

AN OLD WIFE'S TALE.

THE evening at Yoresett House passed with its usual monotonous quietness. Mrs. Conisbrough, weary, and dejected
too, now that she was at home again—now that Aglionby
had gone away, without saying one word of coming again,
without holding out a single hope that he would deal gene-
rously, or, as it seemed to her, even justly, by her and
hers—went to bed early, hoping to find rest and forgetful-
ness. She took a stronger dose than usual of her calming
mixture, and was soon asleep. Rhoda was not long in
following her example. The two elder girls were left alone.
They chatted in a desultory manner, with long pauses, about
all the trivial events which had happened during Judith's
absence. If there were anything remarkable about their
conversation it was, that neither Bernard Aglionby's name,
nor that of Randulf Danesdale, was so much as mentioned.
By degrees their voices ceased entirely ; silence had fallen
upon them for some time before they at last went to their
bedrooms. How different the feelings which caused or
prompted this silence in the one girl and the other ! Delphine's silence was the cloak which hid a happiness tremu-
lous but not uncertain. Looking round her horizon she
beheld a most brilliant star of the morning rising clear,
bright, and prepared to run a long course. She was content
to be silent, and contemplate it.

With Judith it was otherwise. She felt the depression
under which she had lately suffered, but which had been
somewhat dissipated by the strong excitement of the events
which had taken place at Scar Foot. She felt this depression rush over her again with irresistible force, sweeping
her as it were from her feet, submerging her beneath its dark
and melancholy wave. Turn which way she would, she

could see nothing but darkness in her prospects—in the prospects of them all. Hitherto she had fought against this depression; had despised herself for feeling it; and, since her uncle's will had left them penniless, tried to console herself with the reflection that she was no worse off than before, but rather a little better, for that now she might justly go to her mother and claim as a right to be allowed to seek work. To-night she did not feel that consolation; she thought of Bernard Aglionby's eyes, and of the touch of his hand as he had said, 'Good-afternoon, Miss Conisbrough,' and the thought, the recollection, made her throw down her work and pant as if she felt suffocated and longed for fresh air.

By-and-by she went to bed, and, more wearied than she had known she was, soon fell asleep, and had one of those blessed dreams which descend upon our slumbers sometimes when care is blackest and life is hardest, when our weirds, that we have to dree out, look intolerable to us in our weariness and grief. It was a long, rambling, confused dream, incoherent, but happy. When she awoke from it, she could recall no particular incident in it; she did but experience a feeling of happiness and lightness of heart, as if the sun had suddenly burst forth through dark clouds, which she had long been hoping vainly would disperse. And vaguely connected with this happier feeling, the shadow, as it were, the eidolon, or image, of Bernard Aglionby, dim recollections of Shennamere, of moonlight, of words spoken, and then of a long, dreamful silence which supervened.

She lay half-awake, trying, scarce consciously, to thread together these scattered beads of thought, of fancy, and of hope. Then by degrees she remembered where she was, and the truth of it all. But cheered and undaunted still, she rose from her bed, and dressed, and went downstairs, ready to face her day with a steadfast mien.

The morning seemed to pass more quickly and cheerfully

16—2

than usual. Judith was employed in some household work ; that is, her hands were so employed ; her head was busy with schemes of launching herself upon the world—of work, in short. She was reflecting upon the best means of finding something to do, which should give her enough money to let her learn how to do something more. Never before had the prospect seemed so near and so almost within her grasp.

In the afternoon Delphine shut herself up in her den, to paint, and to brood, no doubt, she too, over the future, and its golden possibilities. For, when we are nineteen, the future is so huge, and its hugeness is so cheerful and sunny. Rhoda, inspired with youthful energy, was seen to put on an old and rough-looking pair of gloves, and on being questioned, said she was going to do up the garden. Thus Judith and Mrs. Conisbrough were left alone in the parlour, and Judith offered to read to her mother. The proposal was accepted. Judith had read for some time of the fortunes and misfortunes attending the careers of Darcy Latimer and Alan Fairfax, when, looking up, she saw that her mother was asleep. She laid the book down, and before taking up her work, contemplated the figure and countenance of the sleeping woman. That figure, shapely even now, had once been, as Judith had again and again heard, one of the tallest, straightest, most winsome figures in all Danesdale. Her mother's suitors and admirers had been numerous, if not all eligible, and that countenance, now shrunken, with the anxiously corrugated brow, and the mouth drawn down in lines of care, discontent, and disappointment, had been the face of a beauty. How often had she not heard the words from old servants and old acquaintance, 'Eh, bairn, but your mother was a bonny woman !'

'Poor mother !' murmured Judith, looking at her, with her elbow on her knee, and her chin in her hand ; 'yours has been a sad hard life, after all. I should like to make it gladder for you, and I can and will do so, even without

Uncle Aglionby's money, if you will only wait, and have patience, and trust me to walk alone.'

Then her thoughts flew like lightning to Scar Foot, to Shennamere, to the days from the Saturday to the Wednesday, which she had just passed there, and which had opened out for her such a new world.

Thus she had sat for some little time in silence, and over all the house there was a stillness which was almost intense, when the handle of the door was softly turned, and looking up, Judith beheld their servant Louisa looking in, and evidently wishful to speak with her. She held up her hand, with a warning gesture, looking at her mother ; and then rising, went out of the room, closing the door behind her as softly as it had been opened.

' What is it, Louisa ?'

' Please, Miss Conisbrough, it's an old woman called Martha Paley, and she asked to see the mistress.'

' Mrs. Paley—oh, I know her. I'll go to her, Louisa, and if you have done your work, you can go upstairs and get dressed, while I talk to her, for she will not sit anywhere but in the kitchen.'

Louisa willingly took her way upstairs, and the young lady went into the kitchen.

' Well, Martha, and where do you come from ?' she inquired. ' It is long since we saw you.'

It was a very aged, decent-looking woman, who had seated herself in the rocking-chair at one side of the hearth. Martha Paley had been in old John Aglionby's service years ago. When old age incapacitated her, and after her old man's death, she had yielded to the urgent wishes of a son and his wife, living at Bradford, and had taken up her abode with them. Occasionally she revisited her old haunts in the Dale, the scenes of her youth and matronhood, and Judith conjectured that she must be on such a visit now.

' Ay, a long time it is, my dear,' said the old woman ; she

was a native of Swaledale, and spoke in a dialect so broad, as certainly to be unintelligible to all save those who, like Judith Conisbrough, knew and loved its every idiom, and accordingly, in mercy to the reader, her vernacular is translated : ' I have been staying at John Heseltine's at the Ridgeway farm, nigh to th' Hawes.'

' Ah then, that is why you have not been to see us before, I suppose, as it is a good distance away. But now you are here, Martha, you will take off your bonnet, and stay tea ?'

' I cannot, my bairn, thank you. John's son Edmund has driven me here, so far, in his gig, and he is bound to do some errands in the town, and then to drive me to Leyburn, where my son will meet me and take me home next day.'

' I see. And how are you ? You look pretty well.'

' I'm very well indeed, God be thanked, for such an old, old woman as I am. I have reason to be content. But your mother, bairn—how's your mother ?'

' She has been ill, I am very sorry to say, and she is sleeping now. I daren't awaken her, Martha, or I would; but her heart is weak, you know, and we are always afraid to startle her or give her a shock.'

' Ay, ay ! Well, you'll perhaps do as well as her. I've had something a deal on my mind, ever since Sunday, when I heard of the old Squire's death, and his will. I reckon that would be a shock to you.'

' It was,' replied Judith briefly.

' Ay, indeed ! And it's quite true that he has left his money to his grandson ?'

' Quite true.'

' Judith, my bairn, that was not right.'

' I suppose my uncle thought he had a right to do what he chose with his own, Martha.'

' In a way, he might have, but not after what he'd said to your mother. People have rights, but there's duties too, my dear—duties, and there's honesty and truth. His duty was to deal fairly by those he had encouraged to trust in him, and he died with a lie in his mouth when he led your mother to expect his money, and then left it away. But there's the Scripture, and it's the strongest of all,' she went on, somewhat incoherently, as it seemed to Judith, while she raised her withered hand with a gesture which had in it something almost imposing; 'and *it* says, " for unto him that hath shall be given, and from him that hath not shall be taken away even that which he hath." '

'It is a very true Scripture, Martha, I think—so true that it will scarcely do for us to set ourselves against it in this case. The will is a valid one. Have you seen young Mr. Aglionby?'

'Nay,' she answered, with some vigour; 'when I heard o' what had happened, I couldn't bear to go near the place. And it's the first time I've been in th' Dale without visiting Scar Foot, the bonny place—" Fair Scar Foot " the verses call it.'

'I think that is a pity. You would have found Mr. Aglionby very kind, and most anxious to do all that is right and just.'

'I think, for sure, he ought to be. Why not? It's easy to be just when you have lands and money all round, just as it is hard for an empty sack to stand upright . . . He must be terrible rich, my bairn—that young man.'

'He is as rich as my uncle was, I suppose. He was not rich before; he was very poor—as poor as we are.'

Old Mrs. Paley shook her head, and said decidedly :

'That can't be, honey ! For when his father—poor Ralph—died, his mother's rich relations promised to adopt him ; and they were to look after him, and see that he wanted for nothing. So that with money from them, and the old Squire's money too, he must be a very rich man.'

Such, but more rudely expressed, was old Martha's argument.

Judith felt a wave of sickly dread and terror sweep over her heart. It made her feel cold and faint. This rumour confronted her everywhere, this tale without a word of truth in it. Aglionby's words had been explicit enough. On his mother's side he had no rich relations ; never had possessed even a rich connection. Yet her own impressions, strong, though she knew not whence they were derived ; her own mother's words about ' Bernarda ' and what Bernarda had said (words spoken as she awoke from her fainting fit) ; and now old Martha Paley—on all sides there seemed to be an impression—nay, more, a conviction that he had been adopted by these mythical rich relations. Who had at first originated that report ? Whence had it sprung ? She knew, though she had not owned it to herself—she knew, though she had called herself all manner of ill-names for daring even to guess such a thing. It was because she knew that she had refused Aglionby's overtures.

For a moment or two, cowardice was nearly gaining the victory. Mrs. Paley was an old, feeble woman ; Judith could easily turn her thoughts upon another track ; the worst need never be stated. But another feeling stronger than this shrinking from the truth urged her to learn it, and she said :

' Indeed ; and how do you know this, Martha ?'

' How do I know it, bairn ? Why, from your own mother's lips, as who else should I know it from ? Ay, and she cried and sobbed, she did so, when she brought the news. You know, it was like in this way that it happened. When Ralph got married, and for long before, I was housekeeper at Scar Foot. I well remember it all, and the old Squire's fury, and the names he called the woman who had married his son ; " a low, penniless jade," he called her, ay, and worse than that. He always meant Ralph to have your mother, you know. She was ever a favourite with him. Whether that would have come to anything in any case, I don't know ; for whatever she might have done, Ralph said much and more, that he wouldn't wed her. He went off to London, and married his wife there. The news came, and the Squire was furious. How he raged ! He soon forbade Ralph the house, and cut off his allowance, and refused to see him or hear of him. Two or three years passed ; your mother was married and lived in this house, which had been her mother's before her. I think the old Squire's conscience began to prick, for he got uneasy about his son, and at last would have sent for him, I believe ; but while he was making up his mind Ralph died, and then it was too late. For a time it fairly knocked the old man down. Then he came round, and began to think that he would like to have the boy, and he even made up his mind to make some sort of terms with the wife so as to get the boy into his own care, and "bring him up an Aglionby, and not a vagabond," as he said. It was a great descent for his pride, Miss Judith. He took counsel with your mother, and sent her to Irkford, where Mrs. Ralph lived—that great big town, you know. I've never been there, but they do say that it's wonderful for size and for dirt. He sent her there to see the mother and try to persuade her to let him have the child for the best part of the year, and she was to have it for the rest ; and it was to be brought up like a gentleman, and sent to college, and then it was to have all his money when he died, same as if its father had never crossed him.

' Your mother—she was not a widow then, you know, nor for many a year after—she was away about three days. When she came back she came alone. The old Squire was as white as a sheet with expectation and excitement. I was by at the time, and I saw and heard it all. He said, " Where's the boy?" in a very quiet, strange kind of voice. "Oh, uncle," your mother said, "she's an awful woman—she's like a tigress." Then she cried and sobbed, and said it had been too much for her nerves ; it had nearly killed her. And she told him how Mrs. Ralph had got into a fury, and said she would never be parted for a day from her child, and that she spurned his offer.

'The old Squire said, with his grim little laugh, that perhaps when she was starving, she would not be so ready to spurn. "Oh, she won't starve," your mother said ; "she has plenty of rich relations, and that is partly what makes her so independent. Ralph has left her the child's sole guardian. She scorns and spurns us, and I believe she would like to see us humbled in the dust before her." Then the old Squire let his hatred loose against his son's wife. With his terrible look that he could put on at times, he sat down beside your mother (she was flung on a sofa, you know, half-fainting), and he bade her tell him all about it. He questioned and she answered, and she was trembling like a leaf all the time. He bade me stay where I was, as witness. And at last, when he had heard it all out, he swore a fearful oath, and took heaven and us to witness, that from henceforth, as long as he lived, he would have nothing to do with his grandchild. It might starve, he said, or die, or rot, or anything its mother chose, for aught he cared—*he* had done with it for ever. It was terrible to hear him. And from that day, none of us dared name the child to him. He spent a deal of his time at Yoresett House, with your mother. I heard him many a time tell her, she and hers were all the children he had. And after your father died, he went on purpose to tell her not to be uneasy, but to leave him to do things his own way, and that you children should thrust that brat out of Scar Foot at last. And now he goes and leaves it all his money. Eh, my bairn—that was very wrong.'

Judith, when she answered, spoke, and indeed felt, quite calm : the very hugeness of the effort she had to make, in order to speak at all, kept her calm and quiet. She had never even conceived of anything like the dreadful shame she felt as she said :

'It is a terrible story, Martha. It is very well that you told it to me instead of to my mother, for she is not strong enough to bear having it raked up again. Have you'— her voice almost died away upon her lips—'have you related it to anyone else?'

'Nay, not I! I thought I'd just see Mistress Conisbrough, and ask her if there was nothing to be done. If she was to speak to some lawyer, some clever man—and some of them *is* so clever, you know—happen he might be able to set aside the will.'

'That is what she thought of at first,' said Judith, strenuously keeping her mind fixed upon the subject; battling hard to keep in restraint the sickly fear at her heart lest any of the unsuspecting ones around them should by chance come in and interrupt the interview. 'But Mr. Whaley told her it would not be of the very slightest use. And—and— Martha, I think you are very fond of us all, are you not?'

She came near to the old woman, and knelt beside her, with her hands clasped upon her knee, and she looked up into Martha's face.

'Ay, my bairn, I am so.' She passed her withered hand over Judith's glossy brown braids. 'I am so fond of ye all that I cannot abide to see ye cast out by a usurper.'

'Then if you really care for us, please, Martha, say nothing more to anyone about this, will you? I will tell you why. We have reason to think that Mr. Aglionby's relations were not really so rich as—as was represented; or if they were, they must have changed their minds about adopting him, for he was *very* poor, really, when his grandfather found him. And as it would not be of the least use to dispute the will, we want to keep it all quiet, don't you see? and to make no disturbance about it. Will you promise, Martha?'

'Ay, if you'll promise that if ever I could be of use by telling all about it, as I've told it to you now, that you'll send for me, eh, bairn?'

'Oh, I promise that—yes.'

'Then I promise you what you want. It's none such a pleasant thing that one should want to be raking it up at every turn, to all one's friends and neighbours.'

Judith felt her heart grow cold and faint at the images conjured up by these words of the old woman, who went on, after a pause, during which her thoughts seemed to dwell upon the past, 'Do you know him, my bairn, this young man?'

'Yes,' replied Judith, a flood of colour rushing tumultuously over her pale face. The question was sudden ; the emotion was, for the moment, uncontrollable. Her clear eyes, which had been fixed on old Martha's face, wavered, sank.

Though Mrs. Paley was a withered old woman of eighty, she could read a certain language on a human face as glibly as any young maid of eighteen.

'You do? There's another reason for my holding my tongue. You say he's considerate, and wishful to do right. Is he reasonable, or is he one of them that have eyes, but see not ? If he *has* eyes, he will want never to lose sight of you again. If you and he were to wed—eh, what a grand way of making all straight, and healing all enmities, and a way after the Lord's own heart, too !'

A little shudder ran through Judith. She did not tell old Martha that Aglionby was already engaged ; or Mrs. Paley's indignation would perhaps have loosed her tongue, in other quarters than this, and Judith wished, above all things, and at almost any price, to secure her silence. She knew now that had Bernard been free as air ; had he loved her and her alone, and told her so, and wooed her with all the ardour of which he was capable—after what she had just now heard she would have to say him nay, cost her what it might ; a spoiled life, a broken heart, or what you will.

She rose from her knees, smiled a chilly little attempt at a smile, and said :

' I'm afraid you're a match-maker, Martha.' And then, to her unspeakable relief, she heard the sound of wheels. It was John Heseltine's son Edmund with the gig, coming to fetch Martha away.

The old woman did not ask to see the other girls. The story she had been telling had sent her thoughts wandering back to old times ; she had forgotten Judith's sisters, who were to her things of yesterday. When she departed, Judith shook her withered old hand ; promised to deliver her messages to her mother, led her to the door ; saw her seated in the gig and driven off, sure that she would keep the promise she had given. And thus old Martha Paley disappears from these pages.

Judith returned to the house, and stood in the hall a moment or two, then mechanically took her way upstairs, along the passage, to her own bedroom. She sat down, and folding her hands upon her knee, she began to think. Painfully, shrinkingly, but laboriously, she went in her mind over every detail of this horrible story. She felt a vague kind of hope that perhaps, if it all came to be compared and sifted, the particulars might be found incongruous ; she might be unable to make them agree with one another, and so have a pretext for rejecting it. But as she conned over each one, she found that they fitted together only too well— both her own vague, almost formless suspicions, and the tangible facts which explained them.

Her great-uncle had had an interview with his grandson ; she exactly understood how, talking to Bernard about what he supposed to be his true position, he had been enlightened, and that with a shock. He must have restrained his wrath so far as not to reveal to Aglionby what he had discovered ; he had, as he thought, had pity upon her mother and her mother's daughters. She remembered their journey home from Irkford, and how her uncle's strangely absent and un-genial manner had struck her and chilled her. Then, while she and her sisters were out, on the following morning, he had visited her mother. She could form no idea of what had passed at that interview; it must have been a painful one, for her mother had not mentioned it, but had been left shaken and ill by it. Next, Judith's own interview with her uncle; his extraordinary reception of her; his fury, unaccountable to her at the time, but which was now only too comprehensible; his sinister accusations of herself and her mother, as being leagued together in some plot—some scheme to fleece and hoodwink him; *now* she could interpret this fiery writing on the wall, clearly enough. Her return home; the storm; the apparition of Mr. Whaley driving through it and the night, towards Scar Foot; the hastily executed will; the miserable scene when its contents were made known; her mother's sudden fear and cowering down before Aglionby; her broken words on recovering consciousness—that repetition of the lie told twenty years before, and more. Those words had first aroused her suspicion, her vague fear that all was not so clear and straightforward as it should be.

Now came old Martha, like a finger of some inspired interpreter, pointing out the meaning of each strange occurrence, throwing a flood of light over all, by her grim story of an old man's imperious will thwarted—of a young man's obstinate weakness; of a woman's yielding to temptation, and telling lies for gain. Each detail now seemed to dovetail with hideous accuracy into its neighbour, until the naked truth, the damnable and crushing whole, seemed to start up and stand before her, stark and threatening.

She feebly tried to ignore, or to escape from the inferences which came crowding into her mind—tried piteously not to see the consequences of her mother's sin. That was useless; she had a clear understanding, and a natural turn for logic. Such qualities always come into play at crises, or in emergencies, and she could not escape from their power now. Sitting still, and outwardly composed, her eyes fixed musingly upon a particular spot in the pattern of a rug which was spread near her bedside—her brain was very active. It was as if her will were powerless and paralysed, while her heart was arraigned before her brain, which, with cold and pitiless accuracy, pointed out to that quivering criminal not all, but some portion of what was implied in this sin of her mother ; some of the results involved by it in the lives of herself, her children, and her victims.

As to Mrs. Conisbrough's original motives for such a course of action, Judith did not stop long to consider them. Probably it had occurred to her mother, during that far-back journey to Irkford, that a great deal of power had been intrusted to her, that she did not see why she was to have all the trouble, and Mrs. Ralph Aglionby and her boy all the benefits of this tiresome and troublesome negotiation. Then (according to Judith's knowledge of her mother's character) she had toyed and dallied with the idea, instead of strangling it ere it was fully born. It had grown as such ideas do grow, after the first horror they inspire has faded —'like Titan infants'—and Mrs. Conisbrough had not the nature which can struggle with Titans and overcome them. Judith surmised that her mother had probably gone on telling herself that, of course, she was going to be honest, until the moment came for deciding : she must have so represented her uncle's message to Bernarda, as to rouse her indignation, and cause her indignantly to refuse his overtures. Then she had probably reflected that, after all, it could soon be made right ; she would be the peacemaker, and so lay them both under obligations to her. And then the time had come to be honest ; to confront the old Squire and tell him that she had not been quite successful with Ralph's widow, but that a little explanation would soon make matters right. No doubt she intended to do it, but she did the very reverse, and those sobs, and tears, and tremblings, of which old Martha had spoken, testified to the intense nervous strain she had gone through, and to the violent reaction which had set in when at last the die had been irrevocably cast.

Her lie had been believed implicitly. The wrong path had been made delightfully smooth and easy for her; the right one had been filled with obstacles, and made rough and rugged.

Something like this might, or might not, have been the sequence of the steps in which her mother had fallen. Judith did not consider that; what took possession of her mind was the fact that her mother, who passed for a woman whose heart was stronger than her judgment, a woman with a gentle disposition, hating to give pain—that such a character could act as she had acted towards Bernarda and her boy. It seemed to Judith that what her mother had done had been much the same as if one had met a child in a narrow path, had pushed it aside, and marched onwards, not looking behind, but leaving the child, either to recover its footing, if lucky, or, if not, to fall over the precipice and linger in torture at the bottom, till death should be kind enough to release it.

'We should say that the person was an inhuman monster who did that,' she reflected. 'Yet she knew that if Mrs. Ralph Aglionby's health gave way, if she were incapacitated for work, or work failed, she must starve or go to the workhouse, and the child with her. I cannot see that she was less inhuman than the other person would have been. . . . She has always appeared tranquil; the only thing that troubled her was an occasional fear lest Uncle Aglionby should not leave his property exactly as she desired. Was she tranquil because she knew Mrs. Aglionby to be in decent circumstances? or was it because she knew that she was safe from discovery, and that whatever happened to *them*, she was secure of the money?'

Judith's face was haggard as she arrived at this point in the chain of her mental argument. It would not do to go into that question. She hastily turned aside from it, and began an attempt to unravel some of the intricacies which her discovery must cause in the future for her sisters and herself. She felt a grim pleasure in the knowledge that in the past they had gained nothing from their mother's sin. They had rather lost. In the future, how were they to demean themselves?'

'We can never marry,' she decided. 'As honest women, we can never let any man marry us without telling him the truth, and it is equally impossible for us deliberately to expose our mother's shame. That is decided, and nothing in the heavens above or the earth beneath can ever alter that. We can work, I suppose, and try to hide our heads ; make ourselves as obscure as possible. That is the only way. And we can live, and wait, and die at last, and there will be an end of us, and a good thing too.'

She pondered for a long time upon this prospect; tried to look it in the face. 'Je veux regarder mon destin en face,' she might have said with Maxime, 'the poor young man,' 'pour lui ôter son air de spectre.' And by dint of courage she partially succeeded, even in that dark hour. She succeeded in convincing herself that she could meet her lot, and battle with it hand to hand. She did more ; she conjured up a dream in which she saw how joy might be extracted from this woe—not that it ever would be—but she could picture circumstances under which it might be. For example, she reflected :

'They say there is a silver lining to every cloud. I know what would line my cloud with silver—if I could ever do Bernard Aglionby some marvellous and unheard-of service ; procure him some wonderful good which should make the happiness of his whole life, and then, when he felt that he owed everything to me, if I could go on my knees to him, and tell him all ; see him smile, and hear him say, " It is forgiven," then I could live or die, and be happy, whichever I had to do.'

A calm and beautiful smile had broken over the fixed melancholy of her countenance. It faded away again as she thought, ' And that is just what I shall never be allowed to do. Does he not say himself that there is no forgiveness; for every sin the punishment must be borne. And I must bear mine.'

The dusk had fallen, the air was cold with the autumnal coldness of October. Judith, after deciding that she might keep her secret to herself for to-night, went downstairs to meet her mother and sisters with what cheer she might.

CHAPTER XXIII.

AGLIONBY'S DÉBUT.

AGLIONBY, casting one last look after Rhoda's figure as it disappeared, turned his horse's head, and drove homewards, dreamily. Not a fortnight—not one short fourteen days had elapsed since he had been summoned hither— and how much had taken place since ! He could not have believed, had anyone told him earlier, that he had so much flexibility in his character as to be susceptible of undergoing the change which certainly had taken place in him during that short time. In looking back upon his Irkford life, it appeared like an existence which he had led, say ten years ago, and from which he was for ever severed. The men and women who had moved and lived in it, trooped by, in his mind, like figures in a dream ; so much so, indeed, that he presently dismissed them as one does dismiss a recollected dream from his head, and his thoughts reverted to the present; went back to the parlour at

Yoresett House, to Mrs. Conisbrough's figure reclining in her easy-chair, and to the figures of his three 'cousins.' All over again, and keenly as ever, he felt the pain and mortification he had experienced from Judith's fiat as to their future terms.

'By George !' he muttered, 'I wonder I ever submitted to it ! I can't understand it—only she can subdue me with a look, when anyone else would only rouse me to more determined opposition.'

Arrived at Scar Foot, he entered the house, and in the hall found more cards on the table, of neighbouring gentry who had called upon him. He picked them up, and read them, and smiled a smile such as in his former days of bitterness had often crossed his face. Throwing himself into an easy-chair, he lighted his pipe, and gave himself up to reflection.

'I must decide on something,' he thought. 'In fairness to Lizzie, I must decide. Am I going to live here, or am I not ! I should think the question was rather, " *Can* I ? *will* Lizzie ?" Of course I must keep the house on here ; but I know Lizzie would not be happy to live here. Two houses ? one here and one at Irkford? How would that do ? Whether Lizzie liked it or not, I could always fly here for refuge, when I wanted to dream and be quiet. I could come here alone, and fish—and when I was tired of that, I might go to Irkford, and help a little in political affairs. Perhaps some day I might catch . . . my cousin Judith . . . in a softer mood, and get her to hear reason.'

He looked around the darkening room, and started. There was the soft rustle of a dress—a footfall—a hand on the door—his eyes strained eagerly towards it. Judith always used to come down in the twilight. She enters. It is Mrs. Aveson, come to inquire at what time he would like to dine. He gives her the required information, and sinks discontentedly back into his chair.

'The fact is,' he mentally resumed, 'I am dazed with my new position; I don't know what I want and what I don't want. I must have some advice, and that from the only person whose advice I ever listened to. I must write to Aunt Margaret.'

(Aunt Margaret was his mother's sister, Mrs. Bryce, a widow.)

'I believe,' he then began to think, 'that if I did what was best—what was right, and my duty—I should set things in train for having this old place freshened up. I wonder what Judith would say to that—she has never known it other than it is now—and then I should go to Irkford, tell Lizzie what I'd done; ask her to choose a house there, and to fix the wedding, and I should get it all over as soon as possible, and settle down . . . and that is exactly what I don't want to do . . . I wish I knew some one to whom I could tell what I thought about my cousins; some one who could answer my questions about them. I feel so in the dark about them. I cannot imagine Judith asking things she was not warranted in asking—and yet, blindly to submit to her in such an important matter——'

He spent a dreary evening, debating, wondering, and considering—did nothing that had about it even the appearance of decisiveness, except to write Mrs. Bryce, and ask her to sacrifice herself and come into the country, to give him her company and her counsel, 'both of which I sorely need,' wrote this young man with the character for being very decided and quick in his resolutions. As to other things, he could make up his mind to nothing, and arrived at no satisfactory conclusion. He went to bed feeling very much out of temper, and he too dreamed a dream, in which reality and fantasy were strangely mingled. He seemed to see himself in the Irkford theatre, with 'Diplomacy' being played. He was in the lower circle, in evening dress, and thought to himself, with a grim little smile, how easily one adapted one's self to changed circumstances. Beside him a figure was seated. He had a vague idea that it was a woman's figure—his mother's—and he turned eagerly towards it. But no! It was his grandfather, who was glaring angrily towards a certain point in the upper circle, and Bernard also directed his glance towards that point, and saw, seated side by side, his friend Percy Golding and Lizzie Vane. They looked jeeringly towards him, and he, for some reason, or for none—like most dream reasons—felt a sudden fury and a sudden fear seize him. He strove to rise, but could not. His fear and his anger were growing to a climax, and they at last seemed to overpower him, when he saw Mrs. Conisbrough suddenly appear behind Percy and Lizzie, laughing malignantly. It then seemed to him that in the midst of his fury he glanced from her face towards a large clock, which he was not in the least surprised to see was fixed in the very middle of the dress circle.

'Ten minutes past ten,' so he read the fingers: and his terror increased, as he thought to himself, 'Impossible! It must be much later!' And he turned to the figure of his grandfather by his side, perfectly conscious though he was that it was a phantom.

'Shall I go to them?' he inquired.

'Yes,' replied the apparition.

'But the time!' continued Aglionby frantically, and again looked towards the clock.

'Ten minutes to two,' he read it this time, and thought, 'Of course! a much more appropriate time!'

And turning once more to the phantom, he put the question to it solemnly,

'*Shall I go to them?*'

'N—no,' was the reluctant response. With that it seemed as if the horror reached its climax, and came crashing down upon him, and with a struggle, in the midst of which he heard the mocking laughter of Lizzie, Percy, and Mrs. Conisbrough, he awoke, in a cold perspiration.

The moon was shining into the room, with a clear, cold light. Aglionby, shuddering faintly, drew his watch from under his pillow, and glanced at it. The fingers pointed to ten minutes before two.

' Bah ! a nightmare !' he muttered, shaking himself together again, and, turning over, he tried once more to sleep, but in vain. The dream and its disagreeable impression remained with him in spite of all his efforts to shake them off. The figure which, he felt, had been wanting to convert it from a horror into a pleasant vision, was that of Judith Conisbrough. But after all, he was glad her shape had not intruded into such an insane phantasmagoria.

The following afternoon he drove over to Danesdale Castle, to return the call of Sir Gabriel and his son. It was the first time he had penetrated to that part of the Dale, and he was struck anew with the exceeding beauty of the country, with the noble forms of the hills, and, above all, with the impressive aspect of Danesdale Castle itself.

There was an old Danesdale Castle—a grim, half-ruined pile, standing ' four-square to the four winds of heaven,' with a tower at each corner. It was a landmark and a beacon for miles around, standing as it did on a rise, and proudly looking across the Dale. It was famous in historical associations ; it had been the prison of a captive queen, whose chamber window, high up in the third story, commanded a broad view of lovely lowland country, wild moors, bare-backed fells. Many a weary hour must she have spent there, looking hopelessly across those desolate hills, and envying the wild birds which had liberty to fly across them. All that was over now, and changed. ' Castle Danesdale,' as it was called, was nearly a ruin ; a portion of it was inhabited by some of Sir Gabriel's tenantry ; a big room in it was used for a ball for the said tenantry in winter.

The Danesdales had built themselves a fine commodious mansion of red brick, in Queen Anne's time, in a noble park nearer the river, and there they now lived in great state and comfort, and allowed the four winds of heaven to battle noisily and wuther wearily around the ragged towers of the house of their fathers.

Aglionby found that Sir Gabriel was at home, and, as he entered, Randulf crossed the hall, saw him, and his languid face lighted with a smile of satisfaction.

'Well met!' said he, shaking his hand. 'Come into the drawing-room, and I'll introduce you to my sister. Tell Sir Gabriel,' he added to the servant, and Aglionby followed him.

' For your pleasure or displeasure, I may inform you that you have been a constant subject of conversation at my sister's kettledrums for the last week,' Randulf found time to say to him, as they approached the drawing-room; 'and as there is one of those ceremonials in full swing at the present moment, I would not be you.'

' You don't speak in a way calculated to add to my natural ease and grace of manner,' murmured Bernard, with a somewhat sardonic smile, a gleam of mirth in his eyes. Sooth to say, he had very vague notions as to what a kettledrum might be; and he certainly was not prepared for the spectacle which greeted him, of some seven or eight ladies, young, old, and middle-aged, seated about the room, with Miss Danesdale dispensing tea at a table in the window-recess.

An animated conversation was going on—so animated that Randulf and Aglionby, coming in by a door behind the company, were not immediately perceived except by one or two persons. But by the time that Mr. Danesdale had piloted his victim to the side of the tea-table, every tongue was silent, and every eye was fixed upon them. They stood it well—Bernard, because of his utter unconsciousness of the sensation his advent had created amongst the ladies of the neighbourhood; Randulf, because he was naturally at ease in the presence of women, and also because he did know all about Aglionby and his importance, and was well aware that he had been eagerly speculated about, and that more than one matron then present had silently marked him down, even in advance, in her book of 'eligibles.' Therefore it was with a feeling of deep gratification, and in a louder voice than usual, that he introduced Aglionby to his sister.

Bernard, whose observing faculties were intensely keen, if his range of observation in social matters was limited, had become aware of the hush which had fallen like a holy calm upon the assembled multitude. He bowed to Miss Danesdale, and stood by her side, sustaining the inspection with which he was favoured, with a dark, sombre indifference which was really admirable.

The mothers thought, 'He is quiet and reserved; anything might be made of him, with that figure and that self-possession.' The daughters who were young thought, 'What a delightfully handsome fellow! So dark! Such shoulders, and such eyes!' The daughters who were older thought how very satisfactory to find he was a man whom one could take up and even be intimate with, without feeling as if one ought to apologise to one's friends about him, and explain how he came to visit with them.

Miss Danesdale said something to Aglionby in so low a tone that he had to stoop his head, and say he begged her pardon.

'Will you not sit there?' She pointed to a chair close to herself, which he took. 'Randulf, does papa know Mr. Aglionby is here?'

'I sent to tell him,' replied Randulf, who was making the circuit of the dowagers and the beauties present, and saying something that either was or sounded as if it were meant to be agreeable to each in turn.

'Of course he plants himself down beside Mrs. Malleson,' thought Miss Danesdale, drawing herself up, in some annoyance, 'when any other woman in the room was entitled to a greater share of his attention. . . . Did you drive or ride from Scar Foot, Mr. Aglionby ?'

'I drove ; I don't ride—yet.'

'Don't ride !' echoed Miss Danesdale, surprised almost into animation. 'How very . . . don't you like it ?'

'As I never had the chance of trying, I can hardly tell you,' replied Aglionby, with much *sang froid*, as he realised that to these ladies a man who did not ride, and hunt, and fish, and shoot, and stalk deer, and play croquet and tennis, was doubtless as strange a phenomenon as a man who was not some kind of a clerk or office man would be to Lizzie Vane.

'Were there no horses where you lived ?' suggested a very pretty girl who sat opposite to him, under the wing of a massive and stately mamma, who started visibly on hearing her child thus audaciously uplift her voice to a man and a stranger.

'Certainly there were,' he replied, repressing the malevolent little smile which rose to his lips, and speaking with elaborately grave politeness, 'for those who had money to keep them and leisure to ride them. I had neither until the other day.'

'I beg your pardon, I'm sure,' said the young lady, blushing crimson, and more disconcerted (as is almost universally the case) at having extracted from anyone a confession, even . retrospective, of poverty, than if she had been receiving an offer from a peer of the realm.

'Pray do not mention it. No tea, thank you,' to Philippa, who, anxious to divert the conversation from what she concluded must be to their guest so painful a topic, had just proffered him a cup.

'And do you like Scar Foot ?' she said, in her almost inaudible voice ; to which Bernard replied, in his very distinct one :

'Yes, I do, exceedingly !'

' But you have hardly had time to decide yet,' said the girl who had already addressed him.

Various motives prompted her persistency. First and foremost was the consideration that as in any case she would have a homily on the subject of forwardness, and 'bad form,' she would do her best to deserve it. Next, she was displeased (like Miss Danesdale) to see Randulf seat himself beside Mrs. Malleson, as if very well satisfied, to the neglect of her fair self, and resolved to fly at what was after all, just now, higher game.

' Have I not ? As how ?' he inquired, and all the ladies inwardly registered the remark that Mr. Aglionby was very different from Randulf Danesdale, and indeed from most of their gentleman acquaintances.

They were not quite sure yet, whether they liked or disliked the keen, direct glance of his eyes, straight into those of his interlocutor, and the somewhat curt and imperious tone in which he spoke. But he was, they were all quite sure, the coming man of that part of the world. He must be trotted out, and had at balls, and treated kindly at dinner-parties, and have the prettiest girls allotted to him as his partners at those banquets, and married to one of the said pretty girls—sometime. His presence would make the winter season, with its hunt and county balls, its dinners and theatricals, far more exciting. Pleasing illusions, destined in a few minutes to receive a fatal blow.

' Why, you can hardly have felt it your own yet. We heard you had visitors—two ladies,' said the lovely Miss Askam, from which remark Aglionby learnt several things ; amongst others, that young ladies of position could be very rude sometimes, and could display want of taste as glaring as if they had been born *bourgeoisie.*

'So I have. Mrs. and Miss Conisbrough were my guests until yesterday, when, I am sorry to say, they left me,' he answered.

He thought he detected a shade of mockery in the young lady's smile and tone, which mockery, on that topic, he would not endure ; and he looked at her with such keen eyes, such straight brows, and such compressed lips, that the youthful beauty, unaccustomed to such treatment, blushed again—twice in the same afternoon, as one of her good-natured friends remarked.

Philippa came to the rescue by murmuring that she hoped Mrs. Conisbrough was better.

'Yes, thank you. I believe she is nearly well now.'

'Do you know all the Misses Conisbrough?' pursued Miss Danesdale, equally anxious with Miss Askam to learn something of the terms on which Aglionby stood with those he had dispossessed, but flattering herself that she approached the subject with more *finesse* and delicacy.

Aglionby felt much as if mosquitoes were drinking his blood, so averse was he to speak on this topic with all these strangers. He looked very dignified and very forbidding indeed, as he replied coldly :

'I was introduced to them yesterday, so I suppose I may say I do.'

'They are great friends of Randulf's,' said Miss Danesdale, exasperated, as she saw by a side-glance that her brother was still paying devoted attention to Mrs. Malleson. Also she knew the news would create much disturbance in the bosoms of those her sisters then assembled ; and, thirdly, she had an ancient dislike to the Misses Conisbrough for being poor, pretty, and in a station which made it impossible for her to ignore them.

'Are they?' said Aglionby simply ; 'then I am sure, from what I have seen of my cousins, that he is very fortunate to have such friends.'

'There I quite agree with you,' drawled Randulf, whom no one had imagined to be listening; 'and so does Mrs. Malleson. We've been talking about those ladies just now.'

A sensation of surprise was felt amongst the company. How was it that these Misses Conisbrough had somehow engrossed the conversation? It was stupid and unaccountable, except to Miss Askam, who wished she had never given those tiresome men the chance of talking about these girls.

But the severest blow had yet to come. When the nerves of those present had somewhat recovered from the shock of finding the Misses Conisbrough raised to such prominence in the conversation of their betters, Miss Danesdale said she hoped Bernard would soon come and dine with them. Was he staying at Scar Foot at present? All the matrons listened for the reply, having dinners of their own in view, or, if not dinners, some other form of entertainment.

'I hardly know,' was the reply. 'I shall have to go to Irkford soon, but I don't exactly know when.'

'Irkford! That dreadful, smoky place?' said Miss Askam. 'What possible attractions can such a place have for you, Mr. Aglionby?'

'Several. It is my native place, and all my friends live there, as well as my future wife, whom I am going to see. Perhaps those don't count as points of attraction with you?'

While the sensation caused by this announcement was still at its height, and while Randulf was malevolently commenting upon it, and explaining to Mrs. Malleson what pure joy it caused him, Sir Gabriel entered, creating a diversion, and covering Miss Askam's confusion, though not before she had exclaimed, with a *naïveté* born of great surprise:

'I did not know you were engaged!'

'That is very probable; indeed, I do not see how you possibly could have known it,' Bernard had just politely replied as Sir Gabriel made his appearance.

There was a general greeting. Then by degrees the ladies took their departure. Aglionby managed somehow to get himself introduced to Mrs. Malleson, whose name he had caught while Randulf spoke. Bernard said he had found Mr. Malleson's card yesterday, and hoped soon to return his call : he added, with a smile into which he could when, as now, he chose, infuse both sweetness and amiability, ' Miss Conisbrough told me to be sure to make a friend of you, if I could, so I hope you will not brand me as " impossible " before giving me a trial ;' at which Mrs. Malleson laughed, but said pleasantly enough that after such a touching appeal nothing could be impossible. Then she departed too, and Aglionby felt as if this little aside alone had been worth the drive to Danesdale Castle ten times over.

Sir Gabriel asked Aglionby to stay and dine with them, as he was. They were quite alone, and Philippa would certainly excuse his morning dress. He accepted, after a slight hesitation, for there was something about both Sir Gabriel and his son which Bernard felt to be congenial, unlike though they all three were to one another.

After Philippa had gone, and the wine had gone round once or twice, Sir Gabriel rose to join his daughter, with whom he always passed his evening ; and to do Philippa Danesdale justice, she looked upon her father as the best of men and the finest of gentlemen.

Her one love-romance had occurred just after her mother's death, when Randulf was yet a child, incapable of understanding or sympathising, and when her father was bowed down with woe. Philippa had given up her lover, and remained with her father ; who had not forgotten the circumstance, as some parents have a habit of forgetting such little sacrifices. Thus it came to pass that if ' the boy ' was the most tenderly loved, it was Philippa's word which was law at Danesdale Castle.

'Suppose we come to my room, and have a chat,' suggested Randulf.   'We can join the others later.'

Nothing loth, Aglionby followed him to a den which looked,
on the first view, more luxurious than it really was.   When
it came to be closely examined there was more simplicity
than splendour in it, more refinement than display.   In
after-days, when he had grown intimate as a loved brother
with both the room and its owner, Bernard said that one
resembled the other very closely.   Randulf's room was a
very fair reflex of Randulf's mind and tastes.   The books
were certainly numerous, and many of them costly.   There
were two or three good water-colours on the walls ; some
fine specimens of pottery, Persian, Chinese, and Japanese ;
one or two vases, real Greek antiques, of pure and exquisite
shape and design, gladdening the eye with their clean and
clear simplicity.   In one corner of the room there was an
easel with a portfolio standing on it, and two really comfortable lounging-chairs.

'The rest of the chairs,' said their owner, wheeling up
one for Bernard's accommodation, 'are uncomfortable.   I
took care of that, for I hold that, in a room like this, two
is company, more is none whatever; so I discourage a
plurality of visitors by means of straight backs and hard
seats.'

He handed a box of cigars to Aglionby, plunged himself
into the other chair, and stretched himself.   Somewhere in
the background there was a lamp, which, however, gave but
a dim light.

'Do you know,' said Randulf presently, 'I was in the
same condition as Miss Askam this afternoon.   I didn't
know you were engaged.'

Aglionby laughed.

'She seemed surprised.   I don't know why she should
have been.   I thought her somewhat impertinent, and I
don't see what my affairs could possibly be to her.'

'She is a precocious young woman—as I know to my cost. Of course your affairs were something to her, so long as you were rich and a bachelor. Surely you could understand that.'

'Good Lord!' was all Aglionby said, in a tone of surprised contempt.

'My affairs have been a good deal to her up to now,' continued Randulf tranquilly. 'I was amused to see how she dropped me, as if I had been red-hot shot, when you appeared on the scene and——'

'Don't expose her weaknesses—if she has such weaknesses as those,' said Bernard, laughing again.

'I won't. But she is very handsome—don't you think so?'

'Yes, very. Like a refined and civilized gipsy—I know some one who far surpasses her, though, in the same style.'

'Who is that?'

'The youngest Miss Conisbrough.'

'Yes, you are right. But is it allowable to ask the name of the lady you are engaged to?'

'Why not? Her name is Elizabeth Fermor Vane, and she lives at Irkford, as I mentioned before.'

'It will be a matter of much speculation, amongst those ladies whom you saw this afternoon, what Miss Vane is like.'

'Will it? How can the subject affect them?'

'Well, you see, you will be one of our leading men in the Dale, if you take that place amongst us that you ought to have—and the wife of a country gentleman is as important a person as himself, almost.'

Bernard paused, reflecting upon this. The matter had never struck him in that light before. Lizzie taking a leading part amongst the Danesdale ladies. Charming creature though she was, he somehow failed to realise her doing it. He could have more easily imagined even his little tormentor, Miss Askam, moving with ease in such a sphere. After a pause, he said, feeling impelled to confide to a certain extent in Randulf :

'I had not thought of that before, but of course you are right.   But I am very undecided as to what my future movements will be.   I do not in the least know how Miss Vane will like the idea of living here.   Before I can decide anything, she will have to come over and see the place.   I have asked my aunt, Mrs. Bryce, to come and see me, and I shall try to get Miss Vane to come here soon.   I think she should see the place in winter, so that she can know what she has to expect when it is at its worst.'

'Queer way of putting it,' murmured Randulf, thinking to himself, 'perhaps he wants to "scare" her away.   Why couldn't he have married one of the Conisbroughs and settled everything in that way?'

Bernard proceeded succinctly to explain how Lizzie had become engaged to him under the full conviction that he would always inhabit a town.

Randulf murmured assent, surveying his guest the while from under his half-closed lids, and remarking to himself that Aglionby seemed to speak in a very dry, business-like way of his engagement.

'Influence of Irkford, perhaps,' he thought. 'And yet, that fellow is capable of falling in love in something different from a business-like way, unless I'm much mistaken about him.'

The conversation grew by degrees more intimate and confidential.   The two young men succeeded in letting one another see that each had been favourably impressed with the other ; that they had liked one another well so far, and felt disposed to be friendly in the future.   They progressed so far, that at last Aglionby showed Randulf a likeness of Lizzie, after first almost upsetting his host's gravity by remarking, half to himself :

'If I have it with me.   I may have left it——'

'In your other coat-pocket,' put in Randulf, with imperturbable gravity, whereat they both laughed, and Bernard,
finding the little case containing his sweetheart's likeness (to
which he had not paid much attention lately), handed it to
Randulf, saying:

' Photographs never do give anything but a pale imitation,
you know, but the likenesses, as likenesses, are good. She
" takes well," as they say, and those were done lately.'

Randulf, with due respect, took the case in his hand, and
contemplated the two likenesses, one a profile, the other a
three-quarter face. In the former she had been taken with
a veil or scarf of thick black lace coquettishly twisted about
her throat and head ; the photograph was a good one, and
the face looked out from its dark setting, pure and clear, with
mouth half smiling, and eyelids a little drooping. In the
other, Miss Vane had given free scope to her love for fashion,
or what she was pleased to consider fashion. The hideous,
bushy excrescence of curls bulged over her forehead ; ropes
of false pearls were wound about her neck ; her dress was
composed of some fancy material of contrasting shades, the
most *outré* and unfitting possible to imagine for a black and
white picture. And in that, too, she was triumphantly pretty.

Randulf had asked to see the likeness : he was therefore
bound to say something about it. After a pause he remarked :

' She must be wonderfully pretty.'

' She is a great deal prettier than that,' replied Bernard
amiably, and Randulf, thanking him, returned the case to
him.

Now Randulf had a topic very near his heart too—a
topic which he thought he might be able to discuss with
Aglionby. The two young men had certainly drawn wonderfully near to each other during this short evening of conversation. The fact was, that each admired the other's
qualities. Aglionby's caustic abruptness ; his cool and

18

steady deportment, and his imperturbable dignity and self-possession, under his changed fortunes, pleased Randulf exceedingly. He liked a man who could face the extremes of fortune with unshaken nerve, carry himself proudly and independently through evil circumstances, and accept a brilliant change with calm nonchalance.

Randulf's *sang froid*, his unconventional manner, his independence of his luxurious surroundings, his innate hardiness and simplicity of character, pleased Aglionby. But Bernard's feelings towards Randulf were, it must be remembered, comparatively simple ; Randulf's sentiments towards Bernard were vaguer—he felt every disposition to like him thoroughly, and to make a friend of him ; but he had a doubt or two ; there were some points to be decided which he was not yet clear about. He said, after a pause :

' I was very cool to ask you to show me Miss Vane's likeness. I owe you something in return. Look at these !'

He rose, and opening the portfolio before spoken of, drew out two sketches, and bringing the lamp near, turned it up, and showed the pictures to Bernard.

' What do you think of those ?' he asked.

Aglionby looked at them.

' Why, this is Danesdale Castle, unmistakably ; and well done too, I should say, though I am no judge. It looks so spirited.'

' Now look at the other.'

It was Randulf and his dog. Aglionby, keenly sensible of the ridiculous, burst out laughing.

' That's splendid ! but you must be very amiably disposed towards the artist to take such a " take-off " good-naturedly.'

' Isn't it malicious ? Done by some one, don't you think, who must have seen all my weak points at a glance, and who knew how to make the most of them ?'

' Exactly,' said Bernard, much amused, and still more so to observe the pleased complacency with which Randulf spoke of a drawing which, without being a caricature, made him look so absurd. 'Is he a friend of yours—the artist ?' he asked.

'It was left to my discretion whether I told the name of the artist or not. You must promise that it goes no further.'

'Certainly.'

'They were drawn by Miss Delphine Conisbrough.'

Bernard started violently : his face flushed all over—he laid the drawings down, looking earnestly at Randulf.

'By Judith Conisbrough's sister ?' he asked.

'The same,' said Randulf, puffing away imperturbably, and thinking, 'It is just as I thought. That little piece of wax-work whose likeness I have seen, cannot blind him so that he doesn't know a noble woman when he meets her.' And he waited till Bernard said :

'You amaze me. There is surely very high talent in them : you ought to be a better judge than me Don't you think them very clever ?'

'I think them more than clever. They have the very highest promise in them. The only thing is, her talent wants cultivating.'

'She should have some lessons,' said Bernard eagerly.

'So I ventured to tell her, but she said——' he paused, and then went on, in a voice whose tenderness and regret he could not control, 'that they were too poor.'

He looked at Bernard.

'If he has any feeling on the subject,' he thought, 'that ought to fetch him.'

It 'fetched' Bernard in a manner which Randulf had hardly calculated upon. He started up from his chair, forgetting the strangeness of speaking openly on such a subject to so recent an acquaintance. He had been longing to speak to some one of the griefs connected with his cousins : this was too good an opportunity to be lost.

'Too poor !' he exclaimed, striding about the room.

'She told you that? Good God! will they never have punished me enough?'

The veins in his forehead started out. His perturbation was deep and intense. Randulf laid his cigar down, and asked softly :

'Punished you—how do you mean?'

'I mean with their resentment—their implacable enmity and contempt. To tell you that she was *too poor*—when——'

'It must have been true.'

'Of course it is true; but it is their own fault.'

'I don't understand'

'But I will explain. It is a mystery I cannot unravel. Perhaps you can help me.'

He told Randulf of his desire to be just, and how Judith had at first promised not to oppose his wishes. Then he went on :

'What has caused her to change her mind before I spoke to her again, I cannot imagine. I fear I am but a rough kind of fellow, but in approaching the subject with Miss Conisbrough, I used what delicacy I could. I told her that I should never enjoy a moment's pleasure in possessing that of which they were unjustly deprived—which I never shall. I reminded her of her promise: she flatly told me she recalled it. Well'—he stood before Randulf, and there were tones of passion in his voice—'I humbled myself before Miss Conisbrough, I entreated her to think again, to use her influence with her mother, to meet me half-way, and help me to repair the injustice. I was refused—with distress, it is true—but most unequivocally. Nor would she release me until I had promised not to urge the matter on Mrs. Conisbrough, who, I surmise, would be less stern about it. Miss Conisbrough is relentless and strong. She was not content with that. She not only had a horror of my money, but even of me, it appears. She made me promise not to seek them out, or visit them. By dint of hard pleading I was

allowed to accompany them home, and be formally introduced to her sisters—no more. That is to be the end of it.
I tell you, because I know you can understand it. For the
rest of the world I care nothing. People may call me
grasping and heartless, if they choose. They may picture
me enjoying my plunder, while Mrs. Conisbrough and her
daughters are wearing out their lives in—— Do you wonder
that I cannot bear to think of it?' he added passionately.

'No, I don't. It is the most extraordinary thing I ever
heard.'

'You think so? I am glad you agree with me. Tell me
—for I vow I am so bewildered by it all that I hardly know
whether I am in my senses or out of them—tell me if there
was anything strange in my proposal to share my inheritance
with them—anything unnatural?'

'The very reverse, I should say.'

'Or in my going to Miss Conisbrough about it, rather
than to her mother?'

'No, indeed!'

'It never struck me beforehand that I was contemplating
doing anything strange or wrong. Yet Miss Conisbrough
made me feel myself very wrong. She would have it so, and
I own that there is something about her, her nature and
character are so truly noble, that I could not but submit.
But I submit under protest.'

'I am glad you have told me,' said Randulf reflectively.
'Now all my doubts about you have vanished.'

'Could nothing be done through these drawings?' suggested Aglionby. 'Could you not tell Delphine that some
one had seen them who admired them exceedingly?'

'I see what you mean,' said Randulf, with a smile. 'She
has great schemes for working, and selling her pictures, and
helping them, and so on. But I have a better plan than
that. I must work my father round to it, and then I must
get her to see it. She shall work as much as she pleases

and have as many lessons as she likes—when she is my wife.'

Aglionby started again, flushing deeply. Randulf's words set his whole being into a fever.

' That is your plan ?' said he in a low voice.

' That is my plan, which no one but you knows. However long I have to wait, she shall be my wife.'

' I wish you good speed in your courtship, but I fear your success won't accomplish *my* wishes in the matter.'

' Miss Conisbrough must have some reason for the strange course she has taken,' said Randulf. ' Do you think we are justified in trying to discover that reason, or are we bound not to inquire into it ?'

There was a long pause. Then Aglionby said darkly :

' I have promised.'

' But I have not.'

Bernard shook his head.

' I don't believe, whatever it may be, that anyone but Miss Conisbrough is cognisant of it.'

' Well, let me use my good offices for you, if ever I have a chance. If ever I know them well enough to be taken into their confidence, I shall use my influence on your side— may I ?'

' You will earn my everlasting gratitude, if you do. And if it turns out that they do want help—that my cousin Delphine has to work for money—you will let me know. Remember,' he added jealously, ' it is my right and duty, as their kinsman, to see that they are not distressed.'

' Yes, I know, and I shall not forget you.'

Randulf, when his guest had gone, soliloquised silently :

' That fellow is heart and soul on my side. He doesn't know himself whither he is drifting. I'd like to take the odds with anyone, that he never marries that little dressed-up doll whose likeness he is now carrying about with him.'

CHAPTER XXIV.

'WINTER OF PALE MISFORTUNE.'

AT Yoresett House the winter promised to be a winter indeed ; a ' winter of pale misfortune.' For three days after her conversation with old Mrs. Paley, Judith had maintained silence, while her heart felt as if it were slowly breaking. She had revolved a thousand schemes in her mind. Strange and eerie thoughts had visited her in her desolation. She loved her two sisters with all the love of her intense and powerful nature. She cherished them, and always had done : she was capable of self-immolation for their sakes. But her reason, which was as strong as her heart (which combination made her what she was) told her that in this case self-immolation would be vain. Rhoda might be left unconscious and happy for the present, but Delphine must know the truth, and that soon. Immolation would be required from her also. Judith shuddered as she thought of it. When her younger sisters casually mentioned Randulf Danesdale's name, and laughed and jested with one another about him, Judith felt as if some one had suddenly dealt her a stab, or a blow, which took away her breath.

Was there no help ? she asked herself. Could this sacrifice by no means be avoided ? If *she* kept her lips for ever sealed, sacrificed her own future, let them go their way, and took upon herself never to leave and never to betray that mother who—she resolutely refused, even to herself, to call her mother's deed by any name, repeating, ' It was for our sakes, I suppose ; it was out of love for her children, as she thought.' Would not that do ? Were Delphine and Rhoda to bear the punishment for a sin which had been committed before they were born ?

More than once a gleam of hope crossed her spirit ; she

almost thought that her plan would answer.   Then came the
argument :

'No.   You must not allow this affair to go further.   You
must not allow one of *your* family to enter that of Sir Gabriel
Danesdale, whose unstained name and unsullied honour are
his pride and delight.   You would let your sister marry a
man—for you know he wishes to marry her—she all unconscious, as well as he, of what hung over her.   You might
resolve never to betray the secret, but you can never be perfectly certain that it will not leak out.   Some day Randulf
might discover the truth—and what might he not in his
bitterness do or say?   Besides, it would be wrong ; that is
all that concerns you.   Do not dally any longer with this
chimerical, wicked plan.'

She could see no other solution to the question.   She
closed her eyes—closed her heart, and hardened it against
the contemplation of that anguish which was to come ; and
after waiting three whole days, she went to Delphine on the
afternoon of the fourth, when the girl was upstairs with her
painting.   Rhoda was out.   Mrs. Conisbrough was taking
her afternoon rest.

Delphine turned a smiling face to her sister.   Of late, she
had bloomed out more lovely than ever.   Neither cold, nor
poverty, nor gloomy prospects had had the power to impair
her beauty and its development.   In her heart she carried a
secret joy which was life and light, hope and riches to her.
She was going to spend a very happy afternoon.   But
Judith's presence never disturbed her.   She called to her to
shut the door, because the wind was cold, and to come and
look at her picture, and her voice as she spoke rang clear as
a bell.

'Yes,' said Judith ; 'and I have something to say to you,
which it would not be well for anyone to overhear.'

She closed the door, and sat down.   She trembled and
felt faint : she could not stand.   It was one thing, and one

that was bad enough, to hear the horrid story from other
lips ; it was another—and a ghastly one—to have to tell it
with her own, to her innocent sister.   To speak to Delphine
about such things—to let her see them near—seemed to
Judith to be insulting her.   But it had to be done.   She
gathered up her courage in both hands, as it were, and
began.

The conversation was not a long one.   It was begun in
low tones, which grew ever fainter and more hesitating.
When Judith at last rose again from her chair and looked at
Delphine, the latter looked to her former self exactly what a
dead girl looks compared with one living—as a lily after a
thunderstorm has battered and shattered and laid it low, in
comparison with the same flower in the dewy calm of an
early summer morning.

The elder girl stood with her white lips, and her fixed
eyes, and constrained expression, looking upon the other,
waiting for her to utter some word.   But none came.
Delphine, her face blanched within its frame of waving
golden hair—her eyes fixed as if upon some point thousands
of miles away, to which something she loved had withdrawn
itself, was motionless and silent.

Judith at last stretched out her hands, and exclaimed :

' Delphine, if you do not speak, I shall go mad !   Give
me my due—give me the wretched consolation of hearing
you say that I could not have done otherwise.'

Delphine smiled slightly, and her gaze came abruptly to
earth again.   She saw her sister, and said softly :

' Poor Judith !   No.   You could have done nothing
else.   But you don't expect me to thank you for it, do you ?'

' Delphine !'

' You could have done nothing else.   But you see you
had nothing to lose.   I had all the world—all the world.'

She turned away.   Judith went out of the room, away to
her own chamber—seeing nothing, hearing nothing.   She

locked herself up, and, for the first time giving way, cast herself in an utter abandonment of anguish upon her bed, and buried her face in the pillow ; thinking that it would be good for her if she could never see the sun again. If Delphine had known—but she did not know—she never should know. But if she had known—if the story of her sister's heart for the last fortnight could have been laid bare before her—would she have turned away with a few cold words, as she had done—hugging her own grief—oblivious that others could have any?

No, no ! Judith swore to herself, with passionate fervour, her sweet sister could not have been so wrapped, so engrossed in herself. She should not know—it would only add poignancy to the anguish she was obliged to endure. The worst, surely, had been consummated ; but she did not dare to think of Delphine alone, upstairs.

The worst, morally considered, was perhaps over ; but there were trials yet to come, which were bad to bear. They heard, as in a tiny country-town everything is heard, of Aglionby's departure for Irkford. Then November set in, and the days became shorter, darker, and colder. Mrs. Conisbrough grew more and more fretful and feeble, and still talked sometimes of consulting some other lawyer, of disputing John Aglionby's will, and held forth on Bernard's greed and injustice in a manner which used to send Judith flying upstairs to pace about her room with every feeling in a state of the wildest tumult.

It was too cold for Delphine to pursue her work upstairs. The girls had nothing to do ; nothing on which to spend their energies. When the few domestic things were arranged they had the whole day before them, with absolutely no pressing occupation of any kind. The situation grew hideous and ghastly to Judith. She and her sisters preserved their physical health by means of the regular walks which, so long as it did not actually snow or rain, they took daily.

And Delphine had a fitful gaiety which oppressed her sister, while neither long walks, nor arduous work, nor anything else, put the faintest flush into Judith's cheek, nor called any spontaneous smile to her lips.

She took longer walks than her sisters, went out oftener alone; penetrated to wilder recesses, more desolate spots than they did. She was, in her stature and her strength, a daughter of the gods, and had always been able to tire out both her sisters, while she herself felt no trace of fatigue. She did not fear the strange and lonely hills; they had a weird fascination for her, and in this her trouble she was wont often to seek their silent company.

One afternoon, in a wilder and bitterer mood than usual, she had gone out, and walking fast and far, had found herself at last on the uppermost ridge of a wild mountain road. From where she stood, she could see on the one hand into Danesdale, her home—dear to her, despite what she had suffered there; on the other, into grim Swaledale—always dark and wild, but, in this winter weather, savage and desolate beyond description. Just below her, in the mountainside, were some ghastly holes in the limestone, of the kind known in Yorkshire as 'pots;' all were grim-looking apertures, but close to where Judith sat she saw the jaws of one of them yawning at her: it was the deepest of all—no one had ever succeeded in fathoming it. Both Rhoda and Delphine disliked this spot, which indeed had a bad name, as being dangerous to traverse after twilight, and haunted furthermore by a 'boggart,' who dwelt in this biggest and deepest limestone 'pot.' Judith had never feared the place. She sat there now, casting an occasional glance at the ugly hole, with its ragged jaws, and her thoughts gathered in darkness and bitterness.

She had been reading a book—a biography, one out of several volumes lately lent to her by Dr. Lowther. It was the Letters and Memoirs of a certain great lady, then not long dead. This great lady had been thrown from her earliest youth into the midst of the gay and busy world. She had lived at courts, and for many years her companions had been courtiers. Even that had been a busy life. Even its recital made Judith's heart throb with envy as she read of it ; but when the narrative went on to relate how this lady met a great statesman, politician, and party-leader, and married him, and how her house became a rendezvous for every kind of noted and illustrious man and woman, and how for the rest of her long career, not a day, scarce an hour, remained unoccupied ; how to the very last the game of politics, that most thrilling and best worth playing of all games, remained open to her, and she continued to be an influence in it—then it was that Judith felt her restless longings grow into a desire to *do*, so intense as to be almost torture. This afternoon, alone on the hill-top, she thought of it, and reflected.

'Some women have that—they have everything, and others have *nothing*. I do not want that. I should be thankful for a very little—for a few hours of daily work that must be done, but I cannot get it. It is not right—it is not just that anyone should be doomed to a life like mine. How am I different from others? I am as much like other women as Shylock, though a Jew, was like Christians. Yet I have to do without almost everything which other women of my condition have ; and I may not even work like women who are born to labour. This woman, whose life I have read, was a clever woman—a born woman of the world. I am not that, I know, but I have sense enough and more than enough to do some of the plain rough work of the world, and to do it well, if I had it. And I may not. I may sit here, and wish I were dead. I may take country walks, and save sixpences, and nourish my mind and soul with wool-work. Oh, what *are* women sent into the world for—women like me, that is ? Not even to " suckle fools and chronicle

small-beer" it seems, but to do nothing. To be born, to
vegetate through a term of years—to know that there is a
great living world somewhere outside your dungeon, and to
wish that you were in it. To eat your heart out in weariness ; to consume your youth in bitterness ; to grow sour
and envious, and old and wretched, to find all one's little
bit of enthusiasm gradually grow cold. To care only for
the warmth of the fire, and the creature-comforts that are
left—to linger on, growing more tired and more fretful, and
then to die. It is worse than that iron room which grew
every day narrower, till it closed upon its inmate and crushed
him to death—much worse, for that was over in a few weeks,
this may last fifty, sixty years. If this is to be my life, I
had better read no more. To live that life, and not go
mad, one wants an empty head, an ignorant mind, and a
contempt for all intelligence ; and I am, by some hideous
mistake, destitute of all those qualities.'

She smiled in bitter mockery of herself: she felt a kind
of grim contempt for herself. And she looked again towards
the mouth of the hole in the hillside.

She rose up, went up to it, and stood beside it. A head
that was not very steady must have reeled on looking down
into the silent blackness of the chasm, from whose subter-
ranean depths strangely tortured pillars of grey rock ascended,
clothed near the surface with the most exquisite mosses
and ferns, of that delicate beauty only found in limestone
growths. A few fronds of hart's-tongue fern were yet green ;
a few fairy tufts of the cobwebby *Cystopteris fragilis*, and
some little plumes of the black maidenhair spleenwort.

'You beautiful little fringes round a sepulchre !' thought
Judith. 'If I made a step down there, my grave would
receive me and hush me to sleep in its arms. No one would
ever know. I should rest quietly there ; and who could
have a finer tomb ?'

She looked around again at the wild fells ; still, grand,

and immovable. From her earliest childhood her imagination had always connected certain images with certain hills.
Addlebrough, down below there, at the other side of Danesdale, was like a blacking-brush in some way. Penhill was
smiling; it reminded her of sunny days and picnics. Great
Whernside, looming dim in the far distance, was like an old
bald head of a giant. Great Shunner Fell, at the head of
Swaledale, under one of whose mighty sides she even now
stood, had always put her in mind of secrets, of death,
storm, and darkness; perhaps because of the many tales
she had heard of the treacherous river which was one of
the streams springing from it. Turning again towards Danesdale, she saw a tiny corner of Shennamere, peeping out from
under the shoulder of a great hill. A faint ray of sunshine
touched it. Judith's face changed. Scar Foot was there—
and Bernard Aglionby.

'I'm sure his creed never told him to throw himself into
a hole when things went wrong with him,' she said to herself; and turning her back upon Shunner Fell and the ugly
'pot,' she walked swiftly homewards.

As she arrived at the door of her house a man in livery
rode up with a note. It was one of the Danesdale servants.

Judith took the note from him. He said he had been
told not to wait for an answer, and rode away. The note
was directed to Mrs. Conisbrough. Judith took it in and
gave it to her mother. She opened it, looked at it, and
said :

'It seems like a card of invitation. Read it, Rhoda; I
haven't my glasses here.'

Rhoda read out, in a loud and important voice :

'"Sir Gabriel and Miss Danesdale request the pleasure
of Mrs. and the Misses Conisbrough's company, on the
evening of Thursday, Dec. 31st. Dancing at 8.30.

'"R. S. V. P."

'How absurd to send such a thing !' remarked Rhoda, flicking it with her finger.   'It is that horrid, spiteful Philippa's doing.   I know she hates us, and she knows that none of you can go, so she adds insult to injury in that way.'

'Nonsense, Rhoda !' said Judith.   'She has simply done her duty in sending the invitation.   It is for us to take it or leave it ; and of course that means, leave it.'

'Of course,' echoed Delphine, whose face had flushed, and whose hand trembled so that her work suffered.

'I do wish,' observed Mrs. Conisbrough, in a voice of intense irritation, 'that I might be allowed to have *some* voice in the regulation of my own affairs.   I must say, you all forget yourselves strangely.   The invitation is addressed to me, and it is for me to say whether it shall be accepted or not.   I intend to go to the ball, and I intend you, Judith and Delphine, to go with me.'

'*Mother !*' broke from both the girls at once.

Mrs. Conisbrough's face was flushed.   There was the sanguine hue, the ominous look in her eyes, which, as Judith well knew, betokened very strong internal excitement, and which Dr. Lowther had repeatedly told her was 'bad, very bad.'   She felt it was dangerous to oppose her mother, yet she could not yield without a word, to what appeared to her in her consternation an idea little short of insane.   Accordingly, as Mrs. Conisbrough did not answer their first exclamation, Judith pursued gently, yet with determination :

'How can we possibly go ?'

'What is there to prevent your going ?' asked her mother, trifling nervously with her teaspoon, and with tightened lips and frowning brows.   'We are equal to any of those who will be there, and a great deal superior to *some.*'

'Yes, I know ; but the money, mother, in the first place. We can hardly present ourselves in spotted muslins, and I really do not know of any more elegant garments that we possess.'

She strove to speak jestingly, but there was a bitter earnest in her words.

'Pray leave that to me. I am not so utterly destitute as you seem to imagine. Of course you will require new dresses, and you will have them.'

This information was certainly something unexpected to the girls. Judith, however, advanced her last argument, one which she had been unwilling to use before.

'Mother,' she said, 'you know we—we are in mourning. Uncle Aglionby will not have been dead three months, and —and—everyone will talk.'

Mrs. Conisbrough's eyes flashed fire.

'It is for that very reason that I shall make a point of going,' she said. 'I recognise no claim on my respect in that man's memory. I consider the opportunity is a providential one. Half the county will be at the ball, and they shall know—they shall see for themselves, who it is that has been passed over, in order that an upstart clerk, or shopman, or something, may be raised into the place which ought to have been mine and yours.'

'*Mother!*' exclaimed Judith, in an accent of agony, while the other two girls sat still; Delphine pale again, her eyes fixed on the ground ; Rhoda looking from one to the other with a startled expression, this being the first she had known of any dispute between her mother and sisters.

'Be silent!' said Mrs. Conisbrough, turning upon Judith angrily ; 'and do not add to my troubles by opposing me in this unseemly manner. I intend you to go to the dance, and will hear no further complaints. Please to write to Miss Danesdale, accepting her invitation, and let it go to the post to-morrow. As for your dresses, there is time enough to think about them afterwards.'

Judith felt that there was no more to be said. She was silent, but her distress, as she thought of the coming ordeal, only augmented, until the prospect before her filled her with the most inordinate dread. In anticipation she saw the eyes of 'half the county' turned upon them as they entered, and upon Bernard Aglionby, who of course would be there too. It was exactly the kind of thing from which every fibre of her nature shrank away, in utter distaste which attained almost to horror. The whole exhibition would be useless. It would simply be to make themselves, their poverty and their disappointment, a laughing-stock for the prosperous and well-to-do people who had gossiped over them, and what had happened to them—who would, if they had had John Aglionby's money, have received them with open arms as old friends, just as they had already received Bernard as a new one.

And her mother? That was a terror in addition. She knew that Mrs. Conisbrough could not go through such an evening without strong agitation—agitation almost as violent as that which had made her ill at Scar Foot. Suppose any-thing of the kind happened at Danesdale Castle? The idea was too terrible. It made Judith feel faint in anticipation. But the more she thought of it, the less could she see her way out of it all. She scarcely dared speak to Delphine, who, however, said very little about it. Judith at last asked her almost timidly :

'What is to be done, Del? How are we to escape?'

'We cannot escape,' replied Delphine composedly. 'The only thing is to let mamma have her own way, and say nothing. The more we oppose her, the worse it will be for us.'

She would say no more. After all, thought Judith, it was only natural. She could not expect Delphine to expatiate upon her feelings in advance of the event.

Surely never before was preparation made for a ball by two young and beautiful girls with less lightness of heart. Every-thing about it was loathsome to Judith. Her heart rebelled when her mother informed her, shortly and decidedly, that

out of the small sum of money which she had at different
times saved, she intended to get them what she called
'proper and suitable dresses, such as no one could find any
fault with.'

To Judith's mind it was like throwing so much life-blood
away—not for its own sordid sake, but because of what it
represented. It would have gone a long way towards helping
them to remove from Yoresett, and that was now the goal to
which all her thoughts turned. But Mrs. Conisbrough was
not to be gainsaid. She ordered the dresses from a fashionable milliner in York, and they arrived about ten days before
the ball. The girls looked askance at the box containing the
finery. It might have held a bomb which would explode as
soon as it was opened. Mrs. Conisbrough desired them to
try their gowns on that night, that she might see how they
fitted, and judge of the effect. It was a scene at once
painful in the extreme, and yet dashed with a kind of cruel
pleasure. Mrs. Conisbrough had herself planned and ordered
exactly how the dresses were to be made, and she had a fine
natural taste in such matters.

Judith put on her garment without so much as looking at
herself in the glass, unheeding all Rhoda's enraptured ex-
clamations. Delphine, as her slender fingers arranged the
wreath of dewy leaves upon her corsage, felt her heart thrill
involuntarily, as she caught a glimpse of her own beauty, and
thought of what might have been and what was.

'Now, you are ready. Go down and let mamma see!'
cried Rhoda, who had been acting as Abigail, in an ecstasy.
'Oh, it may be very extravagant, Judith, but surely it is worth
paying something for, to be beautifully dressed and look
lovely, if only for one evening!'

They went into a bare, big dining-room, where there was
less furniture and more room to turn round than in the parlour
they usually inhabited. Rhoda lighted all the available lamps
and candles, and called to her mother, and Mrs. Conis-

brough came to look at her daughters in their ball-dresses, as a happier woman might have done.

Judith's was a long, perfectly plain amber silk, cut square behind and before, with sleeves slightly puffed at the shoulder, and with no trimming except a little fine old lace, with which Mrs. Conisbrough had supplied the milliner. It was a severely simple dress, and in its rich folds and perfect fit it showed off to perfection the beauty of the woman who wore it.

Judith Conisbrough could not help looking like a queen in this brave attire ; she could not help moving and glancing like a queen, and would always do so, in whatever garb she was attired, to whatever station of life she were reduced. She stood pale and perfectly still as her mother came in. She *could* not smile ; she could not look pleased, or expectant.

The mother caught her breath as her eyes fell upon her eldest girl, and then turned to Delphine, whose dress of silk and gauze was of the purest white, enfolding her like a cloud, and trimmed with knots and wreaths of white heather-bells and small ferns : one little tuft of them nestled low down in her hair.

Delphine looked, as Rhoda had once prophesied unto her that she would, 'a vision of beauty.' Her face was ever so little flushed, and in her golden eyes there was a light of suppressed excitement.

'Mother, mother ! aren't they *lovely?*' cried poor Rhoda, her buoyant paces subdued to a processional sedateness, as she circled slowly about the two radiantly-clad figures.

'Of course they are !' said Mrs. Conisbrough curtly, still biting her lip with repressed agitation, but criticising every frill and every flower with the eyes of a woman and a con noisseur. 'I defy any of the girls who will be there to sur- pass them—if they approach them.'

She continued to survey them for some little time, breathing quickly, while Judith still stood motionless, her eyes somewhat downcast, wondering wretchedly whether this horrible finery *must* be worn, if this dreadful ordeal was in no way to be avoided?

Raising her eyes, full of sadness, they met those of her mother. Did Mrs. Conisbrough read anything in them? She started suddenly, drew out her handkerchief, and put it to her eyes, exclaiming brokenly and passionately:

'Why cannot I have this pleasure, like other mothers? Surely I have a right to it?'

A spasm contracted Judith's heart. No—there was the rub. She had no right to it. It was all a phantom-show— all stolen; wrong, from beginning to end. Turning to Delphine, she said rather abruptly:

'Well, I'm going to take my gown off again. Will you come too?'

As they went towards their rooms she thought:

'It cannot be worse. I cannot feel more degraded and ashamed, even at the ball itself.'

During the days that passed between this 'dress rehearsal,' as Rhoda called it, and the ball, Mrs. Conisbrough's health and spirits drooped, but she still maintained her intention of going to Danesdale Castle. Judith said nothing—what could she say? And Delphine was as silent as herself. Once Randulf Danesdale had called. They had been out, and had missed him. Judith was thankful. They had seen nothing of Aglionby, of course. It was understood that he was away from home. It was quite certain that he was away at Christmas-time.

Three days before the ball came off, Mrs. Conisbrough was too ill to rise. Judith began to cherish a faint hope that perhaps after all they might be spared the ordeal. She was deceived. Her mother said to her:

'I want you to go to Mrs. Malleson, and tell her, with my love, that I feel far from well, and would rather not go to

the ball, if she will oblige me by chaperoning you and Del.
If she can't, I shall go if it kills me.'

'Mamma, won't you give it up?' said Judith imploringly.
'For my sake, grant me this favour, and I will never oppose
you again.'

'Certainly not,' said Mrs. Conisbrough angrily. 'Understand, Judith, that I have set my mind on your going to this
ball, and go you shall. Why are you thus set upon thwart-
ing all my plans for your benefit? How can a girl like you
presume to know better than her mother?'

'Don't cry, mother,' said Judith sorrowfully. 'I will go
to Mrs. Malleson this afternoon.'

She kept her word, and found her friend in.

'My dear Judith! What a pleasant surprise! Come to
the fire, and let us have a chat. How cold and starved you
look!'

Judith responded as well as she could to this friendliness,
and presently unfolded her errand, with burning cheeks, and
a brief explanation.

Mrs. Malleson professed herself delighted.

'There is nothing I should like better than to chaperon
you and Del. And you know, my dear, I think you take it
too much to heart; I do really. Would you deprive your poor
mother of all natural feelings—all pride in her handsome
daughters? If I were in her place, I should feel exactly
the same.'

Judith smiled faintly. Of course Mrs. Malleson did not
understand. How could she? She cheered the girl by her
chat; gave her tea, and talked about the ball, and the gossip
of the neighbourhood.

'It is to be a very brilliant affair. Sir Gabriel intends it
for a sort of celebration of his son's return home. It is the
first large party they will have had, you know, since Randulf
came back.'

'Yes, of course.'

'What a nice fellow he is! I do so like him.'

'Yes, so do we,' said Judith mechanically.

'Oh, and we have become quite friendly with Mr. Aglionby of Scar Foot.'

'Have you? And do you like him too?' asked Judith composedly.

'Very much. I couldn't say that to your mother, you know, but I can to you, because you are so good and so reasonable, Judith.'

'Oh, Mrs. Malleson, not at all! The merest simpleton must see that Mr. Bernard Aglionby is not responsible for my grand-uncle's caprice. So you like him? He has been at Irkford, I hear, visiting the lady he is engaged to.'

Judith spoke coolly and tranquilly, crushing out every spark of emotion as she proceeded.

'Yes. Of course he is going to be at the ball, and Miss Vane, his *fiancée*, is going to be there too.'

'Is she?' Judith still spoke with measured calmness. Inwardly she was thinking: 'It will be even worse than I expected. But I am glad I came here and got warned in time.'

'Yes. Mrs. Bryce, Mr. Aglionby's aunt, is staying at Scar Foot. I think he said he wanted her to live there till he was married—if she would. She is very nice. And he is bringing Miss Vane, just for this ball, and the Hunt Ball, on the 3rd of January—and in order that she may see the place, Mr. Aglionby says. He let me see her likeness. She must be wonderfully pretty.'

'Yes, I suppose so.'

'Not to compare with Delphine, though,' pursued Mrs. Malleson warmly. 'But then, there are not half a dozen girls in Yorkshire to compare with her. Oh, I quite long for the ball! I am sure Delphine will make a sensation; and so will you, if only you don't alarm all the men by your dignity, dear,' she added, putting her hand on Judith's shoulder. 'Girls don't go in for dignity now, you know, but for being frank and candid, and knowing everything, and talking with men on their own subjects.'

' I'm afraid Delphine and I will be failures then, for we know so few men, and certainly we do not know what their subjects are.'

' Oh, I didn't say that men liked it ; only that girls do it,' laughed Mrs. Malleson, leading Judith to the door. The latter felt that now their doom was sealed.

Mrs. Malleson would not be so kind as to be taken ill before the dance. She went home and told her mother of the arrangement she had made, and Mrs. Conisbrough professed herself satisfied with it.

CHAPTER XXV.

' A HAPPY NEW YEAR TO YOU.'

BERNARD AGLIONBY's frame of mind was not a happy one on that evening of the 31st of December ; it had been anything but cheerful all day ; it waxed drearier and drearier during his ten-mile drive to Danesdale Castle with his aunt, Mrs. Bryce, and Lizzie, his betrothed. He had brought Miss Vane from Irkford, and introduced her into the halls of his ancestors, and the presence of his mother's sister, last night. The result, he was obliged to own, had hardly been successful. Miss Vane had done little else but shiver since her arrival. She had failed to make a good impression on Mrs. Bryce, whose home was in London, and who had never met her before. She had treated Mrs. Aveson with a vulgar haughtiness, which had galled the feelings of the good woman beyond description. But she had been very amiable to Bernard, and had confided to him that she looked upon this ball as the turning point in her destiny. Perhaps it

was; it was not for him to gainsay it. His moodiness arose
from mental indecision. He had not got to the stage of
absolute confession, even to himself, that his engagement
was a failure. He would not confess it. Much less had he
allowed even the idea distinctly to shape itself in his mind,
that he was, to put it mildly, thinking with deep interest of
another woman. Yet the savage discontent and irritation
which he experienced were due, could he but have known
it, to these two very facts, that his engagement was a failure
and he was beginning to find it out, and that his thoughts,
whenever he allowed them free course, were engrossed with
another woman. He felt all the miserable unrest and irritation which accompanies mental transition periods, whether
they be of transition from good to bad, or from bad to
good.

Thus they were a silent party as they drove along the dark
roads. Lizzie was shrouded in her wraps, and was solicitous
about her dress, lest it should be crushed. Mrs. Bryce was
not a talkative woman. Bernard had never in his life felt
less inclined to speak—less inclined for a festivity of any
kind, for sociability in any shape.

At last they turned in at the great stone gateway at the
foot of the hill, rolled for half a mile up the broad, smooth
drive, and stopped under the large awning filled with servants, light, and bustle.

Poor Lizzie (whom I commiserate sincerely in this crisis
of her fate) felt, as she entered, as if she had crossed the
Rubicon. The fears which she had originally felt for herself
had in a great measure subsided. With the enduing of her
superfine ball-dress, and the consciousness of her triumphant
prettiness, all apprehensions for herself had vanished. With
such a frock and such a face one's behaviour would naturally
adapt itself to that of the very highest circles. All that was
needed was to be fine enough; and on that point she had a
proud consciousness she had never been known to fail.

She felt a little uneasiness about Bernard. She hoped he would tone down his brusque and abrupt manners. She remembered only too well the terrible solecisms of which he had often been guilty at suburban tea-parties, and his reckless disregard of semi-detached villa conventionalities, and a deep distrust of the probable demeanour of her betrothed took possession of her soul.

Bernard at last found himself with Lizzie on his arm, and Mrs. Bryce by his side, in the large drawing-room, approaching Miss Danesdale and Sir Gabriel.

Lizzie Vane's only experience of balls had been such as had taken place amongst intimate friends, the Miss Goldings and such as they, and partaken in by the mankind belonging to them. She had a confused idea, as she went up the room on her lover's arm, that this was in some way different from those past balls.

Bernard noticed that she grew very quiet, and even subdued. He could not know that her soul was gradually filling with dismay as she realised that her pink frock (pink was the colour selected by Lizzie for this her *début* in fashionable society), whether 'the correct thing,' as the Irkford milliner had assured her, or not, was certainly unique : and that she found the crowd of well-bred starers oppressive. Bernard performed the introductions necessary. Mrs. Bryce and Miss Danesdale had already exchanged calls. The latter cast one comprehensive glance over Miss Vane, then, taking the trouble to speak in a voice which could be heard, she expressed her regret that she had not been able to call upon her before the ball, because of her only having arrived so immediately before it ; she hoped to have the pleasure later.

'Oh yes !' murmured Miss Vane, to whom Miss Danesdale appeared a very formidable personage.

Then Bernard led up Randulf and introduced him. Randulf asked if he might have the second dance with her, and, consent having been given, put his name down and departed. Bernard's dancing powers were not of the most brilliant description, but he managed to convey his betrothed safely through the mazes of the first quadrille, and then led her back into the drawing-room. By this time the greater number of the expected guests had arrived, and Miss Vane was beginning to shake off her first timidity. Ambition began to assert itself in her bosom. She looked very pretty. Her face wore a delicate flush, and her blue eyes had grown more deeply blue ; at the end of the first dance everyone had seen her, and everyone who did not know her wanted to know who she was. All the women said, 'What a wonderful dress ! Do look at that pink frock ! Did you ever behold anything like it ?' All the men agreed about the frock (possibly for the sake of peace), but no outlandishly pink raiment could blind them to the charms of its wearer's face. Soon Lizzie was enjoying what was a veritable triumph for her. Her programme was full, to the last dance. Bernard's name was down for one other, a square, towards the end of the evening. He had told her not to refuse any dances on his account, ' because I am such a wretched hand at it, you know,' and she had fully acted up to his suggestion. Randulf took her to dance the second dance, a waltz, with him. After a short time Bernard, seeing that Mrs. Bryce had established friendly relations with a distinguished dowager, and was in full flow of conversation with her, left the drawing-room, and went to the ball-room. There he stopped for a short time, watching the dancers ; noting especially the pink dress and the fleet feet of its wearer. Then he found Philippa Danesdale standing near him, also looking on. (To the last day of his life he remembered every incident and detail of that evening, as if they had happened yesterday.)

'You do not dance, Mr. Aglionby ?' inquired Philippa.

'Very badly. I should not like to inflict myself as a partner on any of the ladies here.'

'Then will you give me your arm to the drawing-room? I just came to see that Randulf was doing his duty; but I know that my guests have not yet all arrived.'

Bernard gave her his arm, and they returned to the drawing-room. He remained by her side, conversing with her in the intervals of receiving her guests : by-and-by the music in the ballroom ceased. The drawing-room was at this time almost empty, and still he stood, his elbow resting on the mantelpiece, talking to Philippa, when the first couples began to come in from the dancing-room. Randulf Danesdale, with Lizzie, was the first to enter. Miss Vane was flushed; her hair had got a trifle disordered; she looked excited. She was now so far at her ease that she had begun to talk, and Randulf had been malign enough to draw her out a little. Her voice, with its unmistakably underbred and provincial accent, was heard upraised : on this vision Bernard's eye rested, till he suddenly awoke to the consciousness of his duties, and going forward, offered Miss Vane his arm.

'You're dreaming, Aglionby,' observed Randulf lightly.

'Am I? Very likely.'

'I can sympathise,' added young Danesdale, 'for so am I.'

'Of what, or of whom?' asked Aglionby, his more genial smile flitting across his face.

Randulf bent forward to him, having first ascertained that Miss Vane's attention was otherwise occupied, and said in a low voice :

'I'm dreaming of dancing with Delphine Conisbrough. She makes me wait long enough, does she not? The ball hasn't begun for me till——why, there they are!'

'With Del——' Aglionby had just ejaculated, electrified, for he had had no forewarning that any of the Conisbroughs were to be there. His glance followed Randulf's, and he had the sensation of starting violently. In reality he turned rather slowly and deliberately, and looked. His face changed. He bit his lips, and became a shade paler. Every pulse was beating wildly. He was in no state to ask himself what it meant. He watched, as if it had been some dissolving view, and saw how Miss Danesdale, with her prim little smile, and her neat little steps, and her unimpeachable etiquette, went forward a little, with outstretched hand, and greeted them. And while she spoke to Mrs. Malleson, Bernard's eyes looked clean over their heads, and met straightly those of Judith Conisbrough. Exactly the same sensation—only far more potent now—as that which had mastered him when he had taken leave of her at her mother's house, seized him—a strong, overwhelming thrill of delight and joy, such as no other being had ever awakened in him. And with it, yet more powerfully than before, he realised that not he alone experienced the sensation. He had the knowledge, intuitive, instinctive, triumphant, that she shared it to the full. He saw how, though she remained calm and composed, her bosom rose and fell with a long, deep inspiration; he saw her eyes change their expression—the shock first, the light that filled them afterwards, and—most eloquent, most intoxicating of all—their final sinking before his long gaze. He lived through a thousand changing phases of emotion while he stood still there, looking at her; he realised with passionate delight, that it was not only he who found her beautiful, but all others who had eyes to see. None could deny that she was beautiful : her outward form did but express her inner soul. A man behind him murmured to another, and Bernard heard him :

'Jove, what splendid-looking girls ! Who are they? Are they from your part of the country too?'

He watched while the two girls shook hands with Miss Danesdale. He saw Randulf go up to them and greet them, and how the first expression of pleasure which had crossed their faces appeared there. Randulf's dream was going to

be realised, Bernard reflected, with wild envy. He could
arrange things pretty much according to his own pleasure.
Delphine had kept him waiting, as he said ; so much the
oftener would he make her dance with him now that at last
she was there.

Then Aglionby became feebly conscious that his arm was
somewhat roughly jogged, and that a voice which he seemed
to have heard fifty years ago sounded in his ear.

' Bernard, are you dreaming ?   Here's a lady speaking to
you.'

With a veritable start this time he came to his senses, and
beheld Mrs. Malleson, in black tulle and *gloire de Dijon* roses,
holding out a hand to him, and smiling in friendly wise.

' Mrs. Malleson, I—— you are late, surely, are you not ?'

' We are, I believe, and I am afraid it is my fault.   I hope
the men are not all so deeply engaged that the Miss Conisbroughs will get no dances.'

Here some one came and said to Lizzie that he thought
it was their dance.   Nothing loth, she suffered herself to be
led away.

' That is Miss Vane, I know,' observed Mrs. Malleson.
' You must introduce her later.   She is wonderfully pretty.'

She was in her turn monopolised and led away. Aglionby
could not have replied had she remained.   If he had never
known, or never admitted the truth to himself until now,
at last it overwhelmed him.   Lizzie Vane beautiful ! Lizzie
Vane *beloved* by him !

It was like awakening from some ghastly dream, to be
confronted by a yet more horrible reality.   He mechanically
passed his hand over his eyes, and shivered.   When he
looked round again he saw that Judith was standing alone.
Philippa was receiving some very late guests.   Delphine
had been led away, so had Mrs. Malleson.   Several groups
were in the room, but both he and Judith were emphatically
alone—outside them all.   Presently he found himself by her

side—how should he not? There was no one else there, so far as he knew. On a desert is land even enemies become reconciled.

'I hope you have not quite forgotten me, Miss Conisbrough.'

His voice was low, and there was no smile on his face, any more than there was on hers. With both of them it was far too deadly earnest to permit of smiles or jests.

'It would imply an unpardonably short memory on my part, if I had,' she answered, very gravely, and looking more majestic than ever.

He felt her gloved hand within his, and for a blessed moment or two he forgot Lizzie Vane's very existence. With the actual touch of her hand, with the sound of her pathetic contralto voice, the spell rushed blindingly over him. How had he lived out these weeks since he parted from her? How had he been able to think it all over, as he had done again and again, calmly and without any particular emotion? In one of Torguéneff's novels he relates the story of a Russian peasant woman, whose only and adored son is suddenly killed. A visitor, calling a week or so later, finds the woman, to his surprise, calm, collected, and even cheerful. 'Laissez la,' observed the husband, 'elle est fossilée!' Now Bernard knew that was exactly what he had been—fossilised; unrealising what had happened to him. For him, as for that peasant woman, the day of awakening had dawned.

He allowed his eyes and his voice to tell Judith that in finding her to-night he had found that which he most desired to see. He allowed his eyes and his voice also to question her eyes and her voice, and in their very hesitation, in their reply, in their very trouble, their abashed quietness, he read the answer he wished for. She had not escaped unscathed from the ordeal which had been too much for him. Twice already to-night he had asked her this question,

and heard this answer—merely with look and tone—without
any word whatever, and he wanted to ask it again and again,
and to have her answer it as often as he asked it.   She was
standing, so was he.   That last long look was hardly over,
when he offered her his arm, and said :
  'You are not dancing ; come to the sofa and sit down.'
  She complied ; mechanically she sat down and he beside
her ; he put his arm over the back of the sofa ; she was
leaning back, and the lace ruffle of her dress just touched
his wrist, and the contact made his blood run faster.
  ' Mrs. Conisbrough is not with you ?' he inquired.
  ' No, she is not well.   She made a point of Delphine's
and my coming.'
  Bernard did not ask her for a dance.   He felt a sympathetic comprehension of her position.   He knew she would
have to dance, unless she wished to be remarkable, which
he was sure was no part of her scheme.   But he knew that
it would be against her will—that she would be more grateful to those who did not ask her than to those who did, and
he refrained.
  ' You said,' he went on, in the same low tone, ' that if we
met in society, we might meet as friends.   I have not troubled
you since you told me that, have I ?'
  Judith paused, and at last said constrainedly : ' No.'
  ' No.   Therefore I claim my reward now.   We are in
society to-night.   It is the time when we are allowed by
your own law to be on friendly terms, and I mean to take
advantage of the fact.   Will you grant me a favour ?   Will
you let me take you in to supper ?'
  Judith, in her simplicity and surprise, was quite bewildered, and felt distracted how to act.   Evidently he had
not given up, and did not intend to give up, any scrap of a
friendly or cousinly privilege which might be open to him.
If her secret in the background had been less terrible and
(to her) tragic, she would have been amused at Aglionby's

determination not to be set aside. As it was, she replied at last, gently :

' Don't you think there is another lady whom you ought rather to take in to supper ?'

He opened his eyes as if not understanding, then re-marked :

' Oh, you mean Miss Vane. Do not imagine that I am neglecting her. Her partner at the supper-table is already selected. She told me so herself. She is to dance an " extra," I think she called it, before supper, or after, I forget which—but with some man who is to take her in to that repast. Therefore, may I hope for the pleasure ? To " confound the politics " of the assembled multitude, if for no other reason,' he added. ' They are sure to look for signs of enmity between us, and I should like to disconcert them.'

' Very well, if you wish it,' said Judith gravely. ' And if I must go in to supper, as I suppose I must.'

' I'm afraid you have not looked forward with any enjoy-ment to this ball ?'

' *Enjoyment!*' echoed Judith drearily ; and added, half forgetting the terms she had herself laid down, ' Do not think it very strange that Delphine and I should be here. Mamma insisted, and we dared not thwart her. You do not know how unwilling we were, and how it has troubled us.'

' I know what it must feel like to you,' he said ; and was going to say more. He was going to say that though he knew what it had cost her, yet that he was not altogether sorry, since it had brought them together, and she would not allow any other kind of intercourse. But just at that moment Sir Gabriel, whom Judith had not yet spoken to, arrived upon the scene. Sir Gabriel had received an inkling of the truth from his son, who had had it from Mrs. Malle-son. Randulf had hastily confided it to Sir Gabriel :

' I wish you'd pay a little attention to the Miss Conis-

broughs, sir. They didn't want to come a bit—to meet
Aglionby, you know, and not three months since their
uncle's death ; but their mother made them, and they dared
not cross her—so if you wouldn't mind——'

The hint was more than enough for the warm-hearted old
gentleman. Despite his real liking for Aglionby, he had
never ceased to shake his head over the will, and to think
that Mrs. Conisbrough and those girls had been very badly
used. He had just had Delphine introduced to him in the
ballroom, and now he made his way to Judith.

' Miss Conisbrough, I'm delighted to see you here. I
have just been talking to your sister, who is the loveliest
creature I've seen for twenty years and more. I may say
that to you, you know. If she doesn't turn some heads to-
night, why, they are not the same kind of heads that used
to be on men's shoulders in my days.'

Judith's face flushed. She smiled a pleased yet nervous
smile. Yes, Delphine was all that the good old man called
her, and how delightful this sweet incense of justice, not
flattery, would have been—how grateful, if—if only ! She
crushed down a desire to laugh, or cry, she knew not which
—an hysteric feeling, and answered Sir Gabriel politely, but,
as he thought, a little indifferently. But, remembering his
son's words, he stood talking to her for some time, and
finally offered her his arm to take her to the ballroom
and dance a quadrille with her. Aglionby went with them
at the same time. So long as he did not exceed the bounds
of politeness, he told himself—so long as his outward
conduct could be denominated 'friendly'—he shook his
head back—he *would* not turn himself into a conventional
machine to say, ' How do you do ?' ' Good-evening,' and no
more.

As they entered the ballroom, they were confronted by
Miss Vane, more flushed now, more at her ease, and arm-in-
arm with a youth who had been introduced to her as Lord

Charles Startforth, and who would by his title alone have fulfilled, to her mind, every requisite necessary to the constitution of a 'real swell !' She saw Bernard, Sir Gabriel, and Judith enter, and at once inquired of her partner .

'Eh, I say, isn't that Sir Gabriel ?'

'That is Sir Gabriel,' replied the young gentleman, with *sang froid.* He had found Miss Vane and her provincialisms a source of the most exquisite entertainment.

'I thought so. And there's my beloved with him.'

'Your beloved—happy man ! Aglionby, I suppose you mean ?'

'Yes,' said Miss Vane, explaining. 'I call him " my beloved," you know, because " Bernard " is too familiar, when you're talking to strangers, and " Mr. Aglionby " sounds stiff, doesn't it ?'

'I quite agree with you. Your beloved's aspect, just at present, is somewhat gloomy.'

'My ! Yes ! He does look as cross as two sticks. But,' with sudden animation, 'I've seen that girl before, who's going to dance with Sir Gabriel. Who is she ?'

'She is Miss Conisbrough, of Yoresett.'

'Conisbrough—oh, of course ! One of those girls who wanted to have Bernard's money,' said Miss Vane, tossing her head. 'Well, just fancy ! only Miss Conisbrough ! From her dress, and Sir Gabriel's dancing with her, I thought she must be a *somebody.*'

'Miss Conisbrough doesn't go out much, I think,' said the young man, instinctively speaking with caution, and unable, for his own part, to resist looking with admiration at the lady in question. 'Your " beloved " seems to know her, though.'

While Lizzie was explaining, her partner advanced, and suggested to Sir Gabriel that he and Miss Vane would be happy to be their *vis-à-vis.* So it was arranged, and Bernard retired, after forcing a smile in answer to a coquettish nod from his betrothed. After this dance Judith found no lack of partners. She was forced to dance, and Aglionby saw her led off time after time, and congratulated himself on having secured her promise concerning supper.

As for Delphine, she had not been in the drawing-room after the first five minutes following her arrival. Judith purposely avoided noticing her. She had a vague consciousness that she was dancing a good deal with Randulf Danesdale, and, while her reason condemned, her heart condoned, and even sympathised with the imprudence. Even she herself, after a time, fell into the spirit of the dance, and began to rejoice in the mere pleasure of the swift rhythmic motion. Though calm and cool outwardly, she was wrought up to a pitch of almost feverish excitement, and, as is often the case with excitement of that kind, she was able distinctly and vividly to note every small circumstance connected with the course of the evening. She remembered her mother's words, ' They shall see who it is that has been passed over,' and she could not but perceive that both she and her sister attracted a great deal of attention ; that men were led up and introduced to them oftener, on the whole, than they were to other girls—that, in fact, they created a sensation—were a success. She supposed, then, that her mother was right. If they had had that 'position' which she so coveted for them, they would not be counted nonentities in it.

Judith also saw, with a woman's quickness in such matters, that which poor Bernard never perceived, the fact, namely, that though Lizzie Vane got plenty of partners, and was apparently made much of, yet that many of her partners were laughing at her, and drawing her out, and that they laughed together about her afterwards ; and lastly—most significant fact of all—that scarce a woman noticed or spoke to her, except Miss Danesdale, who, as hostess, was in a measure obliged to do so.

Gradually she yielded to the spell of the dance, the music,

the excitement of it all; to the unspoken prompting within, ' Enjoy yourself now, while you may. Let to-morrow take care of itself.' Go where she would, dance with whom she would, before the dance was over, sooner or later, once or oftener, as it happened, but inevitably, she met Bernard's dark eyes, and read what they said to her. When supper-time came, and he led her in, and poured out wine for her, and asked her in a low voice if she had ever been to Scar Foot, if she had ever even walked past it since she had ceased to be his guest, Judith answered, with a vibrating voice :

' No, I could not; and, of my own free will, I will not.'

He smiled, but said little more during the meal. The supper was served in brilliant fashion in an enormous room, at numbers of smallish round tables. Those who had time and attention to spare for the arrangements, said it was a fairy scene, with its evergreens, its hot-house flowers, and delicate ferns and perfumed fountains. Judith and Aglionby saw nothing of that ; they forced some kind of an indifferent conversation, for under the eyes of that crowd, and sur-rounded by those brilliant lights, anything like confidential behaviour was impossible. Now and then they were greeted by shouts of especially loud laughter from another part of the room, elicited by some peculiarly piquant sally of Miss Vane's, which charmed the chorus of men around her, and gave a deeper flush of triumph to her cheeks.

Just as the noise and laughter were at their height, and the fun was becoming faster, Aglionby said to Judith :

' Let us go away. This isn't amusing.'

They rose. So did nearly everyone else at the same time, but not to go. Some one had said something, which Judith and Aglionby, absorbed in themselves, had not heard, and a dead silence succeeded to the tumultuous noise. Then a clock was heard striking—a deep-toned stroke, which fell twelve times, and, upon the last sound, the storm of laughter

broke loose, and a tempest of hand-shaking and congratula-
tions broke out.

'A happy new year to you ! I wish you a happy new
year !'

' Here's to the peaceful interment of the old year, and the
joyful beginning of the new one !'

Aglionby looked at Judith. His lips were open, but he
paused. No ; he must not wish her a happy new year. He
knew he must not ; and he was silent. Many others had
now finished supper. They, too, left the room, and seated
themselves, after wandering about a little, in a kind of alcove
with a cushioned seat, of which there were many in the hall.
Then—for they were as much alone as if not another creature
had been near them—Aglionby at once resumed the topic he
had been dwelling on all supper-time.

'You have never been near Scar Foot since that day.
That means that you are still relentless ?' said he, regarding
her steadily, but with entreaty in his eyes, and a decided
accent of the same kind in his voice.

' It means that I must be—must seem so, at least,' she
replied dreamily.

' Pardon me, but I cannot see it in that light.'

' That means, that you do not believe me ?'

'No ; I mean that if you would only state your reasons,
and tell me the obstacle *you* see to our friendship, that I
could demolish it, let it be what it might.'

'Oh no, you could not,' said Judith, her heart beating
with a wild pleasure in thus, as it were, dancing on the edge
of a precipice. ' You do not know : it *could* not be swept
away.'

'And I say it could—it could, Judith, if you would only
allow it.'

She started slightly, as he spoke her name, and bit her
lips ; but she could not summon up her strength of will to
rebuke him.

' What—why do you say such things ? What makes you think so ?' she asked tremulously.

Aglionby took her fan, and bent towards her, as if fanning her with it ; but while his hand moved regularly and steadily to and fro, he spoke to her, with all the earnestness of which he was capable, and with eyes which seemed to burn into hers—yet with a tenderness in his voice which he could not subdue.

' Because you do not trust me. Because you will not believe what to me is so simple and such a matter of course —that no reason you could assert could make me your enemy. Because there is *no* offence I would not condone. Pah ! Condone ?—forgive, forget, wipe clean away, to have the goodwill and the friendship of you and yours. *Now* do you understand ?'

Judith turned pale ; she shut her eyes involuntarily, and drew a long breath. Could it be possible that he suspected —that he had the slightest inkling of her real reason for maintaining the distance between them for which she had stipulated? His words hit home to the very core and eye of her distress. The peril was frightful, imminent, and she had herself attracted it by allowing him to advance thus far, by herself sporting with deadly weapons. He was watching her, with every sense on the alert, and he saw how, unconsciously, her hands clasped ; she gave a little silent gasp and start, and there actually did steal into his mind, only to be dismissed again, the wonder, ' Can it be that there really is some offence which she deems irreparable ?'

' Hush !' she said at last. 'It is very wrong of me to allow the subject to be mentioned. And you do not keep your promise. You know that you promised me at Scar Foot, Mr. Aglionby——'

' You also promised *me* at Scar Foot, and then demanded your promise back again,' said he, resolved that if he had to give way again (and what else could a man do, when a woman appealed to him for mercy?) that she should buy the concession hard.

'I have told you I cannot explain,' she said, almost despairingly. ' Do you mean to make me go over it all again?' A rush of sudden tears filled her eyes. ' Do you mean to make me plead it all a second time ?'

'I should like to make you do it—yes. And, at the end of all, I should like to refuse what you ask,' he said, with a savage tenderness in his voice.

Judith looked steadily at him for a short time, as if to test whether he was in earnest or not, and then said, in a dull, dead voice, ' I wish I were dead ;' and looked at the ground.

This was more than he could bear.

' Forgive me, Judith !' he whispered. ' If you can, forgive me. I will not sin again, but it is hard.'

' Yes, it is hard,' she replied, more composed, as the terror she had felt on hearing him talk about ' offence ' and ' condonation' began to subside. ' It is hard. But making scenes about it will make it none the easier. We have our duties, both of us—you as a man——'

More peals of laughter, as a noisy group came out of the supper-room—half a dozen young men, and Miss Vane in the midst of them, laughing in no gentle tones, and holding in her hand, high above her head, a flower, towards which one of the said young gentlemen occasionally stretched a hand, amidst the loud hilarity of the lady and her companions. The party made their way towards the ballroom, and Miss Vane was heard crying :

' I'm sure I never promised to dance with you. Here's my programme. Look and see !'

They disappeared.

Judith's face burned. She looked timidly at Aglionby, who was gazing after the group, his face pale, his eyes mocking, his lips sneering. He laughed, not a pleasant laugh.

'We all have our duties, as you most justly remark. Mine
is to marry that young lady, and cease to persecute you with
my importunities. I see that is what you were thinking.
And you are quite right.'

'*You* are quite wrong,' said Judith. 'What I do think is
that you are not behaving kindly to her to allow her to—
to—she is so young and inexperienced—and so pretty.'

'And you and your sister are so old and wise, and so
hideous,' he rejoined, with a bitter laugh. 'That alone is
enough to account for your different style of behaviour.
No. Do not try to palliate it.'

'I think you are to blame,' Judith persisted. 'You have
no right to do it—to leave her with all those silly, empty-
headed young men. It is not fair. You ought to take——'

'Take her home—and myself too. A good idea. I am
sure the carriage will be round by now. But you?'

'Take me to the drawing-room, please. I dare say Mrs.
Malleson will also be ready to go.'

He gave her his arm. Mrs. Malleson was soon found,
seated on a sofa, with Delphine beside her, looking a little
pale, and exceedingly tired. Bernard wished them good-
night, and went to the ballroom. He had seen Mrs. Bryce
in the drawing-room, and found that she was quite ready
to go. In the dancing-room there was a momentary pause
between two dances. Bernard saw Randulf Danesdale
promenading with a young lady on his arm, with whom he
seemed to be in earnest conversation. At the further end
of the room he saw that fatal pink dress; heard the same
shrill, affected tones, and the chorus of laughter that followed on them. Nothing could have been more distasteful
to him in his present mood than to have even to speak to
her, after his parting from Judith Conisbrough. But he
walked straight up to the group, most of whom he knew
slightly by this time, and offering his arm to his betrothed,
said gravely :

' Lizzie, I am sorry to break off your amusement, but it is very late ; we have ten miles to drive, and Mrs. Bryce is tired, and wishes to go.'

' Oh, Aglionby, don't take Miss Vane away ! The light of the evening will be gone. Don't look so down, man ! Miss Vane, don't let him drag you off in that way. I am down for a dance.'

' And I,' ' And I,' cried several voices.

Bernard's face did not relax. He could not unstiffen his features into a smile. He looked directly at Lizzie, as mildly as he could, and repeated that he was very sorry, but he was afraid he must ask her to come away.

' Oh, Bernard !' she began ; but then something unusual in his expression struck her. A feeling of something like chill alarm crossed her heart. How dignified he looked ! How commanding ! How different—even she knew—from the feather-brained fops with whom she had even now been jesting and laughing !

' Well, if I must, I must, I suppose,' she said, shrugging her shoulders, and taking his arm. And with a final fare-well to her attendants, she went away with her ' lover.'

' Jove ! but that girl is a caution !' observed one of the young men, giving unrestrained flow to his mirth, as Bernard and his betrothed disappeared. ' I never had such fun in my life !'

' She'll find it a caution, being married to Aglionby,' said a second, looking into the future. ' Didn't you see him as he came up to us ? Lucifer himself couldn't have looked more deuced stiff.'

' Yes—I saw. They don't look exactly as if they were created to run in a pair !' said the first speaker, musingly. ' But why on earth does he leave her to herself in such a way ?'

' He's been dancing attendance on the eldest Miss Conisbrough all evening, and left this little girl to amuse herself with suitable companions.'

'On Miss Conisbrough—why, I thought they were at daggers-drawn.'

'Didn't look like it, I assure you.   I can't make it out, I confess.   Only, on my honour, they were as good-looking a couple as any in the room.   Couldn't help noticing them. But look here, St. John—will you take the odds—ten to one—that it doesn't come off?'

'The wedding?—all right.   At all—or within a year?'

'Oh, hang a year!—at all.   Ten to one that Aglionby and the little dressmaker don't get married at all.'

'Yes; but there must be some time fixed.   Ten to one that it's broken off within a year.'

'In sovs?   Done with you!'

Then the band struck up again for one of the last waltzes, and the young men dispersed to find their partners for the same.

CHAPTER XXVI.

RANDULF.

THE ball had been kept up until morning, if not till daylight. When people began to stroll in to the very late breakfast at Danesdale Castle, not a lady was to be seen amongst them, save one intrepid damsel, equally renowned for her prowess in the chase and her unwearying fleetness in the ballroom.

As she appeared, in hat and habit, she was greeted with something like applause, which was renewed when she announced that she had every intention of sharing the day's run.   Sir Gabriel, in his pink (for no ball would have caused him to be absent at the meet), gallantly placed her beside himself, and apologised for his daughter's absence.

'Philippa has no " go " left in her after these stirs,' he remarked; 'and a day's hunting takes her a week to get over; but I'm glad to see that you are less delicate, my dear.'

'We shall not have many ladies, I think,' said she, smiling, and looking round upon the thinned ranks of the veterans.

Here the door opened, just as breakfast was nearly over, and Sir Gabriel paused in astonishment in the midst of his meal.

'What, Ran? You !' he ejaculated, as his son entered, equipped, he also, for riding to hounds. 'The last thing I should have expected. If anyone had asked me, I should have said you were safe in bed till lunch-time.'

'You would have been wrong, it seems,' replied Randulf, on whom the exertions of the previous evening appeared to have had worse effects than they had upon Miss Bird, the bright-looking girl who was going to ride.

Miss Bird was an heiress; the same pretty girl with whom Randulf had been walking about the ballroom the night before, when Aglionby had come to call Lizzie away.

Randulf himself looked pale, and almost haggard, and was listless and drawling beyond his wont. Sir Gabriel eyed him over, and his genial face brightened. Of course it was bad form to display fondness for your relations in the presence of others. Every Englishman knows that, and Sir Gabriel as well as any of them; but it was always with difficulty that he refrained from smiling with joy every time his eyes met those of his 'lad.' He looked also more kindly than ever upon Miss Bird, who was a favourite of his, more especially when Randulf carried his cup of tea round the table and dropped into the vacant place by her side.

The meet took place at a certain park, a couple of miles from Danesdale Castle, and soon after breakfast a procession of six—Miss Bird, Sir Gabriel, his son, and three other men who were of their party—set off for it. It was a still, cloudy day, with a grey sky and lowering clouds, which, however, were pretty high, for all the hill-tops were clear.

That was a long and memorable run in the annals of Danesdale fox-hunting—'a very devil of a fox !' as Sir

Gabriel said, which led them a cruel and complicated chase
over some of the roughest country in the district.   Sir
Gabriel, as will easily be understood, was a keen sportsman
himself, and had been a little disappointed with Randulf's
apparent indifference to fox, or any other, hunting.   He had
put it down to his long sojourn abroad with people who,
according to Sir Gabriel's ideas, knew no more about hunting than a London street Arab does, who has never stepped
on anything but flags in his life.   He had always trusted
that the boy would mend of such outlandish indifference,
and he certainly had no cause to complain of his lack of
spirit to-day.

Sir Gabriel was lost in amazement.   He could not understand the lad.   Randulf's face—the pale face which he had
brought with him into the breakfast-room—never flushed in
the least : his eyebrows met in a straight line across his forehead.   He seemed to look neither to right nor to left,
but urged his horse relentlessly at every chance of a leap,
big or little, but the uglier and the bigger the better it
seemed, till his father, watching him, began to feel less
puzzled than indignant.   A good day's run, Sir Gabrie
would have argued, was a good day's run ; but to drive
your horse wilfully and wantonly at fences which might have
been piled by Satan himself, and at gaps constructed apparently on the most hideous of man-and-horse-trap principles,
went against all the baronet's traditions ; for all his life he
had been very 'merciful to his beast,' holding his horse in
almost as much respect as himself.   He had always credited
Randulf with the same feelings, and his conduct this day
was bewildering, to say the least of it.

As Sir Gabriel and Miss Bird happened to be running
almost neck and neck through a sloping field—the chase
nearly at an end, the fox in full view at last, with the hounds
in mad eagerness at his heels—suddenly a horseman flew
past them, making straight for a most hideous-looking bit

of fence, on the other side of which was the bed of a beck, full of loose stones, and in which the water in this winter season rushed along, both broad and deep.

All day long a feeling of uneasiness had possessed Sir Gabriel; this put the climax to it. Forgetting the glorious finish, now so near, he pulled his horse up short, crying:

'Good God! Is he mad?'

Miss Bird also wondered if he were mad, but put her own horse, without stopping, at a more reasonable-looking gap, considerably to the left of the fence Randulf was taking.

Two seconds of horrible suspense, and—yes, his horse landed lightly and safely at the other side. Sir Gabriel wiped the sweat from his brow, and, caring nothing for the 'finish' or anything else, rode limply on to where, not Randulf, but another, was presenting the brush to the amiable Miss Bird.

'What the devil do you mean, sir, by riding at a fence like that, and frightening me out of my senses?' growled Sir Gabriel, at his son's elbow.

The latter looked round, with the same white, pallid face, and far-off eyes, which the father had already noticed, and which had filled him with vague and nameless alarm. Randulf passed his hand across his eyes and said:

'What did you say?'

'What ails you, lad? What is the matter with you?' asked poor Sir Gabriel, his brown cheek turning ashy pale, and a feeling of sickly dread creeping over his heart.

'What ails me? Oh, nothing that I know of,' replied Randulf, with blank indifference, and then suddenly heaving such a sigh as comes only from the depths of a sick heart.

The laughter, and jesting, and joyous bustle of the finish were sounding all around them. No one took much notice of the two figures apart, apparently earnestly conversing. Neither Sir Gabriel nor Randulf was given to displaying his feelings openly in public, but Randulf knew, as well as if some one were constantly shouting it aloud from the house-tops, that his father worshipped him—that he was the light of his eyes and the joy of his life, and that to give him any real joy he would have sacrificed most things dear to him. And Sir Gabriel knew that his worship was not wasted upon any idol of clay or wood—that it fell gratefully into a heart which could appreciate and understand it. During the last month it had occasionally crossed his mind that Randulf was a little absent—somewhat more listless and indifferent than usual; but the baronet had himself been unusually busied with magisterial and other concerns, and had scarcely had time to remark the subtle change. Of one thing he was now certain, that Randulf, as he saw him now, was a changed man from what he had been four-and-twenty hours ago. The poor old man felt hopelessly distressed. He knew not how to force the truth from a man who looked at him and said nothing ailed him, when it was patent to the meanest comprehension that, on the contrary, something very serious ailed him. He sat on his horse, looking wist-fully into Randulf's face. The groups were dispersing. The young man, at last looking up, seemed to read what was passing in his father's mind, and said :

' I have something to say to you. Could we manage to ride home alone ? How will Miss Bird do ?'

Sir Gabriel's face brightened quickly. If Randulf had 'something to say' to him, no doubt that communication would quickly put to rights all these shadowy disquietudes which troubled him.

' I'll arrange for Miss Bird to be escorted,' he said ; and, turning round, he requested the man who had already pre-sented her with the brush to see her safely to Danesdale Castle, as a matter of business obliged him and Randulf to ride home by Scar Foot.

The youth yielded a joyful assent, and went off rejoicing

in charge of his 'fair.' Sir Gabriel and Randulf, with a
general 'Good-afternoon' to the rest of the party, turned
their horses' heads in a southerly direction. Scar Foot was
a little distance away, further south, and then there were ten
miles to ride to Danesdale Castle.

They soon found themselves in a deep lane, beneath the
grey and clouded afternoon sky of New Year's Day. Behind
them, Addlebrough reared his bleak, blunt summit, and the
other fells around looked sullen under the sullen sky. It
was Randulf who had proposed the ride, but still he did not
speak, till Sir Gabriel asked, in a voice which he strove to
make indifferent :

'What did you make of the dance last night, Randulf?
Philippa informed me before she went to bed that it had
been a success.'

'A success, was it?' said Randulf indifferently. 'I'm
glad to hear it, I'm sure. I don't know anything about it.'

'What did you think of Aglionby's intended?' pursued
Sir Gabriel.

'Miss Vane? Pooh! She may be his *intended;* it will
never go any further.'

'I should hope not, I'm sure. What a mistake for a man
of that calibre to make! It shows what soft spots there
are in the strongest heads.'

Silence again for a short time, until Sir Gabriel, resolutely
plunging into a serious topic, said :

'Well, surely there were lots of nice girls there. Did
none of them strike your fancy?'

'Surely I've seen most of them before?'

'Well, I'll tell you which girl I like the best of the lot.
I wish you could see her in the light I should like, Randulf.'

'And which was she?' asked Randulf, with a sudden
appearance of animation and eagerness.

'Evelyn Bird.'

'Oh!' There was profound indifference in Randulf's tone.

Sir Gabriel went on steadily :

' It is time, without any jesting, that you began to think about marrying. I've thought about it often lately. An only son is in a different position from——'

Randulf looked drearily around him. They were passing the back of Scar Foot just now, and the profoundest silence seemed to reign there. Slowly their horses mounted the slope of the road which was for Randulf, and for one or two others, haunted with the memories that do not die. The lake lay below them, looking dull and dismal—the ice with which it had been covered turning rapidly to slush in the thaw-wind—its wall of naked fells uncheered by even a ray of sunshine. Randulf remembered certain other rides he had taken along this road, and walks too which he had had there. He glanced towards his father, and in that kindly face he read trouble and perturbation : he knew that that brave old head was filled with plans for his happiness, his welfare—with schemes for securing gladness to him long after those white hairs should be laid low. Yet it was long before he could summon up words in which to answer his father's last remark. At last he said :

' I know what you mean, sir ; I wish I could gratify you, but you must not expect me to marry yet.'

Deep disappointment fell like a cloud over Sir Gabriel's face, as he said :

' Boy, boy ! was that what you brought me out here to tell me ?'

' Partly ; not altogether. It was because I wanted to be alone with you, and make a clean breast of it.'

He paused. ' A clean breast of it ?' Vague visions of dread floated through Sir Gabriel's mind—dreams of foreign adventuresses who entrapped innocent youth into marriages which were a curse and a clog to them all their days. Was his boy, of whom he was so proud, going to unfold some such history to him now? Randulf's next words somewhat relieved him.

'I know you wish me to marry, and I know the sort of girl you would like me to marry, but surely you would not have denied me some tether—some free choice of my own?'

'Bless the lad! Of course not. Every Englishman chooses his own wife, and with the example before me of old John, and the results of his severity——'

'Just so,' said Randulf, with rather a wan smile. 'I've had something on my mind for a good while now. *I* wanted to marry too. My only doubt was, what you would say to the girl I wanted to have, and I had fully meant to talk it all over with you, and tell you all about it, before I did anything.' Randulf raised his eyes full to his father's anxious face. 'I wanted to marry Delphine Conisbrough.'

'Good Lord!' broke involuntarily from Sir Gabriel.

'You don't know her much, I think. I was not going to do anything rashly. For though I love her—better than my life—I knew that whoever I married, you must have a great deal to say in the matter—as it is right you should. I intended to get you to see her, to learn to know her a little better, before you said anything one way or another. You would have consented to my wish—most certainly you would have consented. I heard what you said about her last night, to her sister—about some men's heads being turned by her beauty. Ah, it's not only her beauty—it is everything. But if it were only that, you cannot deny that she surpassed all the women there, in looks?'

He turned to his father with a sort of challenge in his voice and eyes.

'Well, who wants to deny it?' said Sir Gabriel. 'I own I was enchanted with her, and, as you say, not only with her beauty. But you must remember, my boy, that you have to think not only——'

21

'I know, I know,' said Randulf, with a little laugh, not of the gayest description. 'I had to think that if she had been one of this abominable old Aglionby's heiresses it would have been the most suitable thing in the world. But she just missed it—and of course a miss is as good as a mile. She was not so worthy of a wealthy young Admirable Crichton like me, in her poverty, as she might have been *with* the money and the acres. Bah !' He set his teeth, choking back a kind of sob of indignant passion at the picture his own fancy had conjured up, so that Sir Gabriel became very grave, realising that it was more than a mere flirtation or a passing fancy. 'I tell you she would have honoured any man by becoming his wife. But that's not to the point. I had duties towards you—towards the best father a fellow ever had—and I knew it, and was resolved to have it out with you.'

'And suppose I had refused ?'

'But you would have seen her, as I wished ?'

'Naturally. But I might still have refused, finally. What did you propose to do in that case ?'

'I wish you wouldn't ask me. I didn't *propose* to do any-thing—only I felt that if she would be my wife, my wife she should be, against all the world.'

'Well ?' said Sir Gabriel, with a sigh ; 'and what next ?'

'The next is, that last night I lost my head the moment I saw her. From the instant she came into the room, I knew nothing, except that she was there. It was not of my own will that I left her side for an instant. She sent me away many times, and told me to attend to what she called my duties. Well—there's no good in describing it all. I don't know what I may have done, or said, or looked like ; a man doesn't know, when he's off his head like that. But she took the alarm, and asked me to take her back to Mrs. Malleson. She got up, and wanted to go out of the room. We were alone, in my study——'

' The deuce you were !' said Sir Gabriel, in displeasure.

' Yes, I know it was all wrong. I had no business to take her there. I had no business to do anything that I did. I can't exactly remember what I had said, but I saw her turn red and white, and then she started up, and said, " You must not say those things to me. Take me back to Mrs. Malleson, please, Mr. Danesdale." I begged her to wait a moment. She said no ; if I would not take her, she would go alone. I said she should not go yet, and I set my back against the door, and told her she should not leave that room till she had promised to be my wife.'

' Well ?' was all his father said; but he watched askance his son's face.

He could not understand it all. Randulf did not tell his tale by any means joyously. His words came from between his clenched teeth ; his brow wore a dark frown, and his nostrils quivered now and then.

' If I had done wrong,' Randulf went on, ' I got my punishment pretty quickly, for she sat down again and looked at me, and said, as composedly as possible, " No ; that can never be." I had expected a different answer— yes, by ——, I had !' he said passionately. ' I could have sworn, from a thousand signs, that she loved me ; and she is no silly prude—pure-minded women never are prudes. And it was not coquetry. She could not coquette with a man in such a case. I felt as if she had shot me when she said that. There was a scene. I don't deny it. I forgot you— I forgot everything except that I loved her. I couldn't take her answer—I would not. I begged her to tell me why she could not be my wife. First, she made some objections about you ; she said I had done wrong to ask her in that way. What would Sir Gabriel say ? She reminded me that I was an only son '—he laughed again. ' I put all that aside. I told her it was no question of fathers and mothers and only sons, or of anything else, except the success or failure of our two lives. I said that I loved her, and she loved me ; she gathered herself up, as it were, and said coldly, "No; you are mistaken. Now will you let me go?" Oh, sir, I ought to have let her go, I know. But I felt quite beside myself when I heard her say that. I refused to believe her. I repeated that it was not true—that I knew she loved me——'

'You did wrong,' said Sir Gabriel, sternly and coldly ; 'and I cannot understand how a gentleman——'

'Don't say that to me !' said Randulf, looking at him with so haggard a face, lips that twitched so ominously, that his father became silent. 'I cannot understand it now. I must have been mad. I'm concealing nothing from you. I went on telling her that I knew she loved me, and that she should never perjure herself while I could prevent it. I reminded her of this thing and that thing that she had said and done, and I asked her what they all meant, if not that she loved me ? But I came to my senses at last, for I saw that she looked frightened——'

'And it required *that* to bring you to your senses—shame on you !' said his father, very angrily indeed.

'Yes, it required that,' replied Randulf, without noticing his father's tone. 'But when I did come to myself again, I humbly asked her pardon. I threw the door wide open, and said I would take her to Mrs. Malleson, or anywhere that she liked to go. I made her look at me, and I told her, "When I know you married to another man, then I will believe you do not love me, but not till then.'

'And what did she say ?'

Randulf turned his white face towards his father, and said, with a kind of wrathful triumph :

'She said *nothing*—she looked away. She took my arm, and we got into the drawing-room somehow ; and she sat down beside Mrs. Malleson—ah, poor child !—with a white face, and a look in her eyes like you see in a bird's eyes when you've just shot it, and you pick it up and look at it. And I heard Mrs. Malleson say that she looked cold, and she shivered a little, and said yes, she was rather, and very tired. I said nothing. I think I bowed to her, and came away. . . . But I've seen nothing, nothing since, but her eyes and her face, and herself creeping up to Mrs. Malleson. And if I see it much longer I shall go mad,' said Randulf, drawing a long, sobbing breath. ' Right before my eyes it has been ever since, so that I couldn't sleep. It looked at me out of my glass while I dressed, till I flung a handkerchief over it. It was just before my eyes in the field all the morning. Why, do you suppose I rode as I did—not for the pleasure of catching a fox, but because *her face* was there before me, in its misery, just out of my reach, and I felt as if I must catch her, and kiss some life back into her eyes and her lips, or break my neck. And it's here now—there, just before me.'

He shuddered, and drew his hand across his eyes. Sir Gabriel was too disturbed to reply at once; too much astonished, and, as it were, paralysed at the discovery of this fiery drama which had been going on under his very eyes without his knowing it, to speak. Yet he heard Randulf say darkly, half to himself :

' My poor little Delphine ! What have they done to her ? What have they said to her, that she should turn and stab herself and me in this way ?'

Sir Gabriel was still silent, trying in vain to make what he called ' sense ' out of the story. When Randulf had first mentioned Delphine's name, his father's feeling had been one of strong disapproval. Lovely as she was, and charming, she had had neither the training, the position, nor the acquaintance with the world and society which he would have wished for, in a girl who was not only to be Randulf's bride, but, sometime, Lady Danesdale. Be it said for Sir Gabriel that by this time he had forgotten that, and considered only

the deeper issues—his son's future happiness—the question
of his joy or sorrow.   He at last looked up, meaning to ask
another question or two; he met Randulf's eyes, dull and
clouded, now that his narrative was over, looking at him
rather appealingly.   Prudent questions, conventional doubts,
were forgotten.

' My poor lad, I wish I could help you !'

' Ah, I knew *you* would understand,' said Randulf.   ' But
no one can help me now—except time.   If she had consented, then your help would have been everything; now it
is nothing.'

' Suppose I saw her?' suggested Sir Gabriel.   ' Perhaps I
could induce her to state her objection.   It may be a shadow,
after all.   Girls do make important things out of such very
trifles.'

' It was no shadow—to her, at any rate.   It was some
reason which she feels must outweigh all others.   I tell you
she looked like one stricken to death.   It is when I think
of her look, and of her fate, shut up there—horrible !   With
every joy cut off, and in such poverty——'

' They ought not to be in poverty though, if Aglionby's
feelings——'

' Do not misjudge Aglionby.   He has been repulsed too.
He would give his right hand to help them—they are his
kinswomen, as he says.   Every advance he attempts is
repelled.   He is in despair about it.'

' That's very odd.'

' Yes, very.   But I do not know that we have any right
to inquire into their reasons for what they do.'

They rode on in silence again, for a long time, through
Yoresett town and all along the lovely road to Stanniforth,
and thence to Danesdale.   It was shortly before they entered
their own park that Randulf began again :

' And now, sir, you won't resent it, if I am not counted in
the list of Miss Bird's, or Miss Anybody's suitors, at present ?'

'Heaven forbid! We understand one another now. After all, to look at it from a selfish point of view, you will be all my own for so much the longer "My son's my son till he gets him a wife," you know. All I ask, my boy, is that you will be as open with me after a time, when any fresh scheme comes into your mind, or if you decide upon anything. You shall find me more than willing to arrange things as you wish them, if it is possible.'

'I know you will,' said Randulf. 'I suppose these things can be lived down. It pleases me to think that you *would* have done as I wished ; you would have taken into consideration. . . . Sometime, when the time comes, and years are past, I suppose I shall find a wife—not like her, but some one who will marry me.'

Sir Gabriel did not answer this. He did not like it. It did not suit him. He would have preferred almost anything to this calm looking forward to a joyless future.

It had grown dark, and the wind was rising, as they drove into the courtyard of the castle. They had to put on one side all that had passed between them ; their long ride together, and the emotions which filled both their hearts. The house was full of visitors. There would be fifteen or twenty guests at dinner ; all the ball, and the hunt, and the dresses, and the incidents to be discussed. They took their part in it all bravely ; and this courage brought with it balm, as moral courage, well carried out, infallibly does.

CHAPTER XXVII.

LIZZIE'S CONSENT.

TOWARDS noon, on that same first of January, Miss Vane came slowly strolling into the parlour at Scar Foot, yawning undisguisedly, and looking around her with half-open eyes.

'Law, Bernard! you don't need any sleep, I do believe! You look as if nothing had happened.'

Aglionby forced a smile, and touched her forehead with his lips. As is usual in such cases, the less he felt to care for her, the more anxiously did he make himself *aux petits soins* on her behalf, drawing an easy-chair to the fire for her, placing a footstool, putting a screen into her hand—delicate attentions which, a year ago, when he had first had the felicity of calling her his own, it had never entered his head to render.

'I am not fatigued, certainly,' he said. 'My aunt has been downstairs a good while too.'

'Oh, but she wasn't dancing; I was. My word! But it is a grand house, Bernard, that Danesdale Castle; and they are grand people, too. I don't like Miss Danesdale a bit, though. Stiff little thing! And I thought some of the other ladies were very stiff, too. I guess some of them didn't like sitting out when the gentlemen were talking to me.'

'Very likely not,' said Bernard, with a praiseworthy endeavour to appreciate the joke.

'I heard one of them say,' pursued Lizzie, with a musing and complacent smile, 'she said, "Why on earth doesn't Mr. Aglionby look after her? It's atrocious!" So you see you were not considered to be doing your duty. I dare say if you, or anybody else, had been looking after *her*, she wouldn't have felt so ill-tempered.'

Lizzie laughed, and Bernard's face flushed, for he interpreted the remark in a wholly different and less flattering sense than that suggested by Lizzie.

'I hope the Hunt Ball will be half as jolly,' pursued Miss Vane. 'Eh, and did you see those Miss Conisbroughs, Bernard? But of course you did, because I saw you talking to one of them. I wonder you condescended to speak to them, after all their designs to keep you out——'

She paused suddenly, with her remark arrested, her eyes astonished, gazing into Aglionby's face.

'You are quite mistaken,' said he, in a voice which, though quiet, bit even her. 'You must not speak in that manner of my cousins. They had no "designs," as you call them. They have been most shamefully treated; and in short, my dear, I will not allow you to mention them unless you can speak more becomingly of them.'

'Upon my word! Well, they can't be so badly off, anyhow; and look at their dresses! Lovely dresses they were! and that youngest one is sweetly pretty, only she does her hair so queerly; there's no style about it, all hanging loose in loops, when everyone else wears theirs small and neat. But she is pretty, certainly. The eldest one I don't admire a bit; she's like a marble figure.'

'Are you talking about the lady Bernard took in to supper?' asked Mrs. Bryce, joining in the colloquy for the first time.

'Yes, I am, Mrs. Bryce."

'I thought her one of the truest gentlewomen I ever saw,' said Mrs. Bryce, counting the stitches of her knitting. 'Her manners are perfect, wherever they were acquired; but I should say that "grand air" is natural to her, isn't it, Bernard?'

'Entirely, aunt. She always has it.'

'Yes, I thought so. One can see at once when that sort of thing is natural.'

'Well, I thought her the stiffest, proudest creature I ever saw. I couldn't tell why she gave herself such airs,' said Miss Vane. Here Bernard abruptly left the room, unable to bear it any longer, and Mrs. Bryce continued calmly:

'I am afraid you are no judge of manner, my dear; and I wonder at your speaking in that way of Bernard's cousins.'

'Cousins, indeed! Pretty cousins! Much notice they would have taken of him, if they had come into the money.'

'And à propos of manner,' continued Mrs. Bryce, who seemed resolved thoroughly to do her duty as chaperon, 'let me recommend you to tone yours down a little. Try to make it rather more like that of the young ladies we have been talking about, and then perhaps there will not be so many comments passed upon it as I heard last night.'

'Comments !' cried Miss Vane angrily. 'What do you mean ? Does anyone dare to say that I behaved badly ?'

'Not badly, my dear ; but what, in the society you were in last night, means almost the same thing—ignorantly. At the Hunt Ball, if I were you, I would not put on that pink gown, and I would keep a little more with Bernard and myself, and——'

'I'll just tell you this—I won't go to the Hunt Ball at all,' said Lizzie, with passionate anger, wounded in her tenderest feelings. 'I hate all these grand, stuck-up people, with their false ways, like that nasty proud Miss Conisbrough. I won't go near the Hunt Ball. They may whistle for me.' (Mrs. Bryce's face assumed an expression of silent anguish as these amenities of speech were hurled at her.) 'And what's more, I shall tell Bernard, this very day, that I wouldn't live at this horrid, dull old place, if he would give me twice the money he has. I must have society. I must have my f—friends,' sobbed Miss Vane, breaking down.

Mrs. Bryce smiled slightly, but said nothing. She had a strong impression that her nephew, and not Lizzie, would decide, both whether they went to the Hunt Ball or not, and whether they lived at Scar Foot. He came in again at that moment, with a letter-bag. Lizzie speedily dried her eyes, and watched him while he opened it; came behind his chair, in fact, and looked at all the envelopes, as he took them out.

'That's for me,' she said, stretching out a slim hand, from over his shoulder. 'It's from Lucy Golding. She promised to write.'

'Did Percy promise to write, too !' asked Bernard, arrest-

ing the same slim fingers as they made a snatch at the next
letter. ' Because if this isn't Percy's fist, I'll——'

'You need not say what you'll do, sir,' was the coquettish
reply. ' It *is* Percy's " fist," as you call it. Most likely it's
a New Year's card. We are old friends. I sent him one at
Christmas, and I don't see why he shouldn't return the compliment.'

' Oh, certainly. There is absolutely no just cause or im-
pediment, to my knowledge,' replied Bernard, with supreme
indifference. ' There's another—your mother's handwriting,
isn't it ?'

' Yes, it is. I wonder what she's doing with herself, to-day.'

' Aunt, here is one for you, the last of the batch,' he said,
rising, and taking it to her ; while he collected together his
own, which looked chiefly like business letters, newspapers,
etc., and took them to a side-table.

Mrs. Bryce read her letter, and then remarked that she
would go into the drawing-room and answer it at once.
Lizzie and Bernard were left alone. He began to open
his papers : his mind pure of any speculation on the subject
of her correspondence. Why did she take herself as far
away from him as possible, as she opened her letters ? In
perusing one of them, at least, her face flushed ; her foot
tapped the floor. She finished them, put them all into her
pocket, and took up the strip of lace she was supposed to
be working. Perhaps the prolonged silence struck Bernard,
for, suddenly raising his face from the intent perusal of a
leading article, he perceived Lizzie, said to himself, ' Now
for it,' laid his paper down, and went to her side.

During the sleepless vigil he had kept last night, he had
made up his mind as to his immediate course. He would
talk to Lizzie to-day, make her fix the day for their marriage,
as early a day as he could get her to name. Then they
would be married, and he supposed things would somehow
work themselves right after that event. He could live a

calm, if joyless, life; plan out some scheme of work that
would take up a good deal of time. One could not go on
being wretched for ever; and one's feet by degrees harden,
to suit a stony path. He had got engaged to this girl; she
had not refused him in his poverty; he had kept her to himself for a year, and thus hindered her from having any other
chances. To try to break it off now that he was in such
utterly different circumstances would indeed be a pitiful
proceeding. He knew that, and it was a proceeding of
which he was not going to be guilty. He knew now that
she was everything he would rather she had not been. It
was now a matter of constant astonishment to him that he
could ever even have thought himself in love with her. A
sense of shame and degradation burnt through him every
time he realised how easily he had yielded to the sensuous
spell exercised by a pretty face and a pair of beguiling blue
eyes; how densely blind he must have been to have imagined
that the soul, or what did duty for the soul behind that face,
could ever satisfy him. But it was done: it must be carried
through.

Perhaps he began somewhat abruptly. At least she
looked very much startled as he said:

'Put down your work, Lizzie. I want to have a talk with
you. How many months in the year do you think you can
spend at Scar Foot, when we are married?'

'Months, Bernard!' she cried; 'oh, don't ask me to do
that! I'm very sorry, I am really, because I know you like
this place, though I can't for the life of me imagine why,
but I really *couldn't* live here. I should go melancholy
mad.'

'Then you shall not live here,' said he promptly. 'I
shall keep the place up, because I shall often run down
myself and spend a few days at it.' (In imagination, he felt
the soothing influence of the place, the asylum it would be,
the refuge, from Irkford and from Lizzie.) 'But you shall

live in town, since you prefer it, and you shall yourself choose the house and the neighbourhood.'

'Oh, that will be nice!' said Lizzie. 'I shall like that. Then I shall have all my old friends round me. Bernard it's a load off my mind—it is, really.'

He took her hand.

'I am glad if it pleases you, dear. And now, one other thing, Lizzie. Houses can be looked after any time, and there are plenty of them to be had at Irkford. But when will you let me take you to live in that house that we are speaking of?'

She looked at him hastily, and turned first red, then pale, so that he congratulated himself on having taken a straightforward course, for she loved him, poor Lizzie, and it would have been shameful indeed to play her false.

'When?' faltered Lizzie, and looked at him and thought how dark and grim-looking he was, and how much graver and sterner he had become since he left Irkford.

If he were always going to be like this—he never now said anything soothing or pleasant to her; he was dreadfully severe-looking.

'Yes, when, dear? I suppose the house is not to be taken just to stand empty. Some one will have to go and live in it—you and I, surely.'

'Yes, yes; I suppose so,' said Lizzie, slowly and constrainedly, and dropping her eyes.

'Well, all I want to know is, when. Sometime soon, surely. There can be nothing in the way now. For my part, I don't see why it should be put off more than a week or two.'

'Oh, no! Impossible!' she cried, crimsoning, and speaking with such vehemence as surprised him.

'Recollect, we have been engaged more than a year. We have only been waiting till we could be married. Now that we can, why put it off any longer?'

'It is so fearfully sudden,' said she, startled out of her affectation, and fumbling nervously with her handkerchief.

As a lover he was sombre enough. As a husband—almost immediately? There must be no more New Year's cards from old friends, when Bernard was her husband.

'Fearfully sudden—well, say in a month or two, though I call that rather hard lines. But—this is January—why not in the beginning of March?'

'March is so stormy and cold; it would be a bad omen to be married in a storm,' said she, laughing nervously. 'No, a little later than March.'

'Fix your own time, then, dear; only don't put it off too long.'

'Suppose we said the end of May or the beginning of June,' suggested Lizzie, plaiting her handkerchief into folds, which she studied with the deepest interest.

He uttered an exclamation of dismay. Five months longer of unrest, misery, suspense, waiting for a new order of things. The idea was terrible. He felt that he could not face it. He could make the sacrifice if it were to be done at once, but to have to wait—it could not be. He set himself to plead in earnest with his betrothed—at least, with him it was pleading—to her it seemed more like an imperious demand. He said he thought there was a little estrangement between them, which caused him pain.

He begged her not to be so hard. His gravity and earnestness oppressed her more and more. The darkest forebodings assailed Lizzie as to her future happiness with this Knight of the Sorrowful Countenance.

She had no fixed plan; he had : therefore he prevailed. He would have prevailed in any case, by his superior strength of will, as he had done at the very first when his imperious manner and tones had almost repelled her, and when yet he had contrived to gain his own way. He gained it again. He made her promise that they should be married

at the end of April : he promised her on his side all manner
of things. He completely reversed her decision about the
Hunt Ball. She would go with him, she meekly said. All
these things she promised and vowed, and at last he let her
go, having promised, on his part, to take her home to Irkford the day after the Hunt Ball. She said that if they were
to be married so soon she would want all her time for
preparation—and to be with her mother, Lizzie added,
almost piteously. And then she made her escape, looking
exceedingly tired, and very much disturbed. He, being left
alone, realised with a singular clearness and vividness these
comforting facts :

First, that it was with the greatest difficulty that he had
succeeded in maintaining a tranquil and affectionate manner
towards his dearest Lizzie. Secondly, that never had there
been so little sympathy or even mutual understanding
between them as now, when they had just agreed upon the
very day of their marriage. Thirdly, that though she was a
wilful girl, with plenty of likes and dislikes, yet he was
completely her master the instant it pleased him to be so.
That he could make her yield to him and obey him in whatsoever he chose, but that he could not—charm he never so
wisely—make her agree with him by light of reason and
understanding ; could not make her like his way, or like
doing it—could not, in a word, change her nature, though
he could subdue it : a pleasing discovery, perhaps, for the
tyrant by nature, who loves always to have the whip in his
hand, and to see his slaves crouch as he comes in sight, but
a most galling one to Bernard Aglionby.

A cheering prospect! he thought. A wife who, if he left
her entirely to her own devices, would constantly be doing
things which would jar upon all his feelings and wishes—
who had not force of character enough to heartily oppose
him—who would unwillingly, servilely obey, puzzled and
uncomfortable, but not approving. What a noble, elevated

character he would feel himself, with such a life-companion
by his side ! Perhaps in time she would become like some
women whom he had seen now and then—quite broken in ;
having no will or opinion of her own, turning appealing eyes
to their lords upon every question. Hideous prospect !
Would it ever come to that ? Which evil would be the
lesser ? The woman whom he was to marry was a fool—
that fact was clearly enough revealed to him. It depended
upon him whether she should be an independent fool, unrestrained, and at liberty to vaunt her folly ; or whether she
should be a fool tamed and docile, making no disturbance,
but cringing like a spaniel. He had the power to make her
into either of these things. It was not a pleasing alternative.
He would have preferred a companion ; one whose intelligence, even if exerted in opposition to his own, should be
on something like a level with it. But that was never to be.
Lizzie was his : he had wooed her, won her ; since she loved
and trusted in him, he must wear her—and make the best
of it.

  *   *   *   *   *   *

 Less than a week afterwards, Aglionby escorted his betrothed home. The Hunt Ball was over ; it had been more
of a success, so far as decorum and strict propriety of
demeanour went, than that at Danesdale Castle, but Lizzie
had not enjoyed it one half so much. The Miss Conisbroughs, whom she honoured with her peculiar dislike, had
not been there. Randulf Danesdale had, looking very pale,
behaving very courteously ; but, as it seemed to Miss Vane,
chillingly ; dancing very little, and apparently considered a
dull partner by the young ladies whom he did lead out. A
dull ball, she vowed to herself, and she was ready to come
away early. It was on the day following that Aglionby
escorted her home. They had not much to say to one
another on the way. Bernard's thoughts were busied with
the future, and that disagreeably. Lizzie's were engrossed

with a letter which lay at that moment in her pocket. It
had come in an envelope addressed by Lucy Golding, and
when Bernard had given it to her, he had casually remarked:

'You and Miss Golding seem great allies, Lizzie. I didn't
know there was such an affection between you.'

'Oh, she's quite an old friend,' Lizzie had replied.

But the handwriting of the letter was not the handwriting
of the address.

In truth, Lizzie was in greater perplexity of mind than she
ever had felt before. The one thing that bound her to
Bernard was his wealth, and the position he had to offer her.
All her feelings, inclinations, associations, inclined to Percy,
who had lately been raised to a responsible post in the bank
in which he served, and who was now in a position to support
a wife in great comfort. Percy had addressed words of the
deepest pathos and the most heartrending despair to her, and
she was distracted what to do with him—now more than ever,
for her taste of aristocratic society had not altogether been
palatable; and as for Bernard, she felt chilled every time
she looked at him. It was not as if he maintained even his
former brusque fondness and affection. He seemed to have
changed entirely. She had been able to laugh at the brus-
querie, knowing that it needed but a caress on her part to
soften his most rugged mood. But now there was nothing
rugged to be softened—only an imperturbable and majestic
courtesy which literally overwhelmed her; and a gravity
which nothing seemed to have power to lighten. To have
to live with him always—if he were always going to be like
that—was a prospect which appalled her. She shrank, too,
from before his strong will. She did not wish to do the
things he wished her to do; but when he persisted, when he
fixed his eyes upon her, and took her hand in his strong
grasp, and spoke in what no doubt he intended for a kind
voice, but which was a voice that most distinctly said, 'Obey!'

then she felt her heart beat wildly—felt a passionate desire
to angrily fling off his hand and say, ' I will not !' and wrench
herself free ; felt at the same time a horrible hot sensation
which was stronger than she was, so that she always ended
by submitting to him.

He seldom caused her to have this sensation, it is true—
she had felt it when he forbade her to speak slightingly of his
cousins, and in the conversation that followed—but it was a
sensation which left a smart behind it long after the first
rush of it was over : it left her quivering, angry, yet helpless;
confused and miserable.   In a word, it was the sensation of
fear.   She feared her master because she was incapable of
understanding him.   It was not a happy state of things.
Looked at from Lizzie's point of view, she was a misunderstood being—a *femme incomprise.*   And I am not sure that
there was not a great deal of truth in her view of the case.

Bernard only stayed two or three days at Irkford ; long
enough to choose and take a house, and to give Lizzie *carte
blanche* as to the furnishing of it.   He said he would go and
see after Scar Foot being brightened up a little, and Miss
Vane said yes, that was a very good idea.   If she wanted him,
she was to send for him, he said ; and Lizzie said yes, she
would.   He would in any case be sure to come and see her
before April, he added ; and Lizzie said yes, indeed, she
hoped he would ; only he was to be sure and let her know
before he did come, which he promised.

He called to see Percy, and thought his old friend was
stiff and ungenial.   He went to Messrs. Jenkinson and
Sharpe's warehouse and found his old friend Bob Stansfield
there, looking very pale and overworked.   Aglionby carried
him off with him to Scar Foot, and said he had better learn to
be a farmer.   He returned to Scar Foot in the middle of January, found Mrs. Bryce there, and greeted her with the words:

' Aunt, it is good to be at home again.'

CHAPTER XXVIII.

DELPHINE.

WHEN Judith and her sister left Danesdale on the night after the ball, they drove home without exchanging a syllable. Judith was for once too absorbed in herself and her own concerns to notice her companion.

Delphine had folded her cloak around her and crouched, as if exceedingly weary, into one corner of the carriage. With her face turned towards the window, away from Judith, she remained motionless, voiceless, until at last they arrived at Yoresett House. It took a long time before Rhoda could be roused from her sleep by the parlour fire to let them in. At last she opened the door to them, and they went in, and paused in the great bare stone passage. Their candles stood there, and a lighted lamp.

'Well,' said Rhoda, yawning, and rubbing her eyes. 'What sort of a party was it?'

Delphine made no reply, but lighted her candle.

Rhoda was too sleepy to be very determined about receiv-ing an answer to her question, and still stood rubbing hei eyes and inarticulately murmuring that it must be very late.

'Good-night!' observed Delphine, with a shadow of hei usual shadowy smile, and drawing her white cloak about her, her white figure flitted up the stairs.

Then first it was that Judith began to remark something unusual in Delphine's behaviour. She said nothing, but contented herself with telling Rhoda, who had summoned up animation enough again to inquire what sort of a party it was, that it was very large, and very brilliant, and that she was too tired to say anything about it to-night—she would tell her to-morrow. Thereupon she put a candle into the sleepy maiden's hand, and with an indulgent smile bade her go. She would follow when she had looked round the house.

It came as something soothing, after the powerful agitation
of the past hours, to go, candle in hand, through all the dark,
cold passages, trying the doors, and seeing that all was locked
up. Then she put out the lamp in the parlour, and took her
way upstairs. She entered her own room, which, as has
been said, opened into Delphine's, though they both had
doors into the landing. The first thing that struck Judith
was that this door between their rooms was shut. The shut
door chilled her heart. She put her candle down, and stood
still, listening. A silence as of the grave greeted her. Delphine could not, in less than ten minutes, have taken off her
finery, and got into bed, and gone to sleep—*ergo*, she must
be sitting or standing, or at any rate waking, conscious, living,
in that room, behind that closed door.

Dread seized Judith's heart. They were accustomed to
undress with the partition-door open, walking in and out of
each other's rooms, chatting, or silent, as the case might be;
but never debarred either from entering the other's chamber.
And they always left the door open at last, and exchanged a
good-night before going to sleep. What did this miserable,
this unnatural closed door mean ?

' I wonder—I hope—surely it is not anything that Randulf Danesdale has said !' speculated Judith, in great uneasiness. She began to undress, but that closed door
importuned her. Still not a sound from within. She
began to question herself as to what she was to do. To
get into bed and take no notice of Delphine was a sheer im-
possibility. When she had taken off her beautiful frock,
and hung it up, and put on her dressing-gown, and taken
her hair-brush in her hand, she could bear it no longer. If
any sound from within had reached her, she could have
endured it, but the silence remained profound as ever. She
put the brush down, stepped across the room, and knocked
softly at the door. No reply.

Another knock, and ' Delphine !'

She had to knock again, and again to cry 'Delphine!' and then her sister's voice, calm and composed, said : 'Well?'

'May I not come in and say good-night!'

A slight rustle. Then the door was opened—a very little, and Delphine stood on the other side, still fully dressed, and without letting Judith in, said 'Good-night,' and bent forward to kiss her.

'Del, what is this?' asked Judith, in great distress. 'What is the matter?'

'Nothing,' replied the same sweet, composed voice. 'I am a little tired. Let me alone.'

'Tired—well, let me come in and help you to take off your dress, and brush your hair, Del!'

There was an almost urgent appeal in her voice.

'No, thank you. I shall sit by my fire a little while, I dare say. You look tired. Go to bed. Good-night.'

She waited a moment, and then—closed the door again—gently, slowly, but most decidedly.

Judith retired, almost wild with vague alarm. Some great blow had befallen Delphine. She, who was now so well ' acquainted with grief,' was quite sure of that. Who would have supposed that she would take this trouble so coldly and sternly ; so entirely to herself as to shut out even her best beloved, her perfect friend and companion, from participation in it? She passed a sleepless night. She could not tell whether Delphine ever went to bed. She lay awake with her nerves strained, and her ear intent to catch the faintest sound from her sister's room, and still none came. It was a cruel vigil. When it was quite late, though before the late daybreak had appeared, Judith dropped into an uneasy sleep, which presently grew more profound. Wearied out with grief, emotion, and fear, she slept soundly for a few hours, and when she awoke, the daylight made itself visible even through the down-drawn blind.

Feeling that it must be very late, and forgetting for a few

blessed moments the ball, and everything connected with it, she sprang up, and began to dress. Very soon, of course, it all returned to her : the brief flash of hope and new life was over ; grey reality, stony-hearted facts, the clouded future re-asserted themselves, and it was with a heart as heavy as usual that she at last went downstairs.

In the parlour she found that which in nowise tended to reassure her, or brighten her spirits. The breakfast-things were still on the table; Rhoda and Mrs. Conisbrough appeared to have finished. The latter was seated in her rocking-chair by the fire ; the former was at the table, her elbows resting upon it. Both faces were turned towards Delphine, with an expression of pleased interest, who sat at the head of the table, with a face devoid of all trace of colour (but that might easily be fatigue), and looking the whiter in her black dress. She too was smiling : she was talking —she was entertaining her mother and sister with an account of last night's ball—of the company, the dresses, and the be-haviour of those present ; and her descriptions were flavoured with an ill-natured sarcasm very unusual to her. Just now she was describing Miss Vane, and her pink frock, and her manners and conduct in general, holding them up in a light of ridicule, which, could the object have been cognisant of it, must have caused her spasms of mortification.

When Judith came in, she was welcomed also, as being the possible source of more interesting information ; but very soon her mechanical, spiritless recitals and monosyllabic replies drew down Rhoda's indignation, and Judith, with a forced smile and a horrible pain at her heart, said she would not attempt to rival Delphine, for that she had not enjoyed the party and could not pretend to describe it in an amusing manner.

Two or three days passed, and things were still in the same miserable state. Delphine still wore the same blanched face, still continued to show the same spirit of raillery and indifference. When she was with her mother and sisters it was always she who led the conversation, and was, as Rhoda gratefully informed her, the life and soul of the party.

' I wish you could go to a ball every week, Del,' she said fervently. ' It makes you quite delightful.'

To which Delphine replied, with a little laugh, that monotony palled. Rhoda would soon be tired of hearing of balls, which must all bear a strong family resemblance the one to the other. Occasionally Judith had found Delphine silent and alone, and then she realised how completely the other demeanour was a mask, put on to deceive and to cover some secret grief—secret indeed.

There are girls, and girls. Delphine surprised the person who knew her best by the manner in which she took her grief. Whatever it was, she kept it to herself. She had taken it in her arms, as it were, and made a companion of it, of whom she was very jealous. She kept it for her own delectation alone. No one else was suffered even to lift a corner of the thick veil which shrouded it. No one knew what it said to her, or she to it, in the long night-watches, in the silent vigils of darkness, or alone in the daylight hours ; nay, so fondly did she guard it, that none in that house, except Judith, even suspected its existence. Though her mother noted her white face, she was completely deceived by her composed and cheerful demeanour, and said that when the weather was warmer, Delphine would be stronger. It was Judith alone who instinctively felt that never had her sister been stronger, never so strong, as now, when she looked so white and wan. But she also felt it was that terrible kind of strength which feeds upon the spirit which supplies it : when that is exhausted, body and soul seem to break down together in an utter collapse, and this was what the elder girl feared for the younger ; this was why she longed irrepressibly that Delphine would only speak to her—confess her wretchedness—impart the extent and nature of her grief.

CHAPTER XXIX.

' FOR MY SON'S SAKE.'

THE ball had taken place on a Thursday—New Year's Eve. The days dragged on at Yoresett House, in the manner described, until the following Monday. On that afternoon, a dark and cloudy one, the quietness of the village street was broken. Sir Gabriel Danesdale, his groom behind him, rode up to the door. Sir Gabriel inquired if the ladies were at home ; he was told that they were, and he dismounted and went in, leaving his horse to be walked about by his groom, to the great wonderment of the watching population. He was ushered into the parlour, where Judith and her mother sat. Mrs. Conisbrough was fluttered. Only once or twice, since her widowhood, had Sir Gabriel ever entered her house. He had glanced about him as he passed through the hall—he had seen the bareness and the chillness of everything, and his heart was filled with pity and with some self-reproach. Marion Arkendale, with her dark eyes and her light foot, had been so bonny ; 'the Flower of Danesdale' had been her name. He did not know how it was that she had fallen out of the society of the place, had disappeared from the friendly circles, gradually, but surely.

' Poverty, poverty !' he thought to himself. ' It is a shame that she should have been neglected because of her poverty. And it was a rascally trick on old John's part, though he was my friend, to leave her as he did.' Filled with these reflections, he spoke cordially, and almost eagerly, holding out his hand :

' Mrs. Conisbrough, I am more of a stranger in your house than I should be, considering what old friends and neighbours we are. Will you forgive my negligence, and believe that it arises out of anything rather than ill-will ?'

' Ah, Sir Gabriel, I never suspected you of ill-will,' she

said, flushing. 'And when women are alone in the world
their circle must be smaller than when there are men in the
family. Pray sit down. I am glad to see you under my
roof.'

'It gave me hearty pleasure to see your daughters amongst
us on Thursday,' he continued. 'Perhaps, as you say your
circle is so small, you don't know what a sensation they made.
Half the fellows who were there have been talking about
them ever since.'

Mrs. Conisbrough smiled, gratified.

'You are very good. My girls have had no outside
advantages. They have none, indeed, except their youth
and the fact that they are ladies by birth, and, I hope, by
breeding. And that tells, Sir Gabriel—even in these days,
it tells.'

'My dear madam, it is everything,' said he earnestly. 'I
quite agree with you. We'll have a chat about that a little
later ; and meantime, I want to know if I may see your
daughter Delphine, alone, for a short time. I have something that I wish to say to her.'

Mrs. Conisbrough started, paused, then replied :

'Certainly you can see her. Judith, Delphine is in the
other room. Suppose you take Sir Gabriel to her there.'

Judith rose and went across the passage, while Sir Gabriel,
bowing over Mrs. Conisbrough's hand, wished her good-
afternoon, and left her without explaining his errand. He
followed Judith, who was in the room on the opposite side
of the hall. Turning as she saw him come, she remarked :

'Ah, here is Sir Gabriel, Delphine.'

Then she left them alone, and closed the door after her.

Sir Gabriel found himself standing before a pale, composed-
looking young lady, whose hand rested lightly on the mantelpiece, and whose beauty and grace struck him even more in the
dull light of this January afternoon, than they had done in
her radiant ball-dress beneath the lamplight on New Year's

Eve.   Perfectly calm, she turned her large luminous eyes, with their golden reflections, upon him as he entered, and a scarcely perceptible sigh left her lips.

Dark rings encircled those lovely eyes.   Though the delicate white brow was smooth there was a shadow upon it, indefinable, but most palpable.   Sir Gabriel remembered how Randulf had said she looked, and he felt that the lad had been right.   This calm and stillness was not that of repose, but the pallid quietude which follows a mortal blow.   She attempted a faint little smile as he came in which flickered for a moment about her mouth, and then died away again, as if abashed.   Sir Gabriel, whose bosom had been filled with very mingled feelings as he rode hither from Danesdale, no longer felt doubtful as to what emotion predominated.   It was a great compassion that he experienced ; a strong man's generous desire to take to his sufficing protection some weak, and sad, and grieved creature ; to comfort it, to bid it sorrow no more.

Sir Gabriel contemplated the beautiful forlorn figure, and his heart swelled almost to bursting.   Those eyes might well haunt Randulf.   Of course he could not put his arm round her waist, and say, ' My poor child, tell me what ails you, and let me lift this trouble from your shoulders,' as he would have liked to do.   Custom did not permit such a thing, but he took her hand kindly, and looked kindly from his genial, yet commanding eyes into her white face, while he said, kindly too :

' My dear, I have ridden over from Danesdale to have a little chat with you.'

' Yes ; will you sit down ?' said Delphine.

' Yes, if you will take this chair beside me, and listen to me.   I will not delay in telling you my errand.   My boy Randulf tells me that he has fallen very much in love with you, at which fact I certainly cannot pretend to be surprised.   Nay, it is surely not a matter about which to be alarmed !' he added, seeing the agitation on her face, which she could not repress. 'Let me tell you that I know all that has passed between you and Randulf. He told me. He forgot himself the other night—in a very pardonable manner—but he did forget himself, it is quite certain. A man in his position has no business to propose to any lady without consulting his father. From what he told me, I am sure you were sensible of that —were you not? Did you not feel scruples on that point?'

'Yes—that is, I should have done, if——'

'I thought so,' said Sir Gabriel, hearing only that which he wished to hear. 'I told him so. I said I honoured you for those scruples. I thought the matter over very seriously —you will not wonder at that. The marriage of a man's only son is no trivial matter to him. I came to the conclusion that my son's happiness is bound up in this matter— that it stands or falls with it——'

'No, no!' interrupted Delphine, in a quick, gasping voice.

'Yes, my dear child, it does. He loves you with no passing passion. It has made him into a man all at once. I say, his happiness stands or falls with it; and I venture to hope that you feel the same with respect to yourself.'

Silence was the only answer.

Sir Gabriel's face lost none of its kindness, but a troubled expression crept over it, and into his eyes, and he saw the fixed and marble composure of the lovely face before him.

'You do not speak,' he said at last. 'Let me explain as clearly as I can the errand which brought me here. I have come to ask you to reconsider the answer you gave to Randulf the other night. Put away any thoughts of me—ask only of your own heart if it contains that love for my son, which a wife should bear to her husband, and if it answers you yes, give me leave to send Randulf to see you; let him hear from you that you will become his wife, and my daughter.'

Delphine's face had only grown paler. Her hand, which had been resting nervelessly on the table, had slipped down,

and was now fast locked together with the other. She clasped
them tightly upon her lap, looking at him with the same dull,
glazed eyes, the same impassive calm, and speaking at last in
a toneless, mechanical voice, which seemed not to belong to
herself.

'I am very sorry. You are very good to me, but I cannot
marry your son.'

Sir Gabriel was shocked, distressed in the extreme. This
was no refusal from one who was indifferent. Could it
possibly be that the girl was not quite in her right mind? But
that idea was soon cast aside. Nothing could be less agitated,
more reasonable, more sane than her whole manner. He
did not know that she was suffering supreme torture; that
she felt as if every moment she must shriek aloud in her
despair, or burst into a fit of wild, hysterical laughter at the
grim humour of the game of cross-purposes which they were
playing. This he could not know; but he would have been
a fool if he had not read suffering in her blanched face, in
her dull and fixed eyes, in her nervously clasped hands, and
in the dead monotone of her voice. He could only grope
about, pleading Randulf's cause, which had now become his
own; with each word stabbing her afresh, thinking that if
only he could get her to assign the reason for her refusal of
Randulf, he would be able to overcome it.

'You told Randulf that you did not love him,' he went on.
'He told me that he did not believe you.' A rush of colour
surged over her face, and Sir Gabriel went on gently, but
pushing matters as far as he could, to make things straight,
as he thought: 'As to that I can affirm nothing, except
that he spoke from the most reverent and solemn conviction,
and not as a coxcomb. And you will forgive my saying that
there could surely be nothing very remarkable in it—
certainly nothing to be ashamed of, if you did love him, however ardently. I am his father, and consequently prejudiced
in his favour, but I ought to know better than others what

he has been to me. He has been a good son, of whom I am
as proud as I am fond. I think his sister would own that
he is a good brother.' (One of Delphine's hands went up to
her face, and half hid it.) 'His friends, I notice, continue
to be his friends. His dependents are fond of him; they
serve him cheerfully. His dogs and horses love him too,
and that is something to go by. He is no fool; he is a
gentleman by nature as well as by birth.' (Delphine's other
hand had now gone to her face, which was covered completely.) 'And there is no reason why he should not be as
worthy as a lover and husband as he is in these other things.
And added to that, my child, he loves you neither lightly
nor carelessly, but with a love I like to see—with reverence
as well as passion, with a man's love, and the love of a good
and honourable man. Is it really impossible that you can
return his love? Surely you cannot refuse to allow him to
plead his cause! Surely——'

He stopped abruptly, moved, himself, as he dwelt upon
the excellences of that 'boy' who was so dear to him, and
to secure whose happiness he had undertaken this errand.
For the last few minutes Delphine's arms had been stretched
out upon the table, her golden head prone upon them, her
face hidden from sight. Now she suddenly raised it to him
—tearless still, but with her eyes dim with anguish, and
faltered brokenly:

'Oh, Sir Gabriel, have a little pity upon me! Do you
think I do not know what he is!' The words came with
something like indignation, anger, scorn. 'Have I not got
eyes, and ears, and a *heart?* Oh, if it could only turn to
stone this moment! And has he not looked at me, and
spoken to me, and told me he loved me? Has he not been
kind, and gentle, and generous? Has he not I
worship him!'

The last words sprang forth, as it were, involuntarily,
breathlessly. She looked at him for a moment with flashing

eyes, her face transfigured with a beauty which startled him ; her passionate fervour reduced him to silence. That Randulf loved her he wondered no longer. He approved from his heart of hearts.

' *Therefore* I will never marry him,' she went on, and her voice had gained strength. 'Tell him what you please ; that I am a flirt and a jilt—only he will never believe it ; but tell him I will never marry him. And if you knew why,' she added composedly, 'you would not press me either.'

' I do not know that,' he said. ' I see you are oppressed by what seems to you some very painful secret. But you know nothing of the world, my child. I must be a far better judge than you of what does and what does not constitute an insuperable obstacle. Cannot you confide in me ?' '

' No, never, never ! I know nothing of the world, as you say ; but I know the difference between honour and dishonour. It is for your sake, and his—not mine. Do I look as if I were enjoying it ? Do I look happy ? I know what I am doing. Believe that, and in pity's name leave me to my misery.'

He felt that there was no further appeal. He could not be angry with her. He could not resent, though he had spoken quite advisedly when he said that with her answer Randulf's happiness must stand or fall. It would have to fall, but, somehow, the largehearted old man could think at present only of this stricken girl—for he saw she was stricken —not of his own nearest and dearest.

' Then, my child, I must even leave you, though I feel my heart broken to have my errand end so badly. Goodbye, my love ! I would fain have gone home feeling I had gained another child. I would gladly see my son married to a wife like you, if it could have been !'

Sir Gabriel's lips were quivering, as he took her hand, stooped, and gently kissed her forehead. She did not speak, she uttered not a syllable, but sat beside the table still, white

as ever, with her hand drooping beside her. At the door
he turned back once again, and came to her, saying :
'Remember, you can never be indifferent to me. If ever
I can serve you, let me know how, and it shall be done.'

Then he went away, really, and she never moved. She
heard the front door open, the horses' hoofs. Then they
rode away, and she was alone, the fire, burning low, the
early January evening closing in, dank and drear.

To her poignant anguish a great apathy had succeeded.
She had spoken out her whole soul and life as she told Sir
Gabriel, 'I *worship* him !' The whole scene seemed to float
away into the background, like some far-back, half remembered dream. Everything was shadowy and unreal.

Still she sat alone, and her forehead never changed from
its white, stony composure, though it was almost dark, and it
was a long time since Sir Gabriel had gone. She did not
know that. She scarcely heard the door softly open and close,
but she was conscious by-and-by that some one knelt down
beside her—it was Judith, who had taken her drooping
hand, and was speaking to her, in her deep, vibrating tones :
'Delphine, forgive me, but I cannot bear it any longer.
What have I done that you should repel me thus ? If your
heart breaks, let mine break with it. I ask nothing else.
Let us be together, even if it is only in our wretchedness !'

The appeal came at the right moment. Earlier, it would
have irritated. Later, it would have been useless. Just now,
with her great renunciation just consummated, it was salvation ; it enabled her to speak.

'Judith—you are all I have left.'

'And you to me. I have lived with you these two hours,
and suffered with you. Sir Gabriel is a kind old man, Delphine.'

'Poor old man ! Yes, very. He likes to see people
happy. He wants me to be happy—he wants Randulf to
be happy. The other night Randulf asked me to marry him,

and I said no. To-day Sir Gabriel came and asked me to marry Randulf; and told me all about how good he was, and how good it would be —oh, Judith ! how good it would be to be his wife !'

Her head fell upon her sister's neck. Judith knew better than to speak. There was a long silence, during which one suffered perhaps as keenly as the other.

' I said no,' Delphine resumed, at last. 'The worst is over now. I must try to go on as if it had not happened— only, Judith you must promise me one thing.'

' Anything that is in my power to do, my child.'

' Try to keep mamma from talking of it. I fear she will be angry, and I cannot bear it. To wrangle over it, would be like wrangling over the dead body of the person who was dearest to you.'

Judith's brow darkened. There were moments when her large, grave beauty took an expression of kindling anger, and she was not one whose anger is as a summer cloud : it was not an anger to be smiled at.

' I have seen to that,' she said. 'There are limits to childish obedience. For your sake, Delphine, I have done what I never thought to do. My mother was angry. Sir Gabriel just came in and spoke to her. He said it was due to her to say that you had refused Mr. Danesdale, and that he could not oppose your decision. When he was gone, she wanted to know why. She said she must understand what you meant. I could bear it no longer. I spoke : I told her why.'

' You told her ? But that is fearful !' said Delphine, in an awestruck whisper.

' It is fearful. But there was no alternative. I did not openly name the reason ; I said it was for the same reason as that for which Uncle Aglionby had left his money to his grandson. She looked at me in a manner I shall never forget. It was I who felt the criminal ; but you will not be tormented. . . . As for me, I shall soon go away from here. It is not fitting that she and I should be in the same house together, for she will not forgive me. She will forgive you, Delphine. Come and speak to her.'

Delphine complied, without hesitation. It was Judith's turn to be left by herself—the strongest, and therefore the loneliest spirit under that roof.

CHAPTER XXX.

MARAH.

A SAD afternoon at the end of January. The scene was Mrs. Malleson's pleasant drawing-room at Stanniforth Rectory. Stanniforth was an exceeding large and desolate parish; it comprised Yoresett, and Scar Foot, and Danesdale, and many other offshoots and dependencies. Sparse was the population, though the extent was great, for, in the words of the old chronicler, 'Litle corne groweth in Suadale;' and of Danesdale he says, 'Danesdale, and the soile abowt is very hilly, and berith litle corne; but noriseth many bestes;' a description true to this day, to the very letter.

The house belonging to the old 'paroch chirche for alle the aforesaid townes,' was a large, pleasant, modern mansion. Mrs. Malleson's drawing-room faced south, looking across a flower-garden, over some roughly-wooded 'common land,' to rugged grey fells. At this season of the year, the sun set almost exactly opposite the windows of this room. He had been struggling all day to make a way through the clouds, without much success. Just now, however, he had riven the clouds asunder, and was casting an almost lurid glow of farewell splendour; of misty rays like a crown over the rugged ridges of the fells. Indoors, it was not too light. The fire shone on the furniture, and on the keys of the open piano.

The two occupants of the room were Mrs. Malleson and Judith Conisbrough, and they had been drinking four o'clock tea. Judith, who had taken off her hat and mantle, sat in the oriel window, in a low, chintz-covered chair. Her face was turned towards the sunset above the everlasting hills ; and the departing rays caught it, and lit it up with a kind of halo, throwing out into full relief the strong, yet delicate features of her noble face, and showing forth more than usual, both its sadness and its beauty.

Mrs. Malleson, a little bright brunette, with quick, bird-like, graceful movements, looked, beside her visitor, like a robin beside some far-seeing royal bird. She sat behind her tea-table, and laid down the work which her ever-busy fingers had for a long time been plying—for she was an industrious little lady.

'I wish I could have an exact likeness of you as you sit now, Judith, with the sun shining upon your face. The picture would do beautifully for a painted window, if a ring were put round your head, and it was called St. Cecilia, or St. Theresa, or St. Elizabeth, or some of these grand women, you know.'

'Very different from the reality, who is neither grand nor a saint, but who wishes very much that your husband would come in, dear Paulina.'

'I cannot imagine what detains him, I am sure. He knew you were coming, because he made a special note of it, and he has taken such a deep interest in all this affair of yours. But he cannot be long now.'

'And he would not tell you what he had found for me ?' said Judith, and Mrs. Malleson repeated, not for the first time that afternoon :

'No, dear. It was about a week ago that he suddenly said, at breakfast-time, "I have it, I believe, at last." And then I said, "What have you, Laurence ?" he answered, "Some work that will suit Miss Conisbrough." Not another word would he say to me ; but when I asked him if it was anything to do with nursing, he answered mysteriously, "Perhaps—perhaps not." And that is all I know, except that yesterday he told me to write to you, and ask if you would call here, as he was so busy, and didn't wish you to be delayed.'

'I *wonder* what it is !' said Judith, resting her chin upon her hand, and still gazing out towards the hills and the setting sun.

'I hope it will be something you will not mind taking,' said Mrs. Malleson seriously. 'Laurence is such a very matter-of-fact man, you know. He would be quite capable of thinking that when you said you would take *anything*, you meant it.'

'Of course I meant it. I believe there is not any kind of honest work with head or hands that I would not gladly take, to get away from Yoresett.'

'Well, let us hope—there he is !' said Mrs. Malleson, as she heard the loud latch of the vestibule door lift and fall. 'And some one with him. Excuse me, Judith. I'll send him to you here, and tell him to make short work with his business, or he'll have to walk home with you.'

She skimmed out of the room, closing the door after her. Judith, again lost in the absorbing speculation, 'What can it be ?' fixed her eyes upon the now grey and deathly looking sky, over which night was fast casting its mantle, nor noticed any outside sounds, until Mr. Malleson's voice roused her.

The Reverend Laurence Malleson was a favourable specimen of a broad-church clergyman of the Church of England, on the Charles Kingsley lines.

He was some thirty-three or thirty-five years of age, and was dressed in a manner which would not have betrayed to anyone his priestly vocation.

'Miss Conisbrough, I fear I have kept you waiting an unconscionable time,' he began ; 'and I am very sorry for it.

I can only say that I really could not help it, and trust to your good-nature to excuse me.'

'Pray do not mention it, Mr. Malleson. I do not mind waiting if, as Mrs. Malleson leads me to hope, you have a little work waiting for *me*, at the end of the time.'

'I was much puzzled by the circumstances of your case, I confess,' he said. 'I agreed with my wife, that it was not everything that would do for you. I could soon have found you *something*. I could have got you a situation as nursery governess, to take entire charge of three children, and teach them music, French, drawing, and English, at the handsome stipend of twenty-five pounds a year. Would you have taken that ?'

'If there had been *nothing* else—yes. But I would rather have to do with grown-up people than with children.'

'You spoke of nursing. Of course I could have recommended you to different institutions. But there was your "lack of gold !"' (Mr. Malleson spoke plainly, but with as keen an interest as if it were his own case he was describing and providing for, and Judith was far too much in earnest to care if he had been twice as explicit.)

'The most agreeable places as nurses,' he went on, 'are those where you go as what they call a "lady probationer ;" paying about a guinea a week for board, lodging, and practical instruction, until the medical board consider you qualified to take a nurse's place. But you had told me that you must go somewhere where you could earn, not pay money : where services, not a premium, were required.'

'Yes.'

'One morning I bethought myself quite suddenly of Dr. Hugh Wentworth of Irkford. Did you ever hear of him ?'

'No.'

'He has a name, nevertheless. He is an old friend of mine. We were schoolfellows. He is a comparatively young man—about my age, in fact ; but he has taken every

degree that the medical profession has to give, and is
member of I don't know how many scientific societies with
long names.   He is President of the Irkford Royal Infirmary,
and his private practice might be of any extent he chooses.
We used to be great friends, as lads.   Lately, we have lost
sight of one another.   I knew him to be influential, and I
believed him to be rarely good and wise; a man in a
thousand.   Well, I wrote to him; recalled myself to his
memory, and asked him if he cared to do me a favour, as I
thought he could.   Promptly I had a reply.   He remembered all about it, and was glad to hear of me again; and
any favour that lay in his power, he would do me.   I then
wrote to him again.   I told him about you.   I gave him
my impressions as to your character and capabilities.   I
told him that what you wanted was *work*—that you were
desirous to learn anything that you were set to do, and that
whatever it might be, you were resolved to master it.   I
mentioned nursing, and said that your thoughts had turned
towards it, not sentimentally——'

'Ah, I am glad you said that.'

'But as a career—as a practical calling.   In short, I
begged him, if he had any opening for a learner, and was
likely to hear of any, to remember me and you.   And he
has done so.'

Mr. Malleson smiled pleasantly, not adding that he had
spoken of Judith to his friend in terms of praise, such as
those who knew him as Dr. Wentworth did were well aware
he rarely used; that he had wound up his description of
her by saying:

'In short, she is one of those women who would fulfil old
George Herbert's words—who would sweep a room, if she
had it to sweep, to the glory of her God.'

'He has done so?   Oh, Mr. Malleson, what goodness,
on both his part and yours!   And what does he say?'

'He says'—the rector drew a letter from his pocket—

'he says, "The young lady you speak of, Miss Judith Conisbrough, appears to be a—h'm—h'm—character who might
be useful, if her energies were properly directed. Of course
I know, as every medical man of large practice must, that
hundreds, if not thousands, of young women annually die,
or go mad, or sink into hopeless querulousness or hysteric
invalidism, simply because they have nothing to do in the
world. Miss Conisbrough can come to Irkford if she
chooses. I can find some work for her, but I beg you will
explain to her that it is neither light, nor agreeable, nor well-
paid. No nurse's work is agreeable. It is seldom well-paid.
She will find the start, especially, most unpleasant. It would
not be nursing, as I have no room at present for either a
nurse or probationer. By-and-by there will be a vacancy.
What I can give her is this. In the Nurses' Home, in
which my wife and I take a great interest, there is a matron
who wants an assistant. The assistant's duties would be
chiefly of a domestic character at first, and pray do not
delude Miss Conisbrough with the idea that they would be
in any way different from what domestic offices usually are.
She would have various departments to look after—from
the kitchen to the receiving of visitors if necessary, or if the
matron were otherwise engaged. She can try it, if she likes.
It will give her a thorough practical acquaintance with the
arrangements of the house in which, should she ever become
a nurse or a probationer, she would have to live. For her
services in this capacity she would receive eighteen pounds
a year. When an opening occurs, I will, if her conduct
and capabilities have been satisfactory, give her the refusal
of a probationer's place. I have had many applications for
the place, but none which I consider quite suitable. I am
inclined to think that your friend would do, since from what
you say, I gather that she is country born and bred ; that in
tastes she is simple and frugal; is physically strong and
healthy, and in mind steadfast. Pray do not forget to

impress upon her that the work is neither light nor agreeable; or it may be that after five minutes' conversation with her, I may simply have to tell her to go home again. As soon as she decides, let me know. She may come as soon as she pleases; she must come within the next ten days if she decides to come at all.'"

'Now what do you say?' asked Mr. Malleson. 'It is eighteen pounds a year, and work that is evidently neither delicate nor agreeable. The other is five-and-twenty pounds, and much less arduous work——'

'Oh, I will take the Irkford one, please. The work cannot be too arduous for me. Oh, Mr. Malleson, if you only knew what this is to me!'

It was with great difficulty that she refrained from bursting into tears of relief and joy. The tight strain at her heart seemed loosened. The awful tension—the blank unvaried hopelessness of her present and future had changed.

'I am glad if it does please you. But you will forgive my saying—you must allow me, since I am your clergyman, and you are without father or brother—to say that it behoves you to think seriously and long before you take such a step —before you, a lady born and bred, leave your quiet home in this beautiful and healthy spot, to venture out into a great city, where you will have onerous work, which will have to be carried on in the vitiated air of the same city. Remember, you renounce your freedom, your independence; you bind yourself to absolute servitude, absolute obedience, and——'

'Yes, Mr. Malleson; I have reflected upon all those points. I can only say, that you do not know all the motives which prompt me to take this course. You and Mrs. Malleson have known me for some years now; have I ever behaved in a giddy, or unseemly, or irrational manner, during that time?'

'Never, to my knowledge.'

'And I am not doing so now. I have made no light

decision. I came to it on my knees—through fasting and prayer—not from carelessness or love of variety.'

'I will say no more. I trust you fully, and fully appreciate the earnestness of your purpose. It only grieves me to think that one at your age, and in your position, should feel it necessary to come to so stern and sad a decision.'

'You are very kind. I have pitied myself often, in former times, but not now.'

'I hope you have not been without consolation. It is often in such trials that the purest and truest consolation is given; indeed it is doubtful whether those who have not had hard and bitter trials, *can* know what inward peace means. There was a royal lady you know, once, whose crown was a crown of sorrows almost from the first day she wore it, and *she* said constantly :

> 'Who ne'er his bread with tears hath ate,
>   Who ne'er the night's drear watches through
> Weeping beside his bed hath sate,
>   Ye heavenly powers, he knows not *you*.'

'I know,' said Judith. 'But Queen Louise was a braver and a better woman than I am; and in all her sorrows she had work to do. I have sorrowed as she did. I have eaten my bread with tears, and wept on my bed the whole night long; but I have not found much consolation yet. This work, I trust, will help to bring it.'

She rose, as did Mr. Malleson.

'You will not go without telling us—you will see my wife and me again before you leave ?'

'Surely; and I will say good-night to Paulina now. I must take my way home.'

Mr. Malleson preceded her across the passage, threw open the door of a lighted room (for all the sunset had long been over, and darkness had descended); and Judith, entering and screening her eyes from the sudden glare, found herself face to face with her friend Mrs. Malleson, and with Bernard Aglionby, who had risen as she, Judith, came in, and who now stood looking at her.

CHAPTER XXXI.

LOVE AND WAR.

'OH, you are still here !' observed the clergyman to Aglionby. 'Won't you stay and have some dinner with us, as it has got so late ?'

'No, thank you,' replied he, shaking hands with Judith, though neither he nor she spoke. 'I heard from Mrs. Malleson that Miss Conisbrough was here, and would be walking home, so I sent my horse on to Yoresett, and remained here to escort her, if she will allow me to do so.'

'Oh ! I think there is no need,' began Judith.

'My dear, there is !' said Mrs. Malleson decidedly ; 'and, to please me, you will accept Mr. Aglionby's escort. Indeed, I will not invite him to dinner ; and as he will be obliged to walk to Yoresett, that settles the question.'

'Yes, I think it does,' said Judith rather gravely. 'I am only sorry that Mr. Aglionby should have put himself to such inconvenience.'

To this Aglionby made no reply. He had not spoken to her at all. They had all moved towards the hall.

'Are you well wrapped up for the walk, Judith ? Won't you have an extra shawl ?' asked her friend.

'No, thank you. I walk quickly. Good-night, Paulina. Your husband will tell you all about it. And good-night, Mr. Malleson. *I thank you,*' she said, with emphasis, looking earnestly into his face. 'You know what that means with me.'

Husband and wife accompanied them to the hall, opened the door for them, and they stepped out into the mirk.

'Bitter chill it was.'

The door—that hospitable door—was closed after them. It had been thawing during the day, but was now freezing hard. The sky had cleared, and the stars were appearing. Judith's heart was beating fast. However calm and uneventful her outside life might have been, her inner one had been filled with deep and varied emotions. The interview she had just concluded had been to her a solemn one ; it had stirred her spirit to its depths. She had expected a long walk home, alone in the dark, and had promised herself that in its course she would reflect upon all that had passed ; would smooth out the tangled web of conflicting feelings, and plan how best to break her decision to those at home, She felt that she needed this interval : needed this spell of quiet meditation. Now, behold, it was denied her. She was not to be alone. Another was to be her companion : one from whom in spirit she indeed never strayed far, but of whom the shadowy spiritual presence was, compared with the actual bodily one, exactly 'as moonlight is to sunlight, and as water is to wine.' How could she think, how ponder, how become at one with herself, with Bernard Aglionby at her side ? She gave it up at once, thinking, with a kind of moral recklessness which of late had been a frequent visitant with her :

'What does it matter ? Soon it will *all* be at an end. What difference can one pang more make—one other straw ? Let him come ! I shall get through it somehow.'

But as they paced silently down the rectory drive, she began to realise that she had never really conquered him, never induced him to submit to her behests except in so far as words—promises—went. He was like the young man of the parable, who said, 'I go, sir,' but went not. This was the second time he had disobeyed the spirit, if not the letter, of what she required of him. She knew that it was not done innocently or unconsciously. She knew that he was quite aware of his disobedience, and that he did it deliberately and advisedly. It was very wrong of him, with Lizzie Vane in the background on his side, and with, on her side, far worse things than a Lizzie Vane, and things which *must* not be nearly approached. Very wrong; she could in nowise palliate or approve of it ; she felt that she ought to rebuke it, and even while conning over in her mind the best way in which to begin the rebuke, she was conscious of a wild, unlicensed pleasure, on her own part, at the occurrence.

'There is no moon, is there?' were the words which roused her when they had proceeded for some little distance along the road to Yoresett.'

'No ; but it is clear, and the stars are bright. Otherwise, this is a dark, lonely road.'

'It is,' he answered, with considerable emphasis. 'It is no road on which for you to be alone at such an hour. I could scarcely believe Mrs. Malleson when she told me you had got to walk home, and that without an escort.'

'That shows plainly that you have a great deal yet to learn about country habits.'

'I hope so, if that is one of them ; but——'

'Are you going this way?' said Judith, pausing as he made for a narrow lane on the right. 'If we go this way we have to cross the river, and there is no bridge, you know, only the stepping-stones.'

'Well, are you afraid? I thought you were boasting of your country habits. It is starlight ; it is not *quite* the end of daylight yet. "Th' hipping stanes," as they call them here, are solid, high, and dry ; and my hand is a firm one, I assure you.'

Judith said nothing, but followed him down the lane into a road which ran through the bottom of the valley, beside the river for some little distance, till, where it was broad and shallow, a long line of stepping-stones led across it to the other side. It was a weird-looking spot, hardly tempting to one not used to such roads and such 'short-cuts.' Just below the stepping-stones, too, was a ford, and a dangerous ford, since to deviate but a few feet from its course meant—and had proved—certain death to horse and man, by reason of a horrible deep hole shelving suddenly down, deep enough to bury completely, as it had done more than once, horse, driver, and vehicle. Between the 'hipping-stanes' towards this grisly trap the water rushed gurgling along ; the bed of the river was too shallow and broken, the motion too incessant, for the water to freeze. Judith paused as they stood by the first stepping-stone, while, after one or two of the others, the remainder faded and vanished, and the opposite bank of the stream was not discernible.

'It looks—I never crossed them at such an hour, or when it was so dark——' she began.

'Are you afraid to trust yourself on them—with me ? Do you imagine that I should not share any accident which might befall you ?'

He offered her his hand, and again struck dumb, as it were, Judith put hers in it, and allowed him to lead her whither he would. The crossing of the stepping-stones was a slow one, but it was accomplished in safety and in silence. They traversed, silently also, the little lane at the other side, which led them to the high-road to Yoresett, and when they were once more there, and slowly walking through a little dark wood on either side the wall, Aglionby began, slowly :

'Mrs. Malleson tells me that you think of leaving Yoresett.'

'Yes. That is, I have wished to leave Yoresett for a long time. Now I have quite decided to do so, because Mr. Malleson has been kind enough to use his interest with a friend to get me something to do.'

'Ah ! I do not know that such things always *are* kind. Mrs. Malleson said she was jealous of you,' he added, with a forced laugh, 'for that you and her husband had secrets.'

'In other words, you asked her where I was going, and what I was going to do, and she could not tell you.'

'Quite true, though you put it in as disagreeable a manner as you can. You consider my natural interest in your movements to be impertinent.'

'I never said so. I only know that, considering what it was that Mr. Malleson had to say to me, he did perfectly right not to speak of it to anyone until he had seen me.'

'Forgive me; but is it allowable to ask what the work is which is to take you away from Yoresett—a fact which appears to cause you much rejoicing?'

'Oh, quite. I have no wish now to make any secret of it. I was too happy when Mr. Malleson told me of it.'

'Is it something so delightful? You certainly try my patience to the utmost; but perhaps my assurance in asking merits some such punishment.'

'Not at all. I am going to live at Irkford.'

'At Irkford!' First there was a ring of astonishment, then one of irrepressible pleasure, in his tones. 'So am I.'

'Yes, I suppose so.'

'But may I not know what you are going to do at Irkford?'

She told him, briefly enough, and concluded:

'So you see, I shall begin at the beginning, and who knows where I shall end? I am vain enough to fancy that some time I may rise quite high—to the position of matron, or lady-superintendent—who knows?'

He had let her give her account of her future life and duties without uttering a word of interruption. He had heard her out, even to the utterance of the ambitious dream of the last sentence, and then he said, quite composedly:

'I am surprised at Mr. Malleson proposing such a monstrous thing to you, even in a jest. I fancied he had more sense. He must have known how utterly impossible it was for you to accept it. Really, it was almost insulting to you. But I suppose he was trying you.'

'You are strangely mistaken. I have Dr. Wentworth's address in my purse, and shall write to him to-night, and propose to go to him in a week from now.'

'You are jesting,' he said ; and still he spoke composedly, though not so quietly as at first.

'I never was in more solemn and steadfast earnest in my life.'

Another pause.

They walked on side by side, and Judith imagined that he had dismissed the subject from his mind, as not concerning him—as a wilful woman's whim. Suddenly she was startled by hearing him say, in a voice which she hardly recognised :

'You must not : you shall not ! I will not have it !'

His voice quivered uncontrollably. Judith caught her breath : her heart gave a great bound : at the same instant conscience cried, loudly and imperatively :

'That is wrong ! stop it at once !'

'You must be dreaming, Mr. Aglionby, to speak to me in such a manner,' she said coldly.

And that was all that resolution could at first summon to the assistance of conscience. When the head is sick, and the limbs fail, it is hard to march onwards with unchanged front.

'Dreaming, am I ?' he said, with a short, angry laugh. 'I wish to heaven I could think I was !'

They were passing a small lonely farm by the wayside. A bright light shone from one of the windows. He stopped abruptly, and Judith stopped too, as if she had been part of himself.

'Look at me !' he bade her, in a voice choked with anger and sorrow. 'Look at me, and tell me again, *if you can*, that you intend to do this thing.'

'Assuredly, I am resolved to do it,' she answered, raising her eyes to his face, and speaking steadily, coldly, decidedly.

She could, however, scarce endure to encounter the glance she met; it was so wrathful, and withal so wobegone—nor to contemplate his countenance, so pale was it, so transfigured.

'I intend it!' she repeated, averting her eyes, and speaking with desperate haste. 'And more than that, I look forward to it as my salvation, as to a deliverer from a life which I loathe, and from a burden which has grown greater than I can bear.'

'*It must not be!*' said he, in a passionate whisper. 'Judith, it must not be. You must give this up—indeed you must.'

'I quite fail to see why . . . and indeed, I beg you will not enter into your reasons,' she added hastily, seeing he was about to speak. 'My mind is made up, and *you* can have no possible right to meddle in the matter.'

She spoke even more decidedly, but thrilled as she remembered that once or twice already she had made up her mind, without Aglionby's having been much affected by that fact.

'You have treated me hardly from the very first,' he said, and they were still standing in the road, speaking in low, vehement tones. 'You have exacted from me submission in things where most men would have refused to yield it. You have forbidden me to enter your house, to be on friendly terms with you, to do the barest justice to your mother, or your sisters, or yourself. Justice! You refuse to allow me to attempt even any palliation of the manner in which they have been treated. You have already extracted from my inheritance every grain of pleasure which it would have given me, and now to crown all, you turn upon me, and coolly inform me that you—*you*, to save whom from a moment's uneasiness I would give all that I am worth——'

'You have no right to say that to *me*,' said Judith proudly.

'My wrongs give me a right to say that—and more than

that. To crown all, I say, you inform me that you are going to undertake a task which would make a strong man recoil—to be a servant amongst servants, until this doctor, who might be a pope in whom you placed implicit reliance, sees fit in his good pleasure to order you to go to a hospital, and immolate yourself within its walls, amongst horrors of every kind—amongst loathsome wounds, small-pox, fever, perhaps. If they order you to go and nurse a man down with black typhus, you must do it—can you deny it?'

'Deny it—no! Why should I?'

'All this, and all sorts of nameless horrors besides. Any day you may take some horrible disease and die of it. God! it makes my brain reel, only to imagine it! I wish I could have choked Malleson before he ever wrote his disgraceful letter to this cursed doctor!'

Judith had moved on, too agitated, too overpowered and excited to stand still. She had forgotten by now that it was wrong in him to address her thus. She felt only the strong, overpowering joy of finding herself first and foremost in his heart—indubitably, undeniably first.

'And you expect me still tamely to submit to such a proceeding?' he continued, vehemently. 'What do you take me for? A spaniel? A calf? A fool? *You* in such a condition! a woman like you! You must be mad—mad, perfectly mad! And Malleson——'

He stopped.

She was hurrying onward, her hands clasped, her head bent, her heart beating tumultuously, as she heard his hot, rapid words. What was she to do? What to say? She could not stop to consider many alternatives, if they had existed. One thing only remained clear to her mind : she saw it, and strove towards it, as it were ; it was all that she could discern through the tide of emotion which threatened to sweep her away on its rushing waves ; and that one thing was the conviction that she must carry out her purpose.

Not for a second must she entertain the idea of giving it up. She must answer no arguments, notice no side-lights, no incidental modifications of the case, but hold to the one thing, and it would bring her through the peril she was in.

'Do they know—your mother and sisters?' he asked, in a changed, yet eager, tone.

'Not yet. They will when I go in. They know I am going away as soon as I hear of employment.'

'Then, as they do not yet know that you have heard of it, your giving it up can be no disappointment to them. Listen to me! Promise me to give it up; to say nothing to your mother and sisters, and when we get to Yoresett, I will ride back to the rectory, and tell Malleson that you have changed your mind, and do not wish him to take any further steps in the matter.'

'Mr. Aglionby, *you* are dreaming now. I shall do nothing of the kind, for I am quite determined to go to Irkford.'

'One moment,' he said, with forced calm, the nightmare-vision growing every moment more vivid and more horrible, of his queenly Judith becoming, as he had said, a 'servant amongst servants;' and later, exposed to all the horrors and all the dangers of life in a great hospital. It did more than wring his heart; it set his brain on fire, so that he felt scarce master of himself.

'One moment! You force me to take a tone which I am sufficiently ashamed of, but what else is left me? After all I have done in the hope of pleasing you—which in itself is nothing, would be too paltry to mention—but after my sacrifices to please you, surely you will not be ungenerous enough to refuse this little favour to me? It is but a small thing I ask—for you to wait just a little while till something else is found—something, if you *will* wear the yoke, of a more human, less crushing kind than this. Now, you *cannot* refuse me this.'

24

In Aglionby's voice was entreaty of the tenderest and most persuasive nature.

'You ask impossibilities—you do not know what you say. I *must* go through with it,' said Judith, a sob in her voice, her heart like melted wax within her.

A short pause.

'But I cannot endure everything,' then said Aglionby, with constraint. 'There are things which no man with a man's spirit can brook, and one of them is to see a woman whom he lo——, whom he reverences as I reverence you, turned into a beast of burden, a servant, a drudge, while he stands by, without having moved heaven and earth to prevent it. But there is no need for me to do that. You must remember that hitherto I have submitted to your will, and respected your prohibitions. This, however, passes human endurance. You cannot prevent me from seeing Mrs. Conisbrough, and trying whether she is equally hard and implacable as her daughter. I do not believe it, for my part. I do not believe she will treat me as you have done. *She* will not resent and be angry for ever, and if you persist——'

Judith turned cold and faint as she heard these words. The possibility of his proceeding to this extremity had never occurred to her, simple and natural though it was. It must not be done. She herself found it almost impossible to withstand the torrent of Aglionby's will. Her mother would succumb to it at once, and then the shame, and the intolerable degradation which would result !

'Mr. Aglionby, you must not see mamma !' she almost panted—'oh, you must not break your promise !'

'Am I to promise everything, and you nothing? All I ask is that you will yield to me a little. I *must* see Mrs. Conisbrough. I believe I have been very wrong in not doing so before. After all, she is the head of her own house. She, and not her child, possesses the authority to decide whether——'

'Mr. Aglionby—Bernard, oh, *please*, for the love of heaven, do not do this, unless you wish to kill me !' she cried, suddenly clinging with both hands to his arm, and standing quite still again in the darkness.

Aglionby felt a thrill of joy so keen as to be agony, as he felt the clasp of her hands upon his arm, and heard the beseeching accents of her voice. It was very dark ; he could barely discern the dark outline of her figure close beside him, but he could hear her voice, broken and deep, imploring him with passion and with the accents in which, not hatred, but love, entreats a boon. These notes were not in the sweetest of all love's keys, but they were in *one* of love's keys—the only one in which he might hear her voice address him. It was better than silence—he could not forego the delight of it yet. Let her plead ! since neither he nor she might rejoice.

'*I* wish to kill you !' he retorted breathlessly. 'That is a cruel taunt indeed. What have I been doing, but trying to prevent your killing yourself by inches—entombing yourself ! *You* are obstinate, I perceive : but from your very voice I gather that your mother will not be so. I shall see her, and ask her to be reconciled with me.'

'Bernard, *dear* Bernard ! I *implore* you— I implore you !

Her voice broke. She was still clinging to his arm, trembling violently, as he perceived. The chill January night air had become as balmy to him as scented southern gales. The profound sky, the watching stars, the stillness the voice ringing in his ears, intoxicated him. He took her hands; he folded his arm about her, and said, and his voice, too, was broken :

'My child, I believe I can refuse you nothing, though you should break my heart ! What is this thing you implore ?'

'The freedom to do what gives me the least pain in my

wretched life. Do not speak to my mother! Be generous
—you *are* generous. Can you not trust me? Can you not
credit me with having good reasons for what I do? Some
day, perhaps, I can tell you; some day when we are old—it
I am so unhappy as to live to be old. And when I tell you,
you will say I was—I was right.'

She sobbed uncontrollably, Aglionby could not speak.
She tried to turn away. From old habit, she would have
shed her tears, borne her grief, alone and unsupported, but
he would not let her. Because henceforth they were to be
parted, through this crisis he would support her—in it he
would console her; and he clasped his arm yet more closely
about her; while she, feeling little save that he had yielded,
rested her racked and throbbing forehead upon his shoulder,
and wept tears which were not altogether those of bitterness.

He raised his hand at last, and stroked her cheek with it
as one would stroke the cheek of a grieved child. She
raised herself, and stood upright.

'You have the best of all things—strength,' she said; 'as
you are strong, so you will be generous, *I know*,' and carried
the hand which had taken hers to her lips.

'And the reward of this generosity—is it the same which
poor virtue gets?' he asked, almost in a whisper.

'What reward can a poor wretch like me give you?
What can I do, except worship you with all my heart, and
think you the first of men, as long as I live?'

Aglionby was silent, though his heart was on fire. Every
fibre of his nature was appealed to—his love, and his wild
desire to keep her his, as well as his chivalry and generosity.
He said nothing; if he had spoken, it must have been to
call her his heart's delight, and tell her that he could never
let her go again. In silence he conquered, and came
through the ordeal honest—but not unscathed. It was one
of the furnaces seven times heated, which yet are prepared

for men and wonen to pass through ; but from which the
angels are gone who once attended to see that those who
suffered came through unhurt. The crowd is greater and
more ribald ; freer than ever to hoot and jeer at a stumble
or a faltering step ; the flames are eager, as of yore, to lick
up those who retreat. Some come through, firebranded for
the rest of their days ; but, such is the mystery of anguish,
purified too, cleansed as prosperity and success never cleanse
their children.

He presently drew Judith's arm through his own, and in
silence they pursued their way. She was utterly exhausted
by the war of emotions which had shaken her, and could
scarce put one foot before the other. They met hardly a
soul, but walked on along the lonesome country roads like
creatures in a dream-world ; almost as much alone too, until
they arrived in Yoresett, as if the rest of the universe had
been struck dead around them. He accompanied her to
her mother's door, and they paused on the steps. The
flickering light hanging from the market-cross opposite fell
upon both faces, showing them with moderate clearness, the
one to the other. Both were pale and changed. He stood
a step or two lower than she did, and took her hand.

' Have I satisfied you ?' he asked, in a low voice. ' Tell
me the truth ; remember, it has to last me all my life. Are
you satisfied with me ?'

' Perfectly, utterly, and entirely. Can you find any words
to express more than " perfectly "? If so, they express my
satisfaction. But not one exists to describe my gratitude to
you.'

' In the time that is coming for me, I shall suffer,' he said.
' You will not be alone in that ; my sufferings will seem hard,
to me, at least. Will you promise that when you are
attending patients in hospital wards, and feeling compunction
for their sufferings—as I know you will—will you then think
of *me*—alone, wherever I am, and whoever may be with me,

and remember that I suffer from a disease as hard to cure as any of theirs, and give a little of your pity to me, Judith?'

'Do not ask me to pity you. I shall think of you daily till I die; but how can I pity you? You are so strong, and so far above me. I could not pity you any more than I could pity my guardian angel.'

'Well, I know that you will not forget me. Therefore I say, may your path be made smoother for you; and fare you well!'

'God bless you!' was her sole response.

With a last long look at her, from eyes which were full of grief and full of melancholy, he turned away. Judith pulled the bell, and was admitted into the house.

With a vast effort she composed herself so as to join her mother and sisters at tea, when she told them what Mr. Malleson had offered her, and that she had accepted it; upon which information no comments were passed. But as soon as the meal was over she went to her own room, where, cold though it was, she could be alone. There she was free to begin the meditations which should have beguiled her homeward way. Fresh elements made themselves felt in her calculations; new factors appeared in her sum of events.

Was it a victory she had gained, or was it a deliverance through unbounded generosity? The last, the last, she told herself, with tears of joy which streamed down her face in the darkness. She had fought her fight, and she had been conquered; she had measured her will against that of Aglionby, and had very soon been reduced to falling on her knees and crying 'Quarter!' Had it been otherwise she would not have felt as she did now—would have been destitute of that sensation of calm, assured repose in a superior strength which outweighs the feverish joys of a hundred victories to souls like hers, at least.

She had an exceeding great reward in the knowledge that not only was he stronger than she was, but that he was also good, gentle, chivalrous. She was calm, she was free from torturing accusations of conscience. Her heart was sadder and gladder too, than it ever had been before. Her path was yet rough, her future sad, but she had found one who was strong and generous, high-souled and pitiful; and this one had seen her too, and had found in her such harmony with his own soul that he loved her. Their love was to be discrowned; that, in the exaltation of this moment seemed to her a matter of small consequence. What she knew was so full and so satisfying. Her fears were laid to rest. He also had renounced, and she at last felt the most entire confidence in his renunciation. She no longer needed to deny even to herself that she loved him, or to blush guiltily when the knowledge of her love rushed upon and overwhelmed her. There was now no sin and no selfishness in her love. The great peace which follows on the accomplishment of a pure and holy sacrifice was hers; the consolation which Mr. Malleson had wished for her she had received, and in her heart just then was the peace which passeth understanding.

CHAPTER XXXII.

'HER FEET ARE ON THE MOUNTAINS.'

'Et après tout, le rêve, n'est-il pas le pain quotidien de l'existence? La vie, n'est-elle pas l'esperance sans cesse renouvellée du moment qui va suivre? Chaque instant du jour, n'est-il pas une attente, un espoir, un souhait, une fiction? Dépouillez la réalité de cette efflorescence, de cette végétation . . . . et voyez ce qu'il en reste! La réalité n'est que le prétexte de la vie. Ce qui est n'est que la pierre étroite sur laquelle nous mettons le pied pour nous elançer vers ce qui n'est pas.'
LES ETANGS.

DURING some fiery moments, in which soul had been lifted above sense, in which self-abnegation had risen supreme, Aglionby had made *his* 'great renunciation,' and had experienced at the time all the exalted joy which such renunciations bring to those who consummate them. In his walk of an hour with Judith Conisbrough, he, like her, had lived through emotion enough to last him for years; at least, it is very certain that life, if constantly distracted by such emotions, could not be carried on; this poor, imperfect frame, this godlike reason, would succumb under an uninterrupted succession of such excitements. This is so trite as to be a truism. Yet it is a truism we are apt to dispute when the days have to be lived through which follow—as in Aglionby's case they did—upon the few moments, or hours, or days, as the case may be, of intense, highly-strung, mental life : days so grey, so blank and drear, they are like some bare and solitary rock in a northern ocean.

Through such days he had to pass; for a long, blank, uneventful winter followed upon that night of feverish hope and anguish, love and longing and renunciation. He went home and stayed there, and people said how very quiet he was, and how little he cared for any society—except, they added, with surprise, that of Randulf Danesdale. The two men were so utterly dissimilar, said these discerning critics, in tastes, habits, and dispositions, that it was quite marvellous they should have become such sworn allies. So it was however; like or unlike, they were almost inseparable.

The simple fact was that each knew the other's heart. There was something so inwardly similar in their lots, that this likeness alone must have drawn them together; not that any effusive interchange of sentiment, or exchange of confidences, had taken place between them. They had never touched openly on the subjects which lay nearest their hearts. But by bit and bit, over a pipe at this time, during some long dark ride on another occasion, in Bernard's snuggery, or in Randulf's den, they had got pretty clearly to understand what were each other's chiefest hopes and fears, desires or regrets. Randulf knew now that Aglionby's marriage was simply a matter of honour on his side, as to the necessity for consummating which not a doubt had ever entered his mind. Nor had it ever occurred to Randulf to think that there was any way out of it for his friend; they were gentlemen, therefore such a possibility was out of the sphere of their thoughts. That Aglionby was to marry Lizzie Vane, and do all in his power to make her life delightful to her, 'understood itself' with both of them, without their ever saying to themselves, '*Noblesse oblige.*' Aglionby had never in so many words told Danesdale that he loved Judith Conisbrough, but the other guessed it from a thousand slight signs and tokens, which perhaps could not have been read save by a man who was himself in love. He had first felt certain on the point one day in the middle of February, when, sitting with Aglionby over their pipes, he had casually remarked :

'By the way, I happened to be at Hawes Station, yesterday morning, by a strange chance, and I saw Miss Conisbrough and her sisters. They were sending her off to Irkford; she is going to live there, Rhoda told me.'

There was a very long pause before Bernard at length lifted his eyes to his friend's face, and said slowly :

'Yes, I knew she was going; I did not know when.'

Something in eyes and voice told Randulf that her going was no small trouble to Aglionby.

Randulf, for his part, had spoken more openly to Bernard of his troubles and intentions.

'Of course I've given her up for ever,' he said. 'A girl may refuse the man she cares for from a thousand reasons; but she would not have held out against my father, as she did, unless she had been in deadly earnest.'

'No.'

'My father has been goodness itself about it. Not one man in a thousand would have behaved as he has done. He wants me more than anything to get married. I know he is miserable until there are, at any rate, one or two small Danesdales to insure a succession. But he told me—though I know for a fact, you know, that this thing lies nearer to his heart than anything else—he told me, "Don't marry to please me. Wait five years, if you choose. I shall say nothing." Of course,' continued Randulf, with his slowest drawl, as he knocked the ash from his pipe, 'I shall not wait five years—not I! I'll let the worst get over, and then I must look out for a Mrs. Danesdale—a sophisticated young woman, you know, up to everything, who won't care much for me, nor yet expect me to care much for her. One outlives everything, if only one stays above ground long enough. I foresee myself a decent old Philistine, with a stately Philistiness as my consort, and irreproachably well-brought-up daughters coming out at county balls; but '— his mouth twitched—'never one of them all will make me feel as I felt at the bare sight of my little broken-hearted Delphine.'

'Feeling like that has got nothing to with being married,' said Aglionby composedly. 'But, as you say, only keep above ground long enough, and you may calculate on getting not to care, at any rate.'

Adversity did not make Aglionby altogether fuller of sweetness and light than he had been of yore. He told himself, when he thought about it at all, that he was born a crabbed, sour creature; destined to live alone, that he had been too heavily handicapped to go in and win, when the one chance came to him of mating with a spirit which would have softened and made him better. All he could do, had been to glance in at the open gate, to behold the radiant courts of harmony and love, and the soft sunshine within : and then, ere he had had time to stretch his hands towards it all, or to put his foot forward, the gates had been closed again, and he was left shivering outside in the darkness and cold. He retired to his crustiness and abruptness, as a snail to his shell. He showed to Randulf Danesdale alone another side of his nature. For the rest, he did his duties: attended to the social tasks which were set him, all with a sardonic coolness peculiar to himself. Randulf Danesdale did the same. No one could say of them that they absented themselves from the gatherings of their fellow-creatures to which they were bidden. What was said, and that unanimously, was, that they were the most disappointing young men ever known. Mr. Aglionby, it was remarked, had a way of turning the most harmless and amiable feelings into ridicule, and displayed a readiness to see the worst side of things, to look for the meanest motives behind the most innocent actions, and to shrug his shoulders when sinners were found out, in a way that was most painful to sensitive feelings, while Randulf Danesdale did not appear to have any interest in anything; or if he did talk, he talked in a way that no one could understand.

Mrs. Bryce was still at Scar Foot. More than once she had suggested leaving, and still her nephew begged her to remain, if she did not find it too dull. After all, he had not had a stick or a straw altered at the old house. He had reminded himself that Lizzie would never of her own free will come to it; and why, if the furniture pleased him as it was, should he make a great upsetting just because it was usual to upset things on the occasion of one's marriage? He left it. Once or twice his aunt asked him if he did not think of going to Irkford, to which he replied:

'Oh, I shall be running over some time soon, but Lizzie was to send for me if she wanted me; and indeed, she gives me broad hints that when a trousseau is preparing, a man is rather in the way than otherwise.'

With which explanation Mrs. Bryce had to be satisfied. She too knew perfectly well now, that Bernard's heart was not in his marriage. She too shrugged her shoulders, and said within herself:

'What a pity ! But of course he must go through with it.'

Thus he remained at Scar Foot, and watched the winter work out its course ; and felt the first breath of spring blow over the earth; and saw her gradual awakening from her winter sleep—the trees and bushes taking a first faint hue of green ; the skies growing bluer, the days longer ; the airs blowing more rejoicingly ; the seedtime on the farm lands. He watched the ploughman, in the few places where corn was grown—for 'litle corne groweth in Danesdale'—the patient horses toiling in the furrow ; the clank of the plough, the rattle of the harrow, the long ridges ; the rich hue of the mould as it fell from the sharp plough ; the man's voice calling in broad Swaledale dialect to his horses.

He beheld (what he had never seen before) the first spring flowers pushing their way upwards to return the smile of the sun, and the kiss of the westerly breezes. To him it was all miraculous, for he beheld it for the first time. Each flower was a wonder to him, nor did he soon forget how one day he had found himself standing beside glorious Stanniforth Force, hurling itself tumultuously over its rocks, while all the banks were a waste, a rioting wilderness of primrose and cowslip, and fair anemone, and dainty little pink primulas dotted the marshy spots.

Aglionby would have laughed aloud had anyone suggested that he was a poet, yet why, if he were not a poet, did he feel then as if he must shout aloud with the rejoicing waterfall, or fall down and bury himself in those dewy banks of spring flowers ?

He watched, as country folk on their part will watch the garish scenes of a theatre, so he spied out how the feet of the spring gradually stole over the mountains, and how, as she advanced, the leaping becks sprang forth to salute her, and, swollen with melted snow, leaped like melted snow themselves, from steep to steep, shouting with joy.

Though he could wonder, and wonder for ever, he could

but half rejoice, for where was she who had loved these hills and vales, as he well knew, who had loved beyond all this very 'fair Scar Foot'?

Did those eyes of hers turn sometimes with wistful, hungry longing towards the north? Did her feet, as they paced the dingy flags, weary for the springing turf? And when her head ached in the heavy city air, did she not remember the scented breezes that played about the old house beneath the Scar? Did she recall the 'fields bedewed' which surrounded it, and in which he was free to wander?

One day in the middle of April, as he rode out of the courtyard into the road, he saw Rhoda Conisbrough alone, with a basket on her arm. She was walking lingeringly past, gazing with all her eyes at what was to be seen of the house, the orchard, and farm-buildings. When she saw him, she started, blushed guiltily, and hastened her pace. Aglionby dismounted in haste, raised his cap and held out his hand.

'Miss Conisbrough! This is a surprise. Were you coming to Scar Foot?'

'To Scar Foot—no! I'm going to Mereside to find some particular moss for Delphine to paint—so I looked in, that was all. You need not think I was going to trespass,' she added with a look of defiance.

'I wish you had been,' he said wistfully; 'never would trespasser have been so welcome. Since you have come so far, at least step in and rest. Let my aunt entertain you.'

'No, I must not,' said Rhoda, shaking her head. 'But would you really like me to? Would you wish me to enter Scar Foot?'

'More than anything—but there, I must not press you; I know it is against orders. How is Mrs. Conisbrough?'

'Pretty well, thank you.'

'And your sisters?'

'Delphine is pretty well too.'

'And Miss Conisbrough? You have good accounts of her, I hope?'

'Oh, I suppose so. She has begun to nurse in the hospital, and, as she does not like it, it made her very ill at first ; but she is getting over it. Is something the matter with you ?'

'N-no, thank you. I hope nothing serious was the matter with her ?'

'Oh no ! Something that they call hospital sore-throat, I think. Very horrid, but not dangerous, I fancy. They say they all have it.'

'Horrible! Did she not come home to be nursed?

'Judith come home ! Oh dear no !'

'Listen, Miss Conisbrough. At the end of this month I am going away from Scar Foot. I am going to be married, and as my future wife dislikes the country exceedingly——'

'What extraordinary tastes she must have !'

'I do not know when I shall return. Not for a long time, at any rate. Now, seeing that I shall be away, and cannot possibly annoy you by my presence, do you not think you could persuade yourselves to come to Scar Foot now and then, when you wanted snch a walk, and——'

'I should have to come alone, then. Delphine told me that neither she nor Judith ever meant to enter Scar Foot again. I don't know what their reasons may be, I'm sure, but that is what they said. Everything is very stupid—so dismal and mysterious. No, I think I won't promise, Mr. Aglionby, but I see you would not object if I did come.'

'I should feel as if a ban had been lifted from my house and me,' he said.

'It is well you are going to be married,' observed Rhoda composedly, 'for they say there is an old legend that it is dangerous to live alone at Scar Foot.'

'I have found it so,' he replied. And she inclined her head to him, and passed on. Aglionby, as he rode away, wondered how much longer he could endure this sort of thing.

On various pretexts, Lizzie had deferred the date of their

marriage till the middle of May. But the day after his interview with Rhoda, the newspapers brought the announcement that Parliament was to be dissolved in a week. The Government, unable to carry one or two of their favourite measures, had resolved to appeal to the country.

The news acted like magic upon Aglionby's mood. It brought back in a great measure his old eager political bias; his ardour and verve, and zeal for the Liberal cause. Above all, it offered him something to do, something with which to occupy himself during that dreary month of waiting which had yet to elapse before his still more dreary wedding could come off, and his married life, dreariest of all, should commence. Long ago—last year, before the great meeting in October had come off, he and others had agreed, in the event of a general election, to canvass certain districts, and to do their utmost to help forward the cause. What reason was there why he should not even now be as good as his word? He could not merely canvass now, he could help with money. He would revisit his old friends of the Irkford *Daily Chronicle*, and offer his services. His decision was soon taken.

The very idea of sitting inactive at Scar Foot, while all the life and fight and din of battle were going on, was impossible. One fine morning, after recommending Mrs. Bryce to enjoy herself in whatsoever manner seemed good unto her, he drove to Hawes, and took the train from that place to Irkford.

CHAPTER XXXIII.

UNAWARES.

HE arrived at Irkford towards the middle of the afternoon, and drove to the office of his old friend the Irkford *Daily Chronicle*. A few words served to explain his changed

position, and to make it clear that he desired to offer his
money and services to the cause.

Needless to say, that both were rapturously accepted.
Aglionby had an interview with the editor, who remembered
his letters, signed 'Pride of Science,' perfectly, and would
be delighted to receive more communications from the same
able pen.　There was a discussion on ways and means, and
as such vigorous help as Bernard's was particularly welcome
in the 'throng' of work which had so suddenly overtaken
the staff of the *Chronicle*, he was let into all the secrets of
the plan of the campaign, promised to go and dine with the
editor at his club at half-past seven that night, and then,
saying *au revoir*, he departed.

'Where to, sir?' asked the cabman who had been waiting
for him.

'Crane Street — or, stop!　Do you know the Nurses'
Home, Fence Street?'

'Yes, sir.'

'Well, drive slowly past it, and then get on as fast as you
like to 13, Crane Street.'

He had always known vaguely where the Nurses' Home
was; that is, he had passed and repassed it scores and
hundreds of times, almost, without noticing its existence.

It did not take long to get to Fence Street, where the
driver began to slacken his pace.　The Nurses' Home was
almost opposite to his old prison-house, the warehouse of
Messrs. Jenkinson, Sharpe, and Co.　There was little about
it to distinguish it from the other buildings in the street
which, noisy and dirty as it now was, had in former days
been one of the aristocratic quarters of the town, as was
testified by the numerous large, handsome, and massively-
built houses which at one end formed a kind of square
round a black, hideous, and melancholy church.

Many of these houses were the town-residences or con-
sulting-rooms of doctors; on one of the brass door-plates

was the inscription, 'Dr. Hugh Wentworth.' Next door to this was the Nurses' Home, a similar but rather larger house, with very clean steps and brightly-polished windows. Not a face or a form was discernible at any of them. The cabman walked his horse slowly past the house, and then, whipping it up, Bernard was hurried towards the rapturous moment when he should meet his betrothed.

His colloquy with the editor and sub-editor of the *Chronicle* had taken up some time. It was evening, fully half-past six, though of course broad daylight, when he arrived at 13, Crane Street. He would only have time to have a short interview with Lizzie, and leave his portmanteau, and then it would be time for him to go to town again and meet Mr. Williamson, the editor.

As he approached the house, he mechanically felt in his waistcoat-pocket (such is the force of old and long-continued habit) for his latch-key; and was amused to find it there. The garment was one which he must have worn when he had last been staying there, and he had carried the latch-key away without knowing it. Without ringing the bell he ran up the steps, opened the door, and entered.

Was it a dream? Some one ran out of the back-parlour, as of old she used to run, exclaiming in a tone of welcome :

'Oh, here you are! I'm so glad you are early. Come in! Why . . . *Bernard!* I——'

Never blest with a superfluity of wit in an emergency, Miss Vane, white and trembling, leaned up against the wall, pressing her hand to her bosom; and staring at him with wide-open blue eyes, in which blank surprise was gradually giving place to terror.

'Lizzie—what ails you? You look rather horrified than otherwise to see me,' he began; and then, seeing that the driver had placed his portmanteau in the passage, and was standing in the doorway, looking intelligently interested in the whole proceedings, Aglionby paid and dismissed him, pushed the door to without noticing that it was not absolutely shut, and once more turned to Lizzie, who, though she had recovered from her first shock, was still suffering from visible and extreme embarrassment.

'Perhaps I ought to have let you know, Lizzie,' he said, taking her hand, and drawing her into the parlour, where she stood as one paralysed, looking at him blankly and with something like terror—with anything rather than pleasure or welcome. Her hand lay limply in his, she said no word—made no sign. Always, before now, she had made some show of welcoming him. He looked earnestly at her, struck and puzzled by her demeanour, and he discovered that she was elaborately dressed, and that, despite her paleness and disturbance, she looked very lovely in a gown of some soft, forget-me-not-blue stuff, profusely trimmed with silk, and with dainty lace ruffles at the neck and elbows. On the table lay a white fleecy-looking mantle, and a pair of long, pale blue silk gloves, the colour of her dress. The house was very quiet—so quiet that it might have been empty.

'You are going out somewhere!' he said. 'Is Mrs. Vane out?'

'Yes,' came in a low voice from Lizzie's parted lips, as she still seemed almost insensibly to shrink away from him.

He still held her hand, and attempted to draw her nearer to him; but by some slight movement she evaded him, and he continued:

'Where are you off to, and with whom?'

She rallied herself with a great effort, and said, though in a voice which had a strong nervous quiver in it:

'I—we were going to the theatre, the Goldings and I. And—Percy—he was to call for me, and—and——'

'Oh, I see.' He smiled. 'Well, I wish I could join you; but I've come over on electioneering business, and am going to a meeting to-night with Mr. Williamson, so perhaps you will excuse me. And—is it quite convenient to your mother to put me up here, Lizzie? because, if not——But why do you look so nervous and disturbed, child? Surely my coming, even unexpectedly, cannot have upset you in this manner.'

For even he, though in matters of deportment not the most observant, and certainly the least suspicious of men, could not but feel surprised at her continued pallor and nervousness. Lizzie was racking her brains to contrive some means of escaping from him, if only for three minutes, of scribbling a pencil note, and sending her mother's domestic flying with it to the Goldings' house. She could not look unconcerned, while pondering in dire distress of mind upon how best to carry out this scheme. She now stammered :

'Excuse me a moment, Bernard. I have left something upstairs. I must—go——'

'My dear child, you are not fit to move, until you have sat down and rested a little, and taken a little wine, or smelt some salts, or whatever is the proper thing to do. Sit down here, and tell me what's the matter with you.'

He drew her with gentle but irresistible force to an easy-chair, seated himself beside her, and instinctively began to pity her, as it was his nature to pity anything that looked frightened or alarmed, and Miss Vane's countenance at that moment was strongly expressive of both these emotions.

There came a sudden sharp knock at the front door ; then it was pushed open ; a footstep was heard in the passage, and a voice cried : 'Now, Lizzie, where are you ?'

Lizzie started up, visibly in an agony of apprehension. With Bernard, surprise and pity had been transformed like magic into the blackest suspicion.

'Let me speak to him !' said Lizzie breathlessly.

'No ; let him come here,' retorted Aglionby, still holding her hand fast. 'How dare he call you "Lizzie" in that fashion? Come on, Percy !' he cried aloud, in a dry, distinct voice ; 'Miss Vane is waiting for you—and, for the matter of that, so am I !' he added beneath his breath.

There was a momentary pause in the footsteps.   Then they came on again, the door opened, and Percy appeared. When he saw them he looked, first astonished, then appalled, but at last uttered slowly, 'Aglionby—you !' and came to a dead pause.

'Yes, I—why not?' remarked Bernard, never loosing his hold of Lizzie's hand, and seeing clearly enough now that *something* would have to be explained before many minutes should have passed.

He looked steadily at Percy for a little while, and at last observed :

'It's true I've arrived unexpectedly, but I should have looked for a warmer welcome from you both, I must say.'

'Bernard, let go my hand !' suddenly exclaimed his betrothed pettishly.   'What's the use of standing there glaring at me ?   You have frightened me half out of my senses already.   Mr. Golding, did you bring a cab, and is Lucy ready ?'

She looked hard at him as she spoke, as though she would convey some hint to him by her steadfast gaze.   Percy was far too much embarrassed to be able to understand any such subtle modes of communicating ideas, and he replied, lamely :

'Lucy—no—why, did you want Lucy to go?'

A short, sarcastic laugh broke from Aglionby, while Lizzie's fair face was covered with an angry blush.

'Frightened you half out of your senses, have I ?   I'm sorry if that is the feeling with which my coming, however sudden, inspired you, considering that we proposed so soon to be husband and wife.   *Fear* is not exactly the emotion a man would wish to excite in his bride.'

Lizzie had snatched her hand out of his, and, with the angry colour yet high on her cheeks, was looking at him, half with dislike, half with trepidaton—an expression which he did not fail to remark.

'Now for it!' he thought. 'She has cheated me all along, and made a fool of me. Now I am going to be put in the position of the despised and rejected. Good Lord! suppose I cared for her?'

He turned aside, half-seating himself on the edge of a table, and watched the rest of the scene with the sarcastic smile of a looker-on; a smile uncommonly like a sneer, and with a gleam in his eyes as cold and mocking as had ever in his worst days dwelt there. Whatever the inward progress towards 'sweetness and light' which his nature might have made, little of it was visible now—indeed, he felt nothing but contempt for all three of them: for Lizzie's double-dealing; for Percy's dishonest treatment of him, who had been his friend; for himself most of all, and his sublime fatuousness and credulity in imagining that Lizzie was in love with him.

His last remarks, alluding to 'husband and wife,' and to a man and his bride, appeared to goad Percy beyond endurance; for, looking exceedingly agitated, he advanced, stretched out his hands, and cried in a portentous voice:

'Lizzie Vane! The time for playing and trifling is past. I can bear this no longer. I never knew till this moment what it is to confront a friend whom one has deceived——'

Lizzie, not expecting rebuke from Percy, cast herself into a chair, and began to cry.

Mr. Golding proceeded:

'Choose between us! To please you, I have lived in torment for the last six months. You know I adore you, and you have told me you loved me. You must——'

'She has said she loved you?' said Bernard dryly. 'In that case, it is perfectly evident she cannot love me. If I had known this sooner, Percy—it is not exactly what I should have expected from "mine own familiar friend."'

There was a softer tone in his voice as he spoke these words, and when he heard it Percy's emotion (for he was a good creature, and honest, where Lizzie Vane was out of the question) became altogether overpowering.   In a choked voice, he replied :

'I know it, Aglionby, I know it.   It is because I loved her so.   I wanted to speak.   I wanted to be fair and honourable.   But she said she must dismiss you herself. She exacted this silence from me, and——'

Lizzie was here understood to sob out that she had never been so shamefully treated in her life.   But here Bernard interposed, still speaking in the same dry, cold manner.

'There can only be one termination to this affair.   From the manner in which Miss Vane received me this evening, I clearly saw that I was not welcome, though I was far from guessing the reason why.   Now, Lizzie, oblige me by listening to me, and answering me.'

He softened his voice, and took her hand, and honestly tried to look gentle and conciliating.   He could not help it if his face looked black as a thunder-cloud.

Lizzie fixed her frightened, fascinated eyes upon him, half-rising from her chair, as he went on :

'I don't wish to be unjust to you.   I wish to know no particulars.   But tell me this : let us have an understanding. Do you love Percy Golding here, or do you wish to be my wife ?'

As he asked this question, with all the solemnity imaginable, there was borne into his mind a keen sense of the bitter absurdity of the whole affair.   Yet, though it was some time since he had cared for Lizzie, he had honestly and thoroughly believed that she cared for him, and it was not gratifying either to his *amour propre*, or to the feeling of chivalry, of gentlemanly honour, which had kept him loyal to her, when, after looking from one to the other of them, she suddenly darted to Percy's side, saying, in accents that carried conviction to both her hearers :

'I love Percy—I am frightened of you, Bernard. You crush me when you look at me in that way, and I can't marry you—it's no good, I can't, I can't! Oh dear !'

She cast her arms about Percy's neck, laid her head on his shoulder, and cried heartily again.

Percy was agitated, distressed, but triumphant through it all.

Aglionby felt a singular sensation pierce his heart. He knew the girl now exactly for what she was, and valued her accurately at her true worth, or, for him, worthlessness. But once it had been different. He had never seen an intellectual or highly-cultivated woman in her, but he had seen a tender, loving girl, a true and faithful sweetheart. And he had looked to find some consolation in faithfully, on his part, doing his utmost to make her happy.

As he saw her sobbing in Percy's arms, and recalled her look of blank terror and aversion, a thousand signs and tokens rushed into his mind, which went to prove her fear of him, and the oppression she must have felt in regard to him. It was a humiliating, a painful, and a saddening discovery.

He waited for a little while, till her weeping had ceased, and she looked up again, and then he said :

'Nothing is left for me but to say farewell to you. After what I have learnt just now, I cannot suppose that my opinion is of much consequence to you, but let me tell you that I hold you utterly free from blame—utterly. We both made a mistake a year ago, and I have been a blind, conceited fool all this time to imagine that you had not found it out—as I had done. My conscience in the matter is not so pure that I can afford to even whisper a reproach to you ; therefore, Lizzie, will you consent to shake hands with me as a friend ; and when Percy is your husband, will you receive me sometimes as *his* friend ?'

She avoided his eyes, but let him take her hand, and say something further to her; and she murmured something which might be intended for farewell. Bernard looked at Percy, and held out his hand to him. Percy blushed uncomfortably, remembering his own duplicity in the matter; but finally they exchanged a pressure of the hand, and, without speaking, it was understood that they were still friends.

With a slight bow, Bernard left the room, took his small portmanteau in his hand, let himself out of the house, hailed a passing hansom, and told the man to drive him to a certain hotel in town. As he was driven back through the same streets which he had less than an hour ago traversed, he meditated, and by-and-by the feeling of pain he had felt yielded again to that of cynical and bitter amusement. Before he went to the meeting he wrote a letter to Mrs. Bryce, in which he informed her:

'Your astute and worldly-wise nephew has this evening discovered that he has been made an utter fool of —and that by two persons for whose intellect he has always felt, and often expressed, great contempt. That this experience has left him with a feeling of exhilaration rather than one of depression is accounted for by the fact that it is simply the price he has had to pay for his release from a position which was loathsome to him. In other words, my dear aunt, my sweetheart has jilted me, and I am very glad of it. If Randulf Danesdale should happen to call upon you, which he is pretty certain to do, tell him this, and oblige me by making it pretty plain to him, for it is the truth, that it was the lady who would have none of me, not I who was desirous of breaking with her.'

Then he went to the meeting, and by-and-by began to enjoy it. He resolved to stay in Irkford until the election should be quite over.

At night, when he went to bed, he took stock of his own

mental and moral condition, and summed it up thus:
Befooled and jilted by one woman; solemnly vowed to
renounce another—and happier than he ever had been in
his life.

CHAPTER XXXIV.

'*FOR THE REST OF MY LIFE.*'

JULY, more than three years later; the scene, one of the
front rooms at the Nurses' Home, Fence Street, Irkford;
the persons, a man and a woman, alone—he, standing on the
hearth-rug, where he had been waiting some two or three
minutes; she, just closing the door behind her as she
came in.

The man was Dr. Hugh Wentworth; the woman, Judith
Conisbrough.

He was a young-looking man—even surprisingly young
when one considered the high position he held, and the
really vast responsibilities which devolved upon him. But
on looking more closely, one saw that if he were young in
years, yet he was one of those men who are born with
master-minds. One forgot entirely that he was young and
handsome, and pleasant to look upon, so much were these
advantages overweighed by the intellectual ones—by the fire
that dwelt in the deep eyes, by the grand sweep of the mag-
nificent forehead, the mental *power* expressed in every line
and every feature.

Till Judith entered, he had been leaning against the
mantelpiece with his hands clasped behind him, and his
eyes raised to the dingy-looking ceiling above, and he heaved
a sigh. Even those two or three moments of sorely-needed
leisure, of waiting and inaction, were hardly spared and
much grudged.

He had not been kept waiting very long.   In that establishment punctuality and alertness were laws as immutable
as those of the Medes and Persians.   There was she whom
he sought, walking into the room, looking different from her
old self, as you, reader, have known her, because she had a
white cap on her head, a black gown, a white apron of lawn,
with a stomacher, all edged with little plaited frills of the
same material.

'Good-afternoon, nurse,' he observed, holding out his
hand.

'Good-afternoon.   We meet for the first time to-day, I
think ?'

'Yes.   There is a small matter of business which I wish
to discuss with you,' said he, and paused.

She had moved nearer to the window, and now stood beside
it, looking at him.   Then, when the broader light fell upon
her, one saw that the cap and apron, the badges of her
order, were not the only things to distinguish her from the
Judith Conisbrough of three years ago.   She looked, if anything, a little taller, possibly a very little stouter, and her
carriage, if not more stately, was a little more decided than
of yore.

She looked a queenly woman now, in her garb of nursing
sister, just as she had formerly looked a queenly woman in
her shabby old gowns ; in her sorrow, her poverty, her bitter
unhappiness at Yoresett House, when the curse of enforced
idleness, and the grip of a forbidden love, were upon her.
But her face was changed.   It had altered in the way in
which the faces of women do alter, in whom heart is as strong
as head.

No acute or even intelligent observer would have dared
to say that that face wore an altogether happy, or peaceful,
or satisfied expression ; the faces of those who aim high and
feel deeply, seldom, if ever, do look perfectly placid.   There
was a calm and settled power in it, not inferior, in its way, to

that which dwelt in the countenance of Dr. Wentworth himself. The eyes were steady, scrutinising, and critical. It was the mouth which betrayed, more than anything else, the touch of sadness and dissatisfaction. It was when the face was in entire repose that the lips took that curve which makes one feel as if a sigh had either just left, or was on the point of leaving them.

For the rest, one could see that she was in every way developed. She had more ease as well as more dignity of manner. She was more beautiful than before, as well as older ; her face and form now more than ever were such as the most heedless could not fail to observe.

Neither she nor Dr. Wentworth sat down. Each knew the time of the other to be precious.

'You go home for your holiday to-morrow ?' he said half-inquiringly.

'Yes. A fortnight amongst the Yorkshire hills will not be unpleasant.'

'I wish you would take a month,' was his abrupt remark.

'A month—why ?' Her eyes opened a little, as she looked at him in some surprise. 'Not because I look ill, surely— for I never felt better in my life.'

'No ; but because I wish you on your return to take a great deal more responsibility on your shoulders, and you will require some thorough rest and setting up before you undertake it.'

'Indeed. And what is it you wish me to do ?'

'My wife,' said he, smiling, 'charged me to tell you that you were to do as I wished, on pain of forfeiting her friendship. Now, before I explain, let me tell you it is an onerous post I wish you to take. Little rest, and much care and anxiety. Perhaps few friends, and lots of enemies. That for the disagreeable part of it. For the more agreeable : it ought to gratify that ambition of yours, to which you have never yet owned, though it is as patent to me as the sun in a sky without clouds—it ought to gratify that ambition, because it is a post of authority and consequence, and is well remunerated. I want you to become the Matron of the new Hospital at Ridgeford.'

She raised her head quickly; her lips parted, and she looked at him in astonishment for a moment. Then her face flushed deeply, and she turned her eyes to the prospect outside.

Dr. Wentworth watched her unobtrusively, but with the keenest and liveliest interest. He had been her staunch friend ever since the evening he had first seen her, in this very room, standing before him in her bonnet and cloak, to be inspected, when she had said, with a *naïveté* which had amused him, and an earnestness which had gratified him :

' I do not know what you can give me to do, but I beg you will give me something. If it is only sweeping and dusting, let me have it : do not send me back.'

He had not sent her back, for he had correctly discerned (which even genius does not always succeed in doing) that she was one of those tools which will work well, and he had from the first let her see that he expected a gread deal from her. He had not been disappointed, and he had been charmed, like inferior men, to find his own prophetic verdict so thoroughly realised.

The more he asked of work, or study, or observation, or, as he would say in moments of expansiveness to the wife of his bosom, ' of general all-round perfection in her work and her behaviour,' the more she had seemed ready and willing to give him.

Under his influence and by his advice she had received training, not only in nursing, but in some branches of medicine and surgery as well. He had said little to her during her studies in these subjects, but had one day, not long ago, surprised her by proposing to her that she should study medicine thoroughly, and adopt it as a profession, adding that she had nothing to fear, and would make her way.

He had calculated on that ambition, in which he now told her he still believed; but it had not answered to the call. Judith had declined, saying she had no vocation. Mingled motives, so delicately shaded and complicated that she could not possibly have explained their whence or wherefore, had led her to this refusal. He had been as nearly angry with her as possible, saying in remonstrance :

'Scores of women, who really have no vocation for it, who want notoriety, or are curious about things they don't understand, or who want to make a living, and think they have fewer rivals in the medical line than in the schoolmistress one—they all rush into it, pushing to the front, and making themselves a spectacle for gods and men. Here are you— the very sort we want as a pioneer for women-doctors— high-minded and high-hearted, with a pure reverence for science and humanity, with every qualification, mental, moral, and physical. And you will not. You ought to lead the way, to be one of the pioneers on that road where the women who follow after you will some day be great.'

Judith had shaken her head, smiling.

'You are quite mistaken,' she said. 'I lay no claims to a "pure reverence for science and humanity," as you call it. I know nothing about them, except that the one is really great, and the other is thought so by some people. Do you suppose I became a nurse because I wished to do so? Not at all, and I never would have done it if I could have had a happier lot. I "took to it," as they say, because I was miserable, and wanted relief from my wretchedness; I did not like it then, and I do not like it now. You may think me a poor-spirited creature; but I would rather stay here and do as you tell me, and act under orders, than be the first and cleverest woman-doctor of all time.'

You are trying to cajole me by flattery.'

' I am speaking the simple, unvarnished truth.'

' My wife says indignantly—as if it were my fault—that if she had had your qualifications I should never have got her to marry me.'

' Oh, how could she say such a thing! It is almost wicked of her,' Judith had said ; and she had remained immovable. Yes, she thought it a glorious profession, she said ; the noblest that existed——

' Bar the clerical one,' he had suggested, with a malicious smile.

' Bar none,' had been Judith's emphatic retort. And she would honour a really clever medical woman, and would be quite ready to darn her stockings and do her drudgery. The position itself, of a medical woman, she declined. This refusal, and their dispute about it, was in Dr. Wentworth's mind now, as he observed her keenly, and noted every change that passed over her face.

' I shall think you wish to be unfriendly to me, if you re-fuse me this,' he said. ' You are familiar with all the details of the scheme : you have heard them discussed at my house often enough. You know what the duties will be. The salary will be three hundred a year. Now, where is your " Yes " ?'

' " Yes " is sometimes a very hard word to say, Dr. Went-worth.'

' It ought not to be so, when duty cries for it so very loudly, as in this case.'

' You are the chief of the council, and the real head of it, are you not ?'

' I am.'

' And would you always give me your friendship, your counsel, and your advice ?'

' You may depend upon them entirely.'

' It would be a very useful sphere,' she said musingly.

' You, as well as I, know *how* useful. In that place you will be an influence, and a beneficent one, on hundreds.

My dear friend,' he took her hand, ' apart from all other considerations, 'the woman who worthily fills that office, as it will be when it is developed, and as you will fill it—with its trials and its difficulties, its powers and its opportunities for doing good—that woman may, if the right spirit animate her, attain to the rank of the other good women whose names ought to stand opposite saints' days in men's and women's hearts.'

' Then I cannot be worthy of it,' said she, moved.

' And I say you are ; and I say that if you will not take it, I know not where to put my hand on any other woman qualified as you are qualified for it.'

' If I took it, I should have to make up my mind that it should be for the rest of my life.'

' You would.'

A long pause.   He did not interrupt her, nor press her for an answer, for, precious as the time of both was, these moments of reflection and turning over were absolutely necessary.   He leaned against the mantelpiece in silence, and she stood by the window, equally silent, seeing, without heeding them, all the throng of men and vehicles which streamed incessantly up and down the noisy thoroughfare.

What visions did she tear to shreds, he wondered, as he watched her without letting her see his observation—what hopes did she finally immolate ? what bright illusions of girlhood did she lock out of her heart for ever ?   Could he have known, he would have been aware that she had never had any youth, and that she even now inwardly expostulated with her destiny, which had led her up through five-and-twenty years of life without that youth.   Though he and she had grown fast friends, though she and his wife had become almost like sisters, no word had ever passed her lips which could give any clue to the story of sorrow and hopelessness which had driven her forth from her home at twenty-two, a sad, unhopeful woman, and had first led her to

them. That there was a story, he was persuaded; per
suaded, too, that she went over it in her mind as she stood
looking out of the window then, before she answered him—
some story connected with her home in that green dale
which he had never seen, but of which she had once or
twice spoken, in words which, though simple, had been full
of life and fire.

At last her answer came: 'I will do as you wish, Dr.
Wentworth. I will go to Ridgeford.'

In the joy and relief of his heart, he stepped forward and
shook both her hands.

I do thank you—from my heart I thank you. With you
at its head, Ridgeford shall be the first place of its kind in
England—that I swear!'

He laughed with satisfaction. Judith only looked very
grave, and then he said:

'But have you no curiosity to know what my great and
special reason was for wishing you to go?'

'What was it?'

'Just this. I don't want you to be lost to suffering
humanity and the medical profession, whether as a member
of it, or a servant of it. Once safe in that post, you are safe
for life; but, until you are installed there, I have a consuming dread, which haunts me like a ghost, of your breaking away from us, and getting married.'

'You certainly need not fear that,' said Judith, after a
moment's pause, as she looked at him. 'It is one contingency in my life which I am absolutely certain will never
occur. Therefore be reassured.'

'To think of you married,' pursued the fanatic, 'devoted to
one miserable man and his tiresome family, is to think of
something monstrous. Well, good-bye. You'll see my wife
to-morrow, before setting off. And stay at home a month,
while you have the chance.'

He wrung her hand again, and departed.

CHAPTER XXXV.

THE WAY NOT CLEAR.

ONCE more Judith alighted at the well-known station at Hawes, and was met, as of old, by mine host of the King's Arms at Yoresett, and driven home by him. It was the third holiday she had had since first going to her work, but it was now more than a year since she had last been at home. To Judith these home-comings had their terror as well as their joy. Her love of her home, and of every spot of ground for miles around it, was a thing of a deep and ineradicable growth. Therefore there was always a certain delight in returning and beholding the familiar scenes and objects. But the desolation within was so great as almost entirely to counterbalance this joy. Since she had left home no word of leaving Yoresett had ever been spoken either by Delphine or by Mrs. Conisbrough. Each time that she returned it seemed to Judith that Delphine looked more shadowy, more exquisitely lovely, and more unearthly in her fragility. She was particularly struck with that look when she alighted on this occasion, and her sister came forward to welcome her. She formed a striking contrast to the splendid handsomeness of the youngest girl, now a tall and well-developed young lady of nineteen, as full of health, of life, and fire as Delphine seemed shadowy and ghost-like in her beauty.

They welcomed her, Delphine very quietly, Rhoda enthusiastically. Judith had been visited often by a torturing suspicion that Delphine had never regarded her with the same feelings since that afternoon when she had found her in her painting-room, and had told her old Martha Paley's tale. She fancied that Delphine regarded her sometimes with a strangely cold and alien glance, as if she suddenly recollected the mortal blow which Judith's hand had dealt to her happiness, and shivered and feared at the remembrance of it.

26

The idea was almost intolerably painful, and she had never dared to put it into words. Where would have been the use? Delphine could not order her feelings and expression to be exactly that which was most pleasing to others.

Rhoda's cry now, as of old, was for news.

'What's your news, Judith? Surely you have some news?'

'Yes, I have, this time. But I shall not tell it you till I can tell it to mamma as well.'

'She is upstairs,' observed Delphine, 'but I fancy she will come down before long.'

They were in the parlour, and while Judith sat down and rested Delphine remarked:

'Judith, I think you will find mamma looking a good deal changed—I am afraid so. But don't seem to notice it, for there is nothing she dislikes more than for people to make remarks about it.'

'Why—do you mean she is ill, or—or failing, or anything?'

'I don't know, I am sure. She is very much changed. I can hardly describe to you in what way.'

She had scarcely finished speaking when Mrs. Conisbrough came into the room. Judith could not but agree with her sister's words. Their mother looked haggard, worn, and aged, and all these things had greatly increased upon her since Judith had last seen her.

Judith advanced, and greeted her with tender affection; but Mrs. Conisbrough received her coldly. It was one of the girl's heaviest trials, and one which, she felt, was not likely to cease while her mother lived.

Judith had been desperate when she had taken that extreme step of speaking to her mother of the wrong she had done; but she had spoken of it, and as a simple matter of fact Mrs. Conisbrough had never forgiven her for it. They had never been very sympathetic, but that episode had created a breach between them—not very noticeable on the outside, but deep—deep as the respective bases of their own characters.

Judith always felt as if she hardly dared lift her eyes to her mother's face. She always felt as if she were the culprit, and as if she were for ever labouring under the ban of a parent's heavy and merited displeasure. These feelings are settled for us, and arise within us, not at the dictates of reason and justice, but in obedience to inherited traditions, whose beginning has its source somewhere in the dim vista of our ancestors' habits, countless generations back : in obedience, too, to certain instincts in our own individual natures. Such instincts as these it was which made Judith Conisbrough morally cast ashes upon her own head for ever having dared to speak to her mother of her sin ; which made her feel almost as if that mother were justified in treating her with the distant and ceremonious coldness which she had observed to her ever since the first moments of the silence with which she had received her daughter's words.

Delphine also knew the miserable secret, but it did not appear to have caused the same breach between her and her mother. Mrs. Conisbrough spoke almost genially to her, and called her 'my love !' It was three years, Judith reflected, her heart rent with anguish, since that term of endearment, or any like it, had been bestowed upon her. She waited until the evening meal was over, and they were all seated together in the familiar parlour. She had noticed her mother's slight and failing appetite, and how she turned away in distaste from almost everything they tried to tempt her with. Though it was July, there was a small fire, and Mrs. Conisbrough took her place beside it when tea was over. Judith took her position on a stool at her mother's feet, and, clasping her hands on her knee looked up into her face, and said :

'Mother, I have something to tell you.'

' Indeed,' was the listless reply.

' Yes. You know all about Dr. Wentworth now. You have often heard of him from me, and I am sure you have heard his praises sounded by the Mallesons.'

'Oh yes! I suppose he is a very great man. I know he seems to have the art of making people slave for him without giving them much remuneration.'

' It is not always he who decides what the remuneration shall be. He called upon me yesterday. He wants me to take a month's holiday instead of only a fortnight, and then he wants me to undertake a very serious responsibility.'

' Has he any thoughts of paying you for the responsibility?'

'The payment is in the hands of a committee, and it is very liberal. He wants me to be the Matron of the new Hospital at Ridgeford, near Irkford.'

'You?' said Mrs. Conisbrough, looking at her curiously, as if she could not take the idea in. ' Matron of a hospital ––and what did you say?'

'He begged me to go,' said Judith, looking into her mother's face with a great longing. ' He is to be the head of the council, and really the master of it all, and he promised to be my faithful friend if I undertook it. It is an almost terribly responsible post.'

' Ah, indeed ! And pray, what did you decide? I should have felt myself too young and inexperienced had I been in your place,' said Mrs. Conisbrough, almost coldly ; while Delphine, with a sudden rush of surprise and sympathy exclaimed :

' Why, Judith, it will be an immense work ! It will want a woman of great power in every way—a woman like you, and I am sure I think Dr. Wentworth hit upon the right person when he chose you for it.'

' He would not allow me to decline, or to urge any objections,' said Judith, turning to Delphine, almost choked with grief at the manner in which her news was received.

Was it not the turning-point of her whole life? Did not her mother know well its full significance? And had she nothing warmer, nothing more sympathetic to say to it than this? 'I have had great difficulty in believing that I ought to accept it,' Judith went on, 'but at last I felt that I must at least try, and I accepted.'

She turned to her mother again, and said:

'The salary is a good one, mother; it is three hundred a year.'

'Dear me! That is certainly an improvement. The walk in life which you have chosen is not one which would have recommended itself to me; but, since you *have* chosen it, I congratulate you on being successful in it.'

Judith said no more. She had communicated the news somewhat as one does a disagreeable duty, but she had not expected it to be received thus. When Mrs. Conisbrough retired, which she did early, Delphine went with her to her room, and thus Judith and Rhoda were left alone.

'Why didn't you tell me about mamma?' said the former. 'She ought to have a first-rate physician to see her, even if we had to send to London for him. I am perfectly certain she is very seriously out of health. You should not have kept me in the dark, Rhoda.'

'It was Delphine, Judith. She said you had care and trouble enough, without having that added to them. Poor Del! She has been longing for you to come. She has had a dismal time of it with mamma.'

'Why, has mamma been cross?'

'Dreadful! She can't help it, poor thing. I can often see that it is not because she feels unkind or spiteful, but because she is miserable. Uncle Aglionby has a great deal to answer for, and I hope he *will* have to answer for it. I don't despair of *seeing* him brought to account sometime. Meantime it is not very agreeable for us here below. I don't know how Delphine bears it as she does, but mamma has never let her alone about having refused Mr. Danes-dale.'

'Rhoda!'

'You cannot imagine what I have felt sometimes, when I have had to watch Delphine being literally tortured. Of course I don't pretend to understand the facts of the case, or why Delphine refused Mr. Danesdale, but I do know that she adores him, and that her heart is breaking.'

'Oh, Rhoda, it is what I have feared, and what has haunted me again and again, while I have been away. She is one of those who never complain, and *never* get over a thing of that kind. Poor child! But it must not go on. Does she ever see Mr. Danesdale?'

'Oh, at church, sometimes. She never looks at him, but I have seen him look at her, with a look I cannot under-stand. I don't think she has ever spoken to him since that ball you went to. Sir Gabriel has not been well, and they say he is very anxious for Mr. Danesdale to be married, and that he will be soon.'

'Ah! To whom? Do they say that too?'

'Some people talk about Miss Bird. They say she has refused no end of men for his sake.'

'I don't believe it. She is a sweet little thing, but I don't believe she cares, or ever did care, a straw for Randulf Danesdale. No; depend upon it, if he marries, to oblige his father, it will be a different sort of woman—one who will put as little heart into the affair as he will himself. *Poor fellow!*'

'I know nothing about that. I know they say he is going to be married, and if he does marry I believe it will kill Delphine. She says he is quite right—she told mamma so. She says he must marry, but it will kill her all the same.'

Judith sat silent, her heart wrung; and Rhoda, who was, for her, exceedingly subdued, did not enlarge upon the situation. Presently Delphine came downstairs, looking, as Judith's eyes, sharpened by pity and fear, observed, almost transparent in her fragility.

The girls talked about their mother, and Judith found her sisters as anxious as herself to have advice. She said she should write to Dr. Wentworth, and ask his advice, and request him to tell them whom they ought to consult.

Later, when Judith and Rhoda again happened to be alone, the latter said :

' Mr. Danesdale has been abroad for ever so long with Mr. Aglionby.'

' Has he ?'

' Yes ; they are most tremendous friends. People call them Orestes and Pylades. Whenever Mr. Aglionby is at home, Mr. Danesdale is with him, or he is with Mr. Danesdale. But our cousin doesn't spend much of his time at Scar Foot. He's there just now though, and nobody says anything about his getting married. His aunt lives with him and keeps house for him, and some people seem to like him. The Mallesons do. I've seen him there once or twice, and he is fearfully grave and dignified. I can't hate the man, though I should like to.'

Judith was saved from the necessity of a reply, by the entrance of Delphine. She pondered upon all she had heard, and in her mind the situation resolved itself into this, that her mother would not live long. Her eye, now practised in reading the signs of most kinds of disease, beheld the beginning of the end, written very plainly in Mrs. Conisbrough's appearance and expression. With her would die her secret and all chance of its becoming known ; and for them, in their youth and loneliness, would remain nothing in the world but to work out, as best they could, the sad behest :

' Work, be unhappy, but bear life, my son.'

For herself she could answer. She felt within her strength

to meet her fate and master it. She thought she could answer for Rhoda too. No doubt the struggles would be desperate, the torture keen, before conquest was hers, but it would be hers in the end, she felt sure. But for her best-beloved, to whom she was powerless to give hope on the one hand, or callous indifference on the other, or, yet again, the resolve that rides triumphant over death—what remained for her? She dared not attempt to look forward or to answer the question honestly. She had resolution to face most possibilities, but not the one which carried Delphine out of her life.

CHAPTER XXXVI.

'WAIT TILL YOU HEAR FROM ME.'

IT was a little more than a week after Judith Conisbrough's return, a sultry afternoon at the end of July. At Scar Foot all was quiet, except the rooks which wheeled and cawed noisily in the trees. The windows were all open, now that the sun had left the house, after being closed all morning, with the blinds down, to keep the said sun out. In the dining-room the luncheon-table was spread, with Aglionby and Mrs. Bryce at the head and foot of it, and Randulf, as guest, at one side.

The meal was just over, as Aglionby observed:

'You look tired, aunt. Is it the heat?'

'I suppose so. I think it is going to thunder. I generally know by my nerves when it is, and they prognosticate a storm now.'

'Just like Philippa,' said Randulf, with the air of one who has made an interesting discovery. 'She says she always knows when there's going to be a thunderstorm.'

'You don't look too brilliant yourself, Bernard,' observed Mrs. Bryce, laughing. 'Does he, Mr. Danesdale?'

'N—no. A bit thundery (like the weather), as usual, when he doesn't get enough of his own way. I should take no notice of him : he'll come round.'

'Who would not, after hearing such soothing comments passed upon his looks and the causes of them ?' said Aglionby, who had been looking, as a matter of fact, pale, but darkly handsome, as usual, but across whose gravity there now flashed a smile, transforming his whole face. He pushed his chair away as he spoke, and opened the door for Mrs. Bryce, saying :

' I really would go and rest, aunt, if I were you ; or you'll be having one of your headaches.'

' I think I shall,' said Mrs. Bryce, going away.

'Where shall we go ?' said Aglionby to his friend, 'for I'm at your disposal this afternoon.'

'Wherever it's coolest, and wherever it takes least exertion to get to,' was the characteristic reply.

'That's my den, then, across the house-place,' said Bernard, leading the way.

Randulf flung himself at full length on a settee, and began, with the usual promptitude of action which contrasted so oddly with his drawling speech :

' Can you guess what it is I want to have over with you ?'

' I suppose you are really thinking of getting married ?'

' Yes, more's the bad luck, I am. I want you to give me some advice as to a suitable lady.'

' Me—surely you know best yourself.'

' Not I ! My father is anything but well, you know, so he wasn't sorry for the excuse to leave town, and I don't think Philippa minded much. She has got a fancy that he is really failing, and I can see that he is just miserable till I decide upon something. He has sacrificed an awful lot for me ; it is right that I should sacrifice something for him, so I told him I was willing to oblige him.'

' You told me at the time ' (they both seemed to know

what this rather vague expression meant) 'that he had told
you to wait five years if you liked, but that you should do
nothing of the sort.'

'Ah! I fancied my powers of getting over troubles were
greater than they turn out to be. To make a clean breast
of it, I care for that girl as much to-day as I did the day she
refused me—ay, and ten times more. I never shall care for
another girl. My father says I talk cynically. Philippa,
poor lass! turns her eyes towards heaven, and says she
wonders how I *can*'—he laughed. 'She knows nothing
about it. I am going to do it, but I'll never utter one word
of pretence in the whole matter; I won't have "love" so
much as mentioned. Therefore, my dear fellow, think of
money, beauty, rank, cleverness, discretion, dignity, suit-
ability, as much as you please; but for God's sake don't ask
me to marry any girl whom I should have to pretend to care
for, or who would pretend to care for me.'

'You talk as if I could lay my finger on the proper person
at a moment's notice.'

'So you can, if you choose.'

'It's plain to see from that, that you know perfectly well
who is to be the victim of your despair, or the accomplice of
your heartless project—whichever you like to call it. You
mean Miss Askam, I suppose?'

'Well, she is well known to be the most heartless, ambitious, worldly, self-seeking little monkey in the North Riding.'

'So I believe.'

'I thought of her instantly. But I had a scruple.'

'What was that?'

'Some one told me that you admired her.'

'I? Good Lord! Set your mind at rest, I beg; and if
my services can be of the least help to you in the matter,
command them. But I would like to give you a word of
advice.'

'Well?'

'You would do better to look for some one else. I know that Dorothy Askam appears to be exactly what you have said. I don't believe she knows she has got a heart, but I also believe that if you made love to her, she would find it out, and that very soon.'

'Then she won't do. I must have some one to whom I shall not have to pretend even to make love. Make love !' he added bitterly. 'Make *love !* after seeing *her* last Sunday, and her drooping looks ! I know this—I must not see her again if I can help before it's all over, or I shall funk it at the very last. It's hideous—hideous ! I've often heard of girls selling themselves, and seen them do it too, with smiling faces, and take any amount of spooning from fellows whom they may almost loathe ; but I never knew what it must feel like till now.'

'Poor innocent victim ! Poor unsheltered lamb !' was the soothing reply.

'Ah, your sympathy was always of the robust kind,' grumbled Randulf. 'A stroke on the back with one hand, and a cut of the whip from the other.'

'If you drop the whip for long in commiserating either your friend's grief or your own, you find yourself wreathed with weeping willow very soon, and blown out with sentimental sighs,' retorted Aglionby.

'Well, will you think it over, and let me have the result of your meditations ?'

'I will.'

'Do you ever hear anything of Miss Vane "that was," as they say, now ?'

'I have seen her more than once since her marriage, and her husband says that sometimes she tells him what prospects she gave up for his sake. I go over and see them when I want to be reminded that once upon a time I was made a great fool of, all the time that I thought myself a person of the greatest penetration.'

A pause ensued, which was broken by the entrance of a servant with a note for Aglionby.

'The messenger is waiting for an answer, sir.'

He read it through—it was very short—got up, and, without making the slightest observation, scribbled off an answer as short as the note, gave it to the servant, and said :

'Tell William I want Egyptian—he must saddle him at once.'

'Are you mad ?' murmured Randulf. 'To ride—on an afternoon like this.'

'It's a summons,' said Aglionby, 'which may mean a great deal, or perhaps nothing at all. Hark to me, Randulf. Establish yourself here for the night. I can't tell when I may return, but it will be sometime to-night, and I may have news for you.'

'News—about what ?'

'Don't press me ! It is but a chance. But stay—to oblige me, old fellow. And, for Heaven's sake, don't write and propose to Miss Askam, or Miss Anyone, while I am out.'

Randulf shrugged his shoulders.

'Well, to please you. And what am I to say to Mrs. Bryce ?'

'That I was called off on business, and will be back to-night.'

When Egyptian was announced as being ready, Randulf Danesdale, despite the heat, followed his friend into the yard, and stood bareheaded while he mounted, followed him to the gate, and leaned upon it long, watching while Aglionby rode out in the blazing sun, along the road to Yoresett.

'Perhaps the riddle is going to be solved at last,' he said to himself,' as he returned to the house.

CHAPTER XXXVII.

CONFESSION, OR EXPLANATION ?

AGLIONBY rode swiftly under the scorching sun, along the high, wild road to Yoresett.   He went up the village street, and dismounted at the inn, where it was customary for the visitors of all degrees to leave their horses while they transacted their business in the town, and then he walked down the street again to Yoresett House, pulled the bell, and asked to see Mrs. Conisbrough.

The servant seemed to understand that he was expected, for she said ' Yes, sir,' with some alacrity, and admitted him at once, ushering him into the parlour at the left hand of the hall—the one room of that house which he had ever been in.   The light in it was somewhat dim after the blaze of sunshine outside, for the blinds were half-down, and Bernard, as he entered and looked around him, appeared very tall and pale, and rather gaunt, as he had grown to look of late.   He had deluded himself lately into the idea that he was 'getting over' his disappointment about Judith, and that he was becoming reconciled to the position to which she had relegated him ; but he was mistaken, as this afternoon and its occurrences had made him feel.   The mere knowledge that Judith was at home, that he might meet and see her, had excited him ; he could have echoed, with regard to her, all that Randulf had said about Delphine.   Then Mrs. Conisbrough's note coming had made the emotion deeper, and, as it were, given a significance to their conversation.

He found Mrs. Conisbrough alone, and he was shocked to see what an invalid, what a wreck, she had become.   She leaned back in her chair, with a white fleecy shawl round her shoulders, and close beside a small fire, even on this fiery July afternoon.   Her cheeks were wasted ; her eyes were hollow. He had not Judith's practical experience to go upon, but he instinctively felt that he was in the presence of one whose feet were hastening to her grave ; whose spirit must soon say farewell to this life ; to its griefs and joys, and hopes and fears. She looked at him long and steadily, and in silence. There was an expression upon her face which he did not quite understand—a look of coldness, of something like defiance. He laid down his hat, bent over her, and said :

'You sent for me, Mrs. Conisbrough.'

'Yes. I happen to be quite alone to-day, and as I felt a little stronger, and wished to speak to you, I sent for you. I hope I have not inconvenienced you.'

'Your summons' would have been obeyed at whatever inconvenience ; but, as it happens, it caused me none at all.'

'Pray be seated, Mr. Aglionby. We have not seen much of you since my uncle's death. It is long since I even saw you. I have been a great invalid of late, and have not left my house for many months.'

'I heard you had been in ill-health, and was sorry to learn it. I hope there is no cause for any real uneasiness.'

'Not uneasiness,' she replied, with a peculiar smile, which chilled him, he knew not why. 'Oh no ! I have nothing— it is long since I had anything left to be uneasy about. My daughters were uneasy, and last Sunday Judith's great friend, Dr. Wentworth of Irkford, came to see me.'

'Yes.'

'They did not tell me that he had come just for that ; and they imagine that I did not know it. He professed to be staying at the Mallesons', and to have called casually to see Judith on some business ; and then he pretended to think me looking ill, and offered to examine my heart. They think I did not guess it all, and I have not undeceived them. He tired me dreadfully with his stethoscopes and instruments and poking about. I had no breath left in me when

he had done. Such things are very trying in a heart com-
plaint.'

' They must be, indeed,' he said gravely. ' I hope —— '

' Oh, he told them what I could have told him without all
that fuss—that I have not long to live. I have known that
for some time now, but they don't tell me, for fear of upsetting me.'

' It is a most natural feeling. And perhaps, after all—— '

' Oh no !' She smiled in the same chill and weary
manner. ' My days are numbered. I am going to die.
Death has come to my bedside day and night, as I lay awake,
and has taken my hand, and said to me, " Very soon I shall
come and bid you arise, and then you will have to get up and
follow me, willing or unwilling." As it happens, I am willing
—very willing. And knowing that—I have sent for you.'

Aglionby was dumb ; and made no answer to her. She
spoke with perfect calmness, but he realised the entire and
unvarnished truth of all she said. There is no mistaking
the mien of those who have, as she had, held daily com-
munion with Death, and got to look upon him as a friend ;
to wait for his final coming with eagerness, and who have
but one thing to reproach him with—that of not fulfilling
his warnings with greater promptitude.

' I have something to say to you,' she went on presently.
' For a wonder the girls are all out. They are spending a
long day with the Mallesons at Kumer in Swaledale. Mr.
Malleson is taking the clergyman's duty there.'

' Yes, I have been to see them once or twice since they
went.'

' They will not be back till quite late, as Mr. Malleson is
going to drive them over, so I was free to carry out my
purpose. I want to explain to you how it was that your
grandfather left all his money to you instead of to me and
my girls. You must have wondered about it many times,
have you not ?'

'Naturally. And perhaps you on your part have thought me grasping and hard to——'

'No. I did once think so, and expressed an opinion of the kind, but Judith explained. She told me it was not your fault, but hers. She would not allow you to act differently.'

'She would not allow me to speak to you, and I obeyed her.'

'Yes, I know. It is the fashion now to make all your confidences to strangers, and to obey anyone rather than your parents. And yet, had you come to me, *I* could have explained it all, as no one else can. In order to make you understand, I shall have to go back a long way, but I will be as quick as I can about it. I was left an orphan very early, and almost penniless too. I was brought up by my uncle at Scar Foot, with my cousin Ralph, your father. If my uncle had had a daughter, he would have expected blind obedience from her ; so you may imagine what he exacted from me, a niece, and his dependent. He did not mean to be unkind, but no power on earth would ever have convinced him that he did not know people's wants, and wishes too, far better than they did themselves.

'As a rule I managed to get on with him, but I was an Aglionby as well as he—his sister's child—and I had some of the Aglionby spirit in me. There were times when I revolted in secret, but I was afraid of him—I always have been afraid of brute force ; what they call the superiority of sex.

'Sometimes I succeeded in gaining my own ends in opposition to his, but if I did it was by means of subterfuge. I am not going to apologise for that, and I do not feel in the least ashamed of it. I read the other day that that " superiority of sex" argument must always be unanswerable in the hands of a coalheaver. Quite true ; and the man who chooses to treat a woman to arguments of the coalheaver kind, transformed from the physical to the moral side, that man deserves to be cheated, and he may expect to be cheated. I cheated my uncle many a time, in order to obtain things which a generous-minded man would never have needed asking for. I am glad that I did it,' she added slowly, and with cold and concentrated bitterness, while Aglionby sat silent, astounded, and almost aghast at the psychological problem that was gradually being laid bare to him. I just explain this to you to show that with me to deceive him when he oppressed me beyond bounds with his tyranny, had grown into a habit, which I first excused to myself, then justified, and presently realised that it required no justification—it was right. I cheated him as a matter of course, when I should have behaved with transparent honesty to anyone else.

'Ralph was better able to get his own way openly, but he had recourse to subterfuge many and many a time. Often and often have we combined to circumvent the plans of his father, when they were odious to us. We were very good friends, Ralph and I—brother and sister, you understand ; but I cared more for him than he did for me, till the wretched day came on which my uncle took it into his head that we should be married.

' "No sooner said than done," was his motto. He told Ralph privately what he desired, and bade him propose to me. Ralph did not want me, and said so openly—which I did not know till later. It was the first time he had boldly opposed his father, and when he saw the storm of wrath that ensued, he said, by way of excuse, that he was sure I did not wish it either, and that I would not have him if he asked me.

'Now, mark, when he wanted his own way, my uncle could flatter and dissimulate. It was not that he had thought we cared for each other, or that we had struck him as being exceedingly well suited to one another. He wished it, and it should be. He came to me, and said he had reason to think Ralph cared for me—would I marry him if he wished

27

it ? And then he painted the future—how he would provide for us, how one day Scar Foot was to be ours, and so on.

'Ralph was agreeable to me; I was tired to death of being treated as a child without will, or an idiot without reason. I foresaw freedom and independence, and an indulgent young husband, instead of a tyrannical old uncle. I said yes, I would consent. This news was communicated to Ralph, who, for all answer, said that he had given way in many things, but that, as to choosing a wife, he could do that for himself, and that he was not going to marry a woman whom he looked upon as his sister, especially when she did not care two straws for him, nor he for her.

'That answer touched my vanity. I never forgave Ralph for saying it. I was furious at having seemed willing to marry him, even though I had been told he wished me to do so, and I hated my uncle, for having put me into such a position, with a hatred I cannot describe. To gratify his own imbecile self-will, and love of power, I was to be made cheap—to profess myself willing to be forced in marriage upon a man who would not have me.

'Still my uncle would not give up his scheme. He threw us together; his favourite plan was to send us out for walks in the summer evenings. I remember it well—we used to go, one on one side of the lane, and the other on the other; he used to switch off the tops of the flowers and weeds with his cane, and I used to pout, and pluck the grasses, and pull the seeds off, saying, " This year, next year—sometime, never." That was to see when I should be married—not to Ralph.

'We became the talk of the neighbourhood, of course. People laughed at us. My uncle raged; my cousin was sullenly obstinate, as weak characters are, when they get a fixed idea into their heads. I was miserable and furious, and we were all three unspeakably ridiculous.

'At last an opportunity came, which even my uncle

hailed with delight, of sending Ralph away for a few months.

'There was some business in London to be attended to. All would have been well if Ralph had been allowed to go in peace; but his father, with his usual insane spirit of self-assertion, told him, threateningly, that he expected him to come to his senses while he was away, and to return home prepared to obey. It was just a threat—bravado, meant to show that he was the master, which he was not, with all his blustering. Ralph chose to take it in earnest. In London he met Bernarda Long, and the next thing we knew was, that he had married her. He simply sent the news to his father, leaving him to receive it as he chose. I conjecture that your mother's high and resolute character had for the moment inspired him, and rendered him regardless of consequences. He suffered for marrying her, but I think he did well to marry her, and I do not believe he ever really repented having done so.

'I need not go into the details of my uncle's rage when he heard the news. You have heard about it; how he vowed to disinherit Ralph, and said he would never own him. He took possession of me in a savage kind of way— not because he really loved me much, or desired to benefit me, but to make me the instrument of his revenge on Ralph. He made my life a burden to me. Men are brutes—that is all I know about them. *I* had to bear the brunt of his displeasure; I had to listen to all his useless railings and ragings. I hated the Aglionbys, father and son, and nothing will ever make me see that I had done anything to deserve my lot at that time. Two selfish, headstrong men, who, when they could not subdue one another, poured the vials of their wrath upon a poor woman over whom they had fallen out, and who would have asked nothing better than never to see them or hear of them again.

'My uncle made a will in my favour, and told me he had

done so, and never lost any opportunity of impressing upon
me that he had done it out of no superfluous goodwill to
me, but out of hatred to Ralph. That was soothing to my
feelings, as you may suppose. I got to look forward to his
death, and to the distant future, as to the time of my release
and my salvation, and to the possession of the money as my
just indemnification for what I had gone through; and I
see it still in that light.

'I did not marry immediately after Ralph, I lived at Scar
Foot for two long years after that, and went through trouble
and humiliation enough, I can tell you. It hardened me.
Two years after Ralph's marriage I married Mr. Conisbrough, who was the incumbent of this place, which you
know is in the parish of Stanniforth. When you were six
years old, your father died. My first child died an infant.
Judith, when Ralph died, was a little infant. When the
news of your father's death came, it struck my uncle to the
ground; but he was not tamed even then. He knew,
though, that he had done wrong—he had always known it.
The news of his son's death came like a revelation to him, I
suppose. He thought about it, and remembered you. He
imagined that if he could get you into his hands he could
mould you to his will, and then, after all, an Aglionby, flesh
of his flesh, and all that, would have Scar Foot. No sooner
planned than he set about executing his scheme. *I* was
nothing; I was a woman. I had been his dependent; he
had always felt that he might dispose of me much as if I
had been a bale of goods. He had made a will in my
favour and in favour of my children; but what did that
matter? A will can always be altered while a man is in his
right mind, and while he is able to hold a pen and sign his
name. His will should be altered. And with the delicate
consideration which had always distinguished his treatment
of me, *I* was the fortunate person whom he selected to be
the instrument of his purpose. I had the honour of being

ordered to go to Irkford, where Ralph had settled, and
where your mother and you were then living. He would
have gone himself, but he hated your mother so that he
would hold no personal interview with her, and it never
occurred to him that Marion could resent; that Marion
could question his will: she would go and invite another
woman to practically step into her place; she would go and
use every effort to secure to the child of the man who had
scorned her—for Ralph did scorn me—all the advantages
which had been promised to her, and which had been
earned hardly enough, in all conscience, if they had been
ten times as great.

'What a fool he was! What a great, selfish, blundering
fool! Men *are* fools. The great mystery to me is how
they, with their consummate stupidity, have yet managed to
gain the mastery over us. Brute force again, I suppose, is
the only answer to the question. I went to Irkford. I had
to take my nurse and baby with me, of course. My commission was to tell your mother that your grandfather was
wishful to provide for you as if nothing had ever happened,
and, finally, to leave you his estate and property, as he
would have done in the natural course of things. The
conditions attached to this proposal were, that you were to
live with your grandfather eleven months in the year, and
one with your mother, and that no direct communication
was to pass between your mother and your grandfather.
On these conditions she also was to be suitably provided
for, and was to be free as air to follow her own course
in the future ; even to marry again, if she chose to do
so.

' You perceive that this proposal was susceptible of being
made either openly insulting, or, at any rate, fair and politic,
just according to the way in which the messenger delivered
it. I was in no mood to make it smooth, or to deliver it
pleasantly. When I saw your mother, also, I am bound to

say that she received me with a coldness and a haughtiness which were by no means conciliating. Smarting under my wrongs and insults, and indignant at her reception of me, I felt a savage pleasure in delivering the message as rudely and abruptly as possible. I did not for a moment suppose she would refuse my overtures. I told her that Mr. Aglionby, of Scar Foot, wished to have the guardianship of his grandchild, and that he was willing to provide for him on condition that the mother contented herself with seeing him one month in each year, and that she never, under any pretext, sought a personal interview with Mr. Aglionby, or wrote a direct letter to him. All this I told her as if it were a matter of the profoundest indifference to me what course she took, or what became of her and the child.

'You will please understand that I was faithful to the letter of my instructions. I said exactly what my uncle had said, but I said it in a certain way. The effect of it surprised me. Your mother rose up and almost ordered me from her house.

'"Tell him," she said, "that I would rather beg my bread and my child's bread through the streets, than hand him into the power of a man who can behave as he has done. He ruined his own son; he shall not ruin mine; nor shall he insult me with impunity. And you," she added, "how could you, a woman, a mother with a baby at her breast, come and offer such terms to another mother, one who is widowed; one who has *nothing* but her child to make this life worth a moment's purchase to her?"'

'I shrugged my shoulders—how was it likely that she could understand? I took her answer: I came away; I left Irkford. I was not sorry that she had answered me as she had done: it would be a blow to my uncle; it would humble his pride. They would both have to humble themselves—the proud man and the proud woman too, if they were ever to come to anything like an understanding. I had been staying at Scar Foot, when I had been sent to Irkford. I returned straight there.

'Your mother had said to me, that she was not so utterly destitute as I seemed to imagine; that she yet possessed a relation or two, who, even if she died, would not let her child starve. I told this to your grandfather: I said her relations would provide for you rather than that you should get into his hands, and I was happy in saying it.'

(Here Mrs. Conisbrough related the scene which had taken place on her return to Scar Foot, and her narrative agreed in every particular with that given by old Martha to Judith, except that she omitted to mention her own excessive agitation at the time.)

'At times, after that,' she went on, 'I used to amuse myself by thinking that I, if I chose, could bring about a reconciliation—I alone. But I am not so sure now that I should have been able to do so, had I tried. Then my own troubles began, and I gave over thinking of you and your mother.

'Soon after Rhoda's birth, my husband died, and with him, of course, the greater part of my means of subsistence. I was more in the power of my uncle than ever, and that fact hardened me as nothing else could have done. Sordid, grinding poverty oppressed me; forced self-interest ruthlessly to the front, and induced me to keep silence.

'All went well—what I called well—for twenty-two years. Just fancy what a length of time in which to live as I did! But you cannot understand it—men never can understand women's lives and women's trials—it would be as absurd to ask the sea to understand a stagnant pond. Then my uncle went to Irkford, three years ago—simply on a matter of amusement—to attend a political meeting in a town he had once known, and took my daughter Judith with him, "for a change," he said. She had always been his favourite—so far as he had a favourite.

'The day after his return, he came here, and told me that he had seen you, and how deceived he must have been about those relations of your mother's. I knew that my day was over. I do not say I knew I was found out—for I do not see that there was anything to be found out. I had told no lies ; I had kept to the letter of my message. But my day was over, of course. It was my ill-luck. I have been an unlucky woman all my life. He sent for Mr. Whaley that night, and made the will which left everything to you. As to the rest, you know it all.'

She stopped.

Aglionby, his elbows on the table, his chin in his hands, was intently staring at her, honestly but vainly endeavouring to put himself in her place. He did not speak, and by-and-by she went on :

'Different reasons make me wish to tell you this. Not that I am afraid of anything that you can do to me. Do not suppose it for a moment ! Partly, I wish you to understand that it was not out of any sudden affection for you that your grandfather altered his will—it was because I had been too true to him, and he wished to be revenged upon me. He was true to his character to the last : "the ruling passion strong in death" was exemplified in him, if ever it was in anyone.

'When you leaned over the table that day at Scar Foot, and looked at me, you were so strangely like your mother, and your father, and even your grandfather, that I was frightened : it was as if I had seen three ghosts at once—spectres that I hated, all of them. I could not bear it.

'Next, there is one person who in life believed in me, and was good to me—good as a kind angel. If he had stayed with me, I should have been a better woman : I should have confessed my wrong, and he would have forgiven me. It is he alone whom I am afraid to meet. That one is my husband.

' I fear neither my uncle, nor my cousin, nor my cousin's wife. They made me what I was. But I fear lest my husband should turn away from me. You must know that he was the purest and best and gentlest man that ever lived —he was like Delphine, only a man. I am in hopes that his spirit hears me now, and that when I die it is he who will be sent to lead me into the next life—whatever that may be. Therefore, because I feel that he would approve of it, I say, will you forgive me ? I shall soon be out of the way. Perhaps that may make it easier to you.'

' But your daughters—do you not see that it is they whom you have injured irreparably ?' he said, almost breathlessly.

' My daughters,' said Mrs. Conisbrough, her face hardening, ' have behaved unnaturally. They condemned me unheard—at least Judith did ; and Delphine believes in Judith as if she were God—so she condemns me too. They do not know what you know now, yet they condemned me. That is all I have to say about them. I was born to be wretched, and most faithfully has my destiny been carried out.'

Aglionby started up, and began to pace about the room, distracted how to answer her. He wanted, with the instinct of a reasoning animal, to account for her conduct ; to assign some central motive—some ruling idea as the origin and motive-power of her actions during her life. He could find none. He had yet to learn that Mrs. Conisbrough, like many another woman and man who sins, sinned very greatly in consequence of having no ruling motive in her life. That ' commanding voice, which it is our truest life to hear and to obey,' had been absent with her ; as it is with millions of her fellow-creatures, Christians and sceptics alike.

Ruling motives are not so common as the romance-writer in general would have us believe. It would be much easier correctly to portray human nature, and what the author of ' Caleb Williams ' calls ' things as they are,' if they were. A

man or woman with a ruling motive, a supreme passion regu-
lating all his actions, is a fine conception. Provide the ruling
motive : let it be good or bad, according as the romance-
writer feels well and cheerful, or bilious and gloomy ; only
make quite sure that all else is well subordinated to it, and hey,
presto ! your character is bare before you, as plain to read as
the roads and mountains in an ordnance map, and you have
nothing to do but take a clean sheet of paper, and a new
pen, so that your flow of language be not interrupted by
scratches and splutterings, and write it down. A pleasing
idea, for lessening the toils of the scribbler, but unfortunately one which is simply useless to the artist : since chaos,
oftener than order, rules the majority of commonplace lives ;
anarchy, not law, is God. A high emotion here, a low one
there, predominates ; now the soul draws us upwards ; now
the senses drag us downwards—it is one long game of pull
devil, pull baker, between the higher and the lower nature :
sometimes the one has it, sometimes the other ; seldom
does either hold undisputed sway for long. The 'ruling
idea' retires discreetly into the background, and places
itself modestly upon the golden throne which many generations of enthusiastic but deluded story-tellers have combined
to erect for it. The 'ruling motive' is, so far as the millions
are concerned, a beautiful figment of the imagination :
perhaps, in the case of some scores, or more probably tens,
it may become a reality, to be embraced and obeyed.

Aglionby, with the ingenuousness of youth, for he was
young, and he was ingenuous, as surely all his actions here-
tofore must have proved—Aglionby, then, had a vague,
youthful belief in the 'ruling motive' hypothesis. The flat
contradiction given by Mrs. Conisbrough to his precon-
ceived notions staggered him. We often are staggered
when we are confronted in others by the results of principles of which we are ourselves living illustrations.

'Well,' she suddenly broke in upon him, ' you have come

off the victor, as I might have known you would, you being a man, and I a woman. It is always the way. Since you have conquered, surely you can manage to forgive.'

He stopped abruptly before her.

'No, I cannot,' he said curtly. 'At least, not yet. I must first know something which *you* cannot tell me, however much you desired to do so. You must excuse me a short time. I have heard you; you seem only able to see things from one point of view; but you must allow me to see them from one or two others. I trust I may be able to extend my hand to you this very night, and say, " Let us forgive and forget." I hope so. But there *is* a contingency —if it occurs, I cannot—no, by heaven, I cannot and will not forgive you !'

The answer was not what she had expected. The idea that perhaps this forgiveness which she had, as it were, rather demanded than begged, might be refused after all, startled and alarmed her.

'Oh, you must, you must !' she exclaimed, in agitation. 'You must not let me die unforgiven. If I did wrong, see how I have suffered for it—every day, every hour of my life has been a privation, a disappointment, a mortification.'

'That may be,' he said coldly. 'But until I am satisfied on one point, I cannot promise forgiveness. I am human —I am flesh and blood, and not made of wood, or cast iron. I never even pretended to think any man ought to offer his right cheek to him that has smitten his left. You shall know to-night—before the sun sets, I hope. There are others whom you have wronged even more than you have wronged me ; and it is to them I must first appeal. But you shall know before to-day is out.'

He picked up his hat, walked out of the room, and left her.

JUDITH had gone unwillingly with her sisters to the Mallesons' temporary home in Swaledale. They had driven there.
It was only some four miles distant from Yoresett, but the
road was a mountain-pass, going first sheer up, and then
sheer down a steep hill with glorious views of moor and
mountain on every side. The Mallesons made much of the
girls, and were heartily delighted to see them. Delphine
and Rhoda were pleased and touched by this kindness ; so,
too, was Judith, but she could not shake off the weight
which oppressed her spirits. The cause of her unhappiness
was not far to seek. It was the wretched breach between
herself and her mother which took the pleasure from her
life at this time. That breach had only grown deeper during
the week she had been at home, certainly not from any wish
of Judith's. But all her submissiveness, all her eager wish
to please, only seemed to irritate Mrs. Conisbrough further
and further against her daughter. She had parted from her
with marked coldness that morning, and the remembrance
of her alien glance, and of the hard and unfriendly ring of
her voice, lay like a leaden weight at Judith's heart.

All morning the sense of unhappiness had been growing,
until the idea suddenly darted into her mind that her mother
was alone this afternoon. What if she were to return home,
and taking advantage of this solitude, were to plead for forgiveness—though for what fault she could not have told—were to
assure her mother of her deep and unchanging love for her,
and beg her no longer to be so cold and severe with her ?

The desire to act upon this impulse became stronger and
stronger, until at last, as she and Mr. Malleson, to whom
she had been talking about Dr. Wentworth, sat alone upon a
garden bench when lunch was over and while her sisters

and Mrs. Malleson were equipping the children for a donkey-ride to a well-known waterfall, where they were to have a gipsy-tea, she suddenly said :

'Mr. Malleson, will you do me a favour?'

'With pleasure, if I can.'

'Let me go home now, and if the others seem surprised, say I did not like to leave mamma alone all day, but that they are not on any account to follow me—will you?'

'But, my dear Miss Conisbrough, the heat, the long walk over the hill——'

'I am as strong as ever I was. Listen, Mr. Malleson. I have offended my mother; I want to make my peace with her. I must have behaved wrongly in some way—been too proud, or too stiff, or something. She will forgive me, I am sure, if I beg her to do so. She is alone, and I shall have the better chance.'

'In that case, go, by all means, and take my best wishes with you. I will explain what is necessary to the others.'

'Thank you—thank you,' said she, shaking his hand, and adding, with a rather feeble smile, 'I will come to see you and Paulina again before I return to Irkford. You may depend upon me.'

With which, picking up her sunshade, she left him, and set her face towards the hill, in the direction of Danesdale. Her heart was beating with one of those sudden terrors which assail us sometimes, without much cause, perhaps, but none the less potently on that account.

Dr. Wentworth had said her mother was not likely to die at once, or even very suddenly ; but, he had added, she might do so : there was always the possibility of such a thing.

Judith wondered almost wildly why they had consented all to leave her. Who knew what might happen during their absence? It was just at such times that things—by which she meant calamities—so often did happen. And at any rate she must make an effort to put an end to this unnatural hostility between herself and her mother. If the latter were to die without having forgiven her—her heart came to her throat at the mere idea of it.

It had been nearly four when she left the Mallesons' house. The climb to the top of the ridge from Swaledale was a steep one. Then came a rough but more level road, where the moors spread around far and wide, and then the path quickly descended again into Danesdale, and being directly above the town, was known thereabouts as Yoresett Moor, or Common.

She met not a soul as she went up the hill—slowly, in spite of her heart's eagerness; she met not a soul, and she heard scarce a sound, save the melancholy call of the curlew, or the full-throated song of a lark. The shooting season had not begun, so that not even the crack of a sportsman's gun disturbed the quietness. It was almost awfully grand and beautiful to see the sweeping wastes of purple moor—to mark one huge hill-top after another raise itself into the blue ether, each like a great incorporate hymn of praise to That which had planned them ' or ever the world began.'

Judith was not a lover of towns, and it was therefore natural to her mind to institute a comparison—to think how miserable, beside this vast and imposing stillness and calm of eternal nature, appeared the clatter and rattle and bustle of little, fussy, noisy man, with his railways and his commerce, clamouring for his rights, and cheating his fellows, inspired apparently with the ardent desire to resemble a pike as nearly as possible, and to find the rest of his race convenient gudgeons.

It all came home to Judith, whose love for *this* rather than for *that* was innate and hereditary; but it made less impression upon her than usual, because of the fever of her heart and the preoccupation of her mind.

She at last arrived almost at the top of the steep ascent. Here the view on either side was interrupted by high crags of grey limestone rock, rent and torn and tossed, while the herbage could scarce find a place amidst the chaos of huge stones and boulders which lay up and down, like the balls with which giants or demons had been playing some Titanic game. By looking back she could see down into dark Swaledale, from which she had ascended. Many hundreds of feet it lay below her, and looked like a narrow little passage enough, walled in by big black fells, some of the 'greate hilles where they dygge leade,' spoken of by the chronicler, while the 'right noble ryuer, the Swale,' forced its way boisterously through it. This prospect was to the left. To the right there was so abrupt a turn in the road that only a few yards of it were to be seen, and then the crags of lime- stone shut it in. Just here was the green and mossy source of a little dancing rivulet, which came trickling out of the rock with a murmur of endless, low-voiced contentment, at having come safely from the dark womb that bore it, and being free to run into the gay sunshine and over the broad moors.

It was at this point that Judith perforee sat down to rest a few moments before taking her way down the hill to Yore- sett, a descent of two full miles, which was almost more fatiguing than the ascent. The great boulders strewed about offered an abundance of resting-places. She seated herself upon one of them, fixed her eyes upon the little murmuring rill, and waited awhile. The sun had gone behind one of the crags; a fresh, delicate breeze played upon her face; she was literally enjoying the shelter of 'a great rock in a weary land.'

The rocks were so immense, and the bend in the road to the right so sharp, that she neither saw nor heard anything until she suddenly became conscious that a rider was pulling up his horse at her very side. She looked up and half rose, with a smothered cry, as she saw Bernard Aglionby.

' Ha, Judith ! This is greater luck than I expected,' said he, dismounting, and without further ado throwing the bridle over a tall stone pillar which stood hard by. He came to her side, and said abruptly : ' I heard that you and your sisters were with the Mallesons to-day, and I was on my way there.'

' Indeed !'

' But it was you whom I wanted to see,' he added ; and there was a strangely breathless and excited look about him which excited her also, and made her wonder, with a vague alarm, what was coming.

He seated himself beside her, but he had not asked her how she did, nor offered to shake hands with her.

' So you are at home for your holiday ?'

' Yes.'

' Do they loose your chain for long ? How soon have you to be back in prison ?'

' I have a month's holiday.'

' Marvellous ! And then, back you must go, to nurse a lot of sick men and women, whether you like it or not.'

' I am not going to nurse any more myself. I am going to be a matron, and look after the nurses,' she said, essaying a feeble jest.

' Matron !' echoed he, laughing sarcastically. ' And going back, are you ? I suppose that doctor counts upon you as much as we count upon sunrise following sunset ?'

' He certainly expects me back.'

' You _have_ been nursing sick people, though, for three years, have you not ?'

' Yes, I have.'

' And you delight in it, I suppose ?'

' No, I do not.'

' You are wretched in it, then ?'

' Oh no ! You are quite mistaken.'

' Humph ! Neither happy nor miserable. That's an odd state of things. At any rate, you are glad to be at home, and you are happy there.'

' It is just there that I am not happy. If I were, I should not need to go away.'

'An admission at last! And why are you not happy at home?'

' That is my affair,' she replied concisely.

' And mine.'

The answer followed quick as the peal of thunder on the flash of lightning. She scarcely had time to look at him, startled, when he said :

' I know why you are unhappy. Because, twenty-five years ago, your mother told a lie, or acted one, which comes to the same thing, and you have committed the crime of finding her out.'

' Ah—h !' she exclaimed, with a kind of long sigh, as if some great strain or terrible suspense had come to an end ; and then, as though remembering herself, she added quickly: ' I don't know what you mean.'

'Oh yes, you do,' replied Aglionby, smiling, and the accent of his voice belied the accusation contained in his words ; he brought the impeachment against her, which he had been conning over a hundred times during his ride up the hill. 'You know well what I mean. You discovered this wrong that had been done ; you found that you and yours had just escaped profiting by it. The narrowness of the escape made you hard and uncompromising. You told me that the justice I wished to do you would *scorch* you— yes, benefits from my hand were to scorch you—I have not forgotten, you see. The word scorched me, I assure you. And you found my weak points—you found you could twist and turn me to your will; so, instead of trusting me, instead of giving me one moment's credit for a grain of generosity or manly feeling, you tortured me, and banished me, and befooled me, and held me at arm's length, and devoted your self to a martyrdom to expiate the sin. And, above all, you were determined that I should never know it—oh, never ! Hard, pitiless wretch that I was you would never give me,

28

the chance of using the blessed privilege of forgiveness. What do you say? I do not hear you.'

His voice had sunk to a whisper as he bent nearer to her, and thought he distinguished something like:

'You did not believe in forgiveness.'

'Nor you either, it appears,' he said tenderly, though he went on with his accusations. 'You used your power over me—for you had unbounded power over me from the time you became my kinswoman and my guest—and I believe you knew it; you used that power to keep me away from your mother, who could have explained. Ah! she has a tale to tell. I was to suffer, and you were to suffer; Randulf Danesdale, and your sister—you did not mind how many of us suffered——'

'Did not *mind*—oh !'

'We were all to suffer, and I was to remain ignorant. Your plans were well laid, but they were not quite flawless : they have been frustrated, for Mrs. Conisbrough sent for me this afternoon, and told me all about it. She wished to vindicate herself, and to humble me.'

Her face had sunk into her hands, but he could see between her fingers the scarlet flame that covered it. To his last words she made no reply. She gave no sign. Was it shame, or joy, or terror that overcame her? He bent over towards her, and said, softly :

'Judith !'

She only turned aside in silence, and he said :

'All this you have inflicted upon me, and I love you the better for it. It shows me that you thought much of me, or you would not have taken the trouble to do it. I love you the better for it, I say—and I love the pride, and the purity, and the simplicity that dictated your course—and the high-mindedness that carried you through it all; and I shall love them the better when my love has tamed their savageness, for there is something of the savage in the way in which you have treated me—is there not? But not enough of it to repulse me *now*. Your mother asked for my forgiveness, and I, before I could give it her, had to see you.'

He took her hands gently from before her face, and looked into it, feeling as if he had never known what rejoicing was before—looked into it with eyes which claimed as his own every scorching blush, and all the anguish of fear and shame and delight which struggled there.

'You have suffered,' he said. 'It has been my fate to see your wretchedness. It is you who can forgive. What do you say?'

'Do not ask me. I—it is not I. It is you who have been wronged. It is between you and her.'

'It is between you and me,' he replied emphatically. 'From the time I came to Scar Foot, it has been between you and me. Think of the last three years, and tell me, if you dare, that it is not between you and me. Three such years! But I believe this is worth it, after all. If you had wanted to make the possession of you even more precious than it must in any case have been, you could not have succeeded better. It needs a man to win you—I have found that out long ago—a very man ; but, you may believe me, he sits beside you, and holds your hands at this moment.'

He paused an instant, looking at her, and she gave him a glance which made his heart beat more wildly, so exquisite was it to him in its trembling mixture of pride, love, and supplication. He stooped forward, and kissed her parted lips. 'So it was for that, for *that*, that you have mistrusted me, and tortured me,' he said, with almost angry tenderness ; ' oh, I hope and trust you have tortured yourself as well, you " most delicate fiend," or all my sufferings will have gone for nothing, and I must have my revenge.'

There was triumph in his tenderness, and she tried in vain to release a hand, to hide her face, to shelter her grief and her rapture somewhere—for it was rapture she experienced at his imperious wooing, and not distrust ; she knew the love of which it was the almost uncouth expression, and she knew too that he was right : the man to win her was himself, and no other.

'You cannot escape, my well-beloved cousin,' he said, 'till you have answered my question. Tell me—am I to go home with you to your mother, and thank her as well as forgive her? or am I to ride back to Scar Foot, unreconciled still? You only can decide.'

'You mean—you will do—as I wish?' she stammered.

'On one condition.'

She was silent.

'Of course you know what it is,' he went on, with the same little smile of triumph which he could not quite repress. 'Three words—you know what they are '—he bent over her, and whispered, for the delight of whispering:

'Your mother has asked my forgiveness. She knows she has acted wrongly, though she says she has not. But I care not whether she were wrong or right. I say that if you will give yourself over to me for ever, I will forgive her, fifty times over. If you will not—I never will.'

'Never?'

'No, never.'

'Then—I must,' she returned, yielding, as he saw, only inch by inch, but yielding. 'I suppose I must,' she repeated, casting a wavering glance at him ; and then suddenly hiding her face upon his shoulder, 'I must, if you wish it, Bernard. You have made me wish what you wished from the first moment I knew you.'

'It is well to bow to necessity,' he said, in a voice which was not quite steady, as he folded her in his arms, with a sensation of the deepest, profoundest peace and contentment. 'And,' he whispered, with a half-laugh, 'nothing will give me greater joy than to impress that fact upon your friend Dr. Wentworth.'

She pressed his shoulder, as if expostulating, and he said:
' Don't grudge me that bit of malice. No doubt he is
worth a thousand of me. I know he is. But, heaven be
praised, it isn't only the first-rate men who can get good
women to love them—a cross-grained carle like me, even,
has his stroke of luck sometimes, and can induce a woman
more or less like you to take him in hand.'

' When he has left her no choice, because of his goodness
and generosity to those who have wronged him—churl that
he is !' she replied ; and he, looking through her eyes into
her very heart, saw there—his own image.

CHAPTER XXXIX.

GOOD-NIGHT.

' Noch eenmal lat uns spräken,
Goden Abend, gode Nacht.
Di Maand schient up de Däken,
Uns Herrgott hält de Wacht.'

RANDULF kept his promise to his friend, established himself at Scar Foot for the night, and waited for Aglionby's
return. He and Mrs. Bryce dined *tête-à-tête*, and he told
her that Aglionby had been called off to Yoresett on business, but was to return that night, sometime.

It gradually grew apparent that the 'sometime,' whenever it
came, would be late. The evening drew on, and darkness
fell, and still he had not come. Mrs. Bryce, who still felt
languid from the heat, and from her recent headache, went
to bed early. Randulf merely said he would have a smoke,
and wait for Aglionby—the servants need not sit up ; and
presently all the household had retired. It grew so late,
that he knew he must be the only person waking beneath
that roof. He sat in the house-place beside the open door,
for the night was balmy as night could be, and the moon
flooded the earth with her radiance.

Randulf for the most part lay back in his easy-chair ; his

hands clasped behind his head, content to be silent and to
dream. Once or twice he got up, and paced about the
garden, and found his way down to the water's edge; looked
across the motionless lake, and raised his eyes to where, at
the foot of it, Addlebrough, like a grim sentinel, kept
watch. It was very beautiful, but there was also something
irrepressibly weird in it, and he realised this, as he reflected
upon the calm peace and homely shelter of this spot, and
then recalled all the waste of wild, unearthly moors, savage
fells, desolate fastnesses, which spread on every side—all
full of the glamour and mystery of the summer night. A
wild land : and the race that dwelt in it had something of
its own sternness in their nature—especially, he thought,
with a slight smile, that very family under whose roof he was
sojourning this night.

As he stood, motionless, leaning on a rail, he could hear
in the dead silence of the night, the murmur of rushing
waters borne by the faintest breeze to his ear, from the inmost recesses of the hills in which they sprang—cascades
which rush for ever, and for ever tell their tale, whether any
be there to listen or no. He heard the voices of the night
—those weird voices which it would be well for many of us
to hear oftener—and they told an old story to him.

> ' Many voices spake—
> The river to the lake ;
> The iron-ribbèd sky was talking to the sea :
> And every starry spark
> Made music with the dark.

*   *   ·*   *   *   *

> ' When the day had ended,
> And the night descended,
> I heard the sound of streamlets that I heard not in the day.
> And every peak afar
> Was ready for a star,
> And they climbed and rolled about until the morning grey.'

'And I am ready for my star,' thought Randulf, 'if she
would arise for me.'

He did not know how long he had been there; he was not sleepy, and he was not weary. He did not know that it was nearly half-past one in the morning, when at last, a very long way off, in the stillness he heard hoof-strokes. Not another sound interfered to hinder them from being carried to him.

Having once caught the sound of them, he listened, lazily at first, amusing himself by speculating as to whether the rider were in good or bad humour—glad or sorry—excited or depressed. He guessed it to be Aglionby returning. No doubt the turnings and windings of the road, its ups and downs, had something to do with the fact that occasionally the sounds ceased entirely, or again died away into faintness, or seemed to be travelling in exactly the opposite direction. Be that as it may, they came irregularly; and as he listened, his mood, which had at first been simply one of idle specu-lation, grew into one of excitement. He threw his cigar down, stood up, and listened with a gradually increasing anxiety, which presently grew quite breathless.

What news did this rider bring—what cheer? Sorrow or joy—laughter or tears? It was the strangest sensation he had ever had. Nearer came the hoof-strokes, and nearer: slowly, as the horse breasted the rise; quickly, as it de-scended the hill. Randulf at this point made his way speedily round the house into the courtyard. A light was burning in the stables, but the men had gone to bed, as he had desired them to do.

Nearer and nearer those hoof-strokes—loud, hollow, and slowly, through the dark, shaded lane at the back of the house—then Aglionby rode into the yard, drew rein, and flung himself off his horse.

Randulf looked at him, and saw that he was very pale and very grave, but that in his eyes and about his mouth there was a look of wonderful softness, contentment, even sweet ness

'You have sat up for me, old fellow,' he said; 'you expected some news.'

'That tells me that you bring some. Is it good or bad?'

'For me it is good. I know that much. For you—that is as you and your father decide. Just let me give Egyptian a shake-down, and I will tell you all about it.'

A few moments sufficed to attend to the horse, and then they went into the house again.

'You have been long in coming. I had no idea it was all that time,' said Randulf, casting his eyes towards the clock, as they entered the house-place.

'I have. I could not come away before. Randulf, I told you that some day those girls should find out that I was their kinsman, and should treat me as such.'

'And they have done so?'

'They have done so. It's a strange story. But I know all now, and what the blight was that hung over them—or, rather, what they chose to make into a blight. It is all gone now' . . . he paused . . . 'their mother is dead.'

'Their mother!'

Young Danesdale was thunderstruck. No suspicion that Mrs. Conisbrough had anything to do with the proceedings or the fate of her daughters had ever entered his mind.

Aglionby sat down.

'I must own that once or twice lately I have had an inkling that she was at the bottom of it,' he said. Then he told Randulf everything that had passed between him and Mrs. Conisbrough, and dwelt strongly upon the view which she herself had taken of her act. 'Nothing seemed to make her understand,' he went on, 'the significance of what she had done. She is a regular Aglionby, with a weaker stock grafted on her, but she has all our hardness and bitter strength of resentment. I thank heaven for my mother; she gave me a spirit of another sort to counterbalance that one. Well, she seemed unable to comprehend that she had almost ruined her daughters' lives—and there our family spirit crops out again, Randulf—in their conduct, I mean. Who else would have looked upon such a thing as an insuperable bar to allowing themselves to be happy, or to be loved, or to be married? Ridiculous! But I love them the better for it. We are kindred spirits in that as well as in some other things. Mrs. Conisbrough seemed mad with resentment against my grandfather; she had cherished her wrongs till she could see nothing else, poor woman! But she could not utterly blind herself. It was a secret conviction of her sin which had made her send for me, in the first instance. The truth would out, for, with all her fierceness, she was not strong—she dared not die with that burden upon her soul. She waited awhile, as if expecting me to say something. As I didn't, she had to speak. She asked me to forgive her; but it was a demand, rather than a petition. I said I must hear another verdict before I could do that. I felt I must see Judith. I was sorry for the woman, but I felt obliged to make her understand that I did not exonerate her, that I knew she had sinned. I said something, I don't remember what, and rushed off to the inn, got my horse, and set off for Swaledale. I met Judith on Yoresett Moor; she had felt uneasy about her mother, and was returning to see how she was. I stopped, and had it out with her then and there. I told her how simple she had been, and how I loved her for it; that kind of simplicity is a refreshing thing to meet. I won my cause; in mind and body we two shall never wander far apart again. We walked back to Yoresett, and found Mrs. Conisbrough looking much as she had done when I left her; but I suppose she must have been brooding, and got more excited than appeared on the outside. At any rate, when she saw us, her face changed very much. She got up from her chair and cried out: "I *have* sinned: I have sinned against you all." She held out her hands to us, and Judith caught hold of her, crying, "But it is all for

given, mother ; he forgives you freely." I managed to make
her understand that it was so, and that if she would have
told me all, at the very beginning, I would have forgiven her
then, and condoned it ; for though I know I have this hate
ful hardness which belongs to my race, I believe I had it in
me, even then, to have forgiven her——'

'Of course you had.   Well ?'

'As I say, I managed to make her understand this, and
soon afterwards she complained of a terrible pain in her side.
It was getting dark, then.   We laid her on the sofa : even
at that moment I felt that the right I had to be with them
made up for everything we had gone through, and had yet
to endure.   Judith sent off for the doctor, and her mother
presently went off into a kind of stupor.   She scarcely
roused again after that.   She recognised the others when
they came.   Malleson was with them, you know—he
brought them back—and she asked to be left alone with
him for a few minutes.   Of course we don't know what she
said.   I suppose it must have been a sort of confession.   It
was close upon twelve when she died.   She called me to her
again, and looked at me and said : " So you love Judith ?"
I answered, "Yes ;" and she said : "Ah, you are kindred
spirits.   I cannot understand either of you ; but your forgiveness—are you *quite sure ?*"   I knew what she meant, and
said, "Yes, quite."   It was directly after that that she died.'

They were both silent for a little time, till Aglionby said :

'As I rode home, it suddenly flashed upon me—I had
had no time to realise it before—what a miracle it was that I
should at last know all !   Mrs. Conisbrough vacillated for
ever so long before she decided to send me that note, bidding
me go to her.   Suppose she had decided not to do it !   My
last chance would have gone, for those girls would never have
confessed.   There is a kind of touch-and-go in the whole
business which is horrible to me.   I feel as if I had escaped
being drowned, or tumbling over a precipice, by a hair's
breadth.'

'Ay,' responded Randulf absently.

'With me, that sin of Mrs. Conisbrough's weighs nothing —now,' Aglionby went on. 'But it was a sin, all the same. I once had a conversation with Judith, in which I maintained that there is no such thing as forgiveness of sins—and I was right in a way. I meant, that the penalty has to be borne for them by some one. I suppose I expressed myself with my usual ungracious hardness. She took it to mean that I should consider myself justified in punishing anyone who had sinned against me, and that helped to make her see this affair in a morbid light. When she is my wife, I will try to show her that there is another side to my nature. As for you and your father, being both of you what you are, I think I know which way it will go.'

'So do I,' said Randulf. 'I think that before long my father will ride over to Yoresett House again. Perhaps I shall go with him this time, and I believe we shall have a better measure of success. Poor little girl! Well might she droop, while trying to strain her gentle nature to hard thoughts and harder deeds. As for you,' he added, looking with a smile at Aglionby, 'all I can say is, you've had a hard day of it ; therefore I'll leave you, and say, *felicissima notte !*'

THE END.

BILLING AND SONS, PRINTERS, GUILDFORD.

NOVELS BY RHODA BROUGHTON—*continued.*

JOAN.

"There is something very distinct and original in 'Joan.' It is more worthy, more noble, more unselfish than any of her predecessors, while the story is to the full as bright and entertaining as any of those which first made Miss Broughton famous."—*The Daily News.*

"Were there ever more delightful figures in fiction than 'Mr. Brown' and his fellow doggies in Miss Broughton's 'Joan '?"—*The Daily News (on another occasion).*

MRS. BLIGH.

"No one of Miss Broughton's stories has given us so much pleasure as this; not even 'Nancy,' which is probably her best; not even 'Doctor Cupid,' which is no doubt the most interesting of her novels. Rhoda Broughton still takes the form of an analysis of women's feelings, and her greatest successes have been achieved where she has clearly outlined the woman's character, and then limited the rest of the story to circumstances which tend to illustrate that character. In her latest novel she has been truer to this principle than in any other of her works, and it is this quality which makes us say 'Mrs. Bligh' will give more pleasure than any other of the series. The book is a truer picture of woman's love, of her sacrifice of it to a girl, and of the woman's only possible reward, than any Miss Broughton has yet given us. Time, practice, and a sense of literary art have produced in her a form of skill in writing which is apparent upon every page of her new story. How the story is worked out Miss Broughton's readers will see for themselves, and we repeat that she has given them a novel more worthy of remembrance than any she has yet written."—*Pall Mall Gazette.*

NANCY.

"If unwearied brilliancy of style, picturesque description, humorous and original dialogue, and a keen insight into human nature can make a novel popular, there is no doubt whatever that 'Nancy' will take a higher place than anything which Miss Broughton has yet written. It is admirable from first to last."—*The Standard.*

NOT WISELY, BUT TOO WELL.

"Miss Broughton's popularity in all ranks of society shows no sign of decline. A short time ago Captain Markham, of the *Alert*, was introduced to her at his own request. He told her that in some remote Arctic latitudes an ice-bound mountain was christened Mount Rhoda as an acknowledgment of the pleasure which her tales had given to the officers."—*The World.*

RED AS A ROSE IS SHE.

"There are few readers who will not be fascinated by this tale."—*The Times*

SCYLLA OR CHARYBDIS?

"Miss Broughton's new novel is one of her best. The fine story, finely wrought, of deep human interest, with many of those slight side-touches of observation and humour of the kind for which we look in a story by Miss Broughton, is so carefully and so skilfully constructed as to distance its predecessors."—*The World.*

SECOND THOUGHTS.

"I love the romances of Miss Broughton; I think them much truer to nature than Ouida's and more impassioned than George Eliot's. Miss Broughton's heroines are living beings, having not only flesh and blood, but also *esprit* and soul; in a word, they are real women, neither animals nor angels, but allied to both."—ANDRÉ THEURIET.

MACMILLAN AND CO., LTD., LONDON.

Novels by Charlotte M. Yonge.

Crown 8vo. **3/6** *each.*

THE HEIR OF REDCLYFFE.

HEARTSEASE. | HOPES AND FEARS.

DYNEVOR TERRACE. | THE DAISY CHAIN.

THE TRIAL: MORE LINKS OF THE DAISY CHAIN.

PILLARS OF THE HOUSE. Vol. I.

PILLARS OF THE HOUSE. Vol. II.

THE YOUNG STEPMOTHER.

THE CLEVER WOMAN OF THE FAMILY.

THE THREE BRIDES.

MY YOUNG ALCIDES. | THE CAGED LION.

THE DOVE IN THE EAGLE'S NEST.

THE CHAPLET OF PEARLS.

LADY HESTER, AND THE DANVERS PAPERS.

MAGNUM BONUM. | LOVE AND LIFE.

UNKNOWN TO HISTORY.

STRAY PEARLS.

THE ARMOURER'S 'PRENTICES.

THE TWO SIDES OF THE SHIELD.

NUTTIE'S FATHER.

SCENES AND CHARACTERS.

CHANTRY HOUSE.

A MODERN TELEMACHUS.

BYE-WORDS.

BEECHCROFT AT ROCKSTONE.

MORE BY WORDS.

A REPUTED CHANGELING.

THE LITTLE DUKE.

THE LANCES OF LYNWOOD.

THE PRINCE AND THE PAGE.

P'S AND Q'S, AND LITTLE LUCY'S WONDERFUL
    GLOBE.

TWO PENNILESS PRINCESSES.

THAT STICK.

AN OLD WOMAN'S OUTLOOK.

GRISLY GRISELL.

MACMILLAN AND CO., Ltd., LONDON.

www.ingramcontent.com/pod-product-compliance
Lightning Source LLC
Chambersburg PA
CBHW022021110726
47901CB00006B/1607